Books by J.J. Murray

RENEE AND JAY

SOMETHING REAL

ORIGINAL LOVE

I'M YOUR GIRL

CAN'T GET ENOUGH OF YOUR LOVE

TOO MUCH OF A GOOD THING

THE REAL THING

SHE'S THE ONE

I'LL BE YOUR EVERYTHING

A GOOD MAN

YOU GIVE GOOD LOVE

UNTIL I SAW YOUR SMILE

LET'S STAY TOGETHER

NO ORDINARY LOVE

Published by Kensington Publishing Corporation

# no ordinary love

## J.J. Murray

KENSINGTON PUBLISHING CORP.
http://www.kensingtonbooks.com

KENSINGTON BOOKS are published by

Kensington Publishing Corp.
119 West 40th Street
New York, NY 10018

All Kensington Titles, Imprints, and Distributed Lines are available at special quantity discounts for bulk purchases for sales promotions, premiums, fund-raising, and educational or institutional use. Special book excerpts or customized printings can also be created to fit specific needs. For details, write or phone the office of the Kensington special sales manager: Kensington Publishing Corp., 119 West 40th Street, New York, NY 10018, attn: Special Sales Department, Phone: 1-800-221-2647.

Kensington and the K logo Reg. U.S. Pat & TM Off.

ISBN-13: 978-1-61773-482-3
ISBN-10: 1-61773-482-9
First Kensington Mass Market Edition: February 2016

eISBN-13: 978-1-61773-483-0
eISBN-10: 1-61773-483-7
Kensington Electronic Edition: February 2016

10 9 8 7 6 5 4 3 2 1

Printed in the United States of America

*For Amy*

Brooklyn, New York

# 1

On the surface, Anthony "Tony" Santangelo of Cobble Hill, Brooklyn, New York, was a handsome forty-year-old Italian American with wavy black hair, dark blue eyes floating over a clean-shaven face, and broad shoulders topping his sturdy six-foot frame. To anyone seeing him riding the subway or rushing to and from cafés and coffeehouses in Brooklyn, he was an ordinary man.

No one but his brother knew he had made a fortune as a songwriter.

Under the pseudonym "Art E.," Tony had written his first top-forty hit at the age of sixteen and added five dozen more over the next twenty-four years. He had earned thirty-nine Grammy Award nominations, to rank him just behind Eminem, Alison Krauss, Vince Gill, and Barbra Streisand. When he began collaborating with R & B seductress Naomi Stringer in 2011, his songs shot to the top of the charts and earned him three Grammy Awards in a row for best song and yet another nomination this year for Naomi Stringer's "Love Me in the Morning."

Tony had watched Naomi collect all three of his awards on his behalf on television.

"She is pretty," he told his older brother Angelo the first time Naomi accepted his award in 2012.

"Do you want to meet her?" Angelo asked.

"No," Tony said.

"Why not? She owes you. Your songs have put her on the map."

"She is not on any map," Tony said. "A person is not put on a map. Streets and roads and landmarks are put on maps. Mountains and rivers are put on maps. She is not a street or a road. She is too small to be a landmark. She is not a mountain or a river."

Angelo sighed. "It's just an expression, Tony." He pointed at the television. "Look at her, Tony. She's gorgeous, and she's single."

"She wears too much makeup," Tony said. "She wears horse hair instead of her own hair. She does not wear underwear."

Angelo stared at the television screen. "You're right. Look at *that*. You *have* to respect that."

"She should wear underwear," Tony said.

"Come on, Tony," Angelo said. "That *is* kind of hot."

"Naomi should be cold without underwear," Tony said. "She should not be hot."

Tony kept his awards in unopened boxes in the closet in his room, but not because he didn't want fame to go to his head. Fame could never go to Tony Santangelo's head because it was far too congested with music, lyrics, maps, colors, sounds, odors, mostly useless trivia, and forecasts from the Weather Channel.

Tony Santangelo, aka "Art E.," one of America's greatest living songwriters, had Asperger's syndrome, or AS, the mildest form of autism. Although he wasn't physically clumsy and awkward, Tony had enough of the other symptoms to exist in the "mild" range. His voice was a monotone, and his hands were generally at his sides or jammed into his pockets. Until he discovered the piano, he "stimmed" to stay calm by constantly twisting and pulling on his fingers mercilessly while chanting rhymes like a Gregorian monk. He also perseverated, talking endlessly about the same topic for hours or even days at a time.

Tony had difficulty having and maintaining friendships, counting his brother Angelo as his only friend because he had "selective mutism" around women. He could usually talk to other men once he got to know them, but as a child, he would remain completely silent around women, especially with his elementary school teachers and even with his mother.

When he hit puberty and middle school, however, Tony began saying the most inappropriate—though truthful—things to his female classmates:

"You are not ugly. A cockroach is ugly. Dog poop is ugly. Pollution is ugly. What is under my fingernails before I clean them is ugly. You are prettier than a cockroach, dog poop, pollution, and what is under my fingernails . . ."

"You are not black. My shoes are black. My hair is black. My pen is black. You are brown and tan and red and beige and white. You should not tell people you are black when you are not black at all . . ."

"You should not wear a bra yet. You do not have breasts . . ."

Tony often left school with scratches, bruises, and welts.

"I told them the truth," he would say while his mother wearily applied another bag of ice to his cheek or nose after school. "I told them the truth and they hit me."

"You told them too much truth," his mother had said. "You must learn to tell the truth sparingly."

Tony also had the inability to make meaningful eye contact.

"Tony, look at me," his mother had said a few weeks before her death.

"I can hear you," Tony had said. "I do not have to look at you to hear you."

"It is rude not to look at someone who is talking to you," his mother said. "You need to practice looking people in the eye."

Tony had widened his eyes and stared at his mother.

"And it is also rude to stare like that," his mother said.

"I will be rude and not look," Tony had said. "It hurts my eyes to stare."

With Angelo's help, Tony learned to stare *around* a person's face. "At least look in their general direction," Angelo said. "You know, give them the once-over. You don't have to look them directly in the eye. And don't make your eyes so wide when you do. They'll think you're crazy."

As a result, if Tony made eye contact, he did so unintentionally, his eyes sluggishly crawling over another person's face and body. This, unfortunately, made his teachers think he was lazy and inattentive. "He cannot seem to focus," his teachers told his parents. "And when he does focus, he makes rude faces."

Tony also tended to take *everything* literally and had no concept of sarcasm. He had fallen down the stairs as a child, and Angelo had told him, "Smooth move, dork."

Tony had said, "Thank you."

And *meant* it.

A female classmate told him, "Oh, you're *really* funny, aren't you?"

Tony had said, "Thank you."

And *meant* it.

She immediately punched him in the nose for his lack of understanding.

Finally diagnosed with Asperger's syndrome at thirteen, removed from middle school by his parents, and homeschooled by a series of tutors, Tony found refuge in front of an 1883 Mason & Hamlin upright piano that had been quietly gathering dust in the Santangelo cellar.

Tony taught himself to play the piano in three days.

His finger-strangling days diminished drastically.

He became a musical genius in one month.

"He is a prodigy," Ivan Lubitz, his first and only piano teacher, told his parents. "I cannot keep up with him. He has mastered Prokofiev's *Eighth Sonata.* He has reinvented Stravinsky. He plays Boulez's *Second Sonata* and only looks at the music once or twice. He is close to memorizing Ravel's *Gaspard de la Nuit*—in my opinion the single most difficult piano piece ever written. You *must* get him a better piano before he destroys this one."

Tony did his best to make the piano fall apart. He played with such force and power that keys lifted and chipped and the bench splintered, cracked, and eventually imploded beneath him.

Once his father had sold "She's Not Here," a song based on the passing of Tony's mother when he was fourteen, to R & B crooner Walter Little and the song soared into the top ten as a love ballad, his father had a $60,000 Bösendorfer upright, the "upright that sounds like a grand piano," delivered to the cellar.

Tony ignored it.

"Try this one," his father asked.

"This is my piano," Tony said, his fingers flying over the Mason & Hamlin.

"And so is this one," his father said. "This is your piano, too. You can play them both."

"That is not my piano," Tony said.

"It has an incredible sound, Tony," his father said, plinking the keys. "It has a richer, more powerful sound. It is the best piano that money can buy."

"I do not want it."

"I have to pay to have your ugly piano tuned four times a year, Tony," his father said. "And the parts are hard to find. This new one will stay in tune for many years."

"I do not want it."

His father returned the Bösendorfer, and Tony continued to abuse the old upright.

After his father died of pancreatic cancer when Tony was twenty, Angelo became Tony's legal guardian. Angelo sold their parents' brownstone in Carroll Gardens and bought an eight-unit apartment building in Cobble Hill, turning it into "the Castle." Angelo paid numerous contractors to brick in all the windows on the first two floors, gut the interior, and turn the apartment building into a four-floor palace complete with a roof garden, a soundproofed music studio centered around the old upright, a theater with real theater seats and a state-of-the-art television/computer monitor, four bedroom suites with walk-in closets, and an extensive library of map books from around the world.

Angelo was convinced that Tony owned the largest collection of map books in New York City. Tony pored over maps for hours, attempting to memorize every town, road, and hamlet in every country on earth. He was particularly an expert on Brooklyn and knew its every street and alley, from Red Hook to Greenpoint and from the Brooklyn Bridge to Bushwick.

After twenty years of taking complete care of "The Sponge," Angelo's semiaffectionate nickname for his brother, Angelo wrote *Living with the Sponge: A Biography of Art E.* Because he wanted to preserve his brother's anonymity and keep the generally mean-spirited New York media from ruining his and Tony's lives, he signed it simply: "by Art E.'s brother."

It became an international bestseller.

It also won the National Book Award in 2013.

"I wrote your story," Angelo said, handing Tony a copy of the book. "I want you to read it."

Tony read the book in one sitting.

"Did you like it?" Angelo asked.

Tony handed back the book. "You left a lot out."

And that was all Tony would *ever* say about his life story.

The biography chronicled Tony's unconventional life, from his childhood to his most recent top-forty hits. It was hailed as "a bittersweet yet boisterously riotous description of a true American genius" by the *New York Times* and "an ode to brotherly love and affection, an epic tragicomic journey of one of the world's greatest yet least understood lyricists" by the *Village Voice. Publishers Weekly* called it "one of the most inspirational and hilarious biographies of our times," while *Booklist* labeled the Sponge "quirky, peculiar, odd, strange, funny, warped, twisted, and outrageous—yet ultimately endearing and lovable."

Angelo wisely kept Tony from reading the *Booklist* review.

Though Angelo agreed that his brother was different, he didn't think his brother's life was tragic. It was, however, difficult to tell if Tony was happy or unhappy, because of his condition. The only time Tony was visibly unhappy was when someone or something interfered with his routine. Whenever the piano had to be tuned, Angelo had to remove Tony from the Castle for the piano tuner's protection. "But he is doing it wrong!" Tony would shout while pulling and twisting his fingers. "If I had the right tools, I could do it!" During a fierce blizzard in 2010, Angelo had to go outside on the roof with a long broom to dust off the satellite dish every fifteen minutes so Tony could follow the storm's progress on the Weather Channel. When snow-covered Angelo would come inside to get warm, Tony would tell him, "It is still snowing, Angelo." During the lengthy power outage that followed Hurricane Sandy, Tony complained loudly that he couldn't see well enough by candlelight and flashlight to study his maps.

Angelo invested in a propane generator after that.

Tony needed his routines to function. He ate a bowl of Cap'n Crunch with sliced bananas and drank a tall glass of pulp-free orange juice for every breakfast. He ate two pepperoni Hot Pockets and exactly sixteen Cheetos with a bottle or can of Hires Root Beer for lunch. He ate whatever Delores Hill, their cook, prepared for dinner as long as it involved pasta, mozzarella cheese, garlic bread, and meat sauce. Nearly every television was tuned in to the Weather Channel so Tony could watch the weather wherever he was in the Castle.

Tony's daily life followed an exacting schedule. He woke at six sharp for a shave and a shower before brushing his teeth for ten minutes. Angelo bought toothpaste in bulk. Tony put on his underwear first, followed by his left sock and then his right—*never* the other way around—before putting on a T-shirt, pants, and a button-down shirt, which he *always* buttoned from the bottom up. Tony then composed lyrics, put his lyrics to music, studied his maps, or jammed on the piano between meals. He walked their mixed-breed mutt Tonto (and later Silver) five times a day. He went to sleep precisely at eleven.

Under Angelo's guidance, Tony had performed this routine for twenty years, and from all appearances, Tony seemed content.

Late one night a few days after Thanksgiving, Angelo watched Tony using a magnifying glass to study a map of San Francisco on the long, shiny oak table in the library, a green banker's lamp the room's only illumination.

"How's it going?" Angelo asked.

Tony traced something on his map. "I have memorized all the streets in Chinatown."

Angelo had learned that no matter how trivial Tony's pursuits seemed to him, they were *extremely* important to Tony. "That's great," Angelo said. "I wish I had your memory."

Tony opened another map book. "This map shows the earthquake damage in 1906. The earthquake, fires, and dynamite killed seven hundred people and destroyed four and a half square miles of San Francisco in only three days."

Angelo smiled. "Are you planning a trip to San Francisco, Tony?"

"I am not planning a trip to San Francisco." He closed both map books. "I am never leaving Brooklyn."

"I hear San Francisco is a nice city," Angelo said,

slumping into the chair next to him. "Why don't we go there for a vacation so you can walk around Chinatown?"

Tony hesitated for a moment. "I am never leaving Brooklyn."

"Brooklyn will still be here when you get back, Tony."

"Brooklyn will always be here."

Tony left the library, took the elevator to the second floor, and went into the music room.

A moment later, a piano concert began.

*I couldn't be my brother in a million years,* Angelo thought. *I'd go out of my mind from being so much inside my own mind.* He sighed. *And I'd want someone other than me around. I've never been very good company. I'm too busy trying to make normal what can never be normal. I have to sneak women in and out without Tony seeing them so I can have a social life. None of these women have wanted to settle down with me because of the Sponge. He needs me. He needs his routines, and I'm part of those routines. Without routines, he spazzes out. How can I have a normal life without disturbing his?*

*If I could find a good woman for Tony, I would. She'd have to be a canonized saint, and there aren't many of them in Brooklyn or anywhere else in the world for that matter. Tony is work. He's hard to get to know and even harder to talk to.*

*It isn't as if I haven't tried. Not many women respond when you ask them to "come meet my handsome peculiar genius of a brother." All women hear is the word "peculiar." The first time I tried to get him to talk to a woman didn't work out at all. . . .*

# 2

Angelo had had to trick Tony into leaving the Castle that day sixteen years ago.

"I want to stay here," Tony said.

"I know you do," Angelo said. "But don't you want to see how good your memory is?"

"I have a very good memory," Tony said.

"How do you get from here to Angela's Sweet Treats and Coffee on Driggs Avenue in Williamsburg?" Angelo asked.

"Driving, walking, riding the bus, or riding the subway."

"Riding the subway, of course," Angelo said. *I know he knows all the possible ways to get there. If he didn't have Asperger's, Tony could probably run the MTA. Maybe the MTA needs someone like Tony to make travel in New York more efficient.*

"Walk southeast on Baltic Street, northeast on Smith Street to the Bergen Street station," Tony said. "Take the G train toward Court Square, get out at Metropolitan Avenue, walk north on Union Avenue, west on Metropolitan Avenue, northwest on North Sixth, and northeast on Driggs Avenue. It will take twenty-nine minutes."

"Which way is the fastest route during rush hour?" Angelo asked.

Tony thought a moment. "The same way."

"Let's see if you're right."

"I am right."

"Okay," Angelo said. "If you're right, we'll ride the subway for the rest of the evening."

"I want to go to Far Rockaway."

"You want to go way out to Queens?" Angelo asked.

"Yes."

"That's at least an hour-and-a-half ride each way," Angelo said.

"I want to go to Far Rockaway," Tony said.

"Okay, we'll go wherever you want to go," Angelo said.

Tony nodded. "Okay."

"Tony was twenty-four and I wanted him to meet and talk face-to-face with a woman who *wasn't* telling him how much snow Helena, Montana, was getting that day," Angelo wrote in the biography. "Most of the women Tony knew by name were weathercasters he would never meet. I wanted him to talk to a woman who might look past his peculiarities and get to know him—if getting to know anyone with Asperger's is truly possible. Even I barely know my brother, and I've been his constant companion for his entire life."

Angelo had called up an old high-school friend, Jasmine Stanley, to meet them at Angela's Sweet Treats and Coffee to talk to Tony.

"I didn't even know you had a brother," Jasmine said. "What's he like?"

"He's a bit odd."

"How odd?" Jasmine asked.

"You'll see."

Angelo led Tony into Angela's Sweet Treats and Coffee and seated him in a brown vinyl booth where he could watch for Jasmine's arrival while Tony sponged up the décor.

"There is a checkerboard on the floor," Tony said.

"Right," Angelo said. "Imagine playing chess or checkers here. The pieces would be huge."

"There are too many spaces for a checkerboard," Tony said. "A checkerboard has sixty-four spaces. The floor is not square."

"It's a nice place, though, huh?" Angelo asked.

"We can go to Far Rockaway now," Tony said.

"Let's at least get a snack," Angelo said.

"I am not hungry," Tony said. "I want to go to Far Rockaway."

"Why?"

"I like the name," Tony said. "It is a good name. Rockaway, a block away, watch the seagulls flock away, smell the boats a dock away, rock-a-bye-baby Far Rockaway."

Angelo smiled. *My brother and his mumbled word associations that eventually lead to top-forty hits.* "Well, I'm hungry." He went to the counter, bought two house blends and a half dozen oatmeal and raisin cookies, and brought them to the booth.

Tony dug a cookie from the bag. "These raisins are old. They are wrinkled."

"They're supposed to be that way," Angelo said. "Eat up."

"Most American raisins come from California," Tony said. "That is over three thousand miles away from here. These raisins cannot be fresh." He put the cookie into the bag and looked toward the counter. "She is not a barista. She brews and pours coffee."

"Who's she?" Angelo asked.

Tony pointed at the black woman behind the counter.

"Don't point," Angelo said. "It's rude. How do you know she's not a barista?"

Tony pointed at a sign on the far wall. "The sign says she is not a barista."

"Okay, I see it," Angelo said. "And stop pointing."

"I want to go to Far Rockaway now," Tony said.

"We need to soak up the ambiance," Angelo said. "We need to mingle. To see the sights. To eat these cookies and drink the best coffee in Brooklyn."

Tony took a tiny sip of his coffee. "This coffee is good. There are no sights here. We are inside. Sights are outside."

"You need to get out more," Angelo said.

"I go outside to walk Tonto," Tony said.

"You go up to our *roof* to walk Tonto," Angelo said.

"Our roof is outside. I walk him five times a day outside. I get out five times a day."

"True, but there aren't any beautiful women for you to look at on our roof," Angelo said.

"Beautiful women cannot go up to our roof," Tony said. "They do not have a key to the Castle."

Angelo shook his head. "There are a lot of pretty women here, aren't there?"

Tony's eyes roamed the café. "Yes. There are women here."

"And there are some *pretty* women here."

"They are all pretty," Tony said.

"Oh, they all aren't pretty," Angelo said. "Some have some serious mileage on them."

Tony blinked. "Women are not vehicles with odometers."

Angelo laughed. "Some of these women look as if they've been driven many miles."

"If they were passenger vehicles, they would have odometers on them," Tony said. "That is the law. You should not buy a vehicle if the odometer looks as if it has been tampered with."

Angelo smiled. "It might make life easier for men if

women *did* have odometers. They try to cover up their mileage, don't they?"

"You should never do that," Tony said. "You should never tamper with an odometer. It is against the law."

"You got that right."

Angelo smiled as Jasmine came in, held a finger in the air, and walked to the counter. *If I were ever to hook up with a black woman,* Angelo thought, *that woman would be at the top of the list. Jasmine is so sexy.* "Look at her, Tony. That's Jasmine. I went to school with her."

Tony looked at his watch. "I want to go to Far Rockaway now."

"Come on, check her out."

Tony looked up briefly. "I see two women."

"Look at the taller one."

"She is brown," Tony said. "I do not know her."

"Look at that booty," Angelo said.

"That is not honest," Tony said.

"Her booty isn't honest? That booty is the *truth.*"

"It is not honest to stare at her buttocks like that," Tony said.

"I'm not going to wait for her to *see* me looking at her booty," Angelo said. "*That* would be rude."

"It is rude to stare."

"Not if she doesn't know you're staring," Angelo said. "She's looking over here, Tony. I think she's looking at you."

Tony wound his watch. "She is not looking at me."

"She must like what she sees."

"She is not looking at me."

Angelo sighed. "She *is* looking at you, Tony. You're a handsome man."

"I am not handsome."

"Yes, you are," Angelo said. "You're a younger version of me."

"You said we could ride the subway to Far Rockaway," Tony said.

"Jasmine is coming over."

Tony reached into his coat pocket and took out a notepad and pencil.

"Put that away," Angelo said.

Tony shook his head. "I want to write."

"Now? Put it away. You're about to meet a pretty girl."

"I want to write." Tony began scribbling on the notepad.

Jasmine came over to their booth. "Hey, Angelo."

Tony continued to scribble.

"Can I join you two handsome men?" Jasmine asked.

Tony stopped scribbling. "Angelo was staring at your buttocks."

"He was?" Jasmine slid into the booth next to Tony. "Were you, Angelo?"

"Well, you know me," Angelo said.

Jasmine sighed. "See anything you liked?"

Angelo nodded.

"I did not stare at your buttocks," Tony said. "It is rude to stare at other people's buttocks." He resumed his scribbling.

"What are you doing, Tony?" Jasmine asked.

Tony continued to scribble.

"What are you writing?" Jasmine asked.

"Notes," Tony said.

Jasmine leaned closer, shadows forming on the notepad.

Tony moved the notepad away from Jasmine and into the light.

"Is that written in English or Italian?" Jasmine asked.

"It is in English," Tony said. "I do not have good handwriting. English is the only language I know. Your leg is hot. It is firm yet soft. You are sitting too close to me."

"Oh, sorry." Jasmine scooted farther away. "Is that better?"

Tony looked at her leg. "Four more centimeters away is better. This booth is too small."

Jasmine moved farther away. "What do you write about, Tony?"

"Your gum is peppermint," Tony said. "I like spearmint. The flavor in the average piece of gum lasts fifteen minutes."

"I believe it," Jasmine said. "So . . . what do you write about?"

"I write in English," Tony said. "That is the language I speak. I know some Italian from Poppa, but he is dead. We put him in the ground three years, four months, seven days, six hours, and"—he checked his watch—"ten minutes ago. He is buried at the Holy Cross Cemetery."

"Jasmine doesn't want to hear about that, Tony," Angelo said.

"We put a Christmas tree on his grave every year," Tony said. "Someone stole it last year."

"That's terrible," Jasmine said, touching his hand.

Tony jerked his hand away. "This is the cold and flu season."

"My hands are clean," Jasmine said.

"Relax, Tony, geez," Angelo said.

"The average human hand has one hundred and fifty species of bacteria on it at any given time," Tony said.

"I wash them all the time," Jasmine said.

"You cannot kill all the germs," Tony said. "You should not kill all the germs. Some bacteria are good for you." Tony returned to his scribbling.

Jasmine mouthed "wow" to Angelo.

"I told you it wouldn't be easy, Jasmine," Angelo said. "He takes some getting used to."

"Can't he hear you?" Jasmine whispered.

"Not when he's writing like that," Angelo said. "He gets locked in like that sometimes. Poppa called it selective hearing, but I know different. He's beside you, but he's not really there. I have no idea where he goes, but he goes there hard. I call it Sponge World. Something you said or I said or something else he hears sends him there. A car beeps. Someone coughs. He hears some music. He sees a certain color. He smells something. You could tell him this place was on fire, and he wouldn't notice."

"And he's really never talked to a woman before," Jasmine said.

"Nope." Angelo wrapped his knuckles on the table. "Tony?"

Tony looked up. "Are we going to Far Rockaway now?"

"You're being rude to Jasmine," Angelo said.

Tony looked *around* Jasmine's face. "You have an Afro."

"Yes," Jasmine said.

"It is fluffy." Tony reached out his hand. "May I touch it?"

"No," Jasmine said, jerking her head away from his hand, her eyes wide.

"My hands are clean," Tony said. "I use sanitizer. It kills ninety-nine percent of all germs. That leaves me with only one thousand germs on my fingers or two hundred germs per finger. I will only touch your hair with the tip of one finger."

"You can't touch her hair, Tony," Angelo said.

"It is pretty," Tony said. "I like it." He returned to his writing.

"Thank you," Jasmine said.

"He didn't hear you," Angelo said.

"I want him to hear me," Jasmine said.

"Knock on the table," Angelo said. "It seems to work."

Jasmine knocked on the table.

Tony looked up. "Are we going to Far Rockaway now?"

"Thank you for thinking my hair is pretty," Jasmine said.

Tony took a deep breath. "You have nice thighs. They are muscular and smooth and brown. They are hot. You have removed all the hair."

Jasmine laughed. "I try."

"They are not ashy," Tony said. "Many women have ashy thighs. You do not have ashy thighs. You must use lotion."

"I do," Jasmine said. "Lots and lots of lotion."

"You smell like coconut," Tony said. "I am allergic to coconut."

"It's just the *scent* of coconut, Tony," Angelo said.

"If I eat coconut, my throat swells up and I cannot breathe," Tony said. "I will not eat you, Jasmine."

"Um, thanks," Jasmine said.

"I like your eyes," Tony said. "They have gold flecks in them." He blinked rapidly. "Jasmine's eyes, bold gold flecks, cocoa thighs, coconut sex . . ." He flipped to a blank page on his notepad and wrote furiously.

"What was that?" Jasmine asked. "What did he say?"

"He gets stuck in an idea sometimes," Angelo said.

"He does these word association rhyme things all the time. Try to ignore him."

Tony counted on his fingers. "Too many syllables." He marked something out and mouthed the words. "Better."

Jasmine moved farther away from Tony. "He said something about coconut sex, Angelo."

"Compared to some of his other phrases," Angelo said, "that's pretty tame."

Tony began rocking back and forth, mumbling.

"He's beginning to creep me out," Jasmine said. "I should go."

"Don't leave," Angelo said. "Please. He'll be back soon."

Tony stopped rocking and writing and put the pencil and notepad into his coat pocket. "I want to go to Far Rockaway now."

"Tony, do you think Jasmine is pretty?" Angelo asked.

Tony turned slowly and let his eyes wander over Jasmine. "Her lips are plump and red then brown. She has white, shiny teeth. Her nose is smaller than mine. She has a tattoo of a snake tail above her left breast. I do not know where the rest of the snake is. She has furry eyebrows. Her earrings make ding-ding sounds when she talks. Her breasts are in perfect proportion to her ample buttocks. She wears underwear."

Jasmine moved out of the booth. "I'm leaving now."

"Just wait, Jasmine," Angelo said.

"Your brother is a *freak*," Jasmine whispered.

"He tells the truth at all times," Angelo said. "He never lies. He is complimenting you. Really."

"You are very pretty," Tony said.

Jasmine sat. "Thank you, Tony. That's very sweet of you to say."

"Jasmine is a white or reddish flower with a delightful fragrance," Tony said. "It is often seen in gardens of the southern United States. You are not white or red. You are dark brown and tan and black. You are not in the southern United States. Your name is wrong."

"What?" Jasmine cried.

"You have child-bearing hips," Tony said.

"Oh, that's *enough!*" Jasmine left the booth. "I'm outta here."

"Jasmine, give him a chance," Angelo said. "He's harmless."

Tony glanced at her. "Pink."

Jasmine snatched her coffee. "What?"

"Your tongue is pink," Tony said. "I like that color." He stuck out his tongue. "My tongue is red. My dog Tonto has a black and red tongue. He licks his balls with it."

"Yeah, um, right," Jasmine said, backing away from the booth. "You need to keep your brother on a leash. . . ."

Two weeks later, Angelo sold "Coconut Sex" to Jam U, an up-and-coming R & B group from Atlanta.

Four months later, Jam U released it as a single.

It went Platinum.

# 3

Over the next ten years, Angelo helped his brother to become more and more independent. At first, Angelo had to be with Tony wherever they went, mainly to soften and deflect any of the more outrageous things he might say to servers, store clerks, or people on the street or on the subway. Over time, Angelo merely shadowed Tony, making sure he didn't cause too much trouble.

Or cause a woman to punch him out for being too honest.

By the time he was thirty-five, Tony was going out alone to cafés and coffeehouses in every nook and cranny of Brooklyn, his only tether to Angelo a smartphone that Angelo called every hour or so to check up on him. Tony spent his days out in Brooklyn, writing songs on his little notepads while sponging up dialogue and street sounds, later turning them into music using his dusty piano and an old Roland CR-78 drum machine Angelo bought him. Tony enjoyed riding the subway for these adventures and often spent hours listening to subway and street musicians.

"Art E. could be sitting next to you scribbling lyrics on the G train right now," Angelo wrote in the biography. "He could be in front of a violinist in Central Park, seeing the notes in the air as the violinist plays. He might be beat-boxing in his mumbling, stumbling way with a crew on some street corner in Bedford-Stuyvesant. Art E. is always sponging, always searching for music, always soaking up the lives of perfect strangers to give life to his music."

Angelo had tried without success to get Tony to keep a separate notepad for any conversations he might have with women on his travels.

"I do not have conversations with women," Tony said. "I do not talk to strangers."

"Sometimes strange women are fun to talk to," Angelo said. "And after you talk to them, they aren't as strange anymore."

"I will not talk to strange women."

Angelo tried again a few days after Christmas as Tony prepared to go out wearing his favorite Brooklyn Dodgers jacket, black gloves, and a New York Jets knit hat. "Hey, if you talk to any women, write it down."

"I will not talk to any women," Tony said.

"Come on, Tony," Angelo said. "We have to improve your relations with women so you can get a wife one day."

"I do not need a wife."

"If you had a wife," Angelo said, "you'd have someone to love. Then you can have children."

"I do not need someone to love," Tony said. "I do not need children."

"We all need someone to love," Angelo said.

"I do not need someone to love."

"Don't you ever get lonely?"

"No."

*He answered so quickly.* "Not late at night when it's just you in the bed?"

"There is no one else in my bed," Tony said.

"Besides Silver."

"Silver sleeps on the floor now," Tony said. "He licks his balls. He keeps me awake. Tonto licked his balls before he died. Silver is going to die soon."

"Silver isn't going to die soon," Angelo said. "Please do this *one* thing for me. I do everything else around here."

"You do not do everything else," Tony said. "Delores cooks for us. Mrs. Jimenez cleans for us. The garbage men take our—"

"I sell your music, Tony," Angelo interrupted. *I make sure you're safe. I keep the world from messing with you. I supply you with toothpaste, notepads, map books, and Hires Root Beer.*

"I never asked you to sell my music."

"Well, we wouldn't have any of this if I didn't," Angelo said. "We wouldn't have the Castle if I didn't. You wouldn't have a music studio."

"I liked Mama and Poppa's house better," Tony said. "It was smaller. I miss the cellar."

Angelo knew Tony spent some of his days standing in front of the old brownstone in Cobble Hill. *As if he's waiting for Mama and Poppa to open the door for him.*

"Just . . . write down what you say to women and what they say to you today, okay?"

Tony faced the door. "Women do not like me."

"You don't give them a chance to like you, Tony," Angelo said.

"I want to give them a chance," Tony said.

Angelo blinked. *This is new. He normally doesn't care. I have to take advantage of this moment.* "Turn around and look at me."

Tony turned but only looked at Angelo's feet.

"Do you really want to know how to give women a chance?" Angelo asked.

"Yes."

"You're not just pulling my chain, are you?" Angelo asked.

"You have no chain to pull," Tony said. He looked up briefly. "I make jokes."

Angelo smiled. *For a man who's not supposed to have a sense of humor, Tony is pretty funny sometimes.* "Okay, the first thing you have to do to get women to like you is to stop being so honest around them."

"Women do not want to hear the truth," Tony said. "Mama told me that."

"Well, yes and no," Angelo said. "They want you to be truthful with *your* feelings, but they don't want to hear the whole truth about themselves."

"I am truthful with my feelings," Tony said. "A woman should want to know the whole truth about herself."

"The whole truth is too much to handle sometimes," Angelo said. "Say I'm a woman."

"You are a woman."

Angelo smiled.

"I made another joke," Tony said.

"*Pretend* I'm a woman, Tony."

"I cannot pretend you are a woman when you are not a woman. You do not have breasts, a voice of a higher timbre, or . . . the other thing."

*I won't ask, "What's the other thing?" Once Tony learned that girls didn't have penises when he was eleven, he had to tell everybody that girls had vaginas. At Mass. Three weeks in a row. During communion.*

"Okay, *if* a woman asked me how she looked and I thought she *didn't* look good, in order not to hurt her feelings, I might say, 'You look good, baby.'"

"You would lie to her."

"It's a little lie."

"A little lie is still not the truth," Tony said.

"Well, if I say, 'Baby, you look torn up and terrible,' I'll hurt her feelings."

"If she looks torn up and terrible, she should be told she looks torn up and terrible."

"The truth isn't always appreciated, Tony," Angelo said.

"The truth should always be appreciated," Tony said.

*I can't argue with that, but . . .* "Do you remember Jasmine?"

"Jasmine was pretty," Tony said. "She chewed peppermint gum. You liked her buttocks. She was curvy. She used lots of lotion. She smelled like coconut."

*How he remembers so many tiny details after sixteen years, I'll never know.* "Remember how angry Jasmine got when you told her the truth?"

"I told her how pretty she was," Tony said.

"You told her she had child-bearing hips."

"She did have child-bearing hips."

"But that's not something a woman wants to hear." Angelo sighed and stood as close as he dared to his brother. "Tony, look at me. This is important."

Tony raised his head slowly until he focused on Angelo's chin.

"I met someone I really like." *An editor at Random House when my agent and I were pitching the biography. That was about two years ago, but it's taken this long to get Aika to accept me in my role as your caretaker.* "Her name is Aika Saito. Her first name means 'love song.' She's Japanese."

"Japan is an island country in the Pacific Ocean," Tony said. "It lies along the northeastern coast of Asia." Tony tensed and stared at Angelo's nose. "You will move to Japan."

"No. Aika lives here in Brooklyn."

Tony relaxed his shoulders. "She is five feet two with dark hair and dark eyes and wears dark blue underwear that do not fit her buttocks. She runs very fast. She has strong calves and thighs."

*That's Aika!* "Where have you seen her?"

"Here at the Castle. I see her running from the kitchen to your room. Sometimes I see her breasts. They are small but pretty with small brown nipples. She does not wear a bra. She has stayed here forty-three times in the last year. She likes to yell, 'Oh, Angelo, don't stop.' "

*And he's been listening to us! The nerve!*

"I made many notes," Tony said. "Naomi will sing these songs."

"What?"

"I sat outside your door and made many notes," Tony said. "There will be many songs."

"Tony, you can't put what we've been doing in *any* song."

"The song has a nice rhythm." He tapped the rhythm on the front door. "Naomi will like it. You need to fix your bed. It makes too much noise. You will break it."

"We won't break the bed."

"Aika said, 'I am coming.' "

Angelo blinked.

"She was already here," Tony said. "She would not have to come anywhere."

"I have told you about sex," Angelo said. "She said 'I'm coming' because she had an orgasm."

"An orgasm is 'the physical and emotional sensation experienced at the peak of sexual excitation, usually resulting from stimulation of the sexual organ and usually accompanied in the male by ejaculation,' " Tony said, reciting a dictionary definition from memory. "You had . . ." He took out a notepad and flipped through a few pages. "You had three orgasms two nights ago. Aika had one orgasm and you had three orgasms. It does not seem fair."

*Oh my God!* "How long were you outside my door?"

"Four hours, seven minutes, and twenty-four seconds," Tony said. "The average man can have four orgasms in an hour. You are below average. Aika has great stamina. She is very athletic. She has a pretty face when she is not having an orgasm."

"You *watched* her?" Angelo asked.

"The door was open a crack."

"Tony, you really shouldn't do that," Angelo said.

"You should shut the door all the way," Tony said. "There was a draft, and she was cold. Her nipples were very hard."

"*Please* don't mention any of this to Aika," Angelo said.

"If she asks me, I will tell her the truth," Tony said.

"Just don't bring it up," Angelo said. "She's kind of shy."

"I am shy."

*I can't say Aika is as shy as Tony is.* "She's not that shy."

"I did not think Aika had Asperger's," Tony said. "She smiles too much. She also likes to laugh. She likes to be held tightly. You like holding her tightly."

"I do," Angelo said. "Very much. Look at me."

Tony wouldn't raise his eyes.

"Tony, please look at me."

Tony turned his head but kept his eyes on his hands.

"Aika and I are getting serious, Tony," Angelo said. "I think I love her. We may even get married."

"Forty-one percent of all first marriages in the United States end in divorce," Tony said. "A divorce occurs every thirteen seconds in the United States. Only eleven percent of all divorces occur after the age of forty. You are forty-two." He blinked. "You have a good chance to stay married."

"Thanks for, um, your confidence in me," Angelo

said. "Anyway, I want Aika to move in with us. Would that be okay with you?"

Tony stared blankly at the tile floor.

*He's going inert. He's going to count the floor tiles again.* "Tony? Is it okay if Aika moves in with us?"

Tony unzipped his jacket and hung it in the closet. "Her name means 'love song.'"

"Right."

"It is a pretty name." Tony took off his hat and put his gloves inside. He shoved the hat into the sleeve of the jacket. "I am going to play now." He walked to the elevator, took it to the second floor, got out, and went into the music studio, shutting the door behind him.

A few moments later, Angelo smiled. He could hear "their" lovemaking rhythm from the night before. *It sounds good. No, it sounds great. Naomi is going to sing the hell out of this one. Should I ever tell Aika about any of this?*

*No. Never.*

An hour later, Tony flew out of the studio holding a notebook instead of a notepad, bounded down the stairs instead of taking the elevator, and opened the closet door in the foyer.

"Where are you going?" Angelo asked.

"To practice." He took his Brooklyn Dodgers jacket off its hanger, pulling the hat from the sleeve. He put on his Jets hat.

"Practice what?"

"Talking to a woman."

*This is incredible!* "Do you want me to go with you?"

"No." He zipped up his jacket, straightened his Jets hat, and put on his gloves. "You have to help Aika move in. Tell her she does not have to run so fast anymore."

*This is even more incredible.* "So it's okay if Aika lives here with us?"

"She cannot drink my Hires Root Beer."

Angelo smiled. "She won't."

"She has," Tony said. "I counted. She has had fourteen of my root beers."

"I'll, uh, I'll tell her that they're off-limits from now on, okay?"

"She will have to buy her own."

Angelo nodded. "So she can move in with us."

"It is going to be in the upper thirties with a twenty percent chance of rain later today." Tony opened the front door. "You will have enough time to move her in. Tell her . . ."

"What do you want me to tell her?"

Tony stared around Angelo's face. "Tell her she is very pretty."

"I will."

"And tell her . . ." Tony blinked. "She has a pretty voice. It is a small voice like a bird. I like listening to it."

"Where have you heard her talk?"

"After the bed stops shaking, she talks to you," Tony said. "Her voice is softer than cotton balls." He blinked. "Cotton-ball whispers." He took out a pencil and wrote in his notebook. "She is a good person."

"She's an amazing woman, yes," Angelo said.

"She will make you happy." Tony stuffed his notebook inside his jacket. "I am going."

"Where are you going?" Angelo asked.

"Angela's Sweet Treats and Coffee on Driggs Avenue in Williamsburg," Tony said.

*Somehow, that makes perfect sense.* "You remember the way?"

"I never forget the way." Tony stepped outside.

"You have your phone?"

"Yes."

"Is it turned on?"

Tony took his smartphone from his front pocket and pressed and held a button. "It is on."

"Don't be too late, okay?"

"Okay." Tony's eyes flitted up briefly. "Thank you, Angelo."

"For what?"

But Tony had already run off toward the subway.

# 4

Tony took the G train to the Bedford Avenue station and hurried to Angela's Sweet Treats and Coffee. He sat in the same booth where he, Angelo, and Jasmine had sat sixteen years before, the brown vinyl still as shiny, the table just as spotless.

A woman wearing black jeans and a tight white apron over a black sweater approached him. "Can I get you anything?"

Tony opened his notebook and wrote: "She is dark brown. She was here the last time. She is very pretty. I like her."

"Can I get you anything?" she asked again.

Tony looked around her face and then focused on her shoes.

"I'm Angela McConnell," she said. "What's your name?"

Tony scratched out "She" and wrote "Angela M." above it. "My name is Tony Santangelo from Cobble Hill, Brooklyn, New York, USA."

Angela smiled. "Nice to meet you, Tony Santangelo from Cobble Hill. What brings you all the way from Cobble Hill?"

"Angela's Sweet Treats and Coffee on Driggs Avenue," Tony said. "Best coffee in Brooklyn. Put La Estrella out of business. David beat Goliath. Headline in the *Brooklyn Daily Eagle*."

Angela nodded. "That was a couple years ago. You have a good memory."

"I have a very good memory." Tony tried to look into her eyes and failed. "I was here sixteen years ago. I drank the house blend. It was good. I did not eat the cookies. The raisins were old. I remember you."

"Because I am always here," Angela said.

"You are very pretty," Tony said.

"Thank you."

Tony stared at her stomach. "You have a big stomach. You are pregnant."

Angela nodded. "I just started showing. You have good eyesight, too. Can I get you some more house blend? Maybe an apple pastry? They just came out of the oven."

A little girl ran into the café, out of breath and giggling, zipping behind the counter and disappearing into the back.

"She is very fast," Tony said.

"That's my daughter, Angel," Angela said.

A tall man burst through the doors soon after.

"And that's my husband, Matthew."

Tony noticed that Matthew winked at Angela, and Angela winked back.

Tony adjusted his notebook and wrote: "Angela brown, Angel tan, Matthew white. A wink must mean you love someone." He looked up at Angela. "I like your family. It is colorful."

"I like it, too," Angela said. "And it will soon be larger when our son is born."

Matthew kissed Angela on the cheek. "Where'd my little Angel go?"

"Upstairs, I'm sure," Angela said.

Tony watched Matthew's hand slide from Angela's hip to her belly. He wrote: "Matthew is patting his son on the head. I am sure his son is smiling."

Matthew smiled at Tony. "How are you?"

"I am fine," Tony said.

"This is Tony Santangelo all the way from Cobble Hill," Angela said.

Matthew extended his hand. "Good to meet you, Tony."

Tony stared at Matthew's hand. "You have been outside."

"Oh, right," Matthew said. "My hands are dirty." He withdrew his hand and turned to Angela. "I must go find my Angel now."

"Listen for Angel's laughter," Tony said.

Matthew smiled. "That's how I find her *every* time. How'd you know?" Matthew kissed Angela on the lips, winked again, and walked around the counter and into the kitchen.

"I like how Angel laughs," Tony said. He blinked and

wrote: "Angel runs fast, but her laughter runs faster. Angels in heaven are always laughing, but we do not always hear them."

"Tony?"

He looked up in Angela's general direction.

"So, can I get you anything?" Angela asked.

Tony pulled a credit card out of his wallet. "Do you have root beer?"

"I have some Doc's Root Beer."

"I like Hires Root Beer."

"Doc's is better than Hires, in my opinion," Angela said. "And it's made in the Bronx, so you know it's fresh."

Tony nodded. "I will try it."

"How about some cookies?" Angela asked.

"I like oatmeal and raisin but only if the raisins are fresh."

"I just got the raisins in yesterday," Angela said. "They flew in all the way from California, and their little arms are so tired."

"Raisins cannot fly," Tony said.

"Are you sure about that?" Angela asked.

Tony looked at his hands. "I will have the cookies."

"Coming right up."

Tony recorded the entire conversation he had with Angela in his notebook and made a note to research the flying ability of California raisins. He also wrote down lyrics that were forming in his head about Angela and her family. As he ate his cookies and drank his root beer, he tried to make eye contact with the people sitting at the tables near the big front window facing Driggs Avenue. Some noticed him and smiled at him while others did not. Tony wrote: "I made eye contact with two strangers today. The other strangers stayed strange."

A tall tan woman in a snowsuit burst through the door and skipped up to the main counter.

Tony wrote furiously: "She is not white. She is beige. Tall but not as tall as me. Long fingernails." He listened to the woman talking to Angela. "She speaks Spanish. Angela speaks Spanish and English. Their voices sound like the man in Spanish Harlem playing his guitar, like the saxophonist on the G train, like Mrs. Jimenez while she cleans the Castle. Bright yellow jacket. If there is ever an avalanche in Williamsburg, someone will find her. Orange headband holding her black hair in place. Shiny black, glowing black, glistening black hair. White snow boots. In deep snow she would look as if she were floating above the snow. Orange snow pants. White then orange then yellow then orange like an Easter egg you dip in vinegar dye."

He watched the woman carry a tall steaming cup of coffee to the table nearest to his booth. He wrote: "She is pretty. I will speak to her in English. I will say, 'the weather outside is frightful, but the fire is so delightful.' If she does not respond, I will say, '*Feliz Navidad.*' "

"The weather outside is frightful," Tony said, "but the fire is so delightful."

The woman did not respond or look his way.

"*Feliz Navidad.*"

The woman sipped her coffee.

Tony wrote: "She does not speak English or she does not like Christmas carols. The headband is blocking her ears. Maybe it is a large orange rubber band choking her brain. I must talk louder."

"Fourteen point six inches of snow have fallen on the New York metropolitan area since November first," Tony said.

The woman sighed heavily.

Tony wrote: "She sighed like Angelo does when he is frustrated with me. This means she is frustrated with me. I will try to make her smile."

"The snow has been caused by global warming," Tony said. "The world is warming up, but we are getting more snow. This is one of the ironies of global warming."

The woman turned toward him, stared at him briefly, rolled her eyes, raised her eyebrows, and turned away.

Tony wrote: "Frustration flies across her sky-blue eyes. . . . Hispanics genetically do not have sky-blue eyes."

"You wear contacts," Tony said.

"So?" the woman said.

"They are very pretty," Tony said.

"What is your deal?" the woman said.

"I am not a salesman," Tony said. "I do not have a deal."

"Whatever," the woman said.

Tony dutifully wrote down the woman's words. He named her "Angelique" because he liked the sound of the name. "You are angry with me," he said. "When someone says 'whatever,' it is a sign of derision and dismissal when it is clear that rational discussion would be a waste of time and energy according to UrbanDictionary.com."

"Why are you talking to me?" the woman asked.

"My brother Angelo wants me to talk to women," Tony said. "You are a woman so I am talking to you."

The woman waved her free hand. "Poof, be gone."

"I am still here," Tony said. "You are not a magician."

The woman shook her head. "Are you for real?"

"I have mass and take up space," Tony said. "Therefore, I am real."

The woman laughed. "You're a *real* genius."

"Thank you." He stood, gathered his remaining cookies, the bottle of root beer, and his notebook, and he stepped over to her table. "I want to sit with you."

"Are you kidding?"

"I am not kidding," Tony said. "I do not know how to kid. There are three empty seats. There is plenty of room. It will make our conversation easier."

"Get the *hell* outta here. *Now.*"

Tony blinked. "You have cursed. Your curse does not make sense. Hell is not in here. I do not have hell inside me. There is a place in New York City called Hell's Kitchen, but that is not hell either. There is a place called Hell, Michigan. They say Hell does freeze over there. There is a town called Hell, California, too."

"What the . . ." The woman looked around the café. "Can you believe this guy?"

"You can believe me," Tony said. "I always tell the truth."

The woman stared Tony down. "Quit harassing me, man."

"I am not harassing you," Tony said. "Harassment is aggressive pressure or intimidation. I am not aggressive. I am not intimidating. I am talking to you."

"Leave me alone," the woman said.

"If I leave you, you will be alone," Tony said. "I do not want you to be alone. I want to talk to you. You are very pretty. Angela is prettier, but she has a husband, a daughter named Angel, and a son in her stomach."

The woman almost smiled. "Are you crazy or something?"

"No, I have Asperger's," Tony said. "And I am shy."

"Angela," the woman said. "Do you know this guy?"

Angela nodded. "Monique Freitas, meet Tony Santangelo."

"I mean, do you *know* this guy?" Monique asked. "Have you been listening to him?"

"Tony is not dangerous," Angela said.

"I am not dangerous," Tony said. "I do not have any weapons." He held up his pencil. "Just this pencil and it is not very sharp. I press too hard when I write."

"Well, can you get him away from me?" Monique asked. "Please?"

Angela left the counter and moved next to Tony. "Come sit down, Tony. I'll talk to you."

Tony didn't move. "I did not mean to interrupt your day, Angelique."

"Well, you did." Monique turned away from him. "And my name is Monique."

"I hear an angel in you," Tony said. "I do not hear a moan."

Monique moaned.

"I heard a moan that time," Tony said. "You are named correctly."

Monique gathered a green purse and pushed back her chair.

"Your purse does not match your outfit," Tony said. "It should be white, orange, or yellow."

Monique stood. "Get lost, freak!"

"I do not get lost because I have a very good sense of direction," Tony said. "I study maps. I have memorized all the streets in Chinatown in San Francisco. I know Brooklyn very well. If you tell me where you live, I can tell you the best way to get there by walking, bus, car, or train. I am not a freak. I am not horny and I have not had sex yet."

"Holy shit!" Monique cried. "You're out of your *fucking* mind!"

"Shit is not holy," Tony said. "I do not have a fucking mind. The mind does not fuck."

"Wow," Monique said. "You're insane."

"I am not out of my mind," Tony said. "I am inside my mind. And you are very pretty. That snowsuit hides your body. I like your smile."

Monique grabbed her coffee and swept past Tony, slamming her coffee cup into a trash can before banging out the door.

"Her pants made a swishy sound," Tony said. "I do not like her snow pants. They did not let me see her legs. I am sure they are smooth and tan. She is not an Easter egg. She is a frozen striped Popsicle."

Angela gently touched Tony's elbow. "And you have described Monique Freitas perfectly. Would you like to sit with me?"

Tony stared at her finger on his elbow. "You are very brown, Angela. I like dark brown. Dark brown is warm."

"Come on." Angela slid into the booth.

Tony sat opposite her and sipped his root beer. "You are the color of root beer."

"Thank you, Tony," Angela said. "But I'm closer in color to the house blend."

"You have pretty eyes," Tony said. "They are not angry eyes." He looked toward the door. "Monique had angry eyes."

"You kind of surprised her," Angela said.

"I did not mean to," Tony said. "I must write down our conversation."

"Why?" Angela asked.

"My brother wants me to write down conversations I have with women so I can be better at talking to women so I can find a wife and he and Aika can be married. Aika's name means 'love song,' and she has very nice legs. She runs very fast but not as fast as Angel. I have not seen Aika smile yet because the only time I saw her face was when she and Angelo were trying to break the bed. Her face was a frown. Monique's face was a frown, too. I thought her name was Angelique because she was in a snowsuit and she could make snow angels. I am sure Aika's smile is pretty. Her voice is like soft cotton. I saw Aika running from our kitchen to Angelo's bedroom. She wore blue underwear. It was not sky blue like Monique's eyes. I like sky blue. It reminds me of Mama. We buried Mama under a sky-blue sky when I was fourteen." Tony took a deep breath. "I am sorry."

"Why are you sorry?" Angela asked.

"I am talking too much," Tony said.

"It's okay," Angela said. "I'm not busy now." She put her hand on the back of his.

Tony stared at her dark brown hand. He felt the warmth of Angela's fingers seeping into his skin. He also felt tears forming in his eyes. "When Mama died, I did not cry. When Poppa died, I did not cry. When Tonto died, I did not cry. When Silver dies, I will not cry." He stared at her hand. "You touch me and I want to cry."

Angela squeezed his hand. "Are you sad, Tony?"

"No," Tony said. A tear fell. He stared at where it

plopped on the table. "Your hand is warm and brown and soft and strong. I can feel your pulse." He looked at his watch. "You are calm. I am not calm." A flood of tears spilled out of his eyes. "I do not have a warm and brown and soft and strong hand to hold. Delores is brown but she is not warm. She cooks for me and Angelo. She is very old. She laughs all the time. She tries to hug me, but I will not let her."

"Why not?" Angela asked.

"I do not know," Tony said. "Mama used to hug me. Poppa used to hug me. Tonto used to jump up on me. They are all gone."

"Are you afraid if someone hugs you that they'll go away?" Angela asked.

"I do not know."

Angela slid out of the booth, pulling Tony's hand. "Please stand, Tony."

Tony stood.

Angela pulled him close and hugged him.

Tony kept his arms and hands rigid at his sides.

Angela stepped back. "I'm still here, Tony."

"I did not hug you back," Tony said.

"It's okay," Angela said.

"I did not want to hurt your baby and you have a husband," Tony said. "I would not want him angry with me. He has big hands."

"It's okay." She led him back to the booth and slid in next to him.

"I am sorry I did not shake Matthew's hand," Tony said. "His hand was very big. Poppa had big hands. He could not play the piano because his fingers were too wide. I can play the piano because I have Mama's fingers."

"Yeah?"

"And I write songs." He opened his notebook. "I will use my conversation with Monique to compose another song for Naomi Stringer."

"Naomi . . . Stringer."

"I have written lots of songs for Naomi," Tony said. "I want to call Monique's song 'One Hundred Twenty Pounds of Sexy, Sexy Hate.'"

Angela laughed. "That's an accurate title, though that skinny thing probably doesn't weigh more than one-ten."

"Monique had hate for me in her eyes, but she is still sexy," Tony said. "But Naomi will be singing it. She has just had a baby with DC or DQ or QT. I can never keep his names straight. He keeps changing them."

"I think it's CQ now," Angela said.

"So maybe I should title it 'One Hundred Thirty-Five Pounds of Sexy, Sexy Hate.'" He counted the syllables. "Thirteen syllables. Naomi was very big. Maybe I should call it 'One Hundred Fifty Pounds of Sexy, Sexy Hate.'"

"I wouldn't want you to hurt Naomi Stringer's feelings," Angela said. "I'd stick to one-twenty."

Tony made the corrections. "Okay. This is kind of rough." He cleared his throat. "'You interrupt my day, you sure are a sight, you want me to stay, but boy, you ain't bright; you must be crazy to ask me for a date 'cuz I'm one hundred and twenty pounds of sexy, sexy hate.'"

Angela blinked. "That sounds . . . *exactly* like something Naomi Stringer might sing."

"She is a good dancer, too," Tony said. "Sometimes she does not wear underwear."

"Um, okay," Angela said.

"I am also writing a song about you and Matthew

and Angel," Tony said. "I only have a few phrases so far."

"I'd love to hear them," Angela said.

" 'Love is playing hide-and-seek and always being found, a wink and a smile chasing a laughing child, a hug for no reason because love needs no reason, a hand on my hand so warm, soft, and brown.' " He looked briefly into Angela's eyes. "That was the first verse. I think. It might be the bridge. I am sure of this chorus: 'Angel's laughter is the love that I'm after because love is the laughter of angels.' "

Angela touched his hand. "That's . . . that's beautiful, Tony."

"It needs work." He underlined the word "brown."

"And you did all that right here in this booth?" Angela asked.

Tony nodded. "Walter Little could sing it, but he is dead. He sang 'She's Not Here.' "

"I know," Angela said. "I love that song."

"I wrote it when I was sixteen," Tony said. "It is about Mama."

"I thought that song was about a man mourning over a woman who left him," Angela said. "I thought it was a sad love song."

"I was sad Mama left me," Tony said.

"But if you wrote it . . ." She grasped his hand. "You're Art E., aren't you?"

"Please do not tell anyone, Angela," Tony said. "My brother Angelo would not like it. He does not want anyone to know."

Angela looked toward the counter. "Matthew and I both read the book your brother wrote about you. I just finished reading it last week." She turned to Tony and smiled. "I thought I recognized you."

Tony blinked. "You recognized me."

"After reading about you and reading some of the things you've said and the way you compose your music," Angela said, "I feel as if I already know you. It is truly an honor to meet you."

Matthew bounded around the counter with Angel on his shoulders. He extended his hand to Tony. "I have washed it thoroughly."

Tony watched his hand crawl up from under the table to grasp Matthew's hand. "Your hand is big."

"You have a big hand, too," Matthew said. He shook Tony's hand once. "Having a nice conversation?"

"Sit with us," Angela said.

Matthew sat, unloading Angel into the booth, where she stood and looked over the booth cushion at the front window. "It's snowing," she said. "Look, Daddy."

"It is not supposed to be snowing," Tony said. "The forecast is wrong. It is only supposed to rain. There was only a twenty-percent chance. It should not be cold enough to snow."

"They're only flurries," Matthew said.

Tony couldn't take his eyes off Angel. He wanted to write about her in his notebook, but he fought the urge. "She is a snowflake girl," he whispered.

"You're right about that," Angela said. "That child loves snow."

Tony ripped open his notebook and wrote it down. He closed his notebook.

"Matthew," Angela said softly, "I'd like you to meet Art E."

"This . . ." Matthew blinked rapidly. "You're . . ."

Angela nodded slowly.

Tony opened his notebook to a new page. "I have to write now."

"Could you say it as you write it, Tony?" Angela asked.

Tony began to write. " 'Snowflake eyes in a snowflake world, a snowflake palace for a snowflake girl . . .' " He put down his pencil. "I will work on it later. It might make a nice Christmas carol."

"That's *three* songs he's written while he's been sitting in this booth, Matthew," Angela said.

"Amazing," Matthew said.

"It is not amazing," Tony said. "The words and the notes come to me floating on the air. I see them when I close my eyes. I see them everywhere." He nodded for a moment. "I wrote that rhyme when I was ten." He looked briefly at Angela and Matthew, then focused on little Angel. "I am not amazing. Your family is amazing. I wish . . ." He felt tears forming in his eyes again. "I must go. Angelo is probably worried about me. It is not supposed to be snowing. It is supposed to be in the thirties with a twenty-percent chance of rain. I want to meet Aika. She is moving in today. She is Japanese, but she lives in Brooklyn. Sometimes she does not wear a bra. We will watch the Weather Channel together. I will show her my map of San Francisco."

Angel smiled at Tony. "Why are you crying?"

"I have never seen anything so beautiful," Tony said. "Your family is beautiful."

*And I want this,* Tony thought. *I want this.*

*I want a dark brown woman and a snowflake girl.*

*And Angelo is going to help me find her.*

# San Francisco, California

# 5

At 641 O'Farrell Street, Apartment 7, in Nob Hill, San Francisco, in a seismically retrofitted Edwardian building constructed in 1910, Trina Woods woke up at 6:00 AM the day after Christmas.

She had celebrated without a tree by giving herself underwear and a bra.

Trina brushed her teeth first, then showered and shaved her legs in a claw-foot tub surrounded by a clear shower liner. She put on her aqua-blue scrubs in her bedroom, the largest room in her studio apartment, and pulled up the purple-and-white bedspread on her full-size bed. She applied no makeup, not because she never did but because she didn't see the point anymore. She slipped into her scuffed, somewhat white, thin-soled Danskos, ignored the hole near the ball of her right footy sock, and slipped sideways into the tiny kitchen. She grabbed her lunch and a Crock-Pot from the refrigerator, turned on the Crock-Pot, and dropped one piece of bread into the toaster. She left the kitchen and rushed past a small dark purple couch, black wood coffee table, and small television on a black TV stand to the closet near the door, where she threw on a flimsy blue Windbreaker with a broken zipper. After returning to the kitchen to butter her toast and eat it in four bites, she left the apartment for her ten-minute hike up Hyde Street to work at Saint Francis Memorial Hospital.

Five hours later she had emptied a dozen bedpans, switched out eight colostomy bags, cleaned up four incidents of projectile vomiting, transported two dozen patients from the emergency room to the operating room, the intensive care unit, X-ray, or a regular bed, and generally did the scut work assigned to her by nursing supervisor Ellen Sprouse, whom Trina nicknamed "ES" for "evil stepmother."

Trina had already paid her dues. She had learned how not to pee for eight hours at a time and earned several urinary-tract infections along the way. She had done twelve-hour shifts and survived rotating shifts of 6–6 followed by 12–12 followed by 8–8 on consecutive days. She knew a normal workday didn't end until she had passed off her rotation of patients to the next shift. She had dealt with ninety-year-old men and women who were surprisingly strong and who had the ability to break out of restraints and rip out IVs and gastronomy tubes. She had survived, and because of seniority, she had earned a somewhat normal 7:00 AM to 4:00 PM shift.

Once ES took over three years ago, Trina rarely did "normal" RN work. While Trina continued to work with patients nonstop, she rarely did rounds or supervised LPNs or CNAs as she had done for five years before. She rarely kept charts or supervised the direct care of patients. ES had reduced her to a glorified orderly in a matter of weeks, and Trina often found herself working alongside housekeeping instead of doctors, while being watched by Danica Trumbo and Inez Martinez, whom Trina nicknamed "ES2" for "the evil stepsisters." Danica and Inez checked along behind her with clipboards and pens but otherwise did nothing strenuous or patient related.

Trina had been an RN longer than they had. She knew more about caring for patients than all three women combined. She had also been passed over for promotion to nursing supervisor in favor of ES.

Trina took a brief thirty-minute "lunch hour" whenever she could and spent it soaking up a little sun at nearby Huntington Park, where she ate her ham and cheese sandwich with a carton of two-percent milk as cable cars trundled past on California Street.

Six hours later, two of them overtime hours spent in the ER mopping up blood and other fluids from exam-room floors, she walked down Hyde Street for home.

She followed this routine five days a week, fifty-two weeks a year. She often worked weekends.

In her high-ceilinged, four-hundred-square-foot walk-in closet of an apartment, she ate Crock-Pot beef stew with cheddar Goldfish crackers, rested her weary, aching feet, and waited patiently for the Internet to appear on her ancient Apex netbook.

At thirty-two, Trina did not expect to have this lonely, solitary life. Eleven years ago she had buried Grandma Dee, the woman who raised her after her mother had died when she was ten. Two years ago, she had been Katrina Woods Allen, married to Dr. Robert Allen, who had been finishing his surgical residency at San Francisco General. She had scrimped and saved and worked double-shifts to get Robert through med school at the University of California, San Francisco. She had put off having children until Robert was a full-fledged doctor. She had cosigned his student loans and paid on them as often as she could.

Then Robert discovered "Dr. Too White," a long-legged, pasty-skinned, redheaded, green-eyed surgical resident who evidently wanted the Mandingo-warrior experience.

The divorce left Trina with almost nothing. She could no longer get credit of any kind and had to pay for most things with cash or a money order. She had a rudimentary cell phone that only made phone calls. She sold her car to pay down a credit card that Robert had run up on expensive clothing because he had to look "better than good if I want to get anywhere in the white world." She worked ten or more overtime hours a week in the ER to help pay for her "affordable" employee health plan. She had no cable, no satellite, basic DSL, and a nineteen-inch Zenith television with a tiny digital receiver that only picked up local broadcasts. She needed new shoes. She needed a new rain jacket.

She needed a new life.

As she savored her beef stew with her feet propped up on her coffee table, she watched a promo for *Rich Man, Lucky Lady.*

*Whoopee,* she thought. *Another so-called "reality" romance show. Who wouldn't want to marry a rich man? No African American women "win" on those shows anyway. And so few "winners" actually marry the guy, so where's the romance?*

She dreamed of being on a show like *The Bachelorette,* where she could weed men out until she found the right one. *I still have some beauty left. I still get carded, not that I go out much anymore. Maybe I could get on one of those shows.*

She surfed to *The Bachelorette* Web site to find out when the next installment was appearing on television. "Apply now for the fall 2020 show," it said.

*I'd be thirty-six. Terrific.*

She analyzed the next bachelorette. *Creamy white complexion. Long, flowing dark hair with blond highlights. "Come hither" blue eyes. Delicate nose. Pouting lips. Everything I don't have and will never have. But we have something in common, wench. Neither one of us has a man. Ha! I could go out tomorrow and find a man—miracles have been known to happen—but you have to wait at least three months. I wonder how long I will have to wait. I'm a good woman, aren't I? I should be able to find a good man.*

She sighed.

*It would be simpler if a good man found me, a man who is honest, faithful, and true, someone I can trust, someone who can hold my hand and not secretly wish it was white. . . .*

# 6

On a whim, Trina went to the *Rich Man, Lucky Lady* Web site to find out what the rich man wanted.

What she found surprised her.

*This man has simple needs.*

The rich man desired a woman who was single and wanted children.

*So far so good.*

He required a woman who was "fiscally responsible with money."

*If you ignore my credit score, I am fiscally responsible. I'm great with money. I put a man through med school on only an RN's salary.*

The rich man sought a woman who was "trustworthy" and had "a good sense of humor."

*I'm trustworthy to a fault. I trusted the man who married me to honor his vows. I used to have a good sense of humor. I blame the man who didn't honor his vows for my sense of humor's disappearance.*

The rich man wanted a woman who didn't "use drugs, smoke, or drink alcohol to excess" and was "fit and in good health."

*I can't afford to have any vices, not that I ever had many, and I am slim and trim from not eating and being run ragged by ES.*

*I am everything a rich man wants. Lucky me.*

She hit the APPLY NOW button.

The deadline for the show was two months ago.

*His loss.*

She flipped through the few channels she had available for her television and stopped.

*What do you know?* Rich Man, Lucky Lady *is on tonight. Let's see the women I would have beaten out for the rich man's affection.*

"Good evening," the tuxedo-wearing host said. "Welcome to *Rich Man, Lucky Lady.* We are *live* at the equestrian estate of Vincent St. John in the foothills of Boulder, Colorado."

*Hmm. A live show. This could be interesting. No editing to make the romance "real" here. Look at all those windows! They go from the ground to the third floor, so you can probably see the mountains from every room. It must be nice to have money like that. And no neighbors but some horses. That would be so peaceful.*

Steam rose from a large in-ground pool as the camera panned the contestants.

*Those women are shivering! Why did they put this show on in the dead of winter in Colorado?*

The camera zoomed in on several of the women's ample and surgically reconstructed chests.

*Oh, that's why. Girl, look down. One nipple is going south while the other is pointing north.*

"Tonight," the host continued, "Mr. St. John will begin his quest to find a wife." He held up a gold heart pendant. "Unlike other programs of this type, our lucky ladies can opt out of the show completely at any time and even before Mr. St. John starts his selection process. Our hopeful future *Mrs*. St. Johns wear heart pendants like this one. If at any time they want to leave the program, all they have to do is press this button." He demonstrated by pushing the button for the camera. "At that moment, a contestant will forfeit her chance to marry Mr. St. John, exit the pool area to the mansion, and then leave the mansion forever."

*Why would any of them want to leave the mansion? Shoot, I'd stick around for the view. I don't have one. Okay. I have a nice view of the traffic on O'Farrell Street.*

"Now let's meet our twenty-four contestants. . . ."

*Where did they get these women? They look like mannequins. You're too tall for those stilettos, honey. You look like a white stork. And where are your clothes, Miss Thing? It's Colorado in late December, girl. Wear some fur or something. What's wrong with the picture? Is the camera jiggling? No, it's the blonde. She'd give Jell-O a run for its money. The one on the end is already paid. Can you wear any more bling, woman? Like they*

*say, the rich get richer, and the poor get poorer . . .*
*while secretly wanting to be rich.*

"Now it's time to meet our man of the hour," the
host said. "Lucky ladies, please give a warm welcome
to Mr. Vincent St. John."

*How can they give him a warm welcome? It's freez-*
*ing. Are those snowflakes hitting the water? I'd be*
*wearing long johns or leggings at least.*

An ancient matronly nurse with bluish hair rolled an
equally ancient long-haired, scraggly-bearded man in a
wheelchair out to the pool. He wore a fluffy burgundy
robe and bright orange house slippers, a thick brown
fur blanket covering his legs.

Half of the women immediately pressed their "escape" buttons and clicked their heels around him and
into the mansion. One woman shouted, "Oh, *hell* no!"
Another shouted, "This is some serious [expletive]! I
quit my job for this [expletive]!"

Trina laughed so hard she spilled some of her soup.
*Wow! Really? Is this really happening? What did these*
*women expect? It takes time to make money. Mr. St.*
*John really does need a haircut, though. Curly hair*
*down to his shoulders, and that beard looks like a*
*bird's nest.*

Mr. St. John's head whipped back and forth. "What
is happening? Where are they going?"

*Now* I'm *shivering. What a creepy voice, like that*
*Vincent Price guy from* Thriller. *He sounds British.*

"They have opted out of the show, Mr. St. John," the
host said.

"Already?" Mr. St. John cried. "I haven't even spoken a word." He looked up at his nurse, who wore a
starched white uniform. "They only saw me with their
eyes."

*Poor man, but what did he expect? Those women are surface-dwellers who don't know how to dress for the mountains of Colorado. Maybe they were getting frostbite or hypothermia. They obviously had brain lock. Look at his mansion, you fools! That could be your house one day!*

"It's time for your medication," the nurse said.

"Not now, woman," Mr. St. John said.

"You pay me to take care of you," the nurse said, wheeling him around. "It is *time* for your *medication.*"

"Oh, all right."

The camera panned to catch the reactions of the remaining twelve women as the nurse wheeled Mr. St. John back into the mansion. Two more women left, one saying, "No way am I playing nursemaid to that old fart!"

*You'd think that these women would* want *a dying, unhealthy man like that. He dies, and they get his fortune. Wow, that woman is seriously shivering—no, it's the blonde jiggling again. She needs a better bra.* She looked closely at the screen. *She needs to* wear *a bra. She couldn't have been born with those.*

The nurse returned Mr. St. John to the pool. "There were twelve here when I went to take my vitamins," he said.

*Ha! He fooled them. He only had to take some vitamins. Hmm. Maybe that was his purpose. He's weeding them out without actually weeding them out. At the rate they're escaping, this show may end tonight and he'll have his future bride. Crazy! Mr. St. John is indeed the man of the* hour. *Not counting commercials, he could have his wife in forty-four minutes. That has to be a television record.*

"Hello, ladies," Mr. St. John said. "Thank you for being here."

The camera moved from Mr. St. John's smiling face to the host. "We'll be right back with more of *Rich Man, Lucky Lady.*"

During the commercial break, Trina found the Web site for a show called *Second Chances,* described as "a reality TV show where a woman scorned gets a second chance at love with celebrities who are in desperate need of second chances."

*Maybe* this *is the show for me. I've been scorned, and I'm desperate.*

She clicked the APPLY button, found that the deadline was in a week, and began filling out the application.

*Name. Address. Telephone number. Birth date. Social Security Number. This is like applying for a job. Oh, the show's back on. . . .*

"Before I get to know you better," Mr. St. John said. "I have a confession to make." He pointed behind him. "This is not my mansion. The network thought this would be a majestic, romantic backdrop for this show."

Three more women left in a huff, one saying "I knew this was a <expletive> scam!" Another woman said directly to the camera: "That old geezer is probably flat-ass broke!"

Mr. St. John watched them go. Once a large glass door to the mansion shut, he turned and laughed. "Forgive me, ladies. I had to get rid of the, shall we say, *hard-core* gold diggers."

"Ha!" Trina shouted. "That was sweet!" *I'll bet Mr. St. John is in disguise. That was a young man's laugh. I'll even bet he's quite a handsome man under all that hair. That man is crazy like a fox. Only seven left.*

"I'll let you lucky seven in on a little secret," Mr. St. John said. "My mansion is *much* bigger than this little cabin. I live in a *palace.*"

*He's not an old, decrepit, sickly millionaire at all. This man knows what he's doing. He wouldn't have millions if he was a moron. And he definitely knows American women. I wonder why he wants one. At any rate, he's cutting to the chase. He's cutting through the usual reality-TV nonsense and melodrama and getting to the good stuff.*

"No one else is leaving?" Mr. St. John smiled. "Good." The nurse handed him some folders.

"I took the liberty of doing a little research on each of you, using a very discreet, very thorough group of private investigators," Mr. St. John said. "I am a busy man, and as you can see, I am running out of time. Since it's only you seven, let's jump ahead to a little polygraph test. Any objections?"

*Straight to the truth. That's the way to do it. If I were ever on a show like this, I'd do a little research, too. Foolish me. As if they'd ever want me to be on a show like this. A girl can dream, can't she? That's all I have now anyway. Dreams.*

She looked into her soup bowl.

*Dreams, cold beef stew, and soggy cheddar Gold-fish.*

# 7

*A*nd now the fun begins! Trina thought. *Polygraph
tests aren't admissible in court, but we believe in
them on TV shows like this. How gullible are we?*

After technicians seated the first woman, a blonde
with dark roots and even darker eyebrows, and attached wires to her fingers, the host said, "Mr. St. John
will be questioning our lucky ladies while only Mr. St.
John and you at home will know if they are telling the
truth or not."

"May I begin?" Mr. St. John asked.

The technicians nodded.

Mr. St. John rolled up to the blonde and smiled.

*I knew he didn't need that nurse. She's only a prop.
Mr. St. John has some seriously strong-looking forearms.*

"You're Richard P. Johnson of Yonkers, New York,"
Mr. St. John said.

"What?" the woman squealed. "I'm Tammy McGhee
from Calumet City, Illinois."

"LIE!" flashed several times onto the screen in big
bold white letters.

"Ha!" Trina shouted. "You are so busted."

"The Social Security number you provided on your
application matches up to a Richard P. Johnson of
Yonkers, New York," Mr. St. John said.

"There must be some mistake," Tammy said. "I
don't look like a Richard, do I?"

"No, you most certainly do not," Mr. St. John said.

"Thank you, Mr. St. John," Tammy gushed.

*Oh, I hate it when they gush! She was caught in a lie, and she's trying to gush her way out of it.*

Mr. St. John turned to the nurse. "Give me a pen."

The nurse stepped closer and handed him a gold pen.

"I'll make the correction, Miss McGhee," Mr. St. John said.

"I might have messed up a number," Tammy said.

LIE!

"It's okay," Mr. St. John said. "These mistakes happen. I still found out a great deal about you. My investigators use facial recognition software, Miss McGhee. It is *truly* amazing technology. I watched your face match so many pictures."

*Look at her! She knows what's coming. Vincent St. John is giving her a moment to escape, and she's not taking it. What a fool! Press your button, sweetheart.*

"These pictures are in color *and* in black and white," Mr. St. John said. "Hundreds of them. And do you know where we found most of these pictures?"

"On Facebook?" Tammy asked.

"Strangely, you had *no* pictures at all on Facebook," Mr. St. John said. "Not even one selfie. We found these pictures mostly in law enforcement databases."

*Look at her jaw dropping into her cleavage! It's a good thing she has an ample set of breasts or her jaw might have fallen through her chair, hit the ground, and rolled into the pool!*

"You have a number of outstanding warrants, Miss McGhee," Mr. St. John said. He motioned to two men.

*And those men have badges! Oh my goodness! Tammy is about to be arrested on live TV! This has to be a television first!*

"These are federal marshals, Miss McGhee," Mr. St. John said.

"Why are they here?" Tammy asked.

*She can't be that stupid.*

"They are here to collect you and bring you to justice," Mr. St. John said.

The marshals moved around behind her, pulled her to her feet, and handcuffed her.

"There must be some mistake!" Tammy cried.

*Yeah, she's that stupid.*

"There is no mistake," Mr. St. John said. "They're going to charge you with identity theft, Miss McGhee, if that's even your real name. But before you go, I need to tell you something. I would never marry a woman who has allegedly committed fifteen felonies by stealing the identities of others. Nor would I ever marry a woman who isn't content to be herself. Good-bye." He handed the file to the nurse as the marshals hauled Tammy away.

He received another file from the nurse. "Tonya Thomas. You're next."

Technicians attached wires to an overly made-up brunette, her hair immobile, her tan a deep, dark brown. "Hello," Tonya said.

"Hello," Mr. St. John said. "Do you want children, Miss Thomas?"

"Oh yes," Tonya said. "I've always wanted to have a little girl."

LIE!

Mr. St. John flipped a page in the file. "It seems you already have children. Two daughters."

"But I don't!" Tonya cried.

LIE!

"Wench, I want just one, and you deny having two!" Trina shouted. "Trifling, just trifling."

Mr. St. John looked at yet another page. "No. It's right here. It seems you gave them up for adoption. You used an adoption agency twice to 'sell' your children."

"I most certainly did not!"

LIE!

"Miss Thomas," Mr. St. John said, "we have the proof right here."

*There is so much paint on her eyes, and now she's trying to cry it all off. If it were lead-based paint, she'd have more brain damage than she already has. Why do women do that to themselves anyway? Don't most men want to see a woman's eyes and not the tin roof over them?*

"All right," Tonya said. "I had two children, but I was very young."

TRUE!

"How old were you?" Mr. St. John asked.

"I was . . . eighteen."

LIE!

"I was desperate."

TRUE!

"I couldn't support them."

TRUE!

"Didn't you make one hundred thousand dollars from selling your children?" Mr. St. John asked.

"I didn't sell them for a hundred thousand dollars."

LIE!

*She probably bought a tanning bed with the money. I'll bet she sleeps in it every night. She looks like a human football, and her teeth are the laces.*

"Please relax, Miss Thomas," Mr. St. John said.

"This is actually your lucky day. A delightful, enchanting young lady saw your picture online at this show's Web site. She saw a strong resemblance between her and you, so she contacted the show's producer. The producer mentioned this to me, and—"

"Those records are supposed to be sealed!" Tonya cried.

"Well, the young lady is twenty-one now and wanted to meet her birth mother," Mr. St. John said. "I didn't have the heart to deny her." He looked back at the file. "You wrote in your application that you're twenty-five. That would make you a medical miracle, Miss Thomas. Did you really have a child when you were four years old?"

"It must be a misprint," Tonya said.

LIE!

"And *you* misprinted it," Mr. St. John said. "This young lady wants to meet you. Tonight."

A young woman walked out of the mansion. Though she didn't have a tan, her resemblance to Tonya was unmistakable.

"Mama?" she said. "Mama, is that really you?" She ran to embrace Tonya from behind. "I am so glad I finally found you!"

"Oh . . . my . . . God," Tonya whispered.

"Miss Thomas," Mr. St. John said, "I would never consider a woman who didn't want her own children, denied having children, and lied about her age. You two have a lot to catch up on. Good-bye, Miss Thomas."

*That poor child! What this must be like for her. The mother who didn't want me is a football . . .*

# 8

Trina thought that *Rich Man, Lucky Lady* was like the worst of *Maury, Montel,* and *Jerry Springer* all on one show. *The ratings must be off the charts.*

During a commercial, Trina surfed to Facebook and looked at what her friends—all five dozen of them—were already saying about the show:

> "This show is off the chain! This is REAL reality TV! I can't stop laughing!"
> "Is this for real? 'Cuz if it is, I will be watching this show every week!"
> "That man is DESTROYING those women! Those LYING WENCHES are getting what they DESERVE!"
> "Who chooses the women for that show? They're all trifling hos. Let me get up on there."

Trina clicked on a comment below the last post:

> "Girl, you tripping. You know you just got out of jail. LOL!"

*That last woman,* Trina thought. *Just when she thought she had a shot at millions from lying about having children, one of the kids she "sold" robs her of the chance. A fitting end. Life does come full circle sometimes. Karma's gonna get you. I truly like Vincent St. John's methods.*

*Oh, it's the tall woman in the short silver metallic cocktail dress. Stork lady, you're about to be cut down to size.*

"Miss Lauren Gray, you are employed at Bess Baron as a stockbroker, is that right?" Mr. St. John asked.

*That silver swizzle stick is a stockbroker? She looks as if she's getting ready for a New Year's Eve party, not that I'd ever know about going to one of those. I know I won't have a date this year. Geez, I can see the blue veins in her shins.*

"I'm not a stockbroker for Bess Baron anymore," Lauren said. "I'm on my own now."

TRUE!

"But you wrote on this application that you were currently employed by Bess Baron," Mr. St. John said.

"I was employed by them at the time I filled out the application," Lauren said.

TRUE!

"But that was only three months ago, Miss Gray," Mr. St. John said.

"I've been on my own for the last seven days," Lauren said.

TRUE!

"Why aren't you with Bess Baron anymore?" Mr. St. John asked.

"Like I said, I decided to go out on my own," Lauren said. "I have always wanted to be self-employed."

LIE!

*She got fired!*

"Miss Gray, if I gave you a million dollars to invest for me, how would you invest it?" Mr. St. John asked.

"In today's difficult market," Lauren said, "I'd invest in long-term treasury bonds, stocks in businesses like

JCPenney, Sears, and Sonic, and in commodities like corn, wheat, and sugar."

*What the what? Is this woman high? JCPenney, Sears, and Sonic? I know she got fired now.*

"I talked to Mr. Bess and Ms. Baron over at Bess Baron," Mr. St. John said.

Lauren audibly swallowed. "You . . . did?"

*I wish I had a high-definition TV. I know that woman is sickly gray now. She has become her name. She looks like a thin piece of gray chalk with blue veins.*

"He says you lost quite a bit of your clients' money," Mr. St. John said.

"But the market has been volatile," Lauren said.

"It's been steady, Miss Gray, with a slight uptick, actually," Mr. St. John said. "All of my investments are turning a steady, healthy profit."

"You must have a lucky stockbroker, Mr. St. John," Lauren said.

"I'm my own stockbroker, Miss Gray," Mr. St. John said. "I use E*TRADE and make all the transactions myself. Cuts out the middleman—and the costs." He leaned forward in his wheelchair. "So, Miss Gray, how much money did you lose?"

"If they had let me stay, I know I would have gotten it all back for them," Lauren said.

"I'm only curious," Mr. St. John said. "How much money did you lose?"

"Only a couple . . . hundred . . . thousand," Lauren said.

LIE!

"The exact figure was six point two million dollars, Miss Gray," Mr. St. John said.

Trina whistled. "Wow."

"That's more than nothing, especially if your clients trust you to invest wisely for them," Mr. St. John said. "Have you ever made any money for any of your clients?"

Lauren bowed her head. "I guess not."

TRUE!

"We also checked your credit score," Mr. St. John said. "You have the lowest score of anyone who applied to be on this show—and one *thousand* women applied, Miss Gray."

*Maybe it's a good thing I'm not on there. I think I have the lowest credit score you can get.*

"I've had some . . . setbacks," Lauren whispered.

TRUE!

"Why are you really here?" Mr. St. John asked.

Lauren looked up. "To meet you, Mr. St. John. To hopefully be your wife."

"Aren't you really here to use your assets to get my assets?" Mr. St. John asked.

*Good one!*

"But I don't have any assets."

TRUE!

"I had to rent this dress."

TRUE!

*Oh, that's embarrassing. Wait. I'd have to rent a nice dress, too.*

"Miss Gray, I cannot marry a woman who routinely mismanages money, has little business sense, gives ridiculous investment advice, lies often, and has no empathy for her clients. Good-bye."

"Buh-bye," Trina said. *Maybe she'll be able to get a job at JCPenney, Sears, or Sonic to help pay what she owes those people.*

During the commercial break, Trina read the *Second Chances* application's main question: "Why should *you* get a second chance for love?"

*Because I never really had a first chance.*

She started typing:

Robert and I met as undergrads at UCSF. He was going to be a surgeon, and I was going to be a nurse. We married after graduation, I passed the NCLEX on the first try, I became an RN, and I agreed to fund his dream because I believed in him. I worked double-shifts at Saint Francis Memorial Hospital as often as I could for most of our marriage. And then two years ago, he met Dr. Too White.

*Oh, it's back from commercial.*

"Denny Millington," Mr. St. John said. "That's quite an unusual name for a woman."

*That's not a woman. Wow. And she's wearing a turtleneck. Oh man, no fair! Her breasts are bigger than mine are!*

"Denny" cleared her throat and said, "It's a nickname for Denise."

LIE!

"So, Miss Millington," Mr. St. John said.

"Oh, do call me Denny," she said.

"Or *Danny*," Trina whispered.

"Denny, you know we took a blood sample earlier today," Mr. St. John said. "I have to be careful, you know. I had to make sure you ladies had no drugs in your systems and no, shall we say, buns in the oven."

*He knows! Of course he knows!*

"I am *definitely* not pregnant," Denny said.

TRUE!

*Duh.*

"I'll get straight to the point, Miss Millington," Mr. St. John said. "Can you have children?"

"No," Denny said. "I'm not able to have children."

TRUE!

Mr. St. John pulled out a green piece of paper. "This is a certified copy of your birth certificate, and it says your birth name was Dennis."

Denny sighed. "I had sexual reassignment surgery, and I am legally a woman now."

TRUE!

"Denny, I want to have children with my future wife," Mr. St. John said.

"We can adopt," Denny pleaded. "We could get a surrogate."

*But you couldn't supply any eggs, Denny!*

"I'm sure sexual reassignment surgery is quite expensive," Mr. St. John said. "Are you hoping to win my heart so your bills can be paid?"

"It would be a weight off my shoulders," Denny said.

TRUE!

*Smaller breasts would be a weight off your shoulders, Denny.*

"Your honesty is refreshing, Denny," Mr. St. John said, "but your dishonesty is not." He pulled out a thick stack of papers. "On your application, you left the criminal history section completely blank."

"Because I have no criminal history, Mr. St. John," Denny said.

LIE!

"As *Denise* Millington, this is true," Mr. St. John said.

"But as *Dennis* Millington, you have had several felonies, including assault, malicious wounding, and grand theft."

"But I'm a changed woman now!" Denny cried.

*How could you be a changed woman, Denny? You weren't born a woman! You are definitely a changed man!*

"Miss Millington, the rules of the show prohibit anyone with a felony from appearing, no matter if she was a he when she or he did them or not," Mr. St. John said.

"But that was *Dennis,*" Denny pleaded. "That wasn't me. Dennis is *gone.* Denise has a clean record."

"I'm sorry, Denny," Mr. St. John said. "I believe that no matter what you do to your exterior, your interior stays basically the same. I could never marry anyone who believes her exterior is more important than her interior."

*That was deep. And wise. My exterior isn't much, but I'm content with it.*

"Good-bye, Denny," Mr. St. John said. "Who's next?"

Another woman pressed her button and left in a hurry.

*He scared her away! Ha! Serves her right. She had to protect her lying life. There's only two left. One is the human Jell-O girl, an obvious airhead and community chest, and the other is . . . beautiful. The all-American girl. Dark hair, blue eyes, perfect complexion. She'll win. From twenty-four women to two in only forty minutes!*

Trina opened another window on her laptop and again checked Facebook:

"The blonde is toast! Do they have earthquakes in Colorado? That woman can't stay still!"

"He'll pick the cute white girl. They always do . . ."
"He's been saving the best for last. She's the one he's
wanted all along. I'll bet they already hooked up. I
knew this show was rigged."

*Maybe Mr. St. John is saving the brunette for last
because she's the* worst *of the bunch.*

The camera zoomed in on the airhead's chest. *Those
are so unattractive. Maybe they stuffed those fake
things with jumping beans. Are those silver dollar pancakes under there or what?*

"Miss Constance Carroll," Mr. St. John said.

Constance waved, and her breasts seemed to *do* the
wave. "That's me. Hi."

"I have never seen such an extensive curriculum
vitae," Mr. St. John said.

"A what?" Constance asked.

"You are incredibly well-educated, Miss Carroll,"
Mr. St. John said. "Undergrad at Yale, graduated
summa cum laude . . ."

*She probably spelled it "some come loud."*

". . . Harvard Medical, residency at Johns Hopkins,"
Mr. St. John continued. "Served five years with the
Peace Corps, two years with 'Doctors Without Bor-
ders.'"

"Yeah," Constance said, giggling. "Those doctors
were fun."

TRUE!

"And you're currently a heart surgeon at . . ." Mr. St.
John held the page closer to his eyes. "Ciders Sinus."

"I'm a bad speller," Constance said. "It's supposed
to be Cedars-Sinai." She giggled. "I love the field of
medicine."

TRUE!

*She loves to* take *medicine.*

"Do you drink alcohol, use illegal drugs, or smoke cigarettes, Miss Carroll?" Mr. St. John asked.

"Only occasionally," Constance said.

LIE!

"In the first paragraph of the application you filled out," Mr. St. John said, "in big bold letters, it says that I desire a woman who *doesn't* drink to excess, use illegal drugs, or smoke."

"I'm not a very good reader either," Constance said.

TRUE!

"Miss Carroll, have you been drinking, smoking, or using illegal substances while you've been in the mansion?" Mr. St. John asked.

"No."

LIE!

Mr. St. John sighed. "I'd like to show you what we recorded two hours ago."

The screen faded to black and lit up quickly with a split screen, a grand library inside the mansion on the right, and the very bouncy and lively Constance on the left. The camera in the video zoomed in on Constance reading a book.

"Hey, there's me," Constance said. "Look at me reading."

"For the first time," Trina whispered.

In the video, Constance looked side to side then snorted a line of a powdery substance from the book. Then she shut the book, drank from a flask she took from her little purse, and lit up a cigarette.

*Well, at least she can multitask,* Trina thought.

The video faded out, and the split screen disappeared.

"Miss Carroll, can you explain what you were doing?" Mr. St. John asked.

"Well, I was nervous," Constance said. "I had to get right, you know?"

*I avoid those substances to* stay *right,* Trina thought.

"Miss Carroll, did you really go to Harvard?" Mr. St. John asked.

"No," Constance said. "I only wrote that to get your attention."

TRUE!

"And it worked!" Constance shouted. "Here I am on TV." She waved at the camera and blew a kiss.

"Miss Carroll, you lied about your education, your occupation, and you are currently under the influence of several controlled substances," Mr. St. John said. "I cannot abide that in a wife. Good-bye, Miss Carroll."

"Okay." Constance bounced up and wiggled all the way to the mansion.

*And then there was one.*

"Does this mean I win?" the last contestant asked.

"Not necessarily, Miss Wolfe," Mr. St. John said.

"But I'm the last one," Miss Wolfe said.

"Humor me, Miss Wolfe," Mr. St. John said. "I must follow the rules of the show."

As technicians attached the wires, Miss Wolfe said, "You can call me Sheena, Vincent."

"I shall," Mr. St. John said. "Let's see, Sheena, are you currently single?"

"I am."

TRUE!

"Have you ever been married, Sheena?"

"I haven't found the right man yet."

TRUE!

"Have you ever been engaged, Sheena?"

"Yes," Sheena said. "But I became disengaged just last week."

TRUE!

"Oh, you poor, dear girl," Mr. St. John said.

Sheena's eyes filled with tears. "It broke my heart into a million pieces."

LIE!

*A-ha! And now she wants* his *millions.*

"Did you or did he break off the engagement?" Mr. St. John asked. "I'm only asking to make sure that *you* didn't break off an engagement solely to be on this show."

"He said we weren't compatible," Sheena said. "He broke it off, and I was devastated."

LIE!

"So you're here to mend your broken heart," Mr. St. John said.

"Oh yes, Vincent."

LIE!

"How many times have you been engaged, Miss Wolfe?" Mr. St. John asked.

"Three times," Sheena said.

LIE!

"Three strikes and you're out, right?" Sheena said. "I am so unlucky."

Mr. St. John opened a file. "Facial recognition software is very advanced, Miss Wolfe." He held up some newspaper clippings. "The *Clinch Valley Times* from St. Paul, Virginia. The *Jewell County Record* from Superior, Nebraska. The *Feather River Bulletin* from Quincy, California. These are engagement announcements that have appeared in small town newspapers all over the United States. According to these clippings, you've been engaged *sixteen* different times to *sixteen* differ-

ent men from sea to shining sea, from Winter Harbor,
Maine, to Winterhaven, California."

*Oh wow. She's a serial, um, engagement-ist.*

"I'm sorry I lied about that, Vincent," Sheena said.
She fluttered her eyes. "I'm . . . kind of embarrassed. I
mean, who gets engaged and disengaged sixteen times?
I've been so unlucky with men."

LIE!

"I hope I can change my luck with you, Vincent."

TRUE!

"I would think it would be your fiancés who were
unlucky, Miss Wolfe," Mr. St. John said.

"Thank you, Vincent," Sheena said. "That means a
lot to me."

"I wasn't complimenting you, Miss Wolfe," Mr. St.
John said. "You see, we contacted all sixteen of your
ex-fiancés."

*Are they all there? Oh, that would be* fantastic
*drama!*

"Unfortunately, they all declined the offer for us to
fly them here to see you tonight," Mr. St. John said.

*To avoid the national embarrassment for getting
taken by her.*

"You see, Vincent?" Sheena said. "They couldn't
bear to face me after what they did to me."

Mr. St. John pulled out a stack of paper. "They might
not be here, but your sixteen ex-fiancés did give us
sworn affidavits." He smiled. "Do you know the word
these men used the most to describe you?"

"Bitch," Trina said.

"I'll give you a hint," Mr. St. John said. "It begins
with a *B*."

"Beautiful," Sheena said.

*Is she for real?*

"Um, no, Miss Wolfe," Mr. St. John said. "I think you know what they called you. They each also used the phrase 'gold digger' at least once. One man used that phrase twelve times. And according to these affidavits, these men bought you diamond rings with a collective value of over a quarter of a million dollars. Did you ever return any of the rings?"

"No."

TRUE!

*I'll bet she unloaded them on Cash for Gold and eBay. I would be too embarrassed to sell or melt down the pitiful ring Robert got me—that he put on* my *credit card.*

"These men also showered you with lavish gifts, money, cars, paid your bills, took you on exotic vacations, and wined and dined you to the tune of roughly two point nine million dollars," Mr. St. John said.

*Where* are *these men? In* which *small towns? Tell me!*

"And then there's the question of your boyfriend, Freddy," Mr. St. John said.

"I don't have a boyfriend named Freddy," Sheena said.

TRUE!

"That's just one of his aliases, I suppose," Mr. St. John said. "It seems 'Freddy' locates wealthy bachelors and stakes them out. Once he has a mark, he brings you in. Then you give the mark a sob story about your last broken engagement. You even show him the engagement announcement to make it look legit. Then you chew him up, spit him out, and move on to another small town where your former fiancés can't find you. And here you are going for your largest take from me. Isn't that right?"

Sheena hit her button and stormed out.

*It's too late, wench. The whole world knows about you now.*

The camera zoomed in on Mr. St. John's face. "They didn't want me for my appearance or my health. Some ran when they thought I wasn't wealthy. One denied having children. One was seriously bad with money. One woman . . . was not a woman. Another has a serious drug and alcohol problem. And the last woman was a pathological liar and a sociopath."

The host appeared at his side. "I'm sorry you had no success in finding your bride tonight, Mr. St. John."

"Don't be." Mr. St. John *stood.* "It's what I expected."

Then Mr. St. John pushed off his blanket, tore off his robe, removed his beard and a wig, and dived into the pool.

*That man was hot! Whoo! Look at him swim!*

Mr. St. John swam to the other end of the pool and stared into the camera with his striking green eyes. "One has to be careful, doesn't one?"

The host handed him a towel, and Mr. St. John walked, dripping, out of the pool.

*That's what I'm talking about. Look at those cuts!*

"Shall we try again next week, Mr. St. John?" the host asked.

Mr. St. John nodded. "We shall."

"For the next twenty-four hours," the host said, "if you want to be a contestant on *Rich Man, Lucky Lady,* go to our Web site, and apply right now."

"And please," Mr. St. John said, "only apply if you fit the criteria. All I ask is that you be honest, faithful, and true . . ."

# 9

*Mr. St. John seemed a little sad, but if it was what he expected to happen, he shouldn't have been sad at all. If you expect nothing, you'll never be disappointed, right?*

Trina tried to apply to be on *Rich Man, Lucky Lady*, but once she reached the Web site, the page never fully loaded, she could click on nothing, and the screen froze.

*A couple million "honest, faithful, and true" women probably just crashed the server.*

Deciding to try again in the morning, Trina returned to the *Second Chances* application. She stared at the last sentence:

And then he met Dr. Too White.

*I can't put that in there. That makes me look racist. She* was *too white for Robert, but . . .*

She deleted the sentence and continued:

And then my husband met and started an affair with a surgeon at San Francisco General Hospital. "I'm going to be late again tonight," he often told me. "I have a seminar I have to attend over the weekend." I thought he was putting in extra time to be a more skillful surgeon. I thought he was working longer hours so he could better provide for us. I thought he loved me.

I found out about the affair when he told me, "I've found someone who will be better for my career. I hope you understand." And then he filed for divorce, not me, citing irreconcilable differences. Because I couldn't afford a decent lawyer and his mistress could, I didn't get much in the way of alimony. It barely pays one-third of the credit-card bills he left me with.

For the last two years, I have been living in a cramped apartment near where I work because I can't afford a car or even bus fare. I need new work shoes and a rain jacket that doesn't leak here in "sunny" San Francisco. I need a microwave from this millennium that doesn't dim all the lights in my apartment. I need a bigger bed.

I also need a man to keep me company, to keep me warm at night, to talk to me, to listen to me, and to love me.

I gave up ten years of my life so my ex-husband could become a surgeon. I did this by choice. I sacrificed everything for him, and I would do it again. That's the kind of person I am. But all I have to show for our marriage are his bills and some bad memories. I don't have children because we were putting off children until he could support us. I could have had at least two children by now to love.

I have very little. I deserve a second chance at love.

*And I do,* she thought as she hit the SEND APPLICATION NOW! button and got into her bed. *I deserve something more than I got.*

In the morning she tried again to apply to *Rich Man, Lucky Lady,* but the Web site splash page told her it was "Under Construction." She Googled "Rich Man, Lucky Lady application problems" and saw *thousands* of angry posts from frustrated women. One of her Facebook friends, who blamed all of the world's problems on Microsoft, whined, "Damn that Bill Gates! He obviously doesn't want anyone but him to be rich!"

*I guess it's not meant to be for me. I wish I had the chance. If Mr. St. John hooked me up to a polygraph machine, all the audience would see flashing on the screen was the word* true. *And when he asked about my low credit score, I would be able to tell it all and shame Robert at the same time.*

During another horrible morning shift highlighted by forty minutes of sweating and grunting to help an obese male patient use the bathroom, Trina escaped to a break room and sat with Naini Mitra, another dark-skinned RN on ES's scut list. Naini, a petite Bengali woman with a lilting British accent, read the *Chronicle* while Trina glumly looked at a television promo for *Rich Man, Lucky Lady*:

"Last night, he said good-bye to twenty-four ladies," an announcer said, a montage of last night's scenes playing rapidly on the TV screen. "Will twenty-four more ladies break his heart? How many will be arrested? Will they all be women? Will any of them tell the truth, the whole truth, and nothing but the truth? Tune in to *Rich Man, Lucky Lady!*"

"That promo should not be running," Naini said.

"Why?" Trina asked.

"The rich man has already canceled the show," Naini

said. "It is in today's paper." She took apart a newspaper on the table and slid the entertainment section to her. "I will have to remain a humble Hindi now." Naini sighed. "I tried to get on the show but was unsuccessful."

"So did I," Trina said. "The Web site was frozen."

"I stayed up until three in the morning before I gave up," Naini said. "I am such a dreamer."

Trina read Mr. St. John's statement:

I have suspended filming of *Rich Man, Lucky Lady* indefinitely. After last night's parade of femme fatales around the pool and after having my investigators examine five thousand new applications from women trying to marry me, I realize that continuing this show would be an exercise in futility. All five thousand had significant flaws in their applications.

I have learned quite a bit throughout this process. While all people lie from time to time, women who seek a wealthy husband seem to lie more. While some women lie about their ages, gold-digging women seem either to do their best to cover up their ages or have completely *forgotten* their true ages. While some women drink, smoke, and use illegal drugs, a higher percentage of women looking for a life of ease and sloth seem to drink, smoke, and do drugs more.

*All this can also apply to men, too, Mr. St. John. Not all women are like this. If I had been able to get to your Web site, I'd be meeting you soon at your temporary mansion, and I might be the only one there.*

Please do not read this as an indictment of all women. I am only indicting the collective *six thousand* women who applied to meet me.

I am saddened that I have yet to find my soul mate, but it is my sincere hope that one day I will find a woman who is trustworthy, caring, honest, and levelheaded, a woman who will love me first and enjoy the fruits of my labors second. Until such a woman—or a group of such women—exists, *Rich Man, Lucky Lady* will remain off the air.

*I don't blame him at all,* Trina thought. *I hope he does find his soul mate one day.*

*Too bad she can't be me.*

Naini stood and stretched her back, doing nothing to stifle a loud yawn. "I am going back to work now. I will not enjoy it."

Trina smiled and checked the clock. "And I am going on lunch break."

"What was *this* break?" Naini asked.

"The pre-lunch lunch break," Trina said. "You should try it."

While she was eating the last of her ham and cheese sandwich in Huntington Park, Trina's cell phone rang.

"Hello?"

"Hi," an older man said. "I'm Chet Davis, executive producer for *Second Chances.*"

*No way!*

"Am I speaking to Trina Woods?" Mr. Davis asked.

"Yes," Trina said. *I only sent that application last night!*

"Trina, we've reviewed your application," Mr. Davis

said, "and we have selected you to come to LA to audition for the lead role on *Second Chances*."

*Is this really happening?*

"Trina, are you there?"

*No. I'm floating on air!* "Yes, I'm here."

"How soon can you make it to LA?" Mr. Davis asked.

"How soon do you need me?" Trina asked.

"As soon as possible," Mr. Davis said.

"I can be there tomorrow." *I have plenty of vacation days saved up.*

"Morning or afternoon?" Mr. Davis asked.

"Um, let's say, noon," Trina said. *I can't afford a plane ticket to LA. I'll have to take the bus, I'll have to leave tonight, and I'm sure the bus makes plenty of stops between here and LA. I'll be lucky to get there by noon.*

"Great," Mr. Davis said. "We've e-mailed you all the information you'll need to find us. So we'll see you tomorrow at noon?"

"Tomorrow at noon, yes," Trina said breathlessly. "Thank you."

"Bye."

*They chose me!*

"Yes!"

*They chose me—*

*To audition for a role. The role of the jilted lover. The role of the woman scorned. The role of the angry ex. But I'm not furious or even that angry anymore. I am sad, that's all, and mostly because I can't afford a plane ticket to LA.*

*And I'm also sad that I have to inform ES that I will not be working the rest of today and all day tomorrow.*

*Who am I kidding? I'm not sad at all!*
*I am so out of here.*

She marched purposefully to the break room on the second floor, to Nurse Sprouse, who was greedily smacking her bloodred lips on a cheesesteak sub and cackling to Inez and Danica.

*They're obviously on an extended lunch break. It must be nice to be light-skinned and well rested at work.*

"Nurse Sprouse," Trina said, "may I have a word with you?"

"What do you want, Woods?" Ellen asked.

"I'm taking the rest of the day off today and all day tomorrow, Nurse Sprouse," Trina said.

Nurse Sprouse swiveled in her chair to face her. "I can't have that."

Inez and Danica shared a smile. *Light-skinned wenches. Nurse Sprouse has always favored you for your light skin and Caucasian features. ES isn't a racist—she's a colorist. We can't have any white-looking African American nurses getting their hands dirty here at Saint Francis.*

"I am entitled to some time off, Nurse Sprouse," Trina said. "I haven't used a vacation day since I started working here."

"Are you sick?" Nurse Sprouse asked.

*Of you and my "stepsisters," yes.* "No. I need some time off, that's all."

"Times like these make me wonder if I can count on you, Woods," Nurse Sprouse said.

*What times?* "I have not missed a day of work for the last ten years," Trina said. "Even when I was going through my divorce, I was always here for my shift.

That's over twenty-five *hundred* straight days without an absence. Name anyone else on the nursing staff who can say that."

Inez and Danica exchanged puzzled looks. *They share the same brain.*

"It's the impulsive nature of your request, Woods," Nurse Sprouse said. "Had you given me a week's notice, I could have adjusted the master schedule to avoid the problems your absence will create."

"It just came up," Trina said. "Couldn't be helped."

Nurse Sprouse frowned. "Inez, do you have a time-off form handy?"

*Of course she does. Inez has every form known to the medical profession on her clipboard. It's why Inez's left arm is bigger than her right.*

"Right here, Nurse Sprouse," Inez said. She handed the form to Nurse Sprouse.

Nurse Sprouse whipped out a pen. "What is the purpose of your time off?"

"I am not required to tell you that," Trina said.

Nurse Sprouse checked a box. "Would not disclose reason for absence. When will you be back?"

*I already told you.* "The day after tomorrow."

Nurse Sprouse wrote a short narrative on the form. "Before you leave today, I need you to arrange adequate coverage for your absences."

*Say what?* "Isn't that your job, Nurse Sprouse?"

"I make the master schedule," Nurse Sprouse said. "This little adventure you're taking is not on the master schedule. You will have to find someone willing to work in your place during your absence."

"That's not in any of the regulations, Nurse Sprouse," Trina said.

"If you don't find someone to cover for you, I will

have to mark this absence as unpaid," Nurse Sprouse said.

Inez and Danica shared a soft giggle. *Idiots.*

"You can't do that, Nurse Sprouse," Trina said, "and if you do, I will file a grievance. I have sixteen weeks of vacation saved up. That's four months. I am legally entitled to use them whenever and however I want to."

"You're not a team player, Woods," Nurse Sprouse said. "I shall note that on your next evaluation."

*Whatever, ES.* Trina smiled at Inez and Danica. "At least I do nurse work. Oh, is that a paper cut on your finger, Danica? You better not let it get infected."

Before Trina left for the long but happy walk to the Greyhound bus station, she went online and read critical reactions to Vincent St. John's suspension of the show:

> "*Rich Man, Lucky Lady* caters to the least common denominator in our society. We revel in the fall of others, and some of the falls last night are bound to be permanent. How many privacy laws did Mr. St. John break last night? Why is it so wrong for us to have secrets?"

*Because secrets don't remain secrets forever, and people can often get hurt because of them.*

> "While these women did wrong by lying, Mr. St. John has also done wrong by giving all women a bad name on the basis of two dozen misguided souls. Those women were in no way representative of the American woman."

*Um, well, sad to say, they kind of were—for what networks choose to put on television.*

"This is a man who has it going on! If every man investigated the women he dated the way this guy did, the divorce rate would plummet overnight. Forget eHarmony.com or Match.com. Hire yourself some private investigators."

*If you can afford to.*

"It is sad, so sad that a man of means has to resort to Jerry Springer–type tactics to find a wife. Isn't he trying to buy love? What does this say about our society? Where has romance gone?"

*Romance no longer exists. I don't know why people keep looking for it.*
She laughed.
*And here I am about to go to LA for the second chance to find it.*
*I'm either the last romantic soul left on earth . . . or I'm the most foolish woman who ever lived.*

# 10

After sleeping most of the night as the bus sped south through San Jose, Santa Cruz, Salinas, San Luis Obispo, Santa Maria, and Santa Barbara, Trina woke up somewhat wrinkled but hopeful when the bus crept through Oxnard and North Hollywood. She took a cab from the Greyhound station in downtown LA to West Pico Boulevard in Century City.

The cab fare cost more than the round-trip bus fare from San Francisco did.

Once inside the studio, she looked at about one hundred women there for the audition and didn't see a single black woman.

*I know I shouldn't stare or check other women out, but I can't help it. They're obviously checking me out. What is* she *doing here? She's black, and she's not even that cute. This is a white show. She can't be Spanish. She's too dark. With her pores, she won't look good in HD at all. How bad could* her *life be? My boo left me at the altar in front of two thousand wedding guests while Zamfir played the pan flute and Yanni played the piano . . .*

Trina was one of the last women called into Chet Davis's office. After Trina posed for several photos against a tropical beach background, Mr. Davis motioned her to a comfortable chair in front of his massive desk.

"I'm glad you could make it, Trina," Mr. Davis said.

"I'm glad to be here, Mr. Davis."

"Do you have any questions for us?" Mr. Davis asked.

*I thought they were supposed to interview me!* "You don't have any questions for me?"

"Your application was complete and thorough," Mr. Davis said. "You checked out one hundred percent."

"I . . . checked out," Trina said.

"You told us the truth," Mr. Davis said. "About your job, your divorce, your educational background. After what happened on *Rich Man, Lucky Lady,* the network made us go over the applications again. You are who you say you are."

*And all the others who auditioned before me checked out, too? That horde of plastic surgery, tummy tucks, and boob jobs out there? They* all *checked out?*

"So, do you have any questions for me?" Mr. Davis asked.

"Um, when would the show begin?" Trina asked.

"Next week," Mr. Davis said.

*Wow! I made it just in time.* "I have plenty of vacation days saved up," Trina said. "I've, um, never been able to take a vacation since I started working. I worked double-shifts so my ex could get through med school without him worrying about the bills. And I'm the one who's paying. Still paying."

"Any other questions?" Mr. Davis asked.

*Did he hear a word I said?* "When will I find out if I, um, make the final cut?"

"You have already made our final cut, Trina," Mr. Davis said. "You are officially one of the final twelve 'Second Chancers.' "

*I am?* "On the basis of this interview?" *Which really hasn't been much of one.*

"Yes," Mr. Davis said. "This interview and your background check."

*I guess having a low credit score doesn't stop me*

*from getting a second chance in television romance world.* "Do you think I have a real shot?" Trina asked.

"Every one of our twelve finalists has a shot," Mr. Davis said. "And you'll find out soon. The online voting begins in a few hours."

*The . . . online voting.* "What online voting?"

"Online voters will determine who gets a second chance," Mr. Davis said. "And people can vote as often as they want to for the next twenty-four hours. It's one way we gauge interest in the show. The more votes, the more potential viewers." He stood and extended a hand. "It was nice to meet you, Trina. Good luck."

Trina stood and shook his hand. "Nice to meet you, too."

As she sullenly rode the bus out of LA a few hours later, Trina took stock of her situation. *I will have ridden eight hundred miles in a stuffy bus in less than twenty-four hours to be photographed for five minutes and talked to for two minutes, selected as a finalist, probably because I was the only black woman to apply, only to find out that online voters will select the woman who gets a second chance. What a waste of time and money! There's no way this country is going to vote for me. Maybe the producers had to have one black finalist so they didn't get into trouble with the Equal Employment Opportunity Commission.*

The woman sitting next to her played some strange candy game on her smartphone.

"Excuse me," Trina said. "Are you online?"

"I can be," the woman said.

"My phone is pretty basic." She showed the woman her phone. "It's the latest thing in *twentieth* century technology."

"I had one of those *fifteen* years ago," the woman said. "Yours still works?"

"Most of the time," Trina said. "Could you go to the *Second Chances* Web site for me?"

The woman found the Web site and scrolled down. "Hey, isn't that you?"

*There I am, looking wrinkled and tired. Not a bad smile. I didn't know I still could. I wish they had put some makeup on me.* "Yeah, it's me."

"Nice to meet you, Trina Woods," the woman said. "I'm Clara."

"Nice to meet you, Clara," Trina said.

A flashing VOTE NOW! banner crawled across the screen.

Clara clicked on the banner. "I'm going to vote for you."

*At least I'll have one vote.* "Thank you."

"It says I can vote as often as I want to," Clara said. "I'm on my way to Vancouver. I wonder how many times I can vote by then."

"Don't go to any trouble," Trina said.

"It's no trouble," Clara said. "And if you win, I can say, 'I sat with that woman on the bus.'"

"Thank you."

A few hours later a little north of San Luis Obispo, Trina's phone rang. "Hello?"

"I didn't know you were using your maiden name now," a man said.

*Robert.* "Hi, Robert. How's Dr. Too White today? Has her skin blinded you yet? I'd recommend wearing sunglasses. Wouldn't want you to go blind. Blind surgeons don't make any money."

"Putting our business out there like that," Robert said. "You should be ashamed of yourself."

*He's ignoring my every word as usual, but at least I've pissed* him *off for a change.* Trina smiled. "What business, Robert?"

"Our marriage," Robert said. "On the Internet of all places!"

*I'd ask how he found out so quickly, but I don't really want to know.* "I didn't lie about a single thing, Robert."

"Dr. Francis called me," Robert said. "The chief surgeon, Katrina, my *ultimate* boss. He told me there's this nurse from San Francisco on some reality show Web site named Trina, and she looks an awful lot like your ex-wife. You could have warned me, Katrina. I have a reputation to protect."

*Kuh-trina. I have always hated how he said my name.* "You could have warned me that you didn't love me, Robert. You could have warned me that you were sleeping with a skinny albino. If she were a star in the sky, she'd be the brightest one. You could have warned—"

"Telling the world that *I* did you wrong," Robert interrupted.

"You *did* do me wrong and you're *still* doing me wrong," Trina said. "How about being a man and paying me back for paying your way through med school?"

"The judge said that—"

"I know what the judge said," Trina interrupted. "I should have said much worse in that online bio. I could have kept my married name and *named* you and Dr. Too White. I wonder if that would have affected your careers. Hmm. I think I'll call the producers and make some changes in that bio."

"What are you trying to do?" Robert asked. "Shame me? It won't work because you *won't* get on that show. You think America is going to vote for your black ass?"

*No, though my ass is still fairly decent.* "It doesn't matter if they do or don't. I am a finalist for that show. I'm one of twelve women America is voting on right now."

"And you're proud of that?" Robert asked. "The people who run that show saw your black face and said, 'Hey, we *need* one of those.' I thought I taught you better than that. Didn't you listen to me at all during our marriage?"

"I couldn't help listening to you preach at me day in and day out, Robert," Trina said. "That's how you communicated with me. Preaching. You never once simply talked to me."

"You know one of those white girls—"

"That you love so much," Trina interrupted. "I'm not stupid, Robert. I know I don't have a chance, and I didn't learn the reason why from *your* black ass. But how is Dr. Too White? Is she going to marry you? I mean, now that our divorce has been final for so long and all. I thought you'd be calling me from your honeymoon in Ireland or Scotland or one of those Scandinavian countries."

"That's none of your business," Robert said.

*He normally likes to throw her in my face. Yes!* "She dumped you, didn't she?"

"She most *certainly* did not," Robert said. "We are still together. She appreciates how we enhance each other's careers."

"Oh, I know what it is," Trina said. "She *won't* marry you, will she? That's the problem with cheating on your first wife, fool. The second wife already knows you're a cheating asshole. She can't trust you, can she? I'll bet you're banging some other pigment-challenged woman now. Am I right? I'm thinking East Coast WASP with a name like Kitten."

"You're talking gibberish as usual, Katrina," Robert said, "and you're making a fool of yourself for even trying to go on that show."

*I probably am.* "Better a fool for a little while than a fool for life like you." She turned off her phone completely.

"You told him," Clara said.

Trina shrugged. "Not really. He didn't hear me for ten years. I doubt he heard anything I said now."

Clara patted her leg. "Don't you worry, honey. He'll mess up an operation and get sued to the poorhouse."

"I hope it doesn't happen," Trina said. "I don't ever want to feel all the sacrifices I made were a complete waste of time. There aren't that many black doctors in this country, much less black surgeons. I helped make one."

"I hope you get voted onto that show," Clara said. "You deserve a second chance."

"Thank you."

Clara smiled. "I think I've voted for you seven hundred times. I hope it helps."

"I hope so, too."

As the sun rose to her right, Trina lay back and closed her eyes. *I know I won't get enough votes to win, but maybe I can win me a doctor or a surgeon one day, too.* She sighed. *But the only doctors at Saint Francis who are remotely interesting are gay, married, philandering, married and philandering, or socially backward.*

*No. I am in need of an ordinary guy, someone I can trust.*

She bowed her head and prayed: *God, how are You? I'm . . . here. Just sitting here on a bus on the way from a pipedream back to reality. I know I said some harsh things to You the last time I prayed two years ago, and I'm sorry. It wasn't Your fault Robert cheated on me. I still wish You would have struck him with a bolt of lightning or something or at least given him and Dr. Too White one of those Old Testament plagues. And forgive me for hating on Dr. Too White. She saw an opportunity, and she took it. It's my fault I married a weak-minded, spineless, sniveling coward of a man.*

*Okay, God, it wasn't my fault. I just had to remind you of all that Robert is, You know, in case You want to send some thunderbolts or plagues his way.*

*And God, if You're not too busy, could You maybe have me cross paths with an ordinary guy someday? He doesn't have to be buff or superintelligent or rich. He just has to be honest, faithful, and true to me. Thanks. Amen.*

She opened her eyes and smiled at the sunrise.

She closed her eyes. *Oh, one more thing, God. He also has to love me for me. But You already knew that because that's the way You made me. And that's the way You expect all of us to love each other.*

# Brooklyn, New York

# 11

Tony Santangelo adjusted so quickly to Aika Saito's arrival at the Castle that it seemed she had always lived there. They ate Cap'n Crunch with bananas every morning while watching the Weather Channel—and later *SportsCenter*—before she went to work. She sat with or near him while he studied his maps and she edited manuscripts in the library. Tony even stayed in the theater and watched Aika while she and Angelo watched television shows. She said "Good-night, Tony," and he said "Good-night, Aika" every night before he went up to bed. At times, Tony couldn't keep his eyes off Aika and did his best not to let her see him staring.

On a snowy night in early January, Tony stared at Aika's soft lips while she and Angelo curled up on a massive black leather sectional sofa watching a Knicks basketball game.

"Are you trying to flirt with my future wife?" Angelo asked.

Tony's eyes dropped quickly to Pacific Heights, yet another section of San Francisco. "I do not know how to flirt."

"I saw you looking at her," Angelo said. "What were you staring at?"

"Her lips," Tony said. "Aika has soft lips."

"How do you know they're soft?" Angelo asked. "Has she been kissing you?"

"No. They look soft." Tony glanced briefly at Aika. "I am sorry I stared at your lips."

"Don't be, Tony," Aika said. "At least you don't stare at my ass all day."

"Hey, it's my way of flirting," Angelo said. He squeezed her left buttock and kissed her neck.

"But she will be your wife," Tony said. "You should not have to flirt with her anymore."

"Flirting keeps our relationship fresh," Angelo said. "And I don't mind if you look at Aika, Tony. As long as you don't touch her."

"I will not touch her," Tony said. "But you must find someone like Angela and Aika for me who is dark brown."

"Not this again," Angelo said.

"Did you include me with Angela this time, Tony?" Aika asked.

"Yes," Tony said. "You are very pretty."

"Thank you," Aika said. "That's one of the nicest compliments I've ever gotten."

Angelo sat up and rubbed Aika's back. "He still wants me to be his pimp," he whispered.

Aika elbowed Angelo in the ribs. "That was rude."

"He didn't hear me," Angelo whispered. "Ever since he came back from Angela's, that's all he's been talking about. I was hoping he'd get over it."

"I want a dark brown woman so we can have snow-flake children," Tony said.

"It doesn't sound as if he's over it," Aika said.

"Tony, be realistic," Angelo said. "What woman of any color will want to marry you?"

"I do not know," Tony said.

"Well, if you don't know. . . ." Angelo shrugged. "How will I know how to find her for you?"

Tony stood. "I want you to help me find her."

Aika moved to the other end of the couch. "Well? Help him."

"Help him do what?" Angelo asked.

"Help him find a dark brown woman," Aika said. "Let him look at Match.com or something."

"But the Knicks are on," Angelo said.

"They'll fall apart in the fourth quarter as always and lose," Aika said. She hit several buttons on the remote, and the opening Google screen appeared. She typed in "Match.com" on the remote's little keyboard and handed the remote to Angelo.

Angelo rolled his eyes. "I suppose you want me to create a profile for him, too."

"Not yet," Aika said. "Let's see what kind of woman Tony likes first."

After plugging in "11201" for the zip code and selecting "within 10 miles," Angelo stood in front of the television. "Let's talk about age first," he said. "How old or how young do you want her to be?"

"I do not care," Tony said.

"As long as she's dark brown, I know," Angelo said. "Let's make her at least thirty but less than forty, okay?"

"Why?" Aika asked.

"Because she can't be a young thing with no sense and she can't be an old thing who's desperate," Angelo said.

"I'm forty-two," Aika said. "I must be desperate, huh?"

"No, you waited for the right man," Angelo said.

"And where is he?" Aika asked.

"Funny," Angelo said. "Okay, Tony, how tall do you want her to be?"

"I do not care," Tony said.

"Let's make her between five-one and five-ten," Angelo said.

"Why?" Aika asked.

"Are you going to ask 'why' for every category?" Angelo asked.

"Probably," Aika said. "Tony, do you want her to be Angela's height or my height?"

"I like your height," Tony said. "And I like Angela's height."

"Between five-one and five-six," Aika said.

Angelo made the change. "What about her body type, Tony?"

"She must have a body," Tony said.

"I know that," Angelo said. "Do you want her to be skinny, ripped, or stacked?"

"It says 'slender,' 'athletic,' and 'curvy,' Angelo," Aika said.

"I like slender," Tony said. "Aika is slender." He read the screen. "Her eyes must be brown and her hair must be black."

*At least he's sure what he wants there,* Angelo thought. "Okay, let's look at common interests."

Tony scanned the screen. "Music and concerts."

Angelo clicked the box. "Anything else?"

"Coffee and conversation," Tony said.

"How about 'Exploring new areas,' too," Aika said.

"Yes," Tony said. "I like to explore."

Angelo clicked the boxes. "Okay. Ethnicity?"

"Black or of African descent," Tony said. "That is all I need."

"You don't care if she smokes or drinks?" Aika asked.

"I care," Tony said. "No smoking or drinking."

Angelo checked the appropriate boxes and clicked the search button. Eighteen pictures of New York–area black women appeared on the screen.

"Only eighteen," Angelo said. "That's a shame."

"Look at the bottom of the screen," Aika said. "This is page one of six."

"Oh," Angelo said.

"One hundred and eight women," Tony said. He left his chair and stood in front of the television, his eyes moving from photo to photo. He pointed at one woman. "Her ears and nose have too many earrings." He pointed at another. "She has too many teeth." He pointed at another. "That is not her hair."

Aika wrenched the remote from Angelo's hand. "Let *me* help you, Tony." She clicked on one woman's picture. "Oh, shoot. We have to register first." She sighed. "I'll just sign in."

"What?" Angelo said. "You still have a profile there?"

"Yes," Aika said. "And I still get e-mail from men, so you better do right by me." She rubbed her left ring finger.

"Soon," Angelo said. "Very soon."

Aika smiled and signed in, and the first woman's full profile appeared. "What about this woman? She likes singing, taking walks at the beach with her dog, cooking Italian food, and dancing."

"I cannot dance," Tony said.

"She could teach you," Aika said.

"She is too . . . curvy," Tony said.

"There's nothing wrong with curves," Aika said.

"Her body makes me dizzy," Tony said.

Aika returned to the first photoset, clicking on the next woman's picture. "What about her? She is a high-school math teacher who enjoys working out and playing the piano for her church."

"She cannot play my piano," Tony said. "She wears too much makeup. She should not have silver eyelids and silver lips."

"You're being too picky, Tony," Angelo said.

"And you weren't?" Aika asked.

"Well, yeah, of course I was," Angelo said.

Aika sighed. "What *exactly* should she look like, Tony?"

"She must look like Angela McConnell at Angela's Sweet Treats and Coffee on Driggs Avenue in Williamsburg," Tony said. "She must also look like Aika Saito of the Castle."

"I am so flattered, Tony," Aika said.

"There's only one Angela in the world, and there's only one Aika in the world," Angelo said. "They're both one in a million, Tony."

"There are seven billion people on earth," Tony said. "If Angela is one in a million and Aika is one in a million, there are fourteen thousand women like them on earth."

"What Angelo is saying is that Angela and I are unique," Aika said. "There is no one like us *anywhere* in the world."

"But I like Angela," Tony said. "And I like you."

"We know you do," Aika said.

"I must find someone like you and Angela," Tony said. "Click on the next woman."

An hour later, Tony had found something "wrong" with all 108 women. "Show me more," he said.

"This is a longshot, but . . ." Aika typed in "Second Chances" and hit ENTER. "I heard about this show at work. It's like that show we watched the other night, Tony."

"*Rich Man, Lucky Lady,*" Tony said. "I did not like that show. The women told lies. Angela does not tell lies. You do not tell lies."

Angelo had been surprised that the show had held Tony's attention all the way through. He was most surprised when Tony called out "LIES!" or "TRUTH!" before the words flashed onto the screen—and he had been correct *every* time.

"I miss that show," Aika said.

"The rich man did not find love," Tony said.

"True," Aika said, "but it was certainly entertaining, like this show will most likely be. People go on this show to look for love, too."

"I will go on television to look for love," Tony said.

"That isn't happening," Angelo said. "This show is about *second* chances. You haven't had a first chance yet."

"I want a first chance," Tony said.

"This show could be a first chance for him, Angelo," Aika said. "He's famous enough."

"No way," Angelo said.

"Ignore him, Tony," Aika said, reading the screen. "Oh, *this* is different. Viewers get to vote on who gets on this show. Those are the twelve finalists."

"Wow," Angelo said. "Nine white, one Hispanic, one Asian, and one black. Ain't America great?"

Tony zeroed in on the black woman. "I want her. She looks like Angela." Tony blinked. "She has your smile, Aika."

"You want to vote for Trina?" Aika asked.

"I want Trina," Tony said.

"One vote for Trina," Aika said, and she cast a vote. "That Asian girl isn't completely Asian. I'll bet she's half-white or something."

Tony took the remote from Aika. "I want Trina."

"Tony, that's not going to happen," Angelo said. "Never in a million years."

"Let him at least read her bio first," Aika said. "Click on her picture, Tony."

Tony moved the pointer to Trina's picture and clicked ENTER. " 'Robert and I met as undergrads at UCSF.' "

"Let me read it, Tony," Aika said. "It may sound different if you hear a woman's voice reading it."

"I like your voice," Tony said. "It is soft cotton."

"There you go flirting again," Angelo said.

"Thank you for another compliment, Tony," Aika said. "At least I get compliments from him." She turned to the screen. " 'Robert and I met as undergrads at UCSF. He was going to be a surgeon, and I was going to be a nurse. We married after graduation, I passed the NCLEX on the first try, I became an RN, and I agreed to fund his dream because I believed in him. I worked double-shifts at Saint Francis Memorial Hospital as often as I could for most of our marriage.' "

"She works at Saint Francis Memorial Hospital," Tony said. "That is in Nob Hill in San Francisco."

"How do you know that?" Aika asked.

"He has memorized much of San Francisco," Angelo said. "Ask him about Chinatown sometime. Keep reading."

" 'And then my husband met and started an affair'—*figures*—'with a surgeon at San Francisco General Hospital. "I'm going to be late again tonight," he often told me. "I have a seminar I have to attend over the weekend." I thought he was putting in extra time to be a more skillful surgeon. I thought he was working longer hours so he could better provide for us. I thought he loved me.' Wow."

"What is an affair?" Tony asked.

Angelo sat up. *My brother has asked a question. This is . . . rare.* "Her husband cheated on her. Not like cheating in school where you look at someone else's answers. He had sex with another woman."

"When you're married, Tony," Aika said, "you're not supposed to have sex with anyone but the person you marry."

"Oh," Tony said. "Affairs are bad."

"Yes," Aika said. She continued reading. " 'I found out about the affair when he told me, "I've found someone who will be better for my career. I hope you understand.' What a *turd*. 'And then he filed for divorce, not me, citing irreconcilable differences.' Do you know what that means, Tony?"

"I sometimes see what Delores watches," Tony said. "It is called *Divorce Court*. It means they are too different."

"Right," Aika said. " 'Because I couldn't afford a decent lawyer and his mistress could, I didn't get much in the way of alimony. It barely pays one-third of the credit-card bill he left me with.' Poor woman."

"Do you know what alimony is, Tony?" Angelo asked.

"Yes," Tony said. "It is a monthly paycheck the judge orders one spouse to pay another. What is a mistress?"

*Two specific questions,* Angelo thought. "A mistress is a woman a man has sex with who is not his wife."

*J.J. Murray*

Tony nodded. "I do not like Trina's husband."

"Neither do I," Aika said. " 'For the last two years, I have been living in a cramped apartment near where I work because I can't afford a car or even bus fare. I need new work shoes and a rain jacket that doesn't leak here in "sunny" San Francisco. I need a microwave from this millennium that doesn't dim all the lights in my apartment. I need a bigger bed.' "

"I can give her those things," Tony said. "She needs those things." He read the next paragraph. " 'I also need a man to keep me company, to keep me warm at night, to talk to me, to listen to me, and to love me.' " Tony nodded several times. "I can do all those things."

"All except for the love part," Angelo said.

"Angelo!" Aika cried. "That was cruel."

Angelo shrugged. "I'm just saying, and you know it's true."

"I can love someone, Angelo," Tony said.

"Aika, keep reading," Angelo said.

"I can love someone, Angelo," Tony said.

"I heard you," Angelo said. "Keep reading."

" 'I gave up ten years of my life so my ex-husband could become a surgeon. I did this by choice.' " Aika shook her head. "I don't even know this woman, but I like her. She makes no apologies for doing the right thing. 'I sacrificed everything for him, and I would do it again. That's the kind of person I am. And all I have to show for our marriage are his bills and some bad memories. I don't have children because we were putting off children until he could support us. I could have had at least two children by now to love.' "

"I could give her children," Tony said.

"And you'd be her meal ticket for life," Angelo said.

"Angelo, please," Aika said. " 'I have very little. I

deserve a second chance at love.'" Aika flipped the remote to Angelo. "She does, you know."

"She is the one," Tony said. "I want Trina."

Angelo scratched his head. "You don't want Trina, Tony."

Aika flopped onto the couch. "It sounds as if he does."

"She's some random woman on a reality TV show," Angelo said. "I could show him a different woman ten minutes from now, and he'd say, 'I want her.'"

"I want her, Angelo," Tony said. "I really want her."

"Okay, why, Tony?" Angelo asked.

"Trina is honest," Tony said. "She is dark brown. Her face is an angel's face. She has soft brown eyes with flecks of gold."

"Her eyes look so tired," Aika said. "It doesn't look as if she wears any makeup. She's a natural beauty."

"She probably can't afford makeup," Angelo said. "And her ex-husband wasn't a turd, Tony. He was an asshole, but Trina might not be telling the entire truth. Maybe she did something wrong in the marriage."

"Her eyes are tired because of him," Tony said. "I want her. I will be loyal, faithful, and true to Trina."

Angelo laughed. "If she wanted all that, she could buy herself a dog."

Aika threw a couch pillow at Angelo. "Tony, keep ignoring your brother."

"A dog poops and pees outside," Tony said. "I would use the bathroom inside. A dog only lives ten to twelve years. I should live until I am seventy-eight. A dog licks his balls. I do not lick my balls. A dog barks and growls. I would be quiet and whisper. I would keep Trina warm at night."

Aika stood and rubbed Tony's shoulders. "You are a

sweet, sweet man, Tony, and any woman would be happy to have you."

"Aika, really?" Angelo said. "If Trina threw him a ball, Tony would go and fetch it."

"My mouth is not big enough for a ball and I am not a dog," Tony said. "I want Trina. Help me get her." Tony looked directly into his brother's eyes. "Help me, Angelo. Please."

# 12

*I have never seen Tony this focused on anything but his piano and his scribbles,* Angelo thought. *He also said "please." Tony never says "please." I hate to be the bad guy, but I have to nix this latest obsession of his right now before he gets hurt.*

"Tony, Trina might not be available for you to go on a date with anyway," Angelo said. "If enough people vote for her, she'll be on this show. You would have to become a 'Second Chance Suitor' to meet her."

"What is a suitor?" Tony asked.

"A man in competition for a lady's hand in marriage," Angelo said.

"A suitor only wants her hand," Tony said.

"And the rest of her, of course." He held out his hand. "Give me the remote. I want to show you something."

Tony handed Angelo the remote.

Angelo clicked back to the main page. "See these guys? These would be your competition for Trina's hand. Look at these guys. Geez, I haven't seen *him* in fifteen years."

"Who are they?" Tony asked.

*And yet another specific question.* "Tony, you'd be going up against former star athletes, old-school rappers, one-hit wonders, models who have grown old in the tooth and abs, child stars who aren't cute anymore, actors finally clean and out of rehab, comedians who were once funny but can't shake their shtick, you know, men looking for a second chance at fifteen minutes of fame."

Tony looked at the Second Chance Suitors. "They have tattoos and jewelry. I do not have tattoos and jewelry. They have fancy clothes. I do not have fancy clothes. They have big muscles."

"So do you," Aika said. "You're a very strong man."

"Their muscles are bigger," Tony said. He then gazed at the twelve finalists. "Trina will not win."

"She might," Angelo said.

Tony shook his head. "She is the only one with dark brown skin and dark brown eyes. She is unique like Angela and Aika. She is not like the others. She will not win."

"She might win the vote *because* she is unique," Angelo said.

"No," Tony said. "She will not win. Her face is pure. Her face is honest. She deserves a second chance. The other women do not. Therefore, Trina will not win."

"He's probably right," Aika said.

"Find her for me, Angelo," Tony said. "Bring her to Brooklyn."

"It's not that easy, Tony," Angelo said. He pointed at

a woman named Bambi Bennett. "What about her? Will she win?"

"She has big blue eyes," Tony said. "She has big breasts. Her buttocks are not in proportion to her breasts. She has a tattoo above her flat buttocks. She has big hair. She will win the vote."

Angelo clicked on her photo. "Let's see what Bambi has to say. 'I have been beautiful all my life, so beautiful that no boy in high school would ask me out.' Seriously?"

"Let me read the rest," Aika said. "That sounded so creepy coming out of your mouth. 'I didn't go to homecoming. I didn't go to the prom. I thought that in college that would change, but it didn't. I have never been on a single date in my entire life.' Oh come on."

"She is lying," Tony said. "She has been on many dates."

"Of *course* she's been on dates, Tony," Aika said. "She's lying to get sympathy. 'I want to go on this show to get a second chance at romance, the kind of romance that's new, pure, and innocent.'"

"I want that kind of romance," Tony said.

"Bambi is exactly what advertisers want," Aika said. "Can you hear Bambi's voice reading her bio while they film her walking through empty bleachers at a high-school football stadium or wandering through an empty gymnasium where streamers litter the floor?"

"Or having her walk along the beach at sunset in a skimpy bikini all alone," Angelo said.

"Bambi would not walk alone in a bikini," Tony said. "Men would be walking behind her and staring at her buttocks. I sometimes stare at your buttocks, Aika. They are pretty."

"Dude, really?" Angelo said.

"I am sorry," Tony said.

"Don't be, Tony," Aika said. "At least you *tell* me what you appreciate. Unlike your brother."

"I tell you what I like," Angelo said.

"In bed," Aika whispered.

"Well, yeah," Angelo said. "What better place?"

"Bambi is not honest," Tony said. "She lies. She will win, but she will not find love."

"Probably not, but America loves wistful, innocent, doe-eyed beauties like Bambi," Aika said. "She's the all-American girl."

"She has some seriously nice, um, assets," Angelo said.

Aika jumped into Angelo's lap and held him against the couch. "Quit staring at the big-eyed, big-chested Rapunzel who's long on legs and hair and short on intelligence."

"Trina is a pretty name," Tony said. "I want to talk to her." He turned to Angelo. "I will get my phone."

"You don't have her phone number, Tony," Angelo said.

"Get her phone number for me," Tony said.

"I'm not getting her phone number," Angelo said. He kissed Aika forcefully. "I want this little lady's phone number."

"I want her phone number!" Tony shouted.

Angelo looked around Aika. *He asks specific questions and he shouts? Who is this guy in front of me?* "Tony, listen to me. You're not ready for any woman, much less Trina."

"I need more practice," Tony said. He walked quickly out of the theater.

"Where are you going?" Angelo called out.

"I am going to practice with Angela," Tony said.

"Geez," Angelo said. "Aika, if we don't do something, he'll be on the G train and knocking on Angela's shop door in half an hour and Angela has been closed for two hours."

Aika leaped off the couch and met Tony as he was reaching into the closet for his Brooklyn Dodgers jacket. "You could practice with me, right?"

"You are not Angela," Tony said. "You are not dark brown. Trina is dark brown."

"But you like me, don't you?" Aika asked. "You think I'm pretty."

"Yes," Tony said.

She touched his elbow. "Then let's talk." She led him back to the couch in the theater and sat next to him. "Pretend I'm Trina."

"You are not Trina," Tony said.

"Look at her picture on the television then," Aika said.

Tony turned toward the television. "I like looking at Trina's face."

"Okay, let's begin," Aika said. "Hi, my name is Trina. What's your name?"

Tony took a deep breath. "I am Tony Santangelo from Cobble Hill, Brooklyn, New York, USA."

"Just tell her your name is Tony," Angelo said.

"I am more than my name," Tony said.

"I know that, but you're giving her a little too much information all at once," Angelo said, "and you're going to scare the shit out of her."

Tony sighed. "I do not want to scare the shit out of her."

"Let's start again," Aika said. "What's your name?"

"My name is Tony." Tony waited for the next question.

"Now is a good time to ask what her name is," Aika said.

"I know her name," Tony said.

"I *know* you know her name," Aika said, "but you have to act as if you *don't* know her name."

"I do not understand," Tony said.

"If you come up to her and say, 'Hi, Trina,'" Aika said, "she'll ask how you knew her name."

"And I will tell her I saw her story on the Internet," Tony said.

"And she will think you're a stalker," Aika said.

"I do not want that," Tony said.

"Always ask for a woman's name," Aika said. "Trust me on this. You'll be less creepy that way."

"Okay."

"Let's continue," Aika said. "What do you do, Tony?"

"I watch the Weather Channel and walk my dog Silver and play my 1883 Mason & Hamlin piano and ride the subway and write songs and—"

"Trina's running away from you now," Angelo interrupted.

"Simply tell her who you are," Aika said.

"But you asked what I did," Tony said.

"You *are* what you *do*," Aika said. "You write songs and play the piano."

"I am what I do," Tony said. "I write songs and play the piano. Okay. Ask me more."

"Tony, you look familiar," Aika said. "Are you famous?"

"No," Tony said.

"But you are, Tony," Aika said.

"Art E. is famous," Tony said. "I am not."

"Oh, just tell Trina you're Art E. and get on with the conversation," Angelo said. "You're putting her to sleep."

"But I am Tony Santangelo," Tony said. "I want Trina to love me, not Art E. Art E. does not watch the Weather Channel. Art E. does not play the piano. Art E. does not write songs."

"Tony, she might not give you the time of day *unless* you tell her who you are," Angelo said.

"I will buy her a watch so Trina can give me the time of day," Tony said.

"What I meant was, she might not talk to you *at all* unless she knows who you really are," Angelo said. "She might dismiss you in the first ten seconds unless you tell her how famous you are."

"Trina should talk to me whether I am famous or not," Tony said.

"In a perfect world, yes," Aika said. "But the world isn't perfect, Tony."

"Just tell her you're the man whose songs made Naomi Stringer a household name," Angelo said. "You're the man who has won three Grammys."

"Trina will not believe me," Tony said. "No one will believe me."

"He has a point, Angelo," Aika said.

"And that's *my* point," Angelo said. "Unless I'm there *with* Tony to talk to this woman, she's going to think Tony is a nut job. He can't talk to her on his own, Aika. You have to see that."

"I do not want you there," Tony said. "I have to talk to Trina alone."

"Then she won't believe you," Angelo said, "and you'll get to watch her walk away."

Tony started twisting and pulling on his fingers. "I am too different."

Angelo focused on Tony's hands. *Not that again. He hardly does that anymore. At least he's not chanting.*

"Tony, you're wonderfully different," Aika said. She rubbed his thigh.

Tony stopped twisting and pulling on his fingers.

*And Aika stops his stimming by touching him,* Angelo thought. *Mama used to do that, too.*

"You have soul, Tony," Aika said. "You are all heart. Most men don't have half your heart or focus. Including your brother, who is really pissing me off tonight."

"All I'm saying is that if Tony tells Trina all that he is *with* my help," Angelo said, "she *might* become more interested in him."

"What if Trina isn't impressed by that?" Aika asked.

"She has to be impressed by three Grammy Awards," Angelo said. "And hopefully a fourth at the end of the month."

"I do not want Trina to talk to me because of the awards," Tony said. "I do not want Trina to talk to me because I am Art E. I want Trina to talk to me because she likes talking to me. I am Tony Santangelo from Cobble Hill, Brooklyn. Bring Trina to Brooklyn."

"Dude, I can't call up a complete stranger and say, 'Hey, my brother wants to meet you so hop on a plane.'" Angelo smiled. "We have to go *to* her."

"You said you would help me," Tony said.

"I'm trying to help you," Angelo said. "Why don't we all go out to San Francisco so you can meet Trina?"

Tony resumed twisting and pulling on his fingers. "I do not want to leave Brooklyn."

*I hate to keep scaring him like this, but he has to understand how impossible all this is.* "You haven't been out of New York your whole life. Why don't you go to San Francisco? A change of scenery will do you good."

Aika put her hand on Tony's arm, but Tony kept yanking on his fingers. "I will not have the home-field advantage," Tony said. "Home-field advantage is essential to winning championships in the NBA and the NFL."

"How do you know that?" Angelo asked.

"Aika makes me watch *SportsCenter* sometimes at breakfast," Tony said.

"I do not *make* you watch it," Aika said. "You *like* to watch it. You said the 'not top ten' is funny."

"It is funny," Tony said. He shoved his hands into his pockets.

"Home-field advantage is only important in sports, Tony," Angelo said. "Not in romance."

"Well, it kind of is, Angelo," Aika said. "You knew exactly where to take me to impress me the first time we went out. If you didn't know Brooklyn so well, I might not be here now."

"All right, your home turf does play a little role," Angelo said, "but in romance, variety is good."

Tony stood and paced in front of the TV. "I know Brooklyn. Brooklyn is my home."

"San Francisco isn't in a foreign country, Tony," Aika said. "And in some ways, San Francisco is as much if not more of a melting pot as Brooklyn is. You celebrate Brooklyn's diversity so well in your music. Go celebrate the diversity in San Francisco. If nothing else, you'll have the raw materials for more songs."

Tony stopped pacing. "I need to know more about Trina first."

*What just happened? Aika hasn't convinced him to*

*go to San Francisco, has she?* "Why do you need to know more about Trina?"

"So I do not say the wrong thing," Tony said. "I want her to like me."

"You really should learn about Trina on your own," Aika said. "The real joy and wonder of any relationship is the getting-to-know-you part. And even the not knowing and doubt can be wonderful."

"Not knowing is not wonderful," Tony said. "Doubt is not wonderful."

"If you know everything about a person," Aika said, "there are no surprises."

"I do not like surprises," Tony said.

"But if there are no surprises," Aika said, "there may be no fun, no excitement, and no romance. Maybe even . . . no love."

"I want to know all about Trina first," Tony said.

"You mean you want to sponge her," Angelo said.

"Yes," Tony said. "I want to sponge her."

"You shouldn't have to, Tony," Aika said. "You need to wring yourself out and soak up a real person first-hand and face-to-face. You didn't sponge Angela, did you?"

"I found Angela in Brooklyn," Tony said. "I must find Trina in Brooklyn, too."

*This is better,* Angelo thought. *He's talking himself out of it again.*

"But Trina is not in Brooklyn," Aika said.

"Trina will like me in Brooklyn," Tony said.

"Once Trina gets to know you, she will like you any-where," Aika said.

"Trina will not like me in San Francisco," Tony said.

Aika shrugged. "Then she doesn't like you. Move

on and live to love another day. You wrote those lyrics. Put them to use. Follow your own advice. Move on and live to love another day."

Tony ripped his hands from his pockets, pulling and twisting on his fingers. "Okay."

Angelo stood. "Okay what?"

"I am going to San Francisco," Tony said.

*That's not happening.* "To do what exactly?" Angelo asked.

"To find Trina," Tony said.

"And then what?" Angelo asked.

"I do not know," Tony said.

*And I'm glad he doesn't know. That will keep him here. One more scare to seal the deal.* "And that's okay, Tony. One step at a time." Angelo picked up the remote and returned to the Google screen. "I'll check out some flights for us."

"No," Tony said. "I must go by myself."

"Tony," Angelo said, "you need someone—"

"I need Trina," Tony interrupted.

"We'd only go to make sure you were safe," Aika said.

"I must do this alone," Tony said.

"We'll go with you to explain everything to her about you," Aika said. "We'll help her understand."

"No," Tony said. "I will go alone."

"San Francisco is a big city," Angelo said.

"Brooklyn is bigger in land area and population than San Francisco is," Tony said.

"That's no guarantee you'll find her," Angelo said.

"Trina is a nurse at Saint Francis Memorial Hospital," Tony said. "I will find her. I will talk to her. I will get her to like me. I will ask her to marry me."

"Tony, you have to understand," Aika said, "it's not that simple. There are other variables to consider."

"I will be a suitor for her hand," Tony said. "I will win her hand. Buy me a ticket to San Francisco."

"I'm not letting you go by yourself," Angelo said. "Tony, you've never even taken a taxi."

"I do not need a taxi," Tony said.

"You'll need to take plenty of taxis in San Francisco," Angelo said. "It's a very hilly city."

"I will walk," Tony said. "I will wear hiking boots. I will ride the cable cars."

"You'd have to take an airplane to get there," Angelo said.

Tony stopped twisting his fingers. "I will be okay. It is safer to travel on an airplane than on a bus, train, or in a car."

"And you'd have to stay in a hotel," Angelo said. "Hotels are strange places."

"I will stay with Trina," Tony said.

"Oh no you won't," Angelo said. "You'll have to stay in a hotel."

"I want to stay with Trina," Tony said.

"We know you do," Aika said, "but you have to give her a chance to accept you first."

"I do not want her to accept me," Tony said. "I want her to love me. I want her to hold my hand with her dark brown hand."

"We know you do, Tony, and it's so romantic," Aika said. "But you can't just show up and expect someone to love you. Love takes time."

"I will wait two days," Tony said.

"Tony, it doesn't work that way," Aika said.

"I will wait two days, and then I will go to San Francisco." Tony left the theater.

In a few moments, Angelo and Aika heard the hum of the elevator.

"He isn't serious, is he?" Aika asked.

"He will forget all of this in two days," Angelo said. "Don't worry. Tony only has a one-track mind for his music."

"He seems pretty serious," Aika said.

"He'll get over it," Angelo said. "You'll see."

San Francisco,
California

# 13

Three days after her *Second Chances* interview, Trina carried a stack of mail into her bedroom and dumped it onto her bed.

*Bill.*

*Bill.*

*Robert's bill with* my *name on it.*

*"Save the planet!" Oh, no! Not again!*

*Please vote for me in a special election . . .*

*You deserve new vinyl siding!*

*A credit-card application? Are they crazy?*

*Reminder from Hyundai to bring the car I no longer own for a 75,000-mile checkup.*

She stared at the last envelope, postmarked from Century City, California.

*Time to find out what I already know.*

She tore open the envelope and read the enclosed letter:

My dear Miss Woods:
It is with sincere regret that I inform you that online voters did not select you for the leading role on *Second Chances*.

*Shoot. There goes the vinyl siding. Oh well.*

Hopefully this letter has arrived before we have
announced the finalist who received the most
votes. If it hasn't, please accept our sincerest
apologies.

*"The finalist" should read "the white woman."*

I am confident, however, that there is a good
man out there who is going to meet you very
soon. I believe that good people eventually have
good things happen to them. You are a good person, and the world is a better place with you in
it. Though you didn't get on *Second Chances*, I
believe that you will get a second chance for
love very soon.
Sincerely,
Chet Davis
Executive Producer, *Second Chances*

She crumpled up the letter and lay back on her bed.
*Well, no temporary mansion and twenty-four hot men
lusting after me. I'll bet they send that form letter to
everyone who didn't win. Chet, or whoever wrote it,
certainly overused the word "good," though. Was that
an attempt to make me feel good for being a loser? I already know I am a good person. I don't know if I deserve good things happening to me. I hope the world is
a better place with me in it.*
     She watched rain attacking her bedroom window.
*But from now on, I'll be on the lookout for a good
man.*
     She laughed.
*I may be looking for the rest of my life.
I hope I don't go blind. . . .*

Brooklyn, New York

# 14

Tony stayed in the Castle for two days and followed his somewhat "new" routine. He ate breakfast and watched *SportsCenter* with Aika. He walked Silver. He played his piano. He studied his maps.

He also crammed a toothbrush, a tube of toothpaste, a pair of socks, a pair of underwear, a T-shirt, a dozen blank notepads, four black pens, and a map book of San Francisco into a laptop case. He had never used the laptop computer inside the case, but he knew he could find someone on Driggs Street in Williamsburg to help him use it.

After Aika left for work at 8:00 AM, Tony appeared at Angelo's office door. "I am going to Angela's Sweet Treats and Coffee."

Angelo nodded. "Is that the laptop I gave you two Christmases ago?"

"Yes," Tony said.

Angelo smiled. "That's good, Tony. Now maybe you can type your songs so I can read them. Say hello to Angela for me."

"I will," Tony said.

"When will you be back?" Angelo asked.

"I do not know," Tony said.

"You have your watch?" Angelo asked.

Tony showed him his wristwatch.

"You have your phone?" Angelo asked.

Tony nodded.

"Don't be too late," Angelo said.

"Okay," Tony said. "Bye, Angelo."

"Later, dude."

Tony gripped the laptop case firmly as he rode the G train to Williamsburg. By the time he entered Angela's Sweet Treats and Coffee, his hands ached. He waved at Angela, who sat on a stool behind the counter.

"Hey, Tony," Angela said. "You want some house blend?"

Tony sat in a booth and took out the laptop. "No."

"Hey, that's a fancy computer, Tony," Angela said, walking over. "How about some cookies?"

"No," Tony said. "I need you to help me buy a plane ticket to San Francisco."

Angela smiled. "You need me to do what?"

"I need you to help me buy a plane ticket to San Francisco." He pressed the ON button, and the laptop whirred to life.

Angela sat across from him. "Why do you want a plane ticket to San Francisco?"

"I am going to San Francisco to meet Trina Woods," Tony said. "She is a nurse at Saint Francis Memorial Hospital in Nob Hill."

"And how do you know her?" Angela asked.

"I do not know her yet," Tony said. "I am going there to meet her."

Angela started to speak several times. "Um, Tony . . ." She squinted. "Run that by me again."

"I am going to San Francisco to meet Trina Woods," Tony said. "I need you to help me buy a plane ticket."

"Does . . ." She blinked. "Does your brother know about this?"

"No," Tony said. "My brother does not know. I do not want him to know. He wants to go with me to talk to her. I must do this alone."

"Have you ever done anything like this before?" Angela asked.

"No," Tony said. "That is why I came here. I need your help."

Matthew swept out of the kitchen and around the counter. "Hey, Tony. Good to see you." He slid in next to Angela and kissed her cheek.

"Tell Matthew what you're trying to do, Tony," Angela said.

"I am going to San Francisco to meet Trina Woods," Tony said. "I need you to help me buy a plane ticket."

"Does his brother know?" Matthew asked.

"He doesn't know," Angela said. "Tony wants to do all this on his own. For the first time."

Tony turned the laptop around. "Help me."

"Don't you think your brother should know what you're planning to do?" Matthew asked.

"Angelo will come and tell Trina who I am so she will talk to me," Tony said. "I do not want her to talk to me because I am famous. I want her to talk to me because I am me. I need a plane ticket." He took out his wallet and put a credit card and a picture ID on the table. "I know I will need these." He pulled out his toothbrush, socks, underwear, and T-shirt. "I will buy more clothes when I get there."

Angela smiled. "You've really thought this out, haven't you?"

"Yes," Tony said.

She turned to Matthew and whispered, "What do we do?"

"His brother has to be his legal guardian and probably has durable power of attorney," Matthew whispered. "Legally, we can't do anything."

"I can hear you," Tony said.

"Sorry, Tony," Matthew said, "it's just that we're legally unable to help you. Your brother makes all your decisions for you, doesn't he?"

"Yes," Tony said. "But I want to decide. I want to go to San Francisco to meet Trina." He pushed the laptop closer to Matthew. "I do not know how to buy a plane ticket."

"It's not too hard to do, Tony," Matthew said, "but unless we talk to your brother first—"

"I'll help you buy a plane ticket," Angela interrupted, crawling over Matthew to leave the booth and slide next to Tony.

"Angela," Matthew said. "We can't."

Angela turned the laptop around. "We can't what?"

"We can't help Tony escape Brooklyn," Matthew said.

"But we're not helping him escape," she said, smiling at Tony. "We're only showing him how to buy a plane ticket."

Matthew shook his head. "That *could* be construed—"

"Hush," Angela interrupted. "You'll have to ignore my husband, Tony. Sometimes he thinks too much like a lawyer and not enough like a man." She tapped a few keys. "Just connecting you to our Wi-Fi."

"Angela," Matthew said.

Angela widened her eyes. "*Matthew.*" She double-clicked on Internet Explorer. "Tell me more about Trina, Tony."

"She is pretty like you with dark brown skin, dark brown eyes, and black hair," Tony said. "Her ex-husband is a turd and an asshole. She paid for him to go to med school and then he had an affair. She needs new shoes, a new microwave, a new jacket, and a bigger bed."

"Where did you learn all this?" Angela asked.

"On the *Second Chances* Web site," Tony said. "If you go there, you will see her."

Angela found the Web site. "I don't see Trina, Tony."

"She was there two days ago," Tony said. He stared at Bambi Bennett. "I was right. Bambi won."

"Maybe Trina's on this page." Angela clicked on a tab called "Finalists."

Tony pointed at the screen. "There she is."

Angela turned the laptop around. "Does *she* look familiar, Matthew?"

Matthew nodded. "She could be your sister."

"She has Aika's smile," Tony said.

"She's certainly pretty," Angela said. "And you just plan to drop in on her and meet her."

"Yes," Tony said. "I want to talk to her."

"You're playing with fire, Angela," Matthew said.

Angela reached her hand across the table and squeezed Matthew's arm. "You dropped in on me, didn't you? Where's your sense of romance?"

"I still have it," Matthew said, "but that was different."

"Tony," Angela said, "that man who is so worried I'll break some archaic law only he knows about showed up at this shop at six AM one Sunday morning after a date from hell and had some of my coffee a few years ago, and he has been with me ever since."

"But Angela," Matthew said. "We can't be playing matchmaker with a man who is in someone else's *legal* care."

"Who said anything about matchmaking?" Angela said. "We're only showing an old friend how to buy a plane ticket."

"And get a hotel reservation," Tony said. "A hotel near Saint Francis Memorial Hospital."

"Legally, *Angela,* we should be consulting with his caregiver," Matthew said.

"And legally, *Matthew,* Tony is a grown man who should be able to make his own decisions," Angela said. She clicked a few keys. "I think we need to buy a first-class plane ticket, don't you, Tony?"

"I do not know," Tony said.

"First class is nice," Angela said. "Or so I hear. You get a bigger seat, and you get to sit near the front of the plane near the pilot."

"I want first class," Tony said.

"We could be putting Tony in danger, Angela," Matthew said.

"So we'll tell his brother about it," Angela said. "Relax."

"I do not want my brother to know," Tony said.

Angela put her hand on Tony's thigh. "We have to tell him eventually but not right away, okay? How long do you think it will take you to find Trina?"

"One day," Tony said. "I will see her at the hospital."

"So we'll wait a day before informing your brother," Angela said. She stared at Matthew. "Any objections, counselor?"

Matthew sighed. "A lot can go wrong in twenty-four hours, Angela."

"And a lot can go right, too," Angela said.

"His brother is going to be pissed," Matthew said.

"Yes," Tony said. "Angelo will be angry with me."

"But you're not scared of your brother, are you?" Angela asked.

"No," Tony said. "I am not scared of Angelo. I am used to him being angry with me."

"Tony, you are a man who knows what he wants and will do anything to get it," Angela said. "You have to respect that, Matthew."

"I do, but . . ." Matthew sighed. "At least let the airline know about his condition."

"I will." Angela laughed. "We're going to do this, aren't we?"

Matthew slid out of the booth. "Do what? I didn't see anyone ordering plane tickets. Why would anyone order plane tickets to San Francisco from a coffee shop in Brooklyn?" He smiled. "Speaking of coffee, anyone want some coffee?"

"I want root beer," Tony said.

"Me, too," Angela said. She Googled "JFK to San Francisco flights" and watched the screen fill up with airlines and times. "So many choices," Angela said. "This is so much fun, Tony."

Using Tony's credit card, Angela purchased a one-way, nonstop first-class ticket on American Airlines leaving JFK at 5:45 PM. Under special instructions, she typed: "I have Asperger's syndrome and will need special assistance."

"What is 'special assistance'?" Tony asked.

"They'll take good care of you, Tony," Angela said. "Oh." She added: "Please have root beer and cookies available on the flight."

"I can drink root beer and eat cookies on the plane," Tony said.

"Yes," Angela said. "You can listen to music, and you might even get to watch a movie."

"I will get to San Francisco today."

"Right," Angela said. "You will get into San Francisco around ten o'clock tonight, and you can search for Trina tomorrow morning."

"Yes," Tony said. "Tomorrow morning."

"You'll have to get to the airport by three," Angela said, "and Matthew will ride with you in the taxi."

"I will?" Matthew asked.

"You will," Angela said. "And you'll also make sure he gets his ticket at the counter, you'll make sure he gets to his gate, and you'll make sure he gets on that airplane."

"They won't let me back to the gate without a ticket," Matthew said.

"Aren't you his lawyer?" Angela asked.

"I'm sure his brother has retained . . ." Matthew smiled. "Hmm. You're a pretty shrewd woman."

"Yep," Angela said. "Tony, would you like Matthew to be your lawyer?"

"I do not know," Tony said.

"If Matthew is your lawyer," Angela said, "there's a good chance he will be able to stay with you until your plane takes off."

"I would like Matthew to be my lawyer," Tony said.

"I will first need a retainer of some kind," Matthew said.

Tony blinked at him. "You have straight teeth."

"Thanks," Matthew said. "But this kind of retainer is a payment up front to a lawyer for services to be rendered in the future."

"Oh." Tony handed him his credit card. "This is all I have."

"We'll add a dollar to your bill today," Angela said.

Matthew laughed. "A dollar? Really?"

"You're right," Angela said. "Fifty cents. I'm doing all the work here. But we'll need a contract first, won't we? Something simple."

Matthew wrote out a quick contract on a napkin. "This should do for now." He turned it around to Tony. "Sign at the bottom."

Tony read the contract:

I, Tony Santangelo of Cobble Hill, Brooklyn, USA, do retain the services of Matthew McConnell, attorney-at-law, for the sum of fifty US cents on this day, January 3.

Tony signed the contract.

"Now we need to find you a hotel close to the hospital," Angela said. "Looks as if there are two: the Huntington, which overlooks a park, and the Fairmont, which is—whoa. That's expensive."

"I want the one with the park," Tony said.

"The Huntington it is," Angela said. "How long do you think you will be staying in San Francisco?"

"I do not know," Tony said.

"Well, let's make your reservation for a week, just in case," Angela said. In the special instructions section, she typed: "I have Asperger's syndrome. I would prefer a room facing the park." She sat back from the laptop and held the back of Tony's hand. "Mr. Santangelo, you are officially on your way to meet Trina."

"Thank you," Tony said.

"You don't mind hanging out here for a few hours, do you?" Angela asked.

"No," Tony said. "I like being here."

When Angela returned to the counter to prepare for the lunchtime rush, Matthew circled behind her and sat on the stool. "This could backfire in a big way," he whispered.

"Don't be so negative," Angela said. "And quit whispering. Look."

Tony was busily scribbling on a notepad.

"He's not hearing a word we say right now," Angela said.

"I'm worried about him, Angela," Matthew said. "He's so much like a child."

"He came to *us,* Matthew, not to his brother," Angela said. "He trusts us. You remember from reading Tony's biography how long it takes for him to trust people. We can't break that trust."

"This is an entirely different situation," Matthew said.

"It took me months to trust you, and I don't have Asperger's," Angela said. "Tony trusted us after only two visits. That means something."

"I know he'll get there okay, but . . ." Matthew sighed. "I'm scared for the guy for when he gets there."

"I am, too," Angela said, "but you saw how passionate he is about this. That man is going to find and talk to Trina."

"I'm mostly worried how Trina will respond," Matthew said. "I don't want him to get hurt."

"If this Trina Woods is anything like me or Aika," Angela said, "she will find Tony fascinating, lovable, and true."

Brooklyn, New York
to
San Francisco,
California

# 15

Matthew changed into a fancy black suit with a bright red tie and shiny black shoes.

"I am not dressed to fly in the airplane," Tony said.

"You're fine, Tony," Angela said. "Matthew, you're only going to JFK, not to a Broadway show."

"I have to at least *look* like his lawyer, right?" Matthew said.

"I suppose." Angela hugged Tony. "I know you will succeed in finding Trina."

"Thank you," Tony said, his arms at his sides, his eyes flitting to Matthew. "Thank you for helping me, Angela."

Angela released him. "You make sure to call and tell me all about it, you hear?"

"I will call you."

When the taxi arrived, Tony wanted to sit in the front.

"The air bag is in the front," Tony said.

"It is traditional to sit in the back of the taxi," Matthew said. "Besides, we need to discuss some business, Mr. Santangelo."

Tony sat in the back.

"So, you really like Trina," Matthew said.

"Yes," Tony said.

"She seems nice," Matthew said.

"She is nice," Tony said.

"How do you know that Trina is nice?" Matthew asked.

"Her eyes are clear," Tony said.

"That doesn't mean she's nice," Matthew said.

"Angela's eyes are clear," Tony said. "Aika's eyes are clear. They see me with their clear eyes. Trina will see me."

Matthew wanted to tell Tony that Angela and Aika saw him clearly because they were caring, loving people, but he wasn't sure Tony would understand. "Tony, as your lawyer, I have to warn you about something. Some women are not all who they seem to be. I want you to be careful around Trina. While she seems very nice, she might want to take advantage of you."

"I would like Trina to take advantage of me," Tony said. "I have not had sex yet."

*Oh, boy.* "I *meant* that she might act as if she cares about you because you have a lot of money."

"I will not tell her that I have a lot of money," Tony said.

"But if you tell Trina who you really are," Matthew said, "she will *know* that you have a lot of money."

"I will not tell her about Art E.," Tony said. "I am only Tony."

"Only Tony," Matthew said. "That's good. You stay Tony."

Tony sighed. "I am nervous."

"About flying?" Matthew asked.

"No," Tony said. "About Trina."

"It's good to be a little nervous around someone you want to meet," Matthew said. "Nervousness helps you stay quiet and listen."

"I will listen to Trina," Tony said. "I am good at being quiet."

"You're a good man, Tony," Matthew said. "No matter what happens, always remember that you're a good man."

"I will remember," Tony said.

Matthew led Tony to the American Airlines ticket counter. "We're here to pick up a ticket for Tony Santangelo."

The attendant typed on a keyboard. "Yes, sir." She squinted. "We'll get you a cart, Mr. Santangelo." She handed a boarding pass to Matthew.

"I'm Mr. Santangelo's lawyer," Matthew said. "*He's* Tony Santangelo." He put the boarding pass into Tony's hands. "Don't lose this."

They rode the cart to the security checkpoint where Tony had a security guard check out his hiking boots.

"I only put my feet in them," Tony said.

"I've never heard that one before," the man said. "You're very funny."

"Thank you," Tony said.

He then watched his laptop case go on a conveyor belt under a scanner.

"That's to see if you have anything dangerous in there," Matthew said. "And from what you showed me, there's nothing dangerous about some clothes and a toothbrush."

Once they reached his gate, and while Tony watched planes moving around the tarmac and occasionally taking off, Matthew spoke to a woman at the counter. She nodded several times and followed Matthew to Tony.

"Mr. Santangelo, I'm Maggie," she said. "Are you ready to get on the plane?"

"Yes," Tony said.

Matthew placed his hand gently on Tony's shoulder. "It's time for you to fly, Tony."

Tony turned and gradually extended his hand. "Thank you, Matthew."

Matthew shook Tony's hand. "Oh, um, could I get your brother's phone number?"

Tony handed him his cell phone.

Matthew clicked on Tony's contacts and found only two numbers. *Wow. Only two. His brother and Angela. His brother is his lifeline, and I will be cutting off that lifeline for twenty-four hours.* He wrote the number on the back of a business card. "Are you absolutely sure you want to do this, Tony?"

"Yes," Tony said. "Do not call Angelo."

"I won't call him today," Matthew said. "I *will* call him tomorrow."

"Two days," Tony said. "Please."

"I heard you tell Angela that you would find Trina in one day," Matthew said.

"I will," Tony said. "It will take me two days to talk to her. I have to sponge her first."

"Tony, I don't know," Matthew said. "I have to let Angelo know sooner than forty-eight hours. You don't want him to worry about you, do you?"

"He worries about me anyway," Tony said. "I will call Angela when I find Trina. I promise."

"If you don't call Angela, I'll be calling you." Matthew searched for Tony's eyes. "Okay?"

"Okay."

"Go get your girl, Tony."

"Trina is not a girl," Tony said.

"Go get your woman then," Matthew said.

"I will go get my lady," Tony said. "Good-bye, Matthew."

"Good luck, Tony."

Tony walked with a flight attendant through the tunnel.

"I'm Katie," she said.

"I am Tony Santangelo from Cobble Hill, Brooklyn, New York, USA."

"Good to meet you, Tony," Katie said. "Is that your only carry-on?"

"It is a laptop case," Tony said.

"Um, is your laptop case all you have to carry on the plane?" Katie asked.

"Yes," Tony said.

Katie led him into an empty first-class section.

"There is no one else," Tony said.

"We've seated you first, Mr. Santangelo," Katie said. She motioned to a seat, and Tony sat. "You can put your laptop case above you in the bin if you want."

"I will hold onto it," Tony said.

"I understand you like root beer and cookies," Katie said.

"Yes," Tony said. "Hires Root Beer. Oatmeal and raisin cookies."

"We'll get you some," Katie said. "Would you like to listen to some music while we wait to take off?"

"Yes."

She unwrapped and handed a set of headphones to Tony. "Just plug it in there." She pointed toward a plug in the wall. "Then change the channels here." She pointed at a dial on his armrest.

"Thank you," Tony said. "You smell like strawberries."

"It must be my shampoo," Katie said.

"I like strawberries," Tony said.

"Thank you for choosing American Airlines," Katie said.

Tony flipped through the channels, listening to part of a song here, a guitar riff or drumroll there. He froze when he heard Naomi Stringer singing "Love Me in the Morning," and as he listened, he closed his eyes and saw Trina's face. *I would like Trina to sing to me like this,* he thought. *I would like Trina to love me in the morning, too.* When the song finished, he continued flipping through the channels, his mind working overtime to fuse all the sounds he heard into one song.

Then the airplane pulled away from the terminal.

"We are flying now," Tony said.

Katie knelt beside his seat. "We'll be taking off soon, yes," she said.

"What will we be taking off?" Tony asked.

Katie smiled. "Are you flirting with me?"

"No," Tony said. "I only flirt with Aika."

She reached over and fastened his seat belt. "We'll be in the air in a few minutes."

"Okay."

During takeoff and the long climb, Tony twisted and pulled his fingers. When the plane leveled off, he stopped pulling and twisting and looked out the window.

He yanked down the window shade.

*I am in the air, in the air, without a care, do I dare, how's my hair . . .*

"Are you okay, Mr. Santangelo?" Katie asked.

"I am okay."

"I'll get you that root beer and those cookies now, okay?"

"Okay."

Tony blocked out all the other passengers, munched

his cookies, drank his root beer, and continued memorizing the map book of San Francisco. He dozed fitfully somewhere over Chicago and found the courage to peek out the window when the captain said: "If you look out your windows, you'll see the lights of Denver, Colorado, the Mile High City."

He peeked and then jerked down the window shade.

*Fly high, mile high, smile high, style high, while high, pile high, too high . . .*

When the airplane descended, Tony raised the window shade in time to see the lights of San Francisco sparkling around San Francisco Bay. *It is like Christmas down there,* he thought. *I am landing in Christmas town.*

*I hope Trina will be my gift.*

# 16

When the airplane touched down, Tony unfastened his seat belt and stood.

"Tony," Katie called out from her jump seat. "You have to wait until the plane stops."

"I am sorry." He sat.

"It's okay," Katie said, unbuckling and leaving her seat. "You did very well for your first flight."

"Thank you."

"You're going to leave the plane first, okay?" Katie said.

"Yes," Tony said. "I must leave the plane first." He blinked. "But first I have to use the bathroom."

"I'll take you back," Katie said. She led him to the bathroom and opened the door.

"It is small," Tony said.

"It's big enough. Go ahead."

Tony stepped inside. "There is no blue water."

Katie stuck her head inside. "It's a special toilet. It doesn't use water."

"Oh." Tony closed the door and drained off six root beers. He pressed the silver button and listened to the whoosh as his urine disappeared. He turned, washed and dried his hands, and pushed out the door.

"Are you okay?" Katie asked.

"Yes," Tony said. "Toilets should not be so loud."

Katie handed Tony his laptop case. "I put your book inside."

"Thank you," Tony said.

Katie escorted Tony through the tunnel to the terminal, where another uniformed woman waited. "I hope you enjoyed your first flight, Tony."

"I did," Tony said.

"Tony has no luggage, Marie," Katie said. "Tony, Marie will help you from here on."

"Okay." Tony looked at Marie's shiny black shoes. "I am Tony Santangelo."

"Welcome to the City by the Bay, Mr. Santangelo," Marie said as Katie returned to the plane.

"I am not in San Francisco," Tony said.

"You are," Marie said. "That's one of San Francisco's nicknames. It's also sometimes called Fog City."

"That is a good name," Tony said. "It is often foggy here."

"Could I help you get a taxi to your hotel?" Marie asked.

"Yes," Tony said. He saw another cart with a driver. "We will ride the cart."

"Yes, sir," Marie said.

Tony climbed on. "I like riding the cart."

They rode the cart through the crowds to a taxi stand outside. "Where are you staying, Tony?" Marie asked.

"The Huntington," Tony said.

"Follow me," Marie said.

Tony followed Marie to a taxi. "Please take him to the Huntington," she told the driver. "Enjoy your stay in San Francisco, Mr. Santangelo." She opened the back door, and Tony got in.

"Thank you, Marie."

Marie whispered something to the driver, and the driver nodded. "I'll take good care of you, Tony." The taxi pulled away from the curb. "My name's Tino."

"You know my name," Tony said.

"The airlines lady told me," Tino said. "I will need your credit card."

"You will give it back," Tony said.

"I just need to swipe it once, Tony," Tino said.

Tony handed his credit card forward, and Tino swiped and returned it.

"Take me to Saint Francis Memorial Hospital," Tony said.

"You feeling sick, Tony?" Tino asked.

"No."

"The airlines lady told me to take you directly to the Huntington," Tino said.

"I need to go to Saint Francis Memorial Hospital," Tony said.

"Is there someone at the hospital you want to visit first?" Tino asked.

"Yes," Tony said. "Her name is Trina Woods."

"Is she sick?" Tino asked.

"I hope not," Tony said.

Tino smiled. "Oh! Has someone had a baby?"

"Eight babies are born every minute in the United States," Tony said.

"I mean, has *Trina* had a baby?" Tino asked.

"No," Tony said. "Trina wants two daughters. I will give her a snowflake child."

"A what?"

"A snowflake child," Tony said. "Trina is dark brown and I am white. Our daughter will be a snowflake child."

Tino nodded. "So you're in love with Trina, huh?"

"I cannot be in love with Trina," Tony said. "I have not met her yet."

"Oh. Huh?" Tino cruised to a stop at a stoplight. He looked back. "You haven't met her yet?"

"No," Tony said. "I hope to meet her tonight at the hospital."

The taxi pulled through the intersection. "Is she a doctor?"

"She is a nurse," Tony said.

"Okay," Tino said. He pulled up to the curb near the main entrance. "We're here." He opened his door, got out, and opened Tony's door.

Tony stepped out. "Thank you." He stared up at Tino. "You are very big."

"Yeah," Tino said. "I like to eat."

"I like to eat, too." Tony looked at Tino's massive arms. "You are brown."

"Yes," Tino said. "I am Latino."

"You speak Spanish," Tony said.

"*Sí*," Tino said.

"*Gracias,*" Tony said, and he started for the main entrance.

Tino walked beside him.

"I must talk to Trina alone," Tony said, pushing through the double doors.

"I'm going to help you find her, okay?" Tino said. "And if you find her, I'll leave you two alone to talk."

"Okay."

Tino led Tony to the information desk. "My friend Tony here wants to speak to Trina Woods."

"Trina is a nurse here," Tony said. He read her name tag. "Lily Williams."

"Is she expecting you?" Lily asked.

"No," Tony said. "You are brown and have an Afro." Lily widened her eyes. "Um, okay."

"Um, Tony's special," Tino said.

"I have Asperger's," Tony said. "I am not special."

"I'm sorry, Tony," Tino said. "I meant no disrespect."

"It is okay," Tony said. "I need to see Trina Woods."

Lily shook her head. "I can't give out that information, sir."

"I do not understand," Tony said. "Trina works here. She said so on the Internet."

"It's okay, Tony," Tino said. "HIPAA laws, right?"

"Right," Lily said.

"Can you at least tell my friend Tony if she works here?" Tino asked. "He's been in an airplane all day."

"I can't give out that information," Lily said. She then nodded once.

"Thank you, Lily," Tino said. "Is she working now?"

"I can't give out that information," Lily said. She then shook her head.

"Thank you again, Lily," Tino said. "Thanks for not helping." He winked.

"Are you in love with Lily?" Tony asked.

Tino laughed. "This is the first time I've ever met this lovely lady."

"But you winked," Tony said. "A wink means you love someone."

Tino smiled at Lily. "Or it means you like what you see."

Lily smiled.

"Come on, Tony," Tino said. "We can go to your hotel now."

Tony didn't move. "I want to see Trina."

"Didn't you see Lily nodding and shaking her head?" Tino asked.

"No," Tony said. "I have trouble looking at faces."

"Okay," Tino said. "Without saying so to protect her job, Lily told us Trina does work here, and she works during the day."

"I will see Trina in the morning," Tony said.

"Yes," Tino said. "Let's go to your hotel now."

"Okay, Tino."

"It's just around the corner." Tino waved at Lily. "Thank you, Lily."

Lily held out a slip of paper. "In case you don't need any information in the future, Tino."

Tino took the paper. "I think I won't need information very soon." He smiled.

"Bye, Tony," Lily said.

"Bye, Lily," Tony said.

When they reached the Huntington, a doorman wearing white gloves and a dark uniform opened his door. "Welcome to the Huntington," he said.

Tony got out and looked at the cable car going by, its bell clanging twice.

"Those are neat, huh?" Tino said. "You'll have to ride one of those while you're here. They're a lot of fun."

"I will ride one," Tony said. "I know where it goes."

"Come on," Tino said.

Tony walked through the ornate entrance to the reception desk, Tino reaching the desk first. "My friend Tony has a reservation."

Tony read her name tag. "Your name is Jeanie."

"That's right," Jeanie said. "And what is your name?"

"Tony Santangelo, Cobble Hill, Brooklyn, New York, USA."

"One moment," Jeanie said, tapping at her keyboard.

Tino leaned against the reception desk. "I didn't know you were from Brooklyn. I have a cousin who lives in Bushwick. You lived there long?"

"All my life," Tony said.

"You don't have the accent," Tino said.

"It is because I have Asperger's," Tony said. "My brother Angelo has the accent."

"You're staying with us for a week, Mr. Santangelo, and you're already paid in full," Jeanie said. "I'll just need a credit card for any incidental charges you may accrue."

Tony handed her his credit card. "You will give it back."

Jeanie smiled. "Of course I will." She swiped his card and returned it. "If you need anything, Mr. Santangelo, call the front desk and I'll answer."

"Okay," Tony said.

"Are you here on vacation?" Jeanie asked.

"No," Tony said. "I am here to meet Trina Woods."

"Is she a guest at this hotel?" Jeanie asked.

"She is a nurse at Saint Francis Memorial Hospital," Tony said.

Jeanie squinted at the computer screen. "You have requested a room facing the park."

"Yes," Tony said. "I like parks."

"I have just the room." Jeanie swiped, then handed him two key cards. "Here are your room keys."

"They are not keys," Tony said.

"They act like keys," Jeanie said. "You'll see when you get to your room. Are you hungry?"

"Yes," Tony said.

"We can have your food sent up to your room," Jeanie said. "What can we get you?"

"I eat pasta for dinner," Tony said.

"We have plenty of that here," Jeanie said. "We'll send it up to you with some bread, okay?"

"Yes," Tony said. "And Hires Root Beer."

"Fine," Jeanie said. She waved at an elderly bellhop. "Terry, please take Mr. Santangelo and his luggage up to his room."

"He has no luggage," Tino said. "Tony's traveling light."

"I will buy clothes here," Tony said.

"You've come to the right place for buying clothes," Jeanie said.

Tino extended his hand. "Take it easy, Tony."

Tony shook his hand. "Thank you, Tino."

"Good luck with Trina," Tino said.

"Good luck with Lily," Tony said.

Tino laughed. "You saw her give me her phone number."

"I saw you flirting," Tony said.

Tino nodded. "Glad I met you, Tony."

Terry appeared beside Tony. "Right this way, sir."

"I like your uniform," Tony said, following Terry to the elevator.

"Thank you," Terry said.

"You are black," Tony said. "You have no hair. Your head is shiny."

Terry pressed the UP button. "I used to have hair."

"You have freckles on your head," Tony said.

"You're very observant," Terry said. The elevator doors opened. "After you, Tony."

Tony stepped inside, and the doors closed. "I have an elevator in my house in Brooklyn."

"Yeah?" Terry said. "You must have a big house."

"It is called the Castle," Tony said. "The elevator goes up to the roof where I walk Silver." Tony's body shook. "I did not walk Silver five times today."

"You all right, Tony?" Terry asked.

"I must tell Angelo to walk Silver." He pressed the number one and waited. "My phone does not work."

The elevator stopped at the eighth floor. "You don't have a signal. As soon as you get out of the elevator, it should work fine."

Tony pressed the number one again. "Hello? Angelo?"

"It's me, Aika," Aika said. "Tony, where are you?"

"You must walk Silver now," Tony said.

"What?"

"You must walk Silver now," Tony said.

"Tony, where are you?" Aika asked.

"I cannot tell you," Tony said. "I must go now." He ended the call.

"Follow me," Terry said.

Tony walked behind Terry to his room.

"If you give me a key card, I'll show you how to use it," Terry said.

Tony handed Terry a key card and watched him slip it into a slot.

"When you pull it out, the green light goes on." Terry pulled out the card.

"I see a green light."

"That means your door is open," Terry said. "Open it."

Tony opened the door and saw two beds, a couch, two chairs, a wide-screen TV, and a desk. "There are two beds."

"Yes," Terry said.

"I only need one bed," Tony said.

"You didn't request two beds?" Terry asked.

"I will be okay," Tony said. He went to the window. "I can see the park."

"Yes," Terry said, moving beside him.

"I see a fountain," Tony said.

"It's a strange one," Terry said.

"Men are holding up a bowl," Tony said.

"*Naked* men," Terry said.

"Oh," Tony said. "I like the red lights."

"Will you need anything else, Tony?" Terry asked.

"No." Tony extended his hand. "Glad to know you, Terry."

Terry shook his hand. "Glad to know you, too. You have a good stay."

After Terry left, Tony sat on the first bed. *I am here in San Francisco. I am safe. Trina is out there waiting for me.*

He heard a knock on the door.

He opened the door, and a short woman carried a tray inside. It contained a huge plate of pasta with meat sauce, a small plate of bread sticks, and a glass of ice water.

"Where would you like this?" she asked.

He read her name tag. "I do not know, Lu Chu."

"I can set it on the coffee table," Lu said.

"Okay."

Tony followed closely behind her. "You are Japanese."

"I am Chinese," Lu Chu said. She set down the tray.

"You are very pretty," Tony said. "My friend Aika is from Japan, but she lives in Brooklyn. She will marry my brother, Angelo. He looks like me. Aika's name means 'love song.' What does your name mean?"

Lu Chu looked up at Tony and smiled. "Green pearl."

"You are not green," Tony said. "But you are pretty." He picked up the remote. "My name is Tony. I watch the Weather Channel." He turned on the television.

"I can find it for you, Tony," Lu Chu said.

"Okay." He handed the remote to her. "You are short and have brown eyes."

Lu Chu laughed as she found the right channel. "I have always been short." She set the remote on the coffee table. "I'll put this meal on your bill."

"You just put it on the table," Tony said.

Lu Chu squinted. "You're funny."

"Thank you," Tony said.

"I will put the *cost* of this meal on your bill," Lu Chu said.

"Yes." Tony sat. He searched the table. "I need Hires Root Beer."

"We didn't have any, sir," Lu Chu said.

"Do you have Doc's Root Beer?" Tony asked.

"I couldn't find any root beer down there," Lu Chu said. "I could get you a Coke."

"It is okay," Tony said. "I already had too much root beer today." He picked up his fork and started eating. "This is good."

"I'll tell the cook," Lu Chu said. "Enjoy your meal, sir."

Tony shot out his hand. "Thank you, Lu Chu."

Lu Chu shook his hand. "You're welcome, Tony."

He ate most of his pasta and all of the breadsticks while watching an Alberta Clipper speeding across the country toward the Northeast.

His phone rang. "Hello?"

"Tony, where the hell are you?"

"Hello, Angelo," Tony said. "You will have eight to twelve inches of snow in two days."

"I've heard," Angelo said. "Now, where are you?"

"You are angry with me," Tony said.

"I'm not angry," Angelo said. "I'm concerned. I've been worried to death. It's nearly two o'clock in the morning, and you're not home."

"I am safe," Tony said. "Do not worry about me."

"Well, where are you?" Angelo asked. "I'll come get you."

"You cannot come get me," Tony said. "I am meeting Trina tomorrow morning."

"Right," Angelo said. "Just tell me where you are."

"I am in San Francisco," Tony said. "I ate some pasta. It was not the same as Delores makes. They did not have root beer. I drank ice water."

"You're at a restaurant?" Angelo asked.

"No, I am in San Francisco," Tony said. "I can see a

fountain from my window. Naked men are holding up a big bowl."

"Are you on something?" Angelo asked.

"I am on a couch," Tony said.

"I meant . . ." Angelo sighed. "Look. I called Angela, and she said you left her shop around three. Where have you been for the last eleven hours? Did you go over to Mama and Poppa's old house or something?"

"No," Tony said. "I am in San Francisco. I flew in an airplane. I went to Saint Francis Memorial Hospital, but Trina was not there. She works during the day. I will see her in the morning. I am in a hotel. It is very hilly here. The city looks like Christmas."

"Why are you lying to me?" Angelo asked.

"I am not lying," Tony said. "I do not lie."

"Well, then you're pulling my leg or something," Angelo said.

"I cannot reach your leg to pull it," Tony said. "I am over three thousand miles away. I would need very long arms to pull your leg."

"Look," Angelo said, "if you don't tell me where you are, I'm going to call the police."

"They will not help," Tony said. "I am not in Brooklyn, Angelo. I am in San Francisco."

"You expect me to believe that you flew on an airplane all by yourself all the way to San Francisco."

"Yes," Tony said. "I am very tired. I must go to sleep now. I will see Trina in the morning."

"Tony?"

"Yes."

"Are you *really* in San Francisco?"

"Yes."

"I can't believe this!" Angelo shouted. "Who helped you get there?"

"Angela, Matthew, Maggie, Katie, Marie, Tino, Jeanie, Terry, and Lu Chu."

"I know the first two, but who are all the rest?" Angelo asked.

"Angela helped me buy the plane tickets and make a reservation at this hotel," Tony said. "Matthew rode with me in the taxi, and Maggie made sure I got on the airplane okay. Katie was on the plane. She brought me root beer and cookies. She smelled like strawberries. I listened to Naomi with headphones. Marie took me to the taxi. Tino drove me in a taxi. He is very round. He is Latino. He likes Lily. She is brown and has an Afro. Jeanie gave me my room keys. But they are not keys. They are like credit cards. Jeanie had no smell. Terry took me to my room and shook my hand. He had freckles and a bald head. Terry is black. Lu Chu brought me my food. She is Chinese. She is short. Her name means 'green pearl.' She is not green. She is very pretty. She reminds me of Aika."

"You have to be making this up," Angelo said.

"I am not making this up," Tony said. He yawned loudly. "I have to go to sleep now. Say good-night to Aika for me. I will miss saying good-night to her. Good-night, Angelo." He turned off his phone and went to the window.

"Good-night, Trina. I will see you in the morning."

# 17

Tony awoke at 9:00 AM without an alarm clock and realized he couldn't shave.

*I forgot my electric shaver,* he thought. *I cannot shave without my electric shaver.*

He called the front desk.

"Good morning, this is Delia," a woman said. "How may I help you?"

"I need Jeanie," Tony said.

"She worked last night," Delia said. "I can help you . . . Mr. Santangelo. Am I saying that right?"

"Yes," Tony said. "You said it right. I need to shave. I forgot my electric shaver."

"We can give you a razor and some shaving cream, sir," Delia said.

"Angelo does not trust me with a razor," Tony said. "I need an electric shaver, a Remington WetTech Rotary shaver."

"I wish I could help you, sir, but we don't—"

"I must shave," Tony interrupted. "I am meeting Trina today."

"Will one day without shaving be that much of a problem?" Delia asked. "You could always go out and buy an electric shaver, couldn't you?"

"I must shave," Tony said. "I must have a smooth face for Trina."

"You know," Delia said, "lots of women like a man with a little beard on his face."

Tony blinked rapidly. "Women like beards."

"I do," Delia said.

"Okay." Tony hung up.

A minute later he called the front desk. "Delia, I am sorry I hung up. Thank you for helping me."

"It's my pleasure, Mr. Santangelo," Delia said.

"I am hanging up now," Tony said. "Bye."

He showered, using most of the little bar of soap, and washed his hair, using all of the shampoo in the little bottle. He brushed his teeth for ten minutes. He put on clean socks, underwear, a T-shirt, and the clothes he wore the day before. He took the notepads and a pen from his laptop case and put them into the pockets of his Brooklyn Dodgers jacket. He put on the jacket. He turned on his phone but turned off the ringer. He then stared around himself in the mirror.

*I need a haircut,* he thought. He felt his coarse beard. *Women like beards. Trina is a woman. Trina will like my beard.*

He put one key card into his back pocket, turned off all the lights, and left his room. He took the elevator to the lobby and walked by the front desk.

"Have a great day, sir," a woman said.

Tony turned slightly. "Thank you."

"I'm Delia, Mr. Santangelo," she said. "The beard looks good."

"Thank you, Delia."

Tony stepped outside as a cable car rolled by. He saw a map of Nob Hill in his mind, strode through Huntington Park, and arrived at Saint Francis Memorial Hospital at ten-thirty. He walked around to the emergency room entrance on Bush Street and sat in the waiting area, watching every door and several hallways for Trina.

The man snoring next to him had a shaggy beard. "You have a beard," Tony said. "Women like beards."

The man didn't stir.

"You do not have shoelaces," Tony said. He pointed at his hiking boots. "I have shoelaces."

The man shook himself awake. "You talking to me?"

"Yes," Tony said. "You smell like beer."

The man wiped his eyes. "Had a late night."

"You should not drink beer," Tony said. "You should drink root beer."

The man smiled with stained yellow teeth. "I'll try to remember that."

"You should brush your teeth, too," Tony said.

At 11:25 AM, Trina walked by the admission desk carrying a paper bag.

*She is going outside to eat her lunch, but I am frozen,* Tony thought. *I cannot speak.* He cleared his throat and whispered, "Trina."

Trina left the hospital and walked outside.

Tony stood.

"Have a good one," the shaggy man said.

"Thank you," Tony said.

Heart beating wildly, hands sweating, and knees weak, Tony attempted to keep pace with Trina, who strolled fifty feet ahead of him. He pulled out a notepad and scribbled as he weaved his way around other pedestrians on the sidewalk: "Aqua pants and white shoes so fast so strong the hills are steep I have good hiking boots she's in the park I'm in the park she's sitting on a bench on the other side of the naked man fountain I can see the window to my room I should go there to watch her from a safe distance I will buy binoculars."

He glanced at Trina. *She is so pretty. I need to be close to her. I will sit.*

He sat on a bench on the other side of the fountain,

occasionally looking around the shooting and spilling water at Trina. He continued to scribble: "People walk dogs and collect their poop in this park. They do not always do this in Brooklyn. Some Chinese people do slow dances on a hill like slow-motion kung fu. Seagulls drift overhead. They look like Brooklyn seagulls. Trina looks Spanish, French, Cajun, African, and Native American. Bambi is not the all-American girl. Trina is the all-American girl." He looked around the fountain then down to his notes. "Trina has sharp cheekbones. She needs to eat. I am hungry. I need to eat, too. I did not eat breakfast. She is eating a sandwich. It looks like ham and cheese. I like ham and cheese. She is reading a book. It is not the book about me. I am glad. If she reads it, she will not like me."

Trina turned up her face and smiled at the sun making a brief but glorious appearance.

Tony wrote furiously: "I will never forget the way the sun made her face glow as long as I live that was beauty I have seen beauty Trina is beauty." He slowed his breathing and saw the words dancing with notes in his mind. *If you ask me what is beauty, it won't be a woman's booty, it won't be a color or race—it's sunlight's lace on Trina's face.* He wrote down the words. *I have a song, and I have just met her.* He wrote: "I like this park. It is green. The clang of the cable car makes the fountain water dance. Trina's bookmark is a napkin. She rests her feet up on the bench. She reads two pages. She closes her eyes. She is tired. She takes off her white shoes and rubs her feet. Her face is a frown. Her feet hurt. I will get her new shoes."

He widened his thumb and pinkie. "Her foot is nine inches long. She looks my way. I look away. I should have a book to read. I should not be writing. I should get closer to her. I should sit next to her. I should talk to her. I cannot move. She is looking directly at me. I look at the statue of naked men. I should not stare at statues of naked men."

Trina rose and left the park.

Tony saw her aqua legs flashing up a hill and out of sight.

He could not move.

He could not speak.

He wrote: "I have found her. I have not found my voice."

Tony stood and walked over to where Trina was sitting and sat, putting his feet up on the bench as she had. He felt the sun on his face and looked up. *This is what she felt.* He looked past the fountain to where he was sitting before. *She was not staring at me. She was staring at the pretty stained glass of that cathedral. It reminds me of St. Paul's in Cobble Hill. I liked going to Mass. The colors and incense there always whispered soft music to me.*

He took out his phone and called Angela.

"Angela's Sweet Treats and Coffee, Angela speaking," Angela said.

"Angela, I have found Trina," Tony said.

"That's wonderful, Tony," Angela said. "Did you speak to her?"

"No," Tony said. "I followed her from the hospital to the park. She ate a ham and cheese sandwich and read a book. Her feet hurt. She needs new shoes."

"How do you know that?" Angela asked.

"She put her feet up on the bench," Tony said. "She took off her shoes. She rubbed her feet and frowned. Her shoes are old. They are thin on the bottom. I will buy her some new shoes."

"But you don't know her size, Tony," Angela said.

"Nine inches," Tony said. "Her feet are nine inches."

"Are you sure?" Angela asked.

"Yes," Tony said. "I measured them with my eyes."

"Nine inches, huh?"

"Yes."

"Give me a moment," Angela said.

Tony waited, his eyes wandering to the men and women dancing slowly on the hill. *They do not dance with each other and I hear no music. I see their music. It is calm music.*

"Tony, you still there?" Angela asked.

"Yes," Tony said.

"I've been measuring my feet," Angela said. "Mine are eight and a half inches, and I wear a size five. If Trina's are nine inches, you'll have to buy her at least a six, maybe even a seven."

"I will buy several sizes," Tony said. "One will fit." Tony stood. "I am going to the shoe store now."

"But Tony," Angela said, "don't be surprised if Trina doesn't accept them."

"Trina needs new shoes," Tony said.

"Tony, Trina doesn't *know* you," Angela said. "It would be very strange if a strange man brought me shoes."

"Oh."

"You need to talk to her first so you aren't a stranger to her anymore," Angela said.

"I will talk to her after I give her the shoes," Tony said.

"You might want to talk to her *before* you give her the shoes," Angela said. "You know, let her know who you are."

"Okay," Tony said. "I will do that."

"But why didn't you introduce yourself to her when you first saw her?" Angela asked.

"I was scared," Tony said. "I do not like this feeling."

"It's all right, Tony," Angela said. "You were nervous, that's all."

"I need a haircut," Tony said. "And some clothes. I am wearing dirty clothes."

"Your clothes are dirty? What happened?"

"I wore them yesterday," Tony said. "They smell like two taxis and an airplane."

"What are you going to do next?" Angela asked.

"I will find comfortable shoes for Trina," Tony said.

"Sounds like a plan," Angela said. "Call me anytime, okay?"

"I like talking to you," Tony said. "You make me calm."

"I like talking to you, too, Tony," Angela said. "Oh, has Angelo called you today?"

"He called me last night," Tony said.

"He has been calling you today, too," Angela said. "I know this because he's been calling *me*."

"I turned off my ringer," Tony said.

"Well, turn it back on," Angela said. "Your brother is blowing up my phone. Check your messages."

"Angelo is angry," Tony said.

"He's worried about you," Angela said.

"I do not have much time," Tony said. "Angelo will come find me and take me back to Brooklyn."

"Well, get to work," Angela said. "Go get her."

"I will try."

# 18

Tony stared at his phone. He saw many missed calls and messages from Angelo. *I will not listen to them. They are all saying to come home to Brooklyn. I do not want to go home.*

Tony did not turn on his ringer.

He Googled "shoe stores" and saw a map. He decided to try Foot Worship on Sutter Street first since it was closest.

He walked into Foot Worship and saw a display of tall white, black, and red shiny boots with spiky heels to his right and spiked platform shoes with thick clear soles to his left. They reminded him of something Elton John used to wear. *They do not look very comfortable,* Tony thought. *Maybe they have nurses' shoes in the next section.*

The next shoe display to his left featured a sign: THE OUCH DEPARTMENT. A pair of boots nearly three feet tall hung from a hook. *They have ten-inch heels. They would hurt Trina's feet. They would hurt anyone's feet.*

A nearly naked mannequin with an orange wig stared down on him from the second floor. The mannequin wore a fuzzy black and light blue bra, light blue and purple underwear, and purple and light blue criss-crossed hose that stopped above her knees. *She would be cold outside today.*

A large leopard-skin chair in the shape of a high heel sat in front of an ordinary tan couch directly in front of him, a red plush couch with lip-shaped cushions to his left. *Their furniture does not match. I wonder if they know that.*

A woman left her chair at a glass counter in the back. "See anything you like?"

"I am Tony," he said.

"I'm Natalya," she said.

"You are Russian," Tony said.

Natalya laughed. "My grandmother was. I'm plain ol' American now."

"You are very pretty," Tony said.

"Thank you," Natalya said.

"I want shoes for a nurse," Tony said.

"A nurse, huh?" Natalya said. "What kind of fetish does she have?"

"I do not know this word," Tony said.

"You know, fetish," Natalya said. "What's her obsession?"

"I hope it is me," Tony said.

Natalya smiled. "What kind of kink is she into?"

"Trina is not a chain," Tony said. "She does not have a kink."

"I meant . . ." Natalya pointed to the mannequin above her. "How does Trina get her kicks?"

"I do not know," Tony said. "I do not know if she plays soccer."

Natalya shook her head. "Does Trina ever dress like the mannequin up there?"

"No," Tony said. "She wears nurse clothes at Saint Francis Memorial Hospital. They are aqua. I do not know if she wears a fuzzy bra or purple underwear."

Natalya sighed. "You want *real* nurse's shoes."

"Yes," Tony said.

"You want something like Danskos, huh?" Natalya asked.

"I do not know," Tony said. "The shoes I buy for Trina must be comfortable. Her feet hurt."

"You won't find many comfortable shoes here," Natalya said. "This is basically a fetish shoe store."

"I still do not know this word," Tony said.

"I can see that," Natalya said. "This isn't really the store you need, Tony. You want to go someplace like DSW on Post Street."

"Thank you, Natalya," Tony said.

On his way out he stared at the clear platform shoes. *Trina would never wear these to work. They have no grip on the soles. She would slide down the hills of San Francisco. Elton John wore shoes like these in Central Park. He had big sunglasses. He plays the piano. They would not fit me.*

He located Post Street in his head and arrived at Designer Shoe Warehouse after a brisk fifteen-minute walk. He approached a woman, read her name tag, and waited until she turned to face him.

"Bea, I want the best shoes for a nurse," Tony said.

"Then you'll want Danskos," Bea said.

"I have heard of them," Tony said. "I will buy Danskos."

"Unfortunately, we don't carry them," Bea said. "We do carry Sanitas, and they are an excellent shoe for nurses."

"I will get them," Tony said.

"What's your size?" Bea asked.

"Eleven and a half," Tony said.

"We might not have your size," Bea said.

"They are not for me," Tony said. "They are for Katrina Woods. She is a nurse at Saint Francis Memorial Hospital. Her feet hurt."

"What's her size?" Bea asked.

"Nine inches." He stretched out his thumb and pinkie as far as they would go. "About this wide."

Bea wrinkled up her nose. "Um, are you all right?"

"Yes," Tony said.

"I mean, you're buying shoes for a woman and you don't know her shoe size," Bea said.

"Yes," Tony said. "I have not met her yet."

"You lost me," Bea said.

"I am right here," Tony said. "And you are right there."

"I mean . . ." Bea smiled. "I don't understand why you are buying her shoes."

"Trina's feet hurt," Tony said. "I saw her rub them in the park. She needs new shoes. Bigger than a size five. Angela's feet are eight and a half inches and she wears a five. Trina has longer feet."

"And you've never met her," Bea said.

"I have seen her," Tony said. "I want to give her the shoes today."

"Do you even know this Trina?" Bea asked.

"Yes," Tony said. "I know her."

"Okay, okay," Bea said. "Nine inches, right?"

Tony widened his thumb and pinkie again. "Yes."

"I'll bring out a few pairs," Bea said. A few minutes later, she returned with three shoeboxes. "One of these should do. They range in size from six to seven." She opened each box.

"They are black shoes," Tony said. "Nurses wear white shoes."

"Nurses wear all sorts of colors now," Bea said, "and

black shoes seem to hide the blood better. So, which pair will you get?"

"I will buy them all." He handed Bea his credit card. "One will fit."

Bea led him to the checkout counter, swiped his card, returned it, and had him sign the receipt. She put the boxes in a large plastic DSW bag. "I hope she likes them."

"I hope so, too," Tony said. "Thank you, Bea."

"You're welcome," Bea said. "Whatever ones don't fit, you can bring back. Save your receipt."

"Okay."

Outside the wind whipped his hair into his eyes.

*I need a haircut now. I am like the shaggy man at the hospital.*

Tony Googled "barbers" and carried his bag of shoe boxes into Mr. Eckhard's Beauty Salon and Barbershop inside the posh and ornate Fairmont hotel. He stood in front of a brown man who had "Carlos" stitched on his black vest. "I am Tony," he said. "I need a haircut."

"*And* a shave," Carlos said.

"I do not want a shave," Tony said. "Women like a beard."

"Some do," Carlos said, leading him to a shiny silver barber's chair.

Tony set down the bag of shoe boxes and climbed into the chair. "Do dark brown women like a beard?"

"I suppose some do," Carlos said, settling a black cape around him.

"You are dark brown," Tony said.

The barber next to Carlos laughed. "That's not dark brown, honey. That's black."

"Hush, Carmine," Carlos said. "Tony, just because

I'm dark doesn't mean that I know what dark brown *women* like."

"Carlos likes thick beards," Carmine said.

Carlos sighed, fluffed Tony's hair, and ran his soft hands over Tony's beard. "I'll just even up the beard, okay?"

"Okay," Tony said.

Carlos began sectioning and cutting Tony's hair. "So, Tony, where are you from?"

"Cobble Hill, Brooklyn, New York, USA," Tony said.

"I knew you weren't from around here," Carlos said. "Are you here on vacation or business?"

"I am here to talk to Trina," Tony said. "She is a nurse. She is dark brown. I bought her some shoes."

Carlos glanced at the bag. "So I see."

"I do not know her size," Tony said. "One will fit."

Carmine blinked. "Oh, that makes sense."

"Thank you," Tony said.

"You can ignore Carmine," Carlos said.

"I will try," Tony said.

Carlos laughed. "So you're giving Trina some shoes."

"Yes," Tony said. "Her feet hurt."

"That's a good reason to get a woman shoes," Carlos said. "Is she your girlfriend?"

"No," Tony said. "She is a woman. She cannot be my girlfriend."

"Tell me about her," Carlos said.

"Trina is dark brown," Tony said. "She walks very fast. She is divorced. Her ex-husband was an asshole."

Carlos laughed. "Aren't they all?"

"I do not know," Tony said.

"How much do you want me to cut off?" Carlos asked.

"I do not know," Tony said. "Make me handsome."

"You're already a handsome man," Carlos said.

"I do not think so," Tony said. "My brother Angelo is a handsome man. He is marrying Aika. She is Japanese. Women do not like me."

"This Trina does, doesn't she?" Carlos asked.

"I have not spoken to her yet," Tony said.

"Kind of like a blind date?" Carlos said.

"With shoes," Carmine said.

"Hush, Carmine," Carlos said.

"I am not blind," Tony said. "She is not blind. It cannot be a blind date."

"You're funny," Carlos said.

"Thank you," Tony said.

"There's something wrong with him," Carmine whispered.

"I can hear you, Carmine," Tony said. "You whisper too loudly."

"He does everything too loudly," Carlos said. "There's nothing wrong with you, is there, Tony?"

"There is nothing wrong with me," Tony said. "I have Asperger's."

"Oh, I'm sorry," Carmine said, moving closer to Tony. "My little nephew has that. He's an amazing little artist. He draws and paints all day."

"I write songs and play the piano," Tony said.

"My nephew is a very good artist," Carmine said. "I'll bet you're a good pianist."

"My piano is in Brooklyn," Tony said. "I miss it."

"What kinds of songs do you write?" Carlos asked.

"You will not believe me," Tony said.

"I might," Carlos said.

"I wrote 'She's Not Here' when I was sixteen," Tony

said. "It was about my mama. She died. Walter Little sang it. Then Walter Little died. Naomi Stringer will soon sing another song of mine. It is called 'One Hundred Twenty Pounds of Sexy, Sexy Hate.'"

"Naomi Stringer will never weigh a hundred twenty ever again, honey," Carmine said.

"She has won three Grammy Awards with my songs," Tony said. "I keep them in a box in my closet."

"Are you kidding me?" Carlos asked.

"I do not lie," Tony said.

Carmine drifted over to Tony. "My little nephew always tells the truth. He's vile as hell sometimes, but he never, *ever* lies. So you're Art E. You're the Sponge."

"Yes," Tony said. "My brother Angelo calls me that in my book. He does not say it out loud to me."

"And you're here in San Francisco to meet a girl," Carlos said.

"Yes," Tony said.

"That's quite romantic," Carmine said.

"Yes," Tony said. "It is the kind of romance that is new, pure, and innocent."

Carmine laughed. "And you came to San Francisco for *that* kind of romance?"

"Yes," Tony said.

"Don't be rude, Carmine," Carlos said. He spun Tony's chair around. "How do you like it?"

"I look okay," Tony said. "My hair will not cover my eyes."

"You look masculine and rugged," Carlos said. "Trina won't be able to resist you." Carlos removed the cape and cracked it in the air.

"Thank you." He handed Carlos his credit card. "Put the tip on it."

"How much?" Carlos asked.

Tony stared at the masculine, handsome, rugged man in the mirror. "A thousand dollars."

"No, really," Carlos asked. "Five? Ten?"

"A thousand dollars," Tony said. "I like my haircut and face very much."

Carlos stared into Tony's eyes. "I can't take a thousand-dollar tip for a thirty-five-dollar haircut."

"It is a good haircut," Tony said. "I like it."

Carlos sighed. "Okay."

Tony checked to see if his bag was still there.

"Are you really Art E.?" Carmine asked.

"Yes," Tony said. "But I am really Tony."

Carlos rushed back to Tony. "It went through. Carmine, it went through. Um, sign the slip, Tony."

Tony scribbled a reasonable facsimile of his name and left the chair. "Thank you, Carlos." He extended his hand.

Carlos shook it. "Thank you so much for the tip, Tony."

"You are welcome," Tony said.

"Where are you taking Trina?" Carlos asked.

"I am not taking her anywhere," Tony said.

"If you're going on a date, Tony," Carmine said, "you'll want to eat out with her at a restaurant, won't you?"

"Yes," Tony said. "We will eat at a restaurant."

"You have to take her to Cielo Azul," Carlos said.

"Why not Bar Tartine or Aziza?" Carmine asked Carlos.

"Because Cielo Azul is the best restaurant bar none in San Francisco," Carlos said.

Carmine shook his head. "You have to go to Bar Tartine or Aziza, Tony. Cielo Azul is so pretentious."

"I will go to Cielo Azul," Tony said. He let his eyes wander around both barbers. "I like your clothes. I would like to buy clothes like that."

"This is my uniform, honey," Carmine said. "You'd never see me wearing *these* clothes outside of work."

"I like them," Tony said.

"They're made by Banana Republic," Carlos said. "You can find the store over on Grant."

Tony saw Grant Avenue in his mind. "Pine Street to Grant. It is not far away. Thank you, Carlos. Thank you, Carmine." He extended his hand to Carmine.

Carmine shook and held his hand for a few moments. "Are you *really* Art E.?"

Tony nodded.

"I love your music," Carmine said.

"Thank you," Tony said. "I love music." He picked up his bag.

"Good luck with Trina," Carlos said.

"I will not need luck," Tony said, and he left the Fairmont.

When he entered Banana Republic ten minutes later, Tony wandered around until he saw a sign: THE NON-IRON SHIRT. He sat on a bench and let his eyes roam over the clothes. *These are clothes of the earth,* he thought. *Brown and tan and yellow and blue and gray.*

"May I help you, sir?"

"I am Tony. I need new clothes." He read the man's name tag. "William."

"You've come to the right place," William said. "A couple of shirts, some pants?"

"I would like shirts, pants, socks, belts, and shoes," Tony said. He looked again at the racks and displays of clothing. "So many choices." He let the bag drop to the floor and began twisting and pulling on his fingers.

"My brother Angelo buys clothes for me. I do not know what to do. I am sorry. I have Asperger's. I have trouble choosing." He closed his eyes. "I have never bought clothes before."

"Do you know all your sizes?" William asked.

"Yes," Tony said. "Forty-two shirt, thirty-six thirty-two pants, eleven and a half shoes." He opened his eyes. "Will you help me?"

"That's why I'm here, Tony," William said. "What colors do you like?"

"I like all colors," Tony said.

"Let me put together a few outfits for you," William said. "Are you going to be all right while I do that?"

"Yes," Tony said. "I will try not to stare."

Tony watched William putting outfits together, displaying them on top of a rack in front of him. Tan chinos, a solid blue shirt, a brown belt, and brown shoes. Blue chinos, a plaid black shirt, a black belt, and black shoes. White chinos, an orange and red plaid shirt, brown belt, and another pair of brown shoes. William laid three pairs of socks on each of the shoes. "How do these look?"

"They look good," Tony said.

"Do you want to try them on?" William asked.

"Yes," Tony said.

William chose the blue chinos with the plaid black shirt and directed Tony into a changing room. There, Tony took off his old clothes and put them into the DSW bag. When he finished dressing in his new outfit, he stepped outside and looked in a mirror. *This is good,* he thought. *Trina will smile when she sees me. She will see that I know how to dress.*

"You look great, Tony," William said. "That's a good look for you."

"Yes," Tony said. "I want to wear these clothes now."

"Okay," William said. "What about the other outfits?"

"I want them, too." He handed William his credit card.

"I'll ring these up and bag them for you," William said.

*This is a good look for me,* Tony thought. *A good look, a good book, a good cook, a good hook . . .*

"Mr. Santangelo," William said, "your total comes to $750.47."

"Okay," Tony said. He signed the receipt and collected the bags. "Thank you, William."

"Thank you, Tony," William said. "You've made my day."

"God makes days," Tony said.

"You're right, Tony," William said with a smile. "Have a good day."

Tony sped from Banana Republic back to the Huntington Hotel, dropped off his old and new clothes in his room, grabbed the bag of shoe boxes, and stopped by the front desk.

"I am hungry," he told Delia.

"Your brother has been calling you all morning, Tony," Delia said.

"Is Angelo here?" Tony asked.

"No," Delia said. "He's been calling from New York to see how you're doing."

"Oh," Tony said. "I am fine. I am hungry."

"You could eat here," Delia said. "We have a wonderful restaurant with a grand piano."

"It is not my piano," Tony said. "It is too big."

"What kind of food do you like?" Delia asked.

"The kind of food you eat," Tony said.

Delia blinked. "There's a little café not far from here."

"Yes," Tony said. "I will go there."

"It's called the BeanStalk Café," Delia said. "It's over on Bush Street."

"I know where that is," Tony said. "Thank you."

"You're welcome," Delia said. "Don't you think you should call your brother back? He sounded worried."

"He is always worried about me," Tony said. "I will go eat now."

Tony walked briskly to Bush Street and the BeanStalk Café. He approached the counter, where an Asian woman smiled at him.

"I would like to eat lunch now," Tony said.

The woman nodded. "What would you like?"

Tony scanned the menu. "I would like a ham sandwich with lettuce, tomatoes, pickles, onions, mayo, and Dijon mustard."

"Hot or cold?" the woman said.

"It is nice outside," Tony said.

"I meant, do you want the sandwich hot or cold?"

"Hot," Tony said.

"Cheddar, Swiss, or pepper jack cheese?"

Tony hesitated. "Cheddar."

"Horseradish, Korean spicy sauce, jalapeños, peppers, pickled cucumbers, or bacon?"

Tony pulled and twisted his fingers. "Yes."

The woman laughed. "You want all of that?"

Tony stopped pulling on his fingers. "Yes."

"Um, you know you're turning an eight-dollar sandwich into a thirteen-dollar sandwich," the woman said.

"It is okay," Tony said. He pulled out his credit card. "I have this."

"Would you like chips?" she asked.

"Sixteen Cheetos," Tony said.

The woman blinked. "Sixteen."

"Yes."

"What do you want to drink?"

"Hires Root Beer," Tony said.

"For here or to go?" she asked.

"For me," Tony said.

The woman smiled. "I'll bring it out to you."

Tony sat on one of three stools along the wall, a one-foot counter in front of him. *This does not have a good view of the street,* he thought. *Maybe that is a good thing. I am here to eat, not to sponge.*

The woman brought out his lunch.

"You are Chinese," Tony said.

"I am Korean," the woman said.

"My friend Aika is Japanese," Tony said. "Her name means 'love song.' My friend Lu Chu is Chinese. Her name means 'green pearl.' What is your name?"

"Hyun Ae."

"What does it mean?" Tony asked.

"Wise and loving," Hyun Ae said.

"It is a good name," Tony said. "I am Tony. It does not mean anything."

Hyun Ae placed a stack of napkins next to his plate. "Enjoy your meal, Tony. And you'll need these napkins."

Tony spent a full minute deciding how to pick up the overstuffed ham sandwich. He spent another minute deciding where to make his first bite. Once he bit into his sandwich, juices dribbled down his chin to his plate and to the counter. *Hyun Ae is wise to give me so many napkins.*

He put down his sandwich and turned on the ringer of his phone.

It rang immediately.

"Hello, Angelo," Tony said.

"Tony, thank God!" Angelo yelled.

"Thank you, God," Tony said.

"I meant . . ." Angelo sighed. "Never mind. I've been calling your phone and the hotel for the last ten hours. Why didn't you answer me?"

"I turned off the ringer," Tony said.

"Why did you do that?" Angelo asked.

"I do not like how it sounds," Tony said. "It is too demanding."

"Well, change it to something less demanding," Angelo said. "And don't turn off the ringer again."

"But I have been busy," Tony said. "You said I needed to get out more."

"Not all the way to San Francisco," Angelo said.

"You believe me now," Tony said.

"I didn't believe you until I saw your online bank statement," Angelo said. "Three grand for a plane ticket? Fifteen hundred for a hotel? Two hundred for some shoes? A thousand thirty-five for a haircut? Seven-fifty and some change for some clothes?"

"I am only using the credit card," Tony said. "I bought Trina shoes. I got a haircut and a shave. I still have a beard. I am rugged. I have new clothes. I am eating at the BeanStalk Café. I will take Trina to Cielo Azul for dinner tonight."

"Who pays a *thousand bucks* for a haircut?" Angelo yelled.

"It was a good haircut," Tony said.

"Look, I want you to go to the hotel and stay there," Angelo said. "Aika and I are flying out to San Francisco as soon as Aika gets off work tonight."

"I do not need you here," Tony said.

"Tony, I've been worried sick about you," Angelo said.

"Take Pepto-Bismol."

"Not funny," Angelo said. "I'm going out of my mind here."

"I wish I could do that," Tony said.

"Yeah, well, I haven't slept a bit since you disappeared," Angelo said.

"I did not disappear," Tony said. "I am here at the BeanStalk Café with Hyun Ae."

"And I would have *taken* you to San Francisco if you would have let me," Angelo said.

"I am doing this on my own," Tony said.

"There's no doubt about that," Angelo said. "When were you planning to come back to Brooklyn?"

"I do not know," Tony said. "Say hello to Aika for me. Tell her I bought Trina shoes."

"What kind of shoes are they?" Angelo asked.

"Nurse's shoes," Tony said. "They did not have Danskos but Sanitas are excellent. Very comfortable. They are black to hide the blood. I must go give Trina her shoes now."

"No," Angelo said. "You must go to the hotel and stay in your room until I get there."

"I am giving Trina her shoes now," Tony said.

"Tony, you're not hearing me," Angelo said.

"I am hearing you," Tony said. "I do not like what I hear you saying. I am giving Trina her shoes. I will wait outside the hospital for her. There is a bus bench across the street from the emergency room. I will sit and wait until she comes out."

"Wait, Tony," Angelo said. "I don't know if that's a good—"

"Good-bye, Angelo," Tony interrupted. He turned off his ringer and grabbed the bag of shoe boxes.

*I am going to give Trina her shoes.*

*I hope she likes them.*

*I hope she likes me.*

# 19

Trina left the emergency room a little after six and walked with Naini across Bush Street to wait with her until Naini's bus arrived.

"Another day done," Naini said, standing near one end of the bus bench.

"Yeah," Trina said, hovering beside her. "And there will be another one just like it tomorrow."

"Thank you for helping me get some overtime in the ER," Naini said.

"It wasn't hard," Trina said. "I asked if they needed another set of able hands after four o'clock, and they said, 'Please!'" She sighed. "What are you going to do with the extra money?"

"I am putting the money away toward a car," Naini said. "Then I will not *ever* have to take this wretched bus back to Oakland again."

Trina looked at the three people squeezed onto the covered bus bench and noticed a man straining his neck to stare at her. *Is that the guy who was watching me at the park? Same Brooklyn Dodgers jacket. Not many Brooklyn Dodgers fans around here. And he must have gotten a haircut or something. He isn't as shaggy looking. Maybe he has been visiting someone in the hospital.* She glanced behind her to see what the man might have been staring at and saw nothing particularly interesting. When she looked his way again, he quickly turned away.

*That was weird. I hope he's not following me.*

She squeezed Naini's shoulder as the bus rolled up. "I'll see you in the morning."

"No, you will not," Naini said. "I will be working up in acute rehab all day."

"How'd you manage to get that assignment?" Trina asked.

"I have physical therapy skills," Naini said.

"So do I," Trina said. "Put in a good word for me, please."

"I would, but it is only temporary," Naini said. "But at least I will get a few days away from ES."

"You're so lucky," Trina said. "Well, I'll come up to visit you when I can. Bye."

As Trina walked past the bench, toward Hyde Street, she saw the man twisting and pulling at his fingers. *Maybe he got some bad news? Should I talk to him? He looks needy. Maybe he's out here getting some fresh air.*

As Trina turned the corner on Hyde, she saw movement to her left. The man on the bus bench shot to his feet and waved at her with his right hand, shaking a Designer Shoe Warehouse bag of shoe boxes in the air with his left.

*And now he's shaking a bag of shoe boxes at me? Is he trying to sell them to me? You got the wrong customer, pal. I'm broke.*

Trina quickened her step and continued down Hyde Street. *Waving at me. A grown man waving at me! Like Forrest Gump or something. And selling shoes on a bus bench. He actually shook the bag at me. A grown man on a bus bench. What is this world coming to?*

Later at home, Trina read the online version of the *Chronicle*. She scanned the headlines until she saw "Art E. Sighted in Nob Hill?" She clicked on the story and saw two obviously gay barbers out in front of the Fairmont hotel. . . .

A Nob Hill barber got the shock of his life when he received a $1,000 tip for a haircut today from a client asserting that he was Art E., the reclusive songwriter and winner of three Grammy Awards for best song.

"I know it's hard to believe," Carlos Muniz said. "But I have the thousand bucks to prove it."

*Why would the greatest living songwriter get a hair-cut in Nob Hill? If this is true, Art E. was only blocks away from me while I worked. I love that man's music. Unlike most music today, his lyrics make sense and never curse.*

"He was a nice-looking man," Carmine Jenson said. "He was maybe six feet tall with dark eyes. He looked Italian to me."

"I'd tell you what he wrote on the receipt," Muniz said, "but it's unintelligible."

"All he said was that his name was Tony," Jenson said. "And he was from Brooklyn."

"And he was looking for a nurse named Trina," Muniz said.

"He was going to give her some shoes!" Jenson said with a laugh. "I guess her feet hurt."

Trina's body shook.
*What?*
She reread the article.
*Okay. Hmm.*
*This can't be a true story.*
*It's in the entertainment section.*
*Entertainment stories are usually full of rumors and lies.*
*Maybe business is slow at the Fairmont and this is just some free publicity.*
She read the article one more time.
*Brooklyn Dodgers jacket. Tall Italian man with dark hair. Got a haircut. Holding a shoe bag. In Nob Hill. Looking for a nurse named Trina.*
Trina shut off her laptop.
*He couldn't have been looking for me.*
*Nothing that crazy could ever happen to me.*
*Could it?*

# 20

Tony paced his room at the Huntington, twisting and pulling his fingers.
*I waved.*
*I waved at Trina.*

*I should have said hello.*
*I held up her shoes.*
*She did not see them.*
*She did not see me.*
*Her clear eyes did not see me.*
*I could have asked her about the weather. I could have asked her how her feet felt. I could have asked her about the book she was reading in the park. I could have smiled. I could have nodded. I could have tried to flirt. I should have winked. It was dark. She would not have seen me wink. I will see her at the park tomorrow. I will explain everything.*

He called Angela.

"Good news?" Angela said.

"I waved at Trina," Tony said. "I was only two feet from her, and I waved."

"Did you say hello?" Angela asked.

"I was afraid," Tony said. "She is so pretty I could not speak."

"She must be very pretty," Angela said.

"Yes," Tony said. "Her beauty silences me."

"You have to get over that, Tony," Angela said.

"I will try," Tony said.

"What happened after you waved at her?" Angela asked.

"I held up the shoes I bought her," Tony said. "She did not see them."

"I'm sure she did, Tony," Angela said, "but you didn't say anything to her first. I thought you were going to talk to her before you gave her the shoes."

"It is hard," Tony said. "My voice freezes in my throat whenever I see her."

"You don't have to say much," Angela said. "Simply

explain why you got them and then give her the shoes. Go ahead. Say, 'Trina, I got you these shoes . . .'"

"Trina, I got you these shoes," Tony said.

"So that . . ."

"So your feet do not hurt anymore," Tony said.

"That sounds like a great start," Angela said.

"And then I will go to her home," Tony said.

"Um, Tony," Angela said, "let's see how it goes with the shoes first."

"I want to go to Trina's home," Tony said.

"I know you do," Angela said. "Just see if she likes the shoes, okay? And let her *invite* you to her home."

"I cannot go to her home," Tony said.

"Not unless she invites you," Angela said.

Tony looked out the window at Huntington Park. "Help me talk some more. Aika helped me by acting like Trina."

"I will," Angela said, "but you have to go first."

"I will go first," Tony said. "Hi, I am Tony. What is your name?"

"I'm Trina," Angela said.

"It is foggy today," Tony said. "It is like clam chowder without the clams and potatoes. Do you like clam chowder, Trina?"

"Yes," Angela said.

"How do you think the Giants will do this year?" Tony asked.

"What if Trina doesn't follow baseball?" Angela asked. "What would you say next?"

"I do not know," Tony said. "I would probably say nothing and give her the shoes."

"You have to think of something else to say," Angela said. "You know, work your way into giving her the shoes."

"I will tell her I have memorized all the streets in Nob Hill and Chinatown," Tony said.

"Why not cut to the chase and tell her the real reason you came to see her?" Angela asked. "Tell her you're on a quest to meet her."

"Only knights went on quests," Tony said. "I am not a knight."

"You're the most chivalrous man I know," Angela said.

"Trina will think I am crazy," Tony said.

"Or charming," Angela said.

"I am not charming," Tony said.

"I think you are, Tony," Angela said. "Let's try again."

"Hi, my name is Tony," Tony said. "What is your name?"

"I'm Trina," Angela said.

"I have a confession to make, Trina," Tony said.

"Um, no, Tony," Angela said. "That's a bit . . . strange. You just met her. Just say what's in your heart."

"I cannot say what is in my heart," Tony said. "My heart is too confusing. I will say what is in my head."

"Okay," Angela said. "Tell her what's in your head."

"Trina, I feel as if I already know you," Tony said. "In fact, I already know a few things about you. I read your biography on the *Second Chances* Web site, and I took an airplane from Brooklyn to San Francisco to meet you. I think you are very pretty, and I would like to get to know you better. I saw you rub your feet yesterday so I bought you these shoes."

Angela didn't respond immediately.

"Is that okay, Angela?" Tony asked.

"That's great, Tony," Angela said. "That's perfect."

"I will try it tomorrow," Tony said.

"Let me know what happens, okay?" Angela said.

"Okay," Tony said. "Thank you, Angela."

"No, thank you, Tony," Angela said. "You may be the last truly romantic soul left in the universe."

# 21

As Trina entered Huntington Park for her lunch break the following day, she saw the man from the bus bench the night before putting several shoe boxes on the park bench where she usually sat.

*No Brooklyn Dodgers jacket today. Nice clothes. A little wrinkled. Do I stop? He seems harmless. Tall. Italian. Dark eyes. Is he dangerous? Dangerous people don't normally tip barbers a thousand bucks, do they? If this is even the guy.*

Trina approached the bench cautiously. "Are you . . . Tony?"

"Yes," Tony said. He looked in Trina's general direction. "I am Tony. Trina, I feel as if I already—"

"How do you know my name?" Trina asked.

"I read your biography on the *Second Chances* Web site, and—"

"I sounded pretty pathetic, didn't I?" Trina said.

"No," Tony said. "You were honest. Um, I took an airplane from Brooklyn to San Francisco to meet you. I think you are very pretty, and I—"

"Thank you," Trina said.

Tony's eyes moved from her white shoes to her thighs. "I think you are very pretty, and I would like to—"

"Thank you, Tony," Trina said.

Tony's eyes flitted briefly to her face. "You are welcome."

"And you want to . . ."

"Oh," Tony said. "And I would like to get to know you better."

"Really?"

"Yes," Tony said. "I saw you rubbing—"

"Are those Sanitas?" Trina interrupted.

"Yes," Tony said. "I saw you rubbing your feet yesterday so I bought you these shoes." He sighed loudly. "I have said everything now."

"Are you a Good Samaritan or something?" Trina asked.

"No," Tony said. "The Good Samaritan was a man in a parable Jesus told in the Bible in the Gospel of Luke chapter ten. I am not in the Bible."

*This sweet man has something wrong with him. Is he autistic? He seems high functioning, and he's superpolite.* "Well, I think you're a modern-day Good Samaritan, Tony." She stepped closer to the bench and looked at the boxes. "Those are too big—wait. *Those* are my size. Six and a half. How did you know?"

"I measured your feet with my eyes," Tony said. "They were nine inches. I will stand over here while you try them on." He backed several feet away from the bench, toward the fountain.

"Why?" Trina asked.

"I am a stranger," Tony said. "You do not know me."

"You're not a stranger," Trina said. "You're Tony from Brooklyn, and you're giving me shoes I desperately need." She nodded toward the bench. "You can stand closer. I won't bite."

"I will stand closer," Tony said. "I will not bite either."

Trina smiled, slipped off her Danskos, and opened the shoe box. "Did you really fly all the way across the country to meet me?"

"I did not fly," Tony said. "The plane flew."

Trina smiled. "Right." *He takes everything I say literally. What does he have? I should know this.* She put on the Sanitas and danced around the bench. "Oh, these feel like heaven."

"Heaven is where Poppa and Mama are," Tony said. "Tonto may be there, too. I do not know if dogs are allowed in heaven."

"I hope they are," Trina said. "I had a dog named Max when I was little. I still miss him. He was a big old Saint Bernard." She pushed aside the other boxes and sat. "These shoes feel great. And I can just . . . have them?"

"Yes." Tony bagged the other shoe boxes. "I can return these to Bea at DSW if I bring her the receipt." He stared at her photo ID hanging from a lanyard around her neck. "That is not a very good picture of you."

"I know," Trina said. "They caught me first thing in the morning. Pictures should never be taken first thing in the morning."

"You are very pretty in the morning," Tony said, staring at the ground.

"Thank you," Trina said. "You're pretty handsome yourself."

"I look like my brother Angelo," Tony said.

She patted a space next to her on the bench. "Why don't you sit with me?"

"I would like that very much." Tony sat two feet away, the bag at his feet.

"You don't have to sit so far away," Trina said. "I didn't bite you, right?"

"No," Tony said. He twisted his fingers and began pulling them. "I am . . . nervous."

*He is definitely autistic. I've seen autistic kids do that in the children's ward.* "I hope I don't make you feel nervous," Trina said softly.

"You make me feel . . ." Tony stopped pulling on his fingers. "I am not as nervous now."

She slid a few inches closer to Tony. "So you saw me online and just decided to come see me."

"Yes," Tony said, "because the other women were not honest." He looked at her knees. "And you have clear eyes. You have an honest face. Bambi Bennett is . . ." He remembered what Aika said. "Bambi Bennett is a big-eyed, big-chested Rapunzel who is long on legs and hair and short on intelligence."

Trina laughed. "I'll bet she is. Still, she gets to go on television, and I don't."

"You cannot find love on television," Tony said.

"I suppose you're right." She swung her legs back and forth. "This is so nice of you. My feet are happy."

"I have made your feet happy," Tony said.

"And you've made me happy, too," Trina said.

"I am glad," Tony said. He looked at his hiking boots. "My feet do not get happy. They get sweaty."

"So do mine," Trina said. "How long are you staying in San Francisco?"

"I do not know," Tony said.

Trina leaned back on the bench. "So, Tony from Brooklyn, you know a lot about me already. What's your story?"

"It is called *Living with the Sponge, the Biography of Art E.,*" Tony said. "My brother Angelo wrote it."

Trina's arms filled with goose bumps. "What's your last name, Tony?"

"Santangelo," Tony said. "I am Italian. But I am shy. Italians are not supposed to be shy. Angelo is not shy."

Trina moved closer to Tony, her thigh brushing his. "You know, there's nothing wrong with being shy. I'm shy."

"You are not shy," Tony said.

"I really am," Trina said. "It takes me a long time to warm up to people." She smiled. "But here I am warming up to you."

Tony nodded. "I like shy. Shy is good."

"So you're . . . Art E.," Trina said.

"I am Tony Santangelo," Tony said. "I am not Art E. I want you to like me, not Art E. I write music as Art E. It is not my name."

"I like your name," Trina said. "Tony Santangelo. It's easy to say."

"It does not mean anything," Tony said.

"I think it does." *Am I really sitting next to a living legend? I need to read that biography. Naini recommended that I read it, but I turned her down because it sounded too depressing.* "I like your beard."

"It is scratchy today," Tony said. "My face is normally smooth. I forgot my electric shaver. I brought my map book of San Francisco. I have memorized all the streets in Nob Hill and Chinatown. I will not get lost. It is not foggy like clam chowder today." Tony sighed. "I am sorry I am talking too much. I am supposed to be listening."

"It's okay," Trina said. "I want to know more about you. Did you really come out to California to meet me?"

"Yes," Tony said.

"I'm really quite ordinary," Trina said.

"I do not think so," Tony said. "I have learned so much about you since yesterday."

Trina pressed her thigh against his. "What have you learned?"

Tony stared at Trina's thigh. "I have trouble . . . talking to women . . . who are close to me."

Trina moved even closer, sliding her left arm to the back of the bench. "You're doing fine."

Tony looked behind him at Trina's hand. "But I have Asperger's. It is . . . hard. I like you very much, but I do not know how to tell you without saying the wrong thing."

*Asperger's. I should have known that. But Tony knows he has Asperger's. That's good, right? And for a man who often gets lost in his own mind, he's trying to get out of his mind for me. That's so sweet.* "What do you want to tell me?"

"I want to tell you how much I like you," Tony said. "I saw you yesterday on this bench, and when the sun came out and made your face glow, I had never seen anything so beautiful. Your face glowed like an angel, and now your feet feel like heaven."

"Yes, they do," Trina said. *Thank God for that brief sunbeam.*

"I wrote notes about you yesterday." Tony took out several notepads and began to flip through them. "I think I have a song here. 'If you asked me what is beauty, it won't be a woman's booty, it won't be a color or race, it's sunlight's lace on Trina's face . . .'"

*Did he just say . . . booty?*

"Some rapper will do that part," Tony said. "It is the style now. Then a singer will sing, 'Streams of gold shine all around her, I thank God that I have found her, I will remember this sunlight moment as long as I live, as long as I love . . .' It still needs some work."

*Oh my goodness! He's got me tearing up! Is he the real deal? Is he really Art E.?* "That was beautiful, Tony. 'As long as I live, as long as I love.' And you wrote that while you were looking at me?"

"Yes," Tony said. "I may call it 'As Long as I Live, As Long as I Love,' but I might want to call it 'Trina.' "

*A song named for me. Wow.* "You're the songwriter, not me." She looked away.

"You are beautiful, Trina," Tony said. "I look at you and see notes all around you. The words come to me easily. I could write many more songs about you, too."

"I don't know what to say," Trina said. Her eyes filled with tears.

Tony glanced up at Trina's face. "You are crying. I have made you cry. I have just met you and I made you cry."

Trina wiped her eyes. "You're not making me cry, Tony. I sometimes cry when I'm happy. You're making me happy. No one's ever written a song about me before."

"It will sound better with accompaniment," Tony said. "I will be better with accompaniment." He moved a shaking hand to Trina's thigh, lightly touched it, and returned it to his lap. "I will be a better man with accompaniment."

Trina looked into Tony's eyes. "I don't understand."

Tony focused on his feet. "I want to be your second chance, Trina."

*Oh, my heart, my heart, and here come some more tears.* "You do?"

"Yes," Tony said. "You deserve a second chance."

He checked his watch. "You are ten minutes late back to work."

"It doesn't matter," Trina said. She put her hand on his thigh. "I have a really good excuse for being late."

Tony opened a notepad to a blank page, writing as he chanted: "Second chances, sunlight dances, second chances, what romance is."

"Thank Saint Francis," Trina said.

Tony wrote it down. "Yes." He looked at her brown hand on his pants. "I like the way that looks."

"My hand?"

"Yes," Tony said. "I like your hand." He put his notepad away. "I do not want to go back to the shoe store now. I will walk with you."

Trina squeezed his thigh and stood. "I'd like that." She picked up her old shoes. "I won't need these any-more." She walked to a trash can and dropped them in, Tony two steps behind her. "I can't believe you bought me shoes."

Tony moved beside her. "I am glad you like them."

"You know," Trina said, "there are plenty of nurses in the hospital with tired feet who would love to have shoes like these."

"I will give them all shoes," Tony said.

"You'd be a *real* saint if you did that," Trina said. "But there are hundreds of nurses at Saint Francis."

Tony handed the bag to Trina. "It is a start."

"You want me to give these away?" Trina asked.

"Yes," Tony said.

They left the park and turned onto California Street, a cable car clanging as it click-clacked past.

"I'm sure I'll be able to find someone who wants them," Trina said. "I have a friend named Naini who will love these."

As they turned up Hyde Street toward the hospital, Tony walked a few steps in front of Trina and stopped. "I want to see you again, Trina."

*I wish he would look at me.* "I want to see you again, too, Tony." *And I do. He has made my day!*

"I want to take you out to dinner at Cielo Azul tonight," Tony said.

*He wants to make my night, too! Cielo Azul gets incredible reviews. No beef stew tonight!* "I'd like that."

"My barber Carlos said to go there," Tony said. "Carmine said to go to Bar Tartine or Aziza. Carlos said Cielo Azul was the best restaurant in San Francisco bar none."

"Carlos has good taste," Trina said. "I hear it is an excellent restaurant."

"Carlos and Carmine told me where to buy these clothes," Tony said. "I had never bought clothes before. William helped me at Banana Republic."

"William has good taste, too." She reached for his elbow but let her hand drop. *He has issues with contact. I won't push it. I don't want to leave this weirdly fascinating man, but ES and ES2 are probably searching for me.*

"You have a circle on your finger where a ring used to be," Tony said.

Trina nodded. "I want it to fade away."

Tony remembered what Angelo said. "Your ex-husband is an asshole."

Trina laughed loudly.

Tony remembered what Aika said. "What a turd."

Trina grabbed Tony's arm. "He is!"

Tony stared at Trina's hand on his forearm. "I could write a song called 'He Is an Asshole,' but they would not play it on the radio."

"These days, they just might." She tugged his arm gently, and they continued to walk. "They'd bleep out the bad words, of course."

"Not many words rhyme with 'asshole,' " Tony said. " 'Castle' and 'hassle' do. I live in the Castle in Cobble Hill."

*I wish I knew more about this man! I have to find that biography.* "It's not a real castle, is it?"

"No," Tony said. "It is not made of stone. It does not have a moat. It is made of many bricks."

"And you're the knight who lives there," Trina said.

"I am not a knight," Tony said.

Trina turned to face him at the main entrance, letting her hand slide down his arm. "You are a knight to me." She sighed. "Well, we're here."

"We are always here," Tony said.

Trina smiled. *So simple and yet so profound.* "You're right. We are always here." *Now what do I do?*

"Do you think you could ever like me, Trina?" Tony asked.

"I already do, Tony," Trina said. "You have a very kind soul."

"Thank you," Tony said. "I will take you to Cielo Azul for dinner tonight."

"I look forward to it," Trina said.

"But I am nervous," Tony said. "I have never been on a date."

*Will we be going on a date? It feels like one. I'm going to dinner with a good man.* "I haven't been on a real date in a long time."

"But you were married," Tony said.

"That doesn't mean I went on dates," Trina said. "Maybe one or two real dates fourteen years ago *before* I got married, but once I got married . . . nothing."

"I am still nervous," Tony said.

"Just be yourself," Trina said.

"You see how I am," Tony said.

"And that's all you have to be." She touched his hand.

Tony nodded. "That will be another song. 'You see how I am, and that's all I have to be.' Thank you."

*And now I'm supplying him with actual lyrics?* "So, where should I meet you for our date?"

"I will be out here waiting for you." He walked quickly across Bush Street to the bus bench and sat.

Trina waited for traffic to thin before crossing Bush Street. "Tony, I'll be at work for the next four hours," Trina said. *The ER and Naini will have to survive without me tonight because I have a date.*

"It will give me time to write," Tony said. "I have a lot to write about."

"You'll have to make a reservation at Cielo Azul," Trina said. "And since Cielo Azul is a fancy place, I will have to go home to change."

"I do not want you to change," Tony said. "I like you the way you are."

*He's not being funny. He accepts me for me.* "I want to go home to change my *clothes*. I doubt Cielo Azul will let someone wearing scrubs dine there."

"They should let anyone in," Tony said.

"It's a very fancy place," Trina said. "And I want to look good for you."

"You look good," Tony said. "You are good. Do I look okay?"

"Hey, you're Tony Santangelo from Brooklyn," Trina said. "You can wear anything you want. But first we'll need a reservation, and I hear reservations are hard to get there, so . . ." *Take the hint.*

"I will call Cielo Azul and make a reservation for eight o'clock," Tony said. He pulled out his phone and pressed the Google app.

"Hey, that's a smartphone," Trina said. She sat beside him, setting the bag beside her.

"Phones are not smart," Tony said.

"And neither are some people who use them." She stared at the screen. "Wow, you've already found Cielo Azul's Web site. See the number?"

"Yes." Tony pressed on the phone number and waited a few seconds. "Hi, my name is Tony Santangelo. I need a reservation for dinner at eight o'clock tonight."

Trina pressed the speaker button. "I hope you don't mind if I listen in."

"No."

"We have no openings for dinner this evening, sir," a man said. "We won't have any openings—"

"We will only need two chairs and a small table," Tony interrupted. "Trina is slender."

*Well, at least he noticed my body. It's nice to be slender.*

"Sir, this is Cielo Azul," the man said. "We are booked through the end of *next* month, sir. If you would like to dine with us—"

"I have a date with Trina," Tony said. "She is very pretty. I promised her I would take her to dinner at Cielo Azul."

"You should not make promises you can't keep, sir," the man said.

*Pompous ass!* "What if I told you he was Art E., the famous songwriter?" Trina asked.

"You're Art E.," the man said.

"Go ahead," Trina whispered.

"I am Art E.," Tony said.

"I don't believe either of you," the man said.

"Did you see the story about Art E. in the entertainment section of the newspaper this morning?" Trina asked.

"No," the man said.

"I was in the newspaper," Tony said.

"Yes," Trina said. "About you tipping Carlos a thousand dollars. I am sitting next to the subject of that story in front of Saint Francis Memorial."

"I don't believe you for a moment," the man said.

"Okay, it's your loss," Trina said. "Let's try Bar Tartine or Aziza."

"This is a joke, right?" the man said.

"I did not tell a joke," Tony said.

"Wait a minute," the man said. "Am I on the radio?"

"I do not know," Tony said.

"This is some prank call, right?" the man said.

"This is a phone call," Tony said.

"You can't fool me, whoever you are," the man said. "Please don't call again."

*Click.*

"He hung up," Tony said, putting his phone into his pocket. "I did not make a reservation for us."

"We can go somewhere else," Trina said. "It doesn't have to be fancy."

"I want to take you to the best restaurant in San Francisco," Tony said.

"You don't have to, Tony," Trina said. "You could take me to a street vendor, and I'd be content. Tell you what. There's a little Irish pub near where I live called Johnny Foley's. We can go there. They have two pianos in the Cellar."

"I played my piano in the cellar in Cobble Hill," Tony said. "But they will not be my piano."

"Of course not," Trina said. "You would have had to bring your piano on the airplane."

"It would not fit," Tony said.

"And if we go to Johnny Foley's, maybe you could play a song for me." *Maybe my song, the one he wrote for me today.*

"I would like to play a song for you," Tony said.

"I look forward to it." She stood, moved in front of him, and knelt, squeezing both of his hands. "Are you sure you want to wait four hours for me? It might rain."

"There is a twenty-percent chance of rain today with winds from the southwest at seven to ten miles per hour," Tony said. "I watch the Weather Channel."

"It's required viewing around here," Trina said. "Did you have lunch?"

"Oh," Tony said. "You did not eat your lunch at the park."

"It's okay," Trina said. "Are you hungry?"

"Yes," Tony said. "But I can wait."

"Are you sure?" Trina asked. "There are some decent places to eat around here."

"I ate at the BeanStalk Café yesterday," Tony said. "Hyun Ae made me a messy ham and cheese sandwich. Her name means 'wise and loving.'"

"You could go there now," Trina said.

"I will wait for you here," Tony said. "I do not want to miss you again."

*He's worried I won't come back.* She intertwined her fingers with his. "I *will* come back, Tony. I'll be out as soon as I can."

Tony looked down at his lap. "Thank you."

"For what?" Trina asked.

"For holding my hands," Tony said.

*Has anyone* ever *held this man's big, strong hands? I may be the first.* "I'm kind of a touchy-feely, hands-on person."

"Touchy-feely," Tony said.

"I'm a nurse," Trina said. "I have to touch my patients to help them. I hope you don't mind if I touch you."

"I do not mind," Tony said. "Your hands are warm and strong and dark brown. I like your color very much. It is like house blend at Angela's Sweet Treats and Coffee in Williamsburg. It is like Hires Root Beer. It is the color of your eyes."

*He's warming my hands* and *my heart.* "I'll see you in a few hours." She released his hands and stood.

"Okay."

Trina picked up the bag. "I'll be back," she said in her best Arnold Schwarzenegger voice.

"You are not the Terminator," Tony said. "You are too nice."

Trina laughed. "See you soon, Tony."

"Bye."

Tony flipped to a new page and wrote: "I am happy. This is good. This is how two people should . . . be."

*The syllables are wrong, but the words are right. I am happy, this is good, this is how two people should . . . lots of drums . . . be. Naomi will hold this note a long time. Yes. This is good.*

Tony looked at the people around him waiting for the bus.

*Yes, this is very good.*
*Trina will be back.*
He looked at his hands.
*She held my hands.*
*My hands miss her hands very much.*

# 22

Trina sneaked through the halls and took stairways instead of elevators to avoid ES and ES2 and found Naini on the seventh floor helping a double amputee wearing prostheses navigate a set of wooden stairs.

"You are doing fine, Mr. Lewis," Naini said.

The man's T-shirt was drenched in sweat. "Has it been ten minutes yet?"

"No," Naini said.

"I'm done," Mr. Lewis huffed. "I'm toast. I have to rest."

Naini helped him to a chair, handing him a towel and a bottle of water. "We'll try again in a few minutes."

"In a few minutes?" Mr. Lewis wheezed. "You're *killing* me. Marty never worked me this hard."

"It could be why you are still here, Mr. Lewis," Naini said. She smiled at Trina. "You have escaped." She saw the shoe bag. "And you are carrying a DSW bag."

"You still have that book you wanted me to read, the one about Art E.?" Trina asked.

"I loaned it to Tina," Naini said. "What is in the bag, Trina?"

*Lovely. Tina, who has been hitting on me mercilessly since she heard I was getting divorced.* "Why'd you loan Tina that book?"

"She is not a bad person when she is not trying to have sex with you," Naini said.

"She's been hitting on you, too?" Trina asked.

"I am a sexy Bengali woman," Naini said. "What man or woman could resist me?"

"You haven't . . ."

Naini laughed. "No, I have not." She raised her eyebrows. "Not with someone as ordinary as Tina. Now you, on the other hand . . . will now tell me what is in the bag."

Trina opened the bag. "Are either of these your size?"

Naini looked into the bag. "I can squeeze into these and wear two pairs of socks with these."

"Take them both," Trina said.

"There was a three for the price of one sale?" Naini said.

"No," Trina said. "A friend bought me the ones I'm wearing, but he didn't know my size. He bought three pairs to make sure one pair fit me."

"A friend?" Naini smiled. "Who have you been hiding from me and does he have a well-paid brother who wants to satisfy a sexy Bengali woman?"

"I'll have to tell you about him and his brother later," Trina said. "I really need that book."

"Why?" Naini asked.

"You wouldn't believe me if I told you," Trina said.

"I might," Naini said.

Trina pulled Naini to a window overlooking Bush Street and pointed down to the bus bench. "There's a man under the roof of that bench." She squinted. "You can just see his hiking boots."

"He has big feet," Naini said.

"Naini," Trina said, "that man is the composer Art E."

"Oh yes, and I am the goddess Lakshmi," Naini said. "Bow down and worship me. Shower me with lotus flowers."

"Nice to meet you, goddess Lakshmi, because that *is* Art E." Trina bowed once. "I don't have any lotus flowers. The shoes will have to do."

Naini peered down. "Some random man with big feet gives you shoes, and that makes you think he's Art E."

"There's more to it than that," Trina said. "I gotta go find Tina."

"She always seems to prowl around X-ray," Naini said. "She has asked me out twice there."

"I can't believe you turned her down," Trina said.

"She is not my type," Naini said. "She is far too clingy and tall."

"I'll go to X-ray first," Trina said. "Thanks."

"Thank you for the shoes," Naini said.

"Thank the man on the bench."

"I will open a window and shout, 'Thank you, Art E.'," Naini said. "No, I will not. They will send me back to India." She turned to Mr. Lewis. "Rest time is over, Mr. Lewis. Time to climb."

Mr. Lewis moaned.

She winked at Trina. "Go find Tina. I know you will make her day."

Trina took a series of stairs to X-ray and found Tina talking up an LPN, whose eyes seemed to be searching for an exit.

"Hey, Tina." *Please don't hit on me.*

Tina left the LPN in a flash, and the LPN hurried away. "Hey, Trina."

*Tina and Trina. Maybe she wants my body so we can rhyme together.* "Do you have that Art E. book Naini loaned you?"

"Yes," Tina said in a husky voice. "I've been meaning to return it to her. That Sponge guy is a trip."

*I know. I think I've met him. He's on the bus bench outside.* "You have it with you?"

"It's up in my locker," Tina said.

*Yes!* "Could I get it? Naini knows I want to borrow it."

"Sure," Tina said.

*She's making eyes at me.* "Could I get it now?"

"Sure," Tina said, leaning closer and raising a hand.

*Tina wants to pet me now.* Trina backed away to the wall. *I'm touchy-feely. Tina is strictly feely, and that makes me touchy.* "Could we go get it now, please?"

"I'll meet you at my locker in ten minutes," Tina said. "As soon as I unload the old cow in there who broke her hip doing Tai Chi in the park this morning. Can you believe it? Tai Chi."

*Though I want to know how someone could break a hip doing Tai Chi, I will not get into a conversation with this person.* "I'll be waiting."

Tina raised her eyebrows. "I'll hurry."

Trina sat on the bench in front of Tina's locker for only five minutes before Tina crept into the locker room.

"I told you I would hurry." Tina opened her locker

and held out the book. "So are you and Naini . . . a couple?"

*Naini is extremely sexy, but I'm not built that way.* "No."

Tina licked her lower lip. "Are you doing anything tonight? I've been hoping to take someone to this little intimate bar—"

Trina snatched the book. "I have a date."

Tina blinked. "Yeah? Who with?"

*The subject of the book I'm holding.* "His name is Tony. Thanks for the book."

Trina headed straight for the first stall in the nearest staff bathroom, closed the door, and began reading. She skimmed through Tony's childhood, howled with laughter at Tony's encounter with Jasmine, skimmed through Tony's involvement with Naomi Stringer—*she is so overexposed*—and focused on the last two chapters.

*Tony watches the Weather Channel, set in his routines, shy around women, pulls and twists on his fingers when he's nervous—that's Tony all right. "Flinches on contact with people he doesn't know"—but he let me touch him. I guess he's comfortable around me. Either that or he thinks he knows me. "Too polite and accepting of others." That's not a fault. It's a virtue. Unlike so many of us, Tony has an open mind. Tony likes Hires Root Beer, memorizes map books, says inappropriate yet truthful things, has the worst handwriting on earth—*

"Trina, are you in here?" Naini called out.

"Yes," Trina said, opening the stall door and stepping out.

"ES and ES2 have been looking for you," Naini said.

"How did you find me?" Trina asked.

"Tina told me," Naini said. "It seems she was waiting for you to come out of the bathroom for a long time. She is quite a stalker."

"I've been a little sick," Trina said.

"I see," Naini said. "Are you enjoying the book while you are being 'sick'?"

*I'd rather enjoy the Sponge in person.* "I am." She handed the book to Naini. "I'm through with it."

"You could not have read the entire book," Naini said.

"I have been sick a long time," Trina said. *And I'd rather read the man than the book any day.* "Where are ES and ES2 now?"

"On one of their many breaks between breaks," Naini said. "They're on two."

"Good."

Trina went to the nearest waiting area, bought a package of cheese crackers and a can of A&W Root Beer, and took them outside to Tony.

Tony stood. "We can go now."

"Not yet." She handed him the crackers and root beer. "I thought you might be hungry and thirsty."

"I am," Tony said. "Thank you."

"I know it's not Hires," Trina said.

"It is okay," Tony said. "I also like Doc's Root Beer. It is made in the Bronx."

"I'll be out in about two hours," Trina said.

"Okay." Tony sat.

She put her hand on his shoulder. "How's your writing coming?"

Tony showed her a notepad. "I have one notepad left."

Trina turned her head to the side. *Is that written in*

*English? Tony could be a doctor here.* "Do you need more paper? I could get you some."

"I will be okay," Tony said. "My hand is tired."

She backed away from the bench. "See you soon."

"Yes," Tony said.

Instead of going by the nurse's station on the second floor to check in and possibly run into ES and ES2, Trina stood at a hall phone inside the ER and called psych.

"Is this Doc Ramsey?" Trina asked.

"This is she," Dr. Ramsey said.

"Hi, this is Trina Woods, and I'm working with an Asperger's patient." *Well, I am. Sort of.*

"How do you know he has Asperger's?" Dr. Ramsey asked.

"He told me," Trina said.

"That's a good sign," Dr. Ramsey said. "He knows he's different, and he may have already taken steps to function better socially. Is he high functioning?"

"Yes." *He's actually a genius. He has numerous hits and has won three Grammy Awards.*

"What are his strengths as you see them?" Dr. Ramsey asked.

"Music, definitely."

"And his weaknesses?"

"Shyness mostly," Trina said. "Fear of physical contact, too." *Talking to women, but that's not a weakness as long as he only talks to me exclusively.*

"That's par for the course with Aspies," Dr. Ramsey said.

*Aspies? What a strange nickname.*

"He sounds fairly well adjusted," Dr. Ramsey said. "What is he in the hospital for?"

"Um, a routine checkup." *To check up on me!* "Is there anything I should look out for?"

"Well, there's stimming and perseverating," Dr. Ramsey said.

*Those can't be real words.* "What are they?"

"Asperger's sufferers use stimming to calm themselves down," Dr. Ramsey said. "They might pace or rock or make noises that soothe them."

"Or pull on their fingers?"

"Yes," Dr. Ramsey said. "Does your patient do this?"

"I've seen him do it, yes," Trina said.

"What calmed him down?" Dr. Ramsey asked.

*Me!* "Soft words, I guess. I put my hand on his hand, too. What's perseverating?"

"Talking about the same thing for a long time, sometimes all day, sometimes over a number of days," Dr. Ramsey said. "It's a form of fixation, and attempts to change the subject often fail."

*Tony has been fixating on Cielo Azul. Perseverating also sounds like something ES does daily and what Robert did every day for ten years.* "What do I do if that happens?"

"A change of scene sometimes works," Dr. Ramsey said. "Remove the patient from *wherever* he's perseverating, and sometimes he'll snap out of it."

*I don't want to ask this, but . . .* "Could he be dangerous?"

"There's nothing in the medical literature to suggest AS sufferers are inherently dangerous to others," Dr. Ramsey said. "Anything else?"

"Um, no," Trina said. "Thank you, Dr. Ramsey." *You've calmed me down about my date.*

Trina worked the last ninety minutes of her shift on

the fourth floor, helping with a new admittance and watching the nearest clock when she could. At four, she rushed to her locker, collected her jacket and purse, and burst out into the hallway—to be stopped by ES and ES2.

"Where do you think you're going, Woods?" Nurse Sprouse asked.

*On a real date!* "Home. My shift's over." She slipped into her jacket.

"I haven't seen you all afternoon," Nurse Sprouse said.

*I know. Was it good for you, too?* "I've been here."

"Tina Gonzalez said you were in the bathroom for most of the afternoon," Nurse Sprouse said. "Is that true?"

*Tina is a stalking bitch.* "Yes," Trina said. "Well, for about an hour or so."

"Then you should have clocked out and gone home," Nurse Sprouse said. "This hospital is *not* paying you to sit on the toilet all day."

*Just to take patients to and from the toilet when I could be flawlessly managing and charting half a dozen patients.* "I know it isn't." *And this gives me an idea.* "Nurse Sprouse, I'm still not feeling that good. I should probably take the rest of the week off to be sure whatever I have is out of my system."

"Time-off requests must be made—"

"I know the rule, Nurse Sprouse," Trina interrupted. *I helped rewrite that rule six years ago before your anal ass got here.* "But I came down with this today, and you don't want a sick nurse around patients, do you?"

"Of course not, Woods," Nurse Sprouse said.

"I'll be back bright and early on Monday," Trina said, moving around Inez and Danica. "Bye."

"I will remember this during your evaluation," Nurse Sprouse said. "Make a note of it, Martinez."

Inez wrote something down.

Trina stopped. "Remember what? That I got sick?"

"That you, as a nurse, didn't take better care of your health," Nurse Sprouse said. "Trumbo, sign Woods up for a refresher seminar in blood-borne pathogens."

"Yes, ma'am," Danica said with a smile.

"That's not necessary," Trina said. "I just took that course—"

"You're right, Woods," Nurse Sprouse interrupted. "It *isn't* necessary. For a *professional* nurse. For *you*, it is."

Inez and Danica snickered.

*Just you wait, ES2,* Trina thought as she walked out the ER entrance. *In the original* Cinderella, *pigeons pecked out the eyes of Cinderella's evil stepsisters.*

Trina approached the bus bench. "Tony," she whispered.

Tony looked up. "Hi, Trina. It is time to go."

"Yes," Trina said. "It's not a long walk. I live on O'Farrell."

"We will take Hyde Street then," Tony said as he stood. "It is quickest."

She grasped his elbow lightly. "Is it okay if I hold on to your arm as we walk?"

"Yes," Tony said.

A bus pulled up, and a crowd filed around them to get on and off.

"I have written six songs," Tony said as they walked

through the throng at a leisurely pace. "I wrote five about you and one about the bus."

"You wrote a song about the bus," Trina said.

"A bus has music," Tony said. "I hear music everywhere. I listened to people walking all around me today. Each person had a different rhythm."

"What's my rhythm?" Trina asked.

"*Vivace*," Tony said. "You are lively and spirited."

"What's your rhythm?" Trina asked.

"I am *adagio*, slow," Tony said.

"I don't think you're slow at all," Trina said. "You asked me out the first time you met me."

"I did not speak to you the first time I met you," Tony said.

"Because you were sponging me, right?" Trina said.

"Yes," Tony said. "I like to sponge."

"Did you see anything you liked while you were sponging me?" Trina asked.

"Yes," Tony said. "I liked everything."

*I'd ask him to be more specific, but I just met him,* Trina thought. *Oh, it is so nice to be walking with a man.*

Tony's eyes never stayed still during the short walk to Trina's apartment. He stared at a graffiti-covered gray Dumpster and made several notes. He looked up at ancient fire escapes. He seemed to count the metal supports on some scaffolding. He mumbled rhymes as they passed "House of Fans." He turned his head to listen to the swaying leaves of the trees sprouting from the sidewalk. He tried to step only on the darker-colored concrete squares as they turned onto O'Farrell. He counted the windows on her apartment building.

*Tony drinks in and sponges everything, from the sidewalk to the streetlights to the people walking by, as if the whole world is new to him at all times. He is like a child yet he's quiet about it. Children say, "Look! Look!"*

Tony's eyes do the shouting.

*I wish he would look at me.*

*I wish his eyes would shout at me.*

# 23

Tony trailed behind Trina as they climbed the narrow stairs to her apartment door. Once Trina opened the door, ushered him inside, and closed the door behind him, she sighed and said, "So . . . this is where I live."

"It is small," Tony said.

*I'm sure he has closets larger than my apartment,* Trina thought.

Trina took off her jacket and hung it in the closet. "It's all I can afford." *And at only $2,200 a month, which is half my take-home pay.* She dropped her purse onto the couch and went into the kitchen, where she turned off the Crock-Pot. "That *was* my dinner."

"It smells good," Tony said. He stepped into the kitchen. "Your floor is a checkerboard. Angela's Sweet Treats and Coffee has a checkerboard floor."

*And this kitchen has never been so crowded. Tony takes up some serious space.* "Are you hungry? Would you like a bowl of my famous beef stew?"

"Yes."

"Um, go sit on the couch," Trina said. "I'll bring you a bowl."

"Okay."

"That coffee table out there is where I eat all my meals."

Tony took three steps and sat on the couch. "It is purple."

Trina found a clean bowl in a cupboard and filled it to the top. She took a spoon from a drawer, a napkin from a plastic holder, and the bowl to the coffee table.

"I got the couch at a deep discount," Trina said. *I actually found it on the curb on trash day and muscled it up here, where it will forever smell of Crisp Linen Lysol.* "Be careful eating the stew. It's hot."

Tony blew on his first spoonful before devouring it. "It is good."

*Someone likes my cooking. Two miracles in one day.* "Would you like to add some Goldfish crackers?"

"Yes."

Trina added several Goldfish crackers.

"They are swimming." Tony ate another spoonful. "Golden fish. It is good. Crunchy stew. Delores does not make this."

Trina sat beside him. "Who's Delores?"

"Our cook," Tony said.

"I wish I had a cook," Trina said.

"You are a cook," Tony said.

"I warm things up," Trina said. "That's not cooking."

"It tastes like cooking to me." Tony picked up the remote on the coffee table and turned on the television. A multicolored weather map appeared on the screen. "You watch the weather."

"Every morning," Trina said.

"I watch it all day," Tony said. "San Francisco has colorful weather."

Trina watched him empty the bowl in four minutes with an occasional slurp. *He even makes my cooking* sound *good!* "Who do you live with in Brooklyn, Tony?"

"Angelo and Aika," Tony said. "Aika just moved in. She is Japanese. She does not live in Japan. She sleeps in Angelo's bed. She is sometimes loud."

*In bed? No, I can't ask that.* "She has a loud voice, huh?"

"Only when she is in Angelo's bed," Tony said.

*I want to laugh so badly!* "That's . . . that's interesting."

"Aika has a cotton-ball whisper voice," Tony said. "Angelo will marry her. They will have children with cotton-ball voices."

"So it's just the three of you living in the Castle," Trina said.

"Yes," Tony said. "It is very big. It has ten rooms." He stared at the television.

Trina's stomach grumbled. "I'll go change my clothes so we can go eat."

"I have been eating," Tony said.

"Yes," Trina said. "I meant, so we can go eat dinner at Johnny Foley's."

"Yes," Tony said. "I will play you a song."

She put her hand on his thigh, pushed off, and stood. *This man is made of muscle.* "I'll only be a few minutes."

"Okay."

Trina skipped to her room and looked at her meager wardrobe. Whenever she moved her clothes hangers, she heard an echo. *What do I wear? I hope Johnny Foley's isn't too crowded, though Tony didn't seem to mind the crowds flowing around him at the bus stop. He just zoned out completely and wrote songs while all those people were jostling around him. I wish I could focus like that.*

She pushed and pulled the hangers in her closet, frowning at clothes she used to wear in a vain attempt to impress Robert. *I haven't dressed to impress a man in so long, but will Tony even notice? I have nothing in this closet that says, "Look at me!" I have plenty of clothes in this closet that say, "Meh."*

She put on jeans that used to be tight on her legs. *I am no longer sexy. I am slender.* Instead of the Sanitas, she wore some ancient, scuffed hiking boots. *To match his, sort of.* She threw on a white cotton sweater and posed in front of the mirror attached to her closet door with plastic clips. *How plain can I get? Brown and blue and white.* She put on no makeup, spritzed on some citrusy perfume, and fluffed her hair. She sighed. *I guess I'm ready.*

She walked out of her room and stood in front of the television. "Ready?"

Tony looked up briefly before turning off the television.

*No comment. Shoot. I should have worn makeup.*

Tony stood. "You smell like oranges and grapefruits."

*He has a good nose.* "It's my perfume."

"I like it," Tony said. "It smells like calypso music."

*Robert hated my perfume. He said I smelled like a fruit salad. But what about the rest of me, man?* "Tony, how do I look?"

"You look like an angel," Tony said.

*That's . . . that's better.* "What does an angel look like?"

"You."

Trina shook her head. "I'm not an angel, Tony."

Tony stared at the coffee table. "I think you are."

"I sure don't look like an angel," Trina said.

"Yes, you are," Tony said. "Your hair is your own. It is curly and black and shiny. Your eyes are full of golden sunlight. Your ears are brown potato chips. Your nose is small and shiny. Your lips look soft and firm. They are dark brown. Your teeth are white. Your tongue is pink. Your breasts are in proportion to your buttocks. You have strong legs. I like your boots."

*He must have a photographic memory. The breasts and buttocks line was strangely . . . comforting.* "I like *your* boots."

"They are not your size," Tony said. "I can buy you some."

"You already bought me shoes," Trina said. "Let's go eat."

"Okay."

Outside Trina's apartment building, she asked, "May I hold on to your arm?"

"Yes," Tony said. "We are on a date now."

Trina grasped his bicep. *I am holding on to an arm made of stone.* "We are."

Tony took out his phone. "I must call Angela to tell her."

"Who's Angela?" Trina asked.

"My friend." He pressed the number two and waited. "Angela, I am on a date with Trina. We are going to eat at an Irish pub called Johnny Foley's. It has two pianos. . . . Yes, she is here." He handed the phone to Trina. "Angela wants to talk to you."

*This is strange.* "Hello?"

"Is this the Trina from *Second Chances*?"

*Strange question.* "Yes."

"How's he doing?" Angela asked.

*Angela sounds New York and . . . black.* "Fine."

"Define 'fine,' please," Angela said.

"He's actually wonderful," Trina said.

"Did he tell you who he is?" Angela asked.

"Yes."

"Did you believe him the first time he told you?" Angela asked.

"Honestly, no," Trina said. "But then he shared a song he wrote for me, and . . . it was amazing."

"He did the same for me and my family," Angela said.

"And then I read some of Tony's biography, and that cinched it," Trina said.

"And how do you feel about knowing who he really is?" Angela asked.

"I feel great," Trina said. "I have a date with greatness."

"I'm glad Tony called me because his brother Angelo and Angelo's fiancée are on their way to San Francisco," Angela said.

"Why?"

"Tony, kind of, well, escaped from Brooklyn with my help," Angela said. "He didn't tell Angelo he was coming to see you."

Trina gripped Tony's arm more tightly. "So he did all this on his own?"

"Yes, and he sounds as if he's doing very well," Angela said. "Where did you find you?"

"At a park near the hospital," Trina said.

"How close are you to his hotel right now?" Angela asked.

"Where is he staying?" Trina asked.

"The Huntington," Angela said.

"That's right next to the park where we met," Trina said.

"The better to sponge you," Angela said. "I hope you don't think he was stalking you. He is really the sweetest man I've ever known."

*It is so weird to be talking about someone who's walking beside you and who has to hear half the conversation.* "I know he's sweet."

"Could you make sure he gets back to the Huntington after your date?" Angela asked.

"Sure," Trina said. "It's not very far from here."

"I'm warning you, though," Angela said. "Tony may not want to go back to the hotel. He has it in his head that he's going to stay with you. And once he has something in his head, it stays there."

*How do I feel about that? Hmm. That thought hasn't been in my head. It is now.* "What do I do if that happens?"

"Only you can answer that question," Angela said. "Go with your heart."

*My heart says . . . he should stay with me.* "My heart says we go back to my apartment and watch the weather together."

"He's already been to your apartment?"

*Is she accusing me of something? It sounds like it.* "Only so I could change out of my scrubs for our date."

"Well, do your best to get him back to the hotel if you can," Angela said. "Angelo and Aika arrive tomorrow morning. They're going straight to the hotel to collect him."

"Why?" *And why so soon? I just met the guy!*

"He has Asperger's, Trina."

"Okay. And?"

"He needs special care," Angela said. "This is the first time he has ever been out of New York."

"And he's fine," Trina said. "He bought me shoes. He asked me out. He's out on a date."

"He's not normal, Trina," Angela said. "You've noticed that, right?"

"I'm glad he's not normal," Trina said. "A normal man wouldn't have been such a gentleman."

"I am hungry," Tony said.

"It's just a little farther, Tony," Trina said. "He's hungry, Angela."

"Just . . . take good care of him," Angela said.

"Angela," Trina said, "he's taking care of *me*. And if he decides not to go back to his hotel, I will honor his decision to stay with me."

"I just told you that's what he wants," Angela said.

"And that's what I want, too," Trina said. "I do have a couch he can sleep on."

"He has to come back to Brooklyn, Trina," Angela said.

*She's so overprotective!* "He's a grown man, Angela."

"I know that, Trina, but . . ." Angela sighed. "He's not fully grown, if you know what I mean."

"I'm focusing on what he is, not what he isn't," Trina said. "He bought me shoes I really, *really* needed. He says I look like an angel. He likes my cooking." *He likes my . . . proportions.*

"But Trina, seriously," Angela said. "He's like a little boy."

"He's not a child," Trina said. "He is treating me with more respect than any other man I have ever been with in my life. I feel like a lady, a *very* lucky lady. He is polite and kind and honest, and I like him very much."

"There's a lot to like, I know, but . . ."

"He is the perfect gentleman, and I am proud to be on his arm," Trina said.

"You're holding his arm?" Angela asked.

"Yes," Trina said.

"And he didn't flinch or shake off your hand or ask you to wash it?"

"No."

"That's . . . that's good," Angela said. "I tried to hug him once and he was stiff as a board."

"I haven't tried that yet," Trina said.

"You'll want to," Angela said.

*I'm sure I will.*

"But understand, Trina," Angela said. "He may never be able to show you any kind of real affection."

"I feel wanted and needed," Trina said. "A man flew three thousand miles to see me! That's enough affection for me."

"I am hungry, Trina," Tony said.

"I gotta go," Trina said. "I *promise* to take good care of him, Angela."

Angela sighed. "I'm going to hold you to that promise. Let me speak to Tony."

Trina handed the phone to Tony.

"Yes," Tony said. "She is so beautiful, Angela. She is a good cook like you, too. My voice works around her now. . . . Good-bye." He put away his phone.

They continued on O'Farrell.

"Your voice works now," Trina said.

"Yes," Tony said. "I could not speak to you yesterday because of your beauty."

*That's either the greatest compliment a woman can get or . . .* "So I'm not beautiful now?"

"You will always be beautiful, Trina," Tony said.

*It was a compliment. He's not going back to his hotel now because to him I will always be beautiful.*

They arrived outside Johnny Foley's, where Tony read the chalkboard sign on the sidewalk: " 'Guinness Draught sold here. Johnny Foley's presents dueling pianos all request show, no cover.' " Tony blinked. "Pianos do not duel."

"But the pianists sometimes do," Trina said.

"They duel with swords or pistols," Tony said.

"No," Trina said, smiling. "They duel with their fingers on the keys."

"Oh," Tony said.

She led him inside through a tiled hallway that ended at two doors, one marked THE CELLAR and one marked MAIN BAR.

"What is 'all request'?" Tony asked.

"People ask the pianists to play certain songs," Trina said. "The more you tip them, the more likely they'll play the song you want to hear."

"What is 'no cover'?" Tony asked.

"You don't have to pay any money to get in," Trina said. She nodded at the signs above opposite doors. "The Cellar is where the pianos are. They won't start playing for a little while."

"We are eating in the main bar," Tony said.

"Right," Trina said.

"I have never eaten at a bar." Tony opened the door for her.

"Thank you," Trina said.

They walked the length of a long wooden bar and sat at a small circular table looking out onto O'Farrell Street, a series of televisions throughout the bar tuned in to the Lakers-Warriors basketball game.

A server brought them menus. "What can I get you to drink?" she asked.

"Hires Root Beer," Tony said.

"I'll have ice water," Trina said.

The server left.

Tony studied the menu. "Cottage pie."

Trina closed her menu. "I tried it once. It was too bland for me. I always get the fish and chips."

Tony closed his menu. "I will get fish and chips, too."

After the server brought their drinks, Trina felt Tony's knees on hers. *Thank God for small tables.* "So, how long have you known Angela?"

"I saw her sixteen years ago the first time," Tony said. "When I met Jasmine."

*Oh yeah. I read about that, but I have to act as if I didn't.* "Who's Jasmine?"

"I met her at Angela's Sweet Treats and Coffee," Tony said.

"Was she pretty?" Trina asked.

"Yes," Tony said. "Her lips were plumper than yours. She had a snake tattoo on her left breast. I do not know where it ended."

"I don't have any tattoos," Trina said.

"Jasmine's eyebrows were furry," Tony said. "You have thin eyebrows. Her earrings made ding-ding sounds. You do not wear earrings. Her breasts were larger than yours. Her buttocks were larger than yours. She wore underwear."

"I wear underwear, too," Trina said. *I have never said that to anyone in my entire life!*

"I am glad," Tony said. "I do not want you to be cold."

"Do you talk to Angela often?" Trina asked.

"Yes," Tony said. "She helps me talk."

"Angela cares a lot about you," Trina said. "She's a good friend."

"She has only been my friend for two weeks," Tony said.

"You make friends fast," Trina said.

"No, I do not," Tony said.

"I think you do," Trina said. "We're friends in less than a day, right?"

"Yes," Tony said. "It has been a good day."

"Is Angela . . . pretty?" Trina asked.

"Yes," Tony said. "She looks like you. But she has a bigger stomach. She will have a little boy with her husband, Matthew. He has big hands. Their daughter Angel is a snowflake child. I would like to have a snowflake child like Angel."

*A snowflake child. That sounds so . . . nice.* "So you want a little girl."

"I want two little girls," Tony said. "One for each knee. They can play the piano with me."

*And I can see this man teaching them how to play.* "That's a . . . that's something I've always wanted, too."

"Yes," Tony said. "You want children to love."

*I need a man to love first.* She looked at Tony. *I wonder if he's the one.*

When their food arrived, Tony stopped talking and made a plate of fish and chips and a mass of "mushy" peas vanish in less than seven minutes.

Trina tried to engage him with small talk. "Hey," she said, "the Warriors are beating the Lakers again."

Tony didn't look up from his food.

*I know men get into zones while they eat, but when Tony eats, he's gone entirely. Robert was like that, too, and I didn't like it. At least Tony has a valid excuse.*

Tony finished his last bite of fish, downed the rest of his root beer, and looked up at the television. "My brother and Aika watch the Knicks. They always fall apart in the fourth quarter. They are an old team. The Warriors have young players."

*So he* had *heard me. Delayed conversation is better than no conversation at all.* "Yeah," Trina said. "I hope the Warriors make the finals this year."

"I think they will," Tony said.

*Should I tell him that his brother is coming to collect him in the morning? I really should.* "Angela told me that Angelo and Aika are flying to San Francisco tomorrow."

"I know," Tony said. "Angelo told me this morning. He is worried about me. He will take me back to Brooklyn."

"Do you want to go back to Brooklyn, Tony?"

"I want to stay with you," Tony said.

*And that warms up parts of me that haven't even been lukewarm in years.* "They want me to take you back to your hotel tonight."

"The sheets are itchy," Tony said. "I like soft sheets."

"My sheets are soft," Trina said. "I use fabric softener." *And I said this because?*

"I will stay with you and your soft sheets," Tony said.

*If Tony were any other kind of man, I'd think he was asking to sleep with me.* "So you want to stay with me because I have soft sheets."

"I want to talk to you," Tony said. "I have to stay with you to talk to you."

"You could call me on the phone," Trina said.

"I do not want to talk to you on the phone," Tony said. "I like seeing you when we talk."

*But you don't see me! You haven't yet looked into my eyes!*

Tony pushed his chair away from the table. "I am full. This was good. It was not like pasta. I eat pasta for dinner every night. I like fish and chips and mushy peas."

"I'm glad you liked it," Trina said.

"I hear the pianos," Tony said. "They sound like my piano. But they are not my piano."

"They have the same number of keys," Trina said.

"Eighty-eight," Tony said. "I would like to play one of them for you." He stood.

"Um, not yet," Trina said.

Tony sat. "I will wait."

"They have pianists that are paid to play here," Trina said. "Quite a few different ones, actually, and they're all very good. We'll have to see if they could maybe let you play a song during a break or something."

The piano music stopped for a few seconds.

"They are on a break," Tony said, and he stood and moved rapidly out of the bar.

"I guess we're going to the Cellar," Trina said. She threw two twenties—*my last two twenties!*—on the table, grabbed Tony's root beer, and hurried to the Cellar.

By the time Trina entered the dimly lit, sparsely

crowded room, Tony was already seated at a piano bench in front of one of two baby grand pianos, a large flat-screen TV hanging between them. She put Tony's root beer next to a tip jar as Tony began playing "She's Not Here."

Trina's heart thudded. *Wow. That's beautiful.*

"He's making that piano sing," a man beside her said.

Trina turned to him. "Are you supposed to be playing now?"

"Yeah," the man said. "I'm the semifamous Tim Conroy. Who's he?"

*Art E.!* "Tony Santangelo," Trina said. "Do you mind if he plays one song?"

"He's really good," Tim said. "He's playing runs and chords that aren't in the original song. I like his reinterpretation. It's really quite intricate."

*Well, it's because he wrote that song.* "It is." *Look at Tony's hands flow over those keys.*

*My God.*

*I am really on a date with Art E.*

As she watched Tony's hands, Trina saw more people filing into the Cellar, most of them gravitating toward Tony.

"Who is he?"

"That's an old Art E. song."

"I haven't heard that one in years."

"I heard Art E. was in Nob Hill yesterday."

"You saying *this* is the guy? At Johnny Foley's?"

"Yeah. Probably not, but still . . ."

A group of women at one of the tables started singing, and in moments, many people in the Cellar were singing along.

Tony finished the song.

The audience gave him some nice applause.

Tony looked around.

*He's hearing what might be his first ovation.* She stepped onto the small platform. "They're clapping for you, Tony."

"They are clapping for the music," Tony said. "I must make more."

She put her hand on his shoulder. "Tim Conroy, tonight's pianist, is waiting."

Tony stood and pushed back the piano bench. "He will not mind."

Tony took a deep breath . . . and played some old boogie-woogie with a country twang mixed with a hip-hop beat and hard rock bass.

*Oh . . . my . . . goodness! That's . . . wow! I don't know what it is, but it is tight! Whoo! That's* my *date crushing that piano!*

The crowd swayed, clapped, and danced, and in only a few minutes, the Cellar became swaying room only.

"That man can jam!" Tim shouted. "It's like the Grateful Dead, MC Hammer, and Journey had a baby! This is the shit!"

*And Tony is completely oblivious to these people packed around him. Look at his eyes! That's where his eyes focus. They're focused on the keys. They're focused on the music. They're zeroed in on the sound.*

Tony flowed from boogie-woogie to lightning-quick jazz, punctuating the song by pounding a fist on the piano bench behind him, alternating chords and runs with rapid rat-a-tat-tats with his hands on the top of the piano.

*I am witnessing a legend.*

"Dude, he's killing that piano!"

*Literally!* Trina thought. *He's hitting that piano so hard!*

"He's in the zone!"

"That's like nothing I have ever heard before!" Tim shouted to Trina. "Who *is* this guy?"

*I want to tell them all who he really is, but I don't know if it's my place.* "I told you!" Trina shouted. "He's Tony Santangelo!"

"Where's he from?" Tim shouted.

"Cobble Hill, Brooklyn, New York, USA!" Trina shouted.

"I gotta record this." Tim took out his cell phone and began filming. "Go, Tony! Go, man, go!"

Trina saw other cell phones in the air. She felt the floor shaking under her feet. She watched Tony take a swig of his root beer with his right hand while keeping the bass going with his left.

*Tony is who he says he is. He is one with that piano. He is becoming his music. Tony* is *music. I have goose bumps on the tip of my nose!*

"He's making that piano talk!" Tim shouted. "That piano is spilling its guts!"

Tony held out his left hand to Trina.

*He wants to hold my hand? Now?* Trina took hold of Tony's hand.

Tony pulled her behind him and to his right. He placed her fingers on a chord. "Play it as fast as you can," he said.

Trina hit the chord rapidly while Tony added a rolling bass.

*Hey, I'm making music!*

"Faster," Tony said.

Trina stood directly over the chord and hammered away.

"Do you hear the bus, Trina?" Tony asked.

"I hear it!" Trina shouted. She heard the wheels, the tires, and the screech of the brakes. She felt the rumble of the engine.

*We are on the bus!*

Tony lifted her weary hand off the chord a few minutes later. "Rest."

Trina sat on the bench behind him massaging her wrist while Tony's fingers continued to fly until a grand finale finish, where Trina swore he played every key in less than ten seconds.

*Twice.*

The crowd went wild, jumping, shouting, and hooting.

"I will play Naomi's next song now," Tony said to Trina. "It is called 'One Hundred Twenty Pounds of Sexy, Sexy Hate.' Get ready to dance."

"I'm already dancing!" Trina shouted. *I'm doing a piano-bench dance. It's all the rage at Johnny Foley's.*

As Tony played bass runs that made the entire platform shake, the people in the Cellar leaped into the air, drinks spilling, cell phones bouncing, and voices shouting.

*I am seeing history,* Trina thought, holding on to the bench. *I am seeing musical history. Tony knows how to work a crowd! And from what I see of his butt, he knows how to work that, too! Whoo! Dance with that piano, Tony! Show me what you got!*

A series of lightning-like flashes and some seriously bright lights filled the Cellar.

*A TV crew?*

*Oh no!*

Trina looked at Tony, his face serene, his eyes closed, his fingers fused to the keyboard.

*Don't stop playing, Tony!*

*Whatever you do, don't stop playing!*

# 24

A camera crew moved within inches of the platform, and a reporter shouted into Trina's ear: "Are you with him?"

"Um, yes, I—"

"Is that Art E. for real?"

*I'm not sure if I should do this, but . . .* "Yes. But his real name is—"

"What's he doing in San Francisco?"

"He's, um, he's—"

"Are you his girlfriend?"

"Not yet, we just—"

"What's the name of this song?"

" 'One Hundred Twenty Pounds of Sexy, Sexy Hate,' and Naomi Stringer—"

"Why is he suddenly surfacing after twenty-four years?"

*To meet me.* "You'll have to ask—"

"Are you two married? Any kids?"

"No, we just—"

"Where are you from?"

"San Fran—"

"Is he going to do a solo album?"

"I don't—"

"Where has he been hiding?"

"Well, he's been—"

"Will he attend the Grammy Awards this year?"

Trina gave up. *He asks a question and doesn't wait for the answer, and he never even asked for* my *name! What kind of a journalist is he?*

Tony kept playing, transitioning from the sexy hate song to some serious old stomp music, complete with Tony stomping his feet, swaying, and dancing behind the keys.

"Can I interview him after his set's over?" the reporter shouted.

Trina turned on the piano bench to face him. "Will you listen to his entire answer?"

"Yeah," the reporter said.

"I don't know when it's going to end," Trina said. *I don't want it to end! Go, Tony, go!*

Tony held out his empty glass. "More root beer, please."

The reporter wrote it down.

*These will be the first words Art E. will* ever *say in print. An entrepreneur in Omaha, Nebraska, will produce T-shirts with this phrase spelled out in frothy letters and sell them on the Internet. Saturday Night Live will use this phrase as the punch line to a joke. David Letterman will put the phrase into his nightly top ten. The First Lady will use this phrase in her anti-drinking-and-driving campaign.*

Trina took the glass and handed it to a woman in the first row of swaying dancers. "I can't get back to the bar. Could you get Tony some more root beer, please?"

Trina watched the empty glass move above the

crowd's heads to the bar and come back filled and foamy in less than a minute, while Tony played a fast version of the theme from *Jaws*.

"Funny stuff," a reporter said.

Trina handed the glass to Tony, and he guzzled half of it while keeping his right hand doing lilting runs on the high notes. "I will play your song now," Tony said. "I must sit down to play it."

Trina moved the bench forward, and Tony sat.

Tony patted the space to his right.

Trina sat.

"What song is this?" the reporter asked.

*It's my song.*

"It is called 'Trina,' " Tony said.

Trina's song was soft and romantic, light on bass with a melody that rose more than it fell. The crowd fell silent, and many started slow dancing.

*This is my song and only I know some of the words and it's beautiful and beguiling and genuinely moving and I want to cry! His fingers are caressing the keys now, loving them, massaging them. I can almost hear the lyrics in every note: "Streams of gold shine all around her, I thank God that I have found her, I will re-member this sunlight moment as long as I live, as long as I love."*

Tony finished, turned, and winked at Trina.

Trina couldn't find her voice, so she winked back.

As the applause died down, the first reporter and several newcomers surrounded Tony on the platform. Four of them shoved microphones into Tony's face.

*Lord, help us with these vultures.*

"Will that song be on Naomi Stringer's next album?" a reporter asked.

"No," Tony said. "It is only for Trina."

*Take that, Naomi Stringer! Ha! He wrote that song for me!*

"Is Trina your girlfriend?"

"No," Tony said. "Trina is a woman, and she is my friend."

*Which is better than any old girlfriend, thank you very much.*

"Why have you been hiding?"

"I have not been hiding," Tony said. "Many people have seen me. You see me."

"You know what I mean," the reporter said.

"No," Tony said. "I do not know what you mean." Tony sipped some more root beer.

"No one knew who you were for twenty-four years," a reporter said.

"I have known who I am for forty years," Tony said. "I am Tony Santangelo from Cobble Hill, Brooklyn, New York, USA."

"So your brother wrote the book about you," a reporter said.

"My brother Angelo wrote it," Tony said.

"Have you read it?" a reporter asked.

"Yes," Tony said.

The reporter blinked. "So . . . what did you think of it?"

"Angelo left many things out," Tony said.

"Like what?"

"You have heard what he left out," Tony said. He winked again at Trina.

Trina again winked back.

*Angelo left out the music! He wrote the words, the lyrics of Tony's life, but not the music. That is so profound! You have to hear Tony play to truly know Tony.*

*When he was playing my song, it's as if the music hugged me, held me, and wouldn't let me go.*

"What's it like to have Asperger's syndrome?" a reporter asked.

*Jerk! That's like asking a double amputee what it's like not to have legs!*

Tony looked around the crowd until all was silent. "This is what it is like."

*Great answer! Please quote him correctly.*

"What I meant was," the reporter said, "how does it feel to be different?"

"I do not know," Tony said. "I can only be me. I cannot be anyone else."

*Another great answer!*

"Aren't you worried about how people will accept your music now that they know you have Asperger's syndrome?"

"No," Tony said. "Music is music no matter who plays it."

*And Angela was worried about this man? Tony is* killing *this interview.*

"What do you think of San Francisco?" another reporter asked.

"San Francisco is good for my legs," Tony said. "I have to wear my hiking boots. Trina lives here. I like it."

"Are you familiar with San Francisco's great musical heritage?" the reporter asked.

"Yes," Tony said.

"Would you care to . . . *comment* on San Francisco's musical heritage?"

"San Francisco is a musical city," Tony said. "There have been many good musicians here."

"Which ones are your favorites?" a reporter asked.

Tony looked into the cameras. "Jefferson Airplane, Janis Joplin, Jefferson Starship, Pablo Cruise, Santana, Third Eye Blind, Sly and the Family Stone, Grateful Dead, The Steve Miller Band, Journey, Con Funk Shun, Faith No More, Huey Lewis and the News, Creedence Clearwater Revival, Counting Crows, Digital Underground, En Vogue, Green Day, Joe Satriani, MC Hammer, Country Joe and the Fish, The Pointer Sisters, Too Short, and Tony! Toni! Toné!"

*My date is a musical encyclopedia.*

"They're *all* your favorites?" a reporter asked.

"I like them all," Tony said. "I want to synthesize them with my music."

Several reporters shook their heads. "You plan to fuse *all* of San Francisco's music into one song?"

"I already tried tonight," Tony said. "It was the second song I played. I will call it 'Fog City.'"

"Could you give us one more song?" a reporter asked. "For the cameras. We only caught part of the last one."

Tony looked at Trina. "You look tired."

"I'm okay," Trina said. *And I'm taking the rest of the week off, so . . .* "Go ahead."

Tony stood. "I will not need the bench."

Trina pushed it back.

"You will sit on top," Tony said, and he lifted her onto the piano, her feet dangling above the platform.

*So many flashes! Geez, he only lifted me—with ease—onto a piano. But that is because I am slender and Tony has arms of steel.*

"You will have to hold on, Trina," Tony said.

Trina looked for something to grip. *This piano has nothing to grip!* "What are you going to do?"

Tony looked her in the eye. "I am going to play my heart out for you."

*He's looking right at me now. Those eyes, those eyes. He sees me. He really sees me.* "Play your heart out, Tony."

The next fifteen minutes of furious playing would be all over the television, the Internet, and YouTube in less than an hour.

Tony gave the *piano* a lesson.

His fingers flying so fast they became a blur, Tony stomped his feet, slapped the keys, punched the fall-board, and tapped on the music rack. As his sweat sprayed into the glow around him, he rapped on a piano leg while playing thunderous bass and made sounds come out of the piano Trina had never heard before.

Trina felt the vibrations jolting through her feet, her legs, and her soul. *This song is Tony's heart, and he's playing it for me on his only constant companion, his piano, which didn't care if he had Asperger's, which never asked him any strange questions, which simply let him be himself. This song is Tony's heart, and Tony's heart is loud!*

Tony played a series of five-finger chords up and down the keyboard as he leaped into the air until ending the song with one soft, high note.

The ovation shook the piano.

Tony helped Trina down, and Trina hugged him. "That was awesome, that was awesome," she repeated.

Tony remained stiff as a board, his arms rigid at his sides. "I am glad you liked it."

*Angela wasn't kidding about Tony's stiffness.* Trina stepped back. "I *loved* it, Tony. Your heart is so loud."

"Yes," Tony said. "I am quiet, but my heart is loud."

"Thank you," Trina said.

"You are welcome," Tony said. "You are tired now."

"Do you want to go?" Trina asked.

"Yes," Tony said. "I am tired. It has been a good night." He held out his hand.

Trina took it.

"We are leaving now," Tony said.

Reporters surrounded them, shouting more questions as Tony and Trina weaved through a sea of cell phones held high in the air, a camera crew backing away in front of them all the way down Johnny Foley's hallway to O'Farrell Street.

*Now that I know what it's like to be a star,* Trina thought, *I'd much rather never be one. I want some alone time with this star, this man holding my hand.*

Reporters followed them and shouted more questions as they walked to her apartment building.

*I know he hears them,* Trina thought. *But he only sees me. This is how a man should treat a lady. Ignore what doesn't matter and focus on what does.*

One question, though, stopped Trina in her tracks: "Hey, Trina. Are you a friend with benefits?"

"I will answer this one," Tony whispered.

"I'd rather you didn't," Trina whispered.

Tony winked. "It is okay. I know what to say." He turned and addressed the reporters jockeying for position on the sidewalk. "Trina is a friend with many benefits." He turned to Trina and winked.

*Oh, that's going to sound* so *wrong in the newspaper and on TV tomorrow.*

# 25

Once inside Trina's apartment, Tony collapsed onto the couch and became inert, blandly watching the weather on the television.

"Are you okay?" Trina asked.

"I am tired."

"You should be," Trina said. "I am wired."

Tony looked all around her. "I see no wires."

"It means I'm hyped, I'm still full of adrenaline, I'm still excited about the way you played tonight," Trina said.

"I played for you," Tony said.

"And I am so happy you did." She drifted toward the front window and looked down on a group of reporters milling around on the sidewalk, some of the reporters lit up by cameras and speaking into microphones. *My apartment house might be on television right now, but I don't want to change the channel to check. But why is this such big news? Okay, Tony's been incognito his entire life, but why are they jumping on this so hard tonight? There have to be more important stories out there, right?*

"I've never seen it so crowded at Johnny Foley's, and it's not even a Friday or a Saturday night," Trina said. "You are a showman, Tony. A virtuoso."

"I must go to sleep now," Tony said.

Trina moved behind the couch. "Um, where would you like to sleep? The couch or the bed?"

"The bed."

*I hoped he would say that.* "I'll get it ready for you."
*For us.*

"Okay."

*And even if nothing happens, it will be so nice not to sleep alone.*

Trina stripped her bedding and remade the bed with fresh sheets and pillowcases. When she returned to the couch, however, Tony was sound asleep sitting up.

*He is knocked out! He probably burned a thousand calories playing tonight, and he will be so hungry in the morning. I wish I had more than toast and beef stew to offer him. We could go out for breakfast, but I don't have much money, and the media might still be skulking around. I'll let Tony decide.*

She listened to him breathing. *And he doesn't snore. Yes!*

She helped him lie down, nestling a pillow under his head. She removed his boots and sat on the opposite couch arm watching him sleep for several minutes. *He's so peaceful and so calm. It's hard to believe this sleeping angel of a man was trying to kill the piano I was sitting on. I wish there was more room on that couch so I could snuggle up to him.*

Trina left her bedroom door open so she could just see the back of Tony's head on the couch from where she sat on her bed. She turned on her netbook, waited five minutes for Internet Explorer to load, and surfed to YouTube.

*The cell-phone videos are already running,* she thought. *And there I am holding on to that piano for dear life. Maybe I've always been holding on for dear life. Maybe it's time to let go. Look at my face! It's shining! I do have a glow about me.*

She ran a simple Google search for "Art E." and saw

numerous results from eonline.com, Huffingtonpost.
com, and TMZ.com. As she read through a sketchy and
generally fact-free article on TMZ.com, she saw herself listed as the "mystery woman at Johnny Foley's,"
"Art. E's friend," and "Tony Santangelo's gal pal."
*Where did that phrase come from anyway? A gal pal?
At least they didn't call me his "muddy buddy." And
why didn't they use my first name? Tony named a song
after me!*

She typed in "Art E. at Johnny Foley's" and found
numerous "reviews" of Tony's performance, each review making her smile:

> "Shattering, simply shattering! Sheer, utter
> brilliance! Using the piano for percussion—pure
> genius!"
>
> "Art E. plays a synthesis of all that is music,
> and he plays it like nobody else!"
>
> "Where has this man been? He's been keeping
> us from his true musical genius for far too long!"
>
> "Tony Santangelo, aka 'Art E.,' made the piano
> his bitch and taught it a lesson at Johnny Foley's
> in San Francisco tonight. . . ."
>
> "Not since the 'Summer of Love' in 1967 in
> Haight-Ashbury has such live musical talent
> been on display in San Francisco. . . ."
>
> "Look out, San Francisco! There may be an-
> other musical renaissance in our future. Art E. is
> here, and we hope he's here to stay. . . ."

Trina looked at Tony sleeping. *So do I.*

Tony was a hot topic among some of her Facebook
friends:

"He's so cute! I want to kiss him all over!"

"Did you see how big his hands were? I want his hands on me!"

"He is so sweet! And for a white boy, he sure could dance."

"Aren't Italian men hot? I don't care if he's simple. That is a *man*."

*Why isn't anyone specifically talking to me? They saw me on top of that piano, didn't they? I know I'm "Katrina Woods" instead of "Trina Woods" on Facebook, but they had to recognize me. I wish I could do a new selfie so my friends will recognize me as the Trina with Tony. What would I post along with it? "Yes, I'm the one Art E. flew three thousand miles to see. . . . Yes, I'm the one he named a song after. . . . Yes, I'm the one he played his heart out for." I hate when people toot their own horns on Facebook, selling themselves and all their daily and often hourly "accomplishments." I need to let someone else do it for me. But who would do that for me? The media outside aren't doing their jobs! I'm only Tony's "gal pal"!*

She looked at her profile picture. *I had that taken when I could afford to get my hair done regularly. No wonder none of my Facebook friends have recognized me yet. Man, I need a trim.*

She returned to the TMZ.com article and read comments rolling in nonstop under the allegedly "updated" story:

"That black woman he was with is so average. You think Art E. could be with someone who at least looked good. Hiking boots, baggy jeans, and an over-sized white sweater? Maybe he's blind or something."

*Hater*.

"That wench has to only be after his money. Art E. is a nut. Who would date a nut but a gold digger?"

*Bitch*.

"He didn't even hug her back so they're not really to-gether. She's probably a groupie or a hook-up. They can't really be friends. Hey, Art E., I'm available! You can play your fingers on me all night long!"

*Not gonna happen*.

"Wasn't she the same woman who didn't get voted onto that *Second Chances* show? As if she could ever get on that show. What a fame whore! What an oppor-tunist!"

*I'm so glad I didn't get voted onto that show! I might have had to leave Tony in less than a week!*

"This is yet another sad example of a black sister suckered into eternal sin and damnation by the White Devil. When are black women going to learn that nothing good can come of any relationship with our tormentor?"

*Troll*.

"It's a dam shame he has Assburgers. Otherwise, he'd be the perfect man."

*Ditz! He already* is *the perfect man. And learn how to spell!*

Trina went to the couch to check on Tony and found him sleeping soundly. *I'm an average, opportunistic, gold-digging fame whore of a woman watching a nut sleep on my reclaimed-from-the-curb-and-drowned-in-Lysol purple couch.*

*And I can't remember when I've been so happy.*

She settled a blanket around him. *I don't mind holding him with my hands and arms as long as he holds me in his mind. Maybe Tony can only love me in his mind. Strange, but that kind of love has to be purer because it isn't marred by emotions or urges or whims or moods. It just . . . is. Mind love, the purest form of love.*

*And Tony Santangelo, aka Art E., seems to have this kind of love for me.*

She went to her bedroom, disrobed, and put on shorts and a baggy T-shirt. As her head settled into her pillow, she whispered, "Good-night, Tony. Sweet dreams."

*You deserve them because you made this night a dream come true for me.*

# 26

At 6:00 AM, Trina awoke to the sound of her shower.
*And I'm not in it.*

She looked through her doorway at the empty couch.
*Tony is in my shower.*
*What do I do?*

She crept to the bathroom door. *Do I knock? I don't want to startle him.* "Tony, are you okay?"

"I like your soap," Tony said.
*It's only Dove.*

"I like your shampoo, too," Tony said. "It is thick and smells like flowers."

*I hope he left me some. I need to wash my hair to-night.*

The water stopped.

"Tony, there are some towels—"

The door opened to reveal Tony in only a medium-sized purple towel.

*He fills that towel completely.* "Oh, you . . . found the towels."

"Yes," Tony said. "I need my toothbrush."

*This man is all muscle and hair from his navel to his neck. Look at those powerful shoulders! No piano will ever stand a chance against this man.*

*No woman either.*

*Especially me.*

"Trina," Tony said, "I need my toothbrush."

*Sorry, I am sponging you, and you give me so much to sponge.* "I don't think I have an extra toothbrush.

You can use mine if you want to." *I can't believe I said that! It must be all those delicious-looking muscles, I swear!*

"Thank you." Tony turned and stood in front of the sink.

*I have just seen Tony's buttocks because my towels are cheap and tiny. I, um, I like his . . . proportions very much. So those were dancing in front of me under his pants last night. Very nice.* "My toothbrush is in the medicine cabinet behind the mirror."

Tony opened the medicine cabinet, found the only toothbrush, filled the bristles with Crest toothpaste, and began brushing.

*Look at his legs, all sinewy and long and hairy and only two mere feet from my itching hands—*

*I have to get a grip on myself.*

"I don't have much to offer you for breakfast."

Tony continued to brush.

"We could eat some more beef stew."

Tony continued to brush.

"Or we could go out for breakfast."

Tony continued to brush.

"It's up to you."

*Four* minutes later, Tony spat into the sink. "I like beef stew."

"Beef stew it is," Trina said. *No wonder his teeth are so white. He is a dentist's dream patient.*

Tony dropped the towel at his feet and stepped over to his clothes, piled neatly on the floor near the bathtub.

*I didn't need to see all that manliness. I have never seen anything so magnificent. If it weren't for this doorframe, I'd be passed out on the floor.*

Tony put on his underwear.

*His poor underwear! My God, he's beautiful. Robert never dressed or undressed in front of me in ten years of marriage, and I see all of Tony in less than a day.*

Tony put on his left sock and then his right.

*Tony had no hesitation, no shyness, and no worry. Doesn't he know I'm watching his every move? Doesn't he know I haven't had a man in my life—*

*I have never had a real man in my life.*

*That's a real man.*

Tony put on a T-shirt, his pants, and his button-down shirt, buttoning it up from the bottom.

*I hope this is one of his routines. I am going to like this routine, but I need to be completely awake for the next performance.* "Did you sleep well?"

"Yes," Tony said. He tightened his belt. "You have to go to work."

"I took the rest of the week off," Trina said. *Because I'm sick. Can't you tell? I almost passed out from what I just witnessed. I'm sure I have a fever. Even my toes are sweating.*

"We will go to Cielo Azul tonight," Tony said.

*Is he perseverating?* "But they wouldn't let us eat there last night," Trina said.

"It is the best restaurant in San Francisco," Tony said.

*He's perseverating. I need to get him into a different room.* "Come into the kitchen with me."

Tony followed Trina into the kitchen.

"We can probably eat anywhere now, and without a reservation, too," Trina said. "Because you've come out, so to speak, all we have to do is show up and we can probably get a table wherever you want to eat."

Tony blinked.

*He doesn't understand the doors that fame can*

*open—which is cool. Tony will never be an asshole celebrity who thinks he or she is entitled to everything and anything.* "We can go to Cielo Azul, *or* we can go to any restaurant in San Francisco on just your name alone."

"I want to take you to Cielo Azul."

*That didn't work. Maybe the kitchen isn't a large enough change of scenery.* Trina smiled. "We'll go to Cielo Azul then."

"Yes."

Trina fixed Tony a bowl of stew and put it into the microwave. She pressed a few buttons, and it whirred and sputtered to life. "I'm going to take a shower now. When you hear the beep, your breakfast is ready. The spoons are in the drawer underneath the microwave."

"Okay." Tony went to the couch, sat, and turned on the television. "I will watch the weather."

Trina collected a clean bra, T-shirt, and a pair of white underwear with brown polka dots and took them into the bathroom. After spraying away some of Tony's hairs, she went to the doorway. "What will the high temperature be today, Tony?"

"Fifty-five," Tony said.

*Not exactly shorts weather, but I want to look better than "average" today. The media will likely notice Tony again wherever we go and I'd love to silence some of the haters with my slender, smooth legs.* "Thank you." She shut the door. *Should I lock it? I don't want him to think I don't trust him.*

She left it unlocked, took off her clothes, got into the shower, closed the curtain around her, and lathered up her legs. She had just finished shaving her legs when the door opened. She watched Tony step up to the shower, part the curtain, and thrust her cell phone in front of her face.

"A man named Robert is on your phone," Tony said.

Trina aimed the spray away from her and took her phone. "Thanks."

Tony turned and left the bathroom, closing the door behind him.

*Tony didn't even look at me! His eyes looked every-where* but *me. I know he tries to be polite, but that was no time to be polite! That was the time to stare!*

She pressed the speaker button and set the phone on the edge of the tub. "What do you want, Robert?" She soaped up a washcloth and bathed quickly.

"And you brought him home," Robert said. "You brought Art E. home."

"So?"

"You let that mindless robot stay overnight with you," Robert said.

"He is not mindless and he's not a robot," Trina said. "He is a man, and he is a genius." She rinsed quickly and turned off the water.

"Are you in the shower?" Robert asked.

"Yes," Trina said.

"And he just brought the phone to you while you were in the shower?" Robert asked.

"Yes," Trina said. "And now I'm getting out." She took another purple towel from a stack and began drying off.

"So he has seen you naked?" Robert asked.

*Duh.* "What do you want, Robert?"

"I can't believe this," Robert said. "You have lost your mind."

Trina wrapped the towel under her arms and lotioned her legs and thighs. "Actually, I've found my mind. It took me two long years, but I'm finally sane again."

"It isn't sane to shack up with a mentally defective white man," Robert said.

"Tony is a genius," Trina said, lotioning her buttocks, stomach, and breasts, "and he's more of a man in a day than you were in ten years."

"Oh, I seriously doubt that," Robert said.

Trina opened and peeked through the bathroom door. *Tony already finished his stew. I love cooking for that man. But his eyes are glued to that television. Maybe if I stomp my feet as I go from the bathroom to my bedroom, he'll turn his head to see me.* She picked up the phone and turned off the speaker. "What do you care anyway, Robert?" She gathered her clean clothes, took a deep breath, and dropped her towel. She walked on her heels into the hallway and stopped. *Look this way, man! Slender Trina in all her naked glory! Check out this profile! Look at my perfectly proportional breasts and buttocks!*

Tony didn't turn his head.

Trina sighed and put on her panties and bra. *Over here, Tony! I'm dressing leisurely and seductively for you.*

Tony's head stayed focused on the television.

"I read up on Asperger's syndrome, Katrina," Robert said.

Trina sighed and dragged her feet into her room, where she put on a pair of baggy tan shorts. "So reading a page or two at WebMD-dot-com makes you an expert."

"He will never have any real feelings for you, Katrina," Robert said. "He can never show you any empathy."

"I've already seen different." She put on some deodorant then picked out an orange and black flannel shirt. "He saw me rubbing my feet at the park and he bought me shoes. That's empathy. He listens—"

"That isn't true empathy," Robert interrupted.

"Let me finish," Trina said, buttoning up her shirt. "Unlike *you,* Tony listens to me and values what I have to say. That's empathy."

"That is not the definition of empathy, Katrina," Robert said.

"Whatever, Robert." She slid on some tan wool socks. "Tony has plenty of feelings for me, especially last night."

"He is simple and genetically defective, Katrina," Robert said.

"He's simply wonderful and isn't simply defective like you are." She turned off her phone. *That felt good.* She put on her hiking boots, fluffed her hair once, and left the bedroom. "You okay, Tony?"

"Yes," Tony said.

*His eyes are still fused to that television.* "That was my ex-husband."

"What a turd," Tony said.

*A normal man would ask why my ex called, but not Tony. "Live and let live" must be his motto. I like that kind of freedom.* "Are you ready to see the sights?"

Tony turned off the television and stood. "You are a sight."

"Thank you."

"I like your stomach," Tony said. "It is flat and brown. You have a small belly button. It is pretty."

*He* did *see me. I wonder what else he saw while he was trying to be polite.* "You saw me?"

"I did not stare," Tony said. "Staring is rude."

"It's okay to stare at someone you like," Trina said. "Did you like what you saw?"

"Yes," Tony said.

"What did you like?" Trina asked.

"I like your breasts. They are firm. Your nipples are brown. They are the size of dimes. Your nipples were sticking out. Your buttocks are firm. They have some freckles on them. Your legs are smooth and shiny. Your other thing is dark brown."

*My other thing?* "What other thing?"

"I am not allowed to say that word anymore," Tony said.

"It's okay," Trina said. "I'm a nurse. I know all the parts of the body."

"Angelo would be mad," Tony said.

"I won't be," Trina said. "What's my other thing?"

"Your vagina," Tony said. "It is pretty. It is darker brown. It looks smooth and silky."

*This man has very fast eyes. When he looks as if he's not looking at me, he really is. And all of this is exciting me.* "Thank you. No one has ever complimented me like that before." *Should I return the favor and say he has a nice penis? I want to, but . . . no.*

"I like your shirt," Tony said. He reached out to put his right hand on her shoulder. "It is soft."

"Because it's threadbare and old," Trina said.

"I like the colors. The colors have music." Tony put his left hand on her other shoulder and squeezed gently with both hands. "You are symmetrical and strong. I want to touch your hair."

*Please.* "Go ahead."

Tony smoothly ran his fingers through her hair. "Soft. Strong. Silky."

*I am getting excited. His fingers feel like feathers.*

"It is not an Afro," Tony said.

"I relax my hair."

"It is relaxed," Tony said.

*I'm not! If he does this any longer, my hands will be feeling on his chest.* "What do you want to do today?"

Tony dropped his arms to his sides. "I want to feel your face."

"I meant . . ." *A man wants to put his big old strong hands on my face. Who am I to deny him?* "Oh, go for it."

Tony's hands caressed her face tenderly. "Soft. Hot. Getting hotter."

*Because I'm getting even more excited!*

Tony rubbed her lips with his fingers, tracing her smile. He ran his thumbs up and down her neck.

*This is the best foreplay I have ever had, and I am fully clothed!*

Tony pressed his fingers into her neck. "I feel your pulse. It is very fast."

*Because a man is touching me, a man is appreciating me, and a man is igniting my body. This man cares about me. . . .*

*And now I'm crying.*

"You are crying," Tony said. He dropped his hands to his sides.

*How can I make him understand what makes absolutely no sense?* "You make me feel so good, Tony. I haven't felt this good in a long time. I'm happy. I'm crying because I'm happy."

Tony nodded. "When Angela touched my hand, I cried. I was happy, too."

She put her hands on his face. "I've been touching on you since I met you, and you haven't cried at all."

"Your touch does not make me cry." He reached up and touched her nose, ears, and chin with his fingertips. "I like touching you."

She slid her hands down his face to his chest. "I like you touching me, Tony."

"You are touchable." He moved his hands to her shoulders and felt his way down her biceps and forearms. He squeezed her palms and each finger individually.

*I'm about to have an orgasm fully clothed, and he hasn't even touched anything erogenous!* Trina closed her eyes and moaned softly.

"You closed your eyes," Tony said.

"Because your touch feels good," Trina whispered.

"You feel good."

*Does he know what he's doing to me? Should I care?* "When you touch me, I feel . . . happy inside." *From my lips to my "other thing."*

She felt his hands moving from her fingers to her hips, to the tops of her buttocks, to her lower back, to her shoulder blades and shoulders. "You are hot."

*I am actually on fire.* "You're making me hot."

"You should wear a T-shirt," Tony said.

"It's only going to be fifty-five today," Trina said.

"It is warm enough."

Trina felt Tony's hands massaging her buttocks. *I can't believe I'm about to come. Geez!*

"Round," Tony said. "So round. And symmetrical. They are the same."

*I am so close to orgasm! I don't want to scare him when I scream!* She opened her eyes. "Tony, that feels really good. Thank you for doing that."

"Does it feel better when you close your eyes?" Tony asked.

"Yes," Trina said, and she closed her eyes.

She felt Tony's hands on her chest. "So round. And symmetrical. They are the same, too."

*I may have to change my underwear!*

She then felt his hot hands moving down her stomach to her hips before running down the front and climbing up the back of her legs.

*I shouldn't have put on these boots. My feet could use a massage, too.*

"I am touching an angel," Tony said. "Thank you."

Trina opened her eyes and hugged him tightly, resting her head on his chest. "For what?"

"For letting me see you," Tony said.

She looked up into his eyes. "I didn't think you noticed."

"I did," Tony said. "I want to touch you again. You make my fingers warm."

*His fingers make my entire body vibrate!* "I want you to touch me again." *Any time, any place, twenty-four seven. I will, of course, be wearing fewer clothes, and so will you.*

Tony placed his hands on her hips. "I like touching you, Trina."

*I want to kiss him so badly, but his face is still made of stone.* "Maybe we should go now." *Before I drag you to my bed, rip off your clothes, and take complete and total advantage of you.*

"I will go with you anywhere, Trina," Tony said.

*My bedroom is free, the sheets are extremely soft, and I am already wet. . . . No. Not yet.* "Would you like to ride the cable cars?"

"I have seen them," Tony said. "I know where they go. I have the map in my head."

She stepped back and held his hands. "Then let's go."

There was a loud knock at the door.

"Trina, it's me, Angelo. Open up."

*Oh . . . shit.*

"Angelo sounds angry," Tony said.

*Tony's brother is here to collect him. How did he find us?*

"He has come to take me back to Brooklyn," Tony said.

*He can't go now! Not now!*

"Don't let him take me back to Brooklyn, Trina," Tony said.

*I don't know what to do!*

"Please, Trina."

# 27

Trina opened the door, and Angelo stormed inside.
"Hi," she said to Angelo's back. *That is one pissed-off yet handsome Italian man.* She smiled at a petite Japanese woman with long, dark hair and luminous eyes. "You must be Aika."

"Hi, Trina," Aika said, stepping inside.

Trina closed the door. *Wow, it's crowded.* "Why don't we, um, hmm." She pointed to the couch. "I suppose you and I can sit on the couch, Aika."

Aika hugged Tony before sitting on the couch.

Trina sat next to her.

Angelo faced Tony. "Are you okay?"

"Yes," Tony said. "I am fine, Angelo. Trina and I are riding the cable cars today."

Angelo wheeled and stared at Trina. "You *said* you'd take him back to the hotel. That's where we've been *not* finding him for the last two hours."

*Attitude, in my house? This has been an attitude-free zone since Robert left.* "I told Angela I'd *try.* It was Tony's decision to stay here. How did you find us anyway?"

"You haven't looked outside," Angelo said.

"No," Trina said. "Obviously."

Angelo went to the window and opened the curtains. "Your apartment building is live on CNN. They have 'Art E. Watch' or some such nonsense on the screen."

"Must be a slow news day," Trina said.

Aika laughed. "That's what I said."

Angelo closed the curtains. "Do you know what you've done, Trina? You've exposed my brother to that *mess* out there. Do you know the damage all this could cause him?"

"Angelo, you *told* Tony to tell Trina who he is," Aika said.

"Yeah, but she didn't have to go blabbing it to the world the first time a camera was on her," Angelo said. "Twenty-four years I have protected him, and with one answer to some no-name reporter, you destroyed all that."

"Oh yes," Aika said. "Tony certainly looks destroyed. Nice clothes, Tony."

"Thank you, Aika," Tony said.

"Tony always looks uninvolved that way," Angelo said.

"I don't know," Aika said. "I think something's changed."

"Nothing has changed," Angelo said. "He's still the same old Tony. Come on, Tony. Let's go home."

"I am riding the cable cars with Trina," Tony said.

"I *told* you something's changed," Aika said.

*I'm in the middle of an argument in my own house, and I'm not saying a thing!* Trina thought. *And I think I'm winning the argument!*

"No, you're not riding any cable cars, Tony," Angelo said. "You're going home with us."

"No," Tony said. "I am staying here. I am riding the cable cars with Trina."

"Tony, you can't stay here," Angelo said. "You've already stayed one night too many."

"Yes, I can," Tony said. "Trina invited me. Angela said if Trina invited me, I can stay."

"Well, I'm saying you can't," Angelo said.

Tony shook his head. "I will stay." He squeezed in between Aika and Trina on the couch.

Angelo sighed. "What, did you give him some, Trina?"

"Angelo!" Aika shouted.

*Time to join the argument.* "I most certainly did *not* give him some. Tony slept right here on this couch. He was out like a light after his performance."

"I was tired," Tony said. "I wanted to sleep in Trina's bed. She has soft sheets. I fell asleep on the couch. She put a blanket over me."

"Apologize to Trina, Angelo," Aika said.

"Why should I?" Angelo asked.

"Because what you said was uncalled for and rude," Aika said.

Angelo pointed at Trina. "What *she's* doing is uncalled for, too."

"It is not polite to point," Tony said.

Angelo withdrew his hand. "We're going now, Tony."

"No," Tony said. "You said a change of scenery will do me good."

Aika smiled. "That's what you told him, Angelo, and this is definitely a change of scenery." She patted Tony's leg. "I wish I had your memory."

"I know I told him that, but I didn't expect him to get on a plane and fly across the country to get it," Angelo said. "Tony, you've had your change of scenery, and now it's time to go home."

"No," Tony said. "We are riding the cable cars."

"No, you're not," Angelo said.

"You cannot make me go back to Brooklyn," Tony said. "I will not go."

Angelo gripped the back of the couch. "Tony, the whole television world is camped out there waiting to ruin your life some more."

"I was on TV last night," Tony said. "They asked me questions. They liked my songs."

"And they made you look stupid, Tony," Angelo said.

"I am not stupid," Tony said. "They cannot make me look stupid."

"I thought he did great with the reporters last night," Aika said. "You were wonderful, Tony. I'm proud of you." She squeezed his leg. "You're a natural on camera."

"I'm proud of you, too, Tony, *geez,*" Angelo said. "Can we go *home* now?"

"No," Tony said. "You are not proud of me. You are angry I came here."

"You left without telling me where you were going," Angelo said. "Can you blame me for being angry?"

Tony nodded. "I can blame you for not liking Trina. I like Angela and you like Angela. I like Aika and you love Aika. I like Trina and you do not like Trina."

"I just met her, Tony," Angelo said. "I'm sure she's a *wonderful* woman."

"Quit being such a sarcastic ass, Angelo," Aika said.

"I just met Trina, too," Tony said. "Trina is wonderful. She is what I said she was. She has clear eyes. She cooks stew. I had beef stew for breakfast."

*Oh, did you have to tell him that?*

"Beef stew?" Angelo huffed. "Really? For breakfast?"

"I like it, Angelo," Tony said. "We are riding the cable cars now." He held his hand out to Trina.

"No, you're not," Angelo said.

Tony withdrew his hand.

"Angelo, now you're being an absolute asshole," Aika said.

Tony started pulling and twisting his fingers. "No, Aika. Trina's ex-husband is an asshole. Angelo is not an asshole. Angelo is my friend. Angelo is my brother. Angelo is not an asshole."

Aika rubbed Tony's leg. "I'm sorry, Tony. I meant that your brother is being *extremely* unreasonable. I know you care about Angelo."

"I do," Tony said. He settled his hands on his knees. "I wish he would care more about me now."

"If I didn't care, I wouldn't have come all the way out here in an airplane," Angelo said.

"To take me back to Brooklyn," Tony said. "I want to stay, Angelo. Let me stay."

Aika looked up at Angelo. "What's the harm, Angelo? He seems fine."

"The media is out there waiting to turn Tony into a sideshow," Angelo said.

"They want to put me in a circus," Tony said.

"Yeah," Angelo said. "They want to turn you into a clown."

"I do not wear makeup," Tony said.

"They want to make a fool out of you," Angelo said. "There's a sea of cynical shitheads hoping for the chance to—"

"Their heads are shit," Tony interrupted, jumping up and going to the window. He pulled back the curtain. "Their heads are not shit. Their heads are heads. There are many heads out there."

Trina rose and joined him at the window. "Angelo thinks they will be mean to you."

"They will not be mean," Tony said. "They are curious. They do not know me. They want to know me."

*Kind of true.* "I like the way you think, Tony." Trina rubbed his shoulders. "Look at that camera. I think it's pointing up at us."

Tony waved.

Angelo stomped over to the window and shut the curtains. "Cut that out!"

Tony stopped waving.

"Angelo, you're overreacting," Aika said. "Tony did fine in his first interview. You're just mad you weren't there when he did it."

"That's not true," Angelo said.

*I'll bet it is,* Trina thought. *Angelo wanted to be*

*there to take some of the credit. I don't blame him a bit. He helped make Tony who he is.*

"I need my new clothes," Tony said.

"They're in the taxi outside," Aika said, "along with your laptop case."

"I want to change my clothes to ride the cable cars," Tony said.

"You don't need to change your clothes," Angelo said. "You're only getting on an airplane."

"I do not want to ride on the airplane," Tony said. "I want to ride on the cable cars with Trina."

*Keep on perseverating, Tony,* Trina thought. *I think you're wearing your brother down.*

"You don't belong here, Tony," Angelo said. "You belong in Brooklyn."

"I belong here," Tony said.

"No, you don't," Angelo said.

"I belong in Brooklyn," Tony said. "I belong in San Francisco. I belong at Johnny Foley's. I belong with Trina."

"You don't know anything about her!" Angelo shouted.

"I know she is an angel," Tony said. "I know she likes me."

Trina squeezed Tony's hand. "And I do. You have an amazing brother, Angelo."

"Tony, you'll forget about her the second you're back in Brooklyn," Angelo said. "Trust me, Tony. The second you're back to your coffeehouses and cafés, you'll—"

"I know I will cry if I leave Trina," Tony interrupted.

*If that isn't a show of feelings, I don't know what is,* Trina thought. *He's making me tear up again.*

"You'll what?" Angelo shouted.

"I will cry if I leave Trina." Tony batted at a tear slid-ing down his nose. "I am already crying."

*I want to kiss that tear away so badly!* Trina thought.

"Angelo, why can't he stay?" Aika asked.

"For one, because of the bottom-feeders outside," Angelo said. "And two, because I don't trust *her.*"

*Okay. I've been quiet long enough.* "What? Trust me? Is your brother safe? Has he been fed? Did he get a good night's sleep? Is he clean? Is he dressed? Did anything bad happen to him?"

Angelo stepped within inches of Trina's toes. "You tried to go on television to find a man. And then on television last night, you told the world my brother is Art E. What kind of a woman does that? I'll tell you. A narcissistic, egotistical, self-serving, vain, gold-digging—"

"Did I get voted onto that show?" Trina interrupted.

Angelo blinked. "That's not the—"

"Did I get voted on that show?" Trina interrupted again. "I didn't, so I must *not* be that kind of woman. You don't know a thing about me."

"And neither does Tony," Angelo said.

"Trina is an angel," Tony said.

"Who wants to take advantage of you, Tony," An-gelo said.

"She did not take advantage of me," Tony said. "We did not have sex."

Aika laughed and slapped the couch cushion. "Sorry! Ignore me, Tony."

"I cannot ignore you, Aika," Tony said.

*Tony sure likes Aika. I can see why. She's sweet and she's gorgeous.* "How am I taking advantage of him?" Trina asked. "You see where I live. You see *how* I live.

In less than two minutes you can see everything I own."

"And it wouldn't hurt to have a sugar daddy in your life to change all that, would it?" Angelo asked.

"Angelo!" Aika shouted.

"What is a sugar daddy?" Tony asked.

"Your brother thinks that *you* are a sugar daddy," Trina said. "A sugar daddy is a rich man who gives his money away to women in exchange for something that *did* not happen here last night."

"I saw you living it up with him last night," Angelo said.

"Living it up?" Trina shook her head and sighed. "We went to Johnny Foley's. It's not exactly the world's most expensive restaurant. The whole meal cost me forty dollars with tip and five root beers included."

"Trina paid," Tony said. "I will pay for dinner tonight, Trina."

"Thank you, Tony," Trina said. *Because I'm nearly broke, and I can't even afford an appetizer at Cielo Azul*.

"What about the shoes he gave you?" Angelo asked. "What about them?"

"I accepted Tony's gift," Trina said.

"Those are some expensive shoes," Angelo said.

"That will last me for years." *What a jerk!* "But I'll pay you back, Tony. I get paid Friday, and I'll pay you back."

"No," Tony said. "I gave the shoes to you, Trina. They are yours."

"No, it's okay," Trina said. "I wouldn't want your brother to think I was using you for your money." She opened the closet and took out her purse. "If I have the money now, I'll give it to you." *I don't know why I'm looking in my purse. I only have some loose change and some expired coupons in here.*

"No," Tony said. He closed Trina's purse. "Trina, I gave you the shoes. It is wrong to take money for a gift."

"And I agree," Aika said.

"Aika," Angelo said, "whose side are you on?"

"Tony's and Trina's," Aika said.

"You're not seeing what's going on here," Angelo said.

"Sure I am," Aika said. "I know it's wrong to take money for a gift. And I know why you *don't* know that—because *you* have been doing that for years."

"Hey now, that's not fair," Angelo said.

"You've been taking money for Tony's gifts since he was sixteen," Aika said.

*Oh, I love Aika,* Trina thought. *She's a feisty little thing. She is officially my friend for life.*

"I did what I had to do to give Tony a better life," Angelo said. "If it weren't for me, where would he be?" He sat next to Aika. "I could have . . . put him away somewhere, right? But I didn't. I gave him a home."

"The world of music is so much richer because of your sacrifice, Angelo," Aika said. "I am in awe that you gave up much of your life for him. You love him so much. That's one of the reasons I'm attracted to you. You put your family first—where it belongs. But now Tony wants to have his own life. Isn't that what you've always wanted for him?"

"Well, yeah, of course, but not this way," Angelo said. "Never *this* way."

"Then what way?" Aika asked. "He has to start somewhere, and he's made a huge first step. And from what I see, he's stepping just fine. And he did it all on his own." Aika smiled at Trina. "I'm sorry we brought all this drama into your home."

"It's okay," Trina said. "Drama is much better than silence." She returned her purse to the closet and rubbed Tony's arm. "Thank you for standing up for me. You know I love those shoes."

"I am sorry I yelled," Tony said.

*I didn't know he did!* "It's okay."

"Well," Aika said, standing and stretching, "now that that's settled, we can—"

"What's settled?" Angelo interrupted.

"Trina is obviously not out to use Tony," Aika said.

"Yet," Angelo said.

"Oh, Angelo, please stop it," Aika said.

"She's an opportunist," Angelo said.

"You're right, Angelo," Trina said, moving in front of him. "I am. I met a wonderful man, and I took the *opportunity* to get to know him. I liked him as Tony long before I was sure he was Art E."

"Oh, right," Angelo said. "Tell me anything."

"I did like him," Trina said. "I do like him. I have been waiting two years for someone like Tony to come along."

Angelo frowned. "You've been waiting for a man who has Asperger's syndrome to come along."

Trina turned to Aika. "Is he always like this?"

"No, and it pisses me off," Aika said. "He needs to take some lessons in manners from Tony."

"Who do you think taught him those manners?" Angelo asked.

"Then *do* what you taught him and behave," Aika said.

"I have been waiting for a man who is kind, honest, and caring," Trina said, "and here he is."

"Tony is all of that, all the time," Aika said. "You know this, Angelo. You raised him to be that way, didn't you?"

"And he's like no man I've ever known," Trina said. "He doesn't play mind games, and don't you make some smart remark, Angelo."

Angelo shrugged. "I wasn't going to."

"Tony has an *amazing* mind," Trina said. "I know he spends a lot of time inside his mind sometimes, but that's not wrong. He's thinking life through. He's making connections I can only dream of making."

"And now you're an *expert* on Tony's condition," Angelo said.

"I'll never know all you know about Asperger's, Angelo," Trina said, "but what I know about Tony I like very much. Tony doesn't disrespect me. He treats me like a lady is supposed to be treated. He doesn't lie to me. He tells me the truth. He doesn't force me to do things I don't want to do. He doesn't try to make me think like him. I spent ten years with a man who did that. Tony doesn't ignore me, either. Even if he doesn't look me in the eye, I know he's listening to my every word. On top of that, he has a great sense of humor. I have never laughed and smiled so much in my life."

"But Tony has *never* laughed, *really* laughed, a day in his life," Angelo said.

"I can laugh," Tony said. "Ha."

Trina and Aika laughed.

"See?" Aika said.

"I like to make Trina laugh," Tony said. "Her laughter makes me feel warm."

"That's your hormones talking, Tony," Angelo said.

"Hormones do not talk," Tony said. "They do not have mouths or vocal cords."

"Your brother's do," Aika said, laughing. "Trust me."

Angelo scratched his head with both hands. "This is crazy."

"It is crazy and it is normal," Tony said.

"There's nothing normal about any of this, Tony," Angelo said.

"It is crazy and it is normal," Tony said. "It is crazy normal. It is romance." He held his hand out to Trina. "We are going to ride the cable cars now."

Trina grasped his hand. "Yes, we are."

Angelo looked wide-eyed at Tony. "Since when do you . . . hold hands?"

"I like holding Trina's hand," Tony said. "It is soft and warm and strong."

*This must be some breakthrough,* Trina thought. *Angelo looks amazed. And to think Tony is making this breakthrough with me. I'm not letting this man's hand go for the rest of the day.* "Are there any more objections?"

"None from me," Aika said. She took Angelo's hand and swung it back and forth. "This is so sweet! Are you going to take me on the cable cars, too?"

"This is nuts," Angelo said.

Trina reached into the closet with her free hand and grabbed her purse and jacket. "You really should go with us, Angelo. You know, to keep an eye on me, to make sure I don't take advantage of Tony. How are book sales, anyway?"

"Hey, twenty-five percent of the sales of that book go to Asperger's research," Angelo said.

"I was just *saying,* you know," Trina said, smiling. *I can be Brooklyn, too.*

Angelo shook his head. "You're really holding her hand, huh, Tony?"

"Yes," Tony said. "It is dark brown. It is warm. I like how it looks holding my hand."

"And you didn't sleep in her bed?" Angelo asked.

"I wanted to," Tony said. "I fell asleep on the couch. I did not get to say good-night to Trina."

Angelo squinted at Tony. "Okay. I believe you." He turned to Trina. "But I still don't trust you."

"Yet," Trina said.

Angelo rolled his eyes. "Whatever. Let's get out of here."

"We are riding the cable cars," Tony said.

"Yes, Tony," Angelo said. "We're riding the cable cars now."

"Thank you, Angelo," Tony said.

"Yeah, whatever," Angelo said. "Let's go."

Trina smiled at Aika, and Aika nodded.

*She saw Angelo almost smile, too,* Trina thought. *There's a nice guy under all that testosterone, and it's our job to bring him out.*

Trina closed her eyes briefly. *Thank you, God, for sending me a good man, and please help Angelo accept me, amen.* She opened her eyes and smiled at Tony. "Are you ready?"

"Yes," Tony said. "I am ready for anything."

*So am I.*

# 28

"A rt E.! Art E.! Over here!"
"Why are you in San Francisco?"
"Is she your girlfriend?"
"Is that your brother?"
"Why have you both been hiding from the world?"

The camera crews and reporters surrounded the quartet on their way to the taxi.

"Don't say anything, Tony," Angelo said, holding Aika's hand and parting the way ahead of them.

"What about me?" Trina asked as she tried desperately to keep hold of Tony's hand as reporters crowded around them.

"You've already said too much, *obviously,*" Angelo said.

A reporter stood in front of the taxi's back door. "Angelo, did you write Tony's biography to make yourself rich and famous?"

"What do you think?" Angelo said.

"I don't know," the reporter said. "That's why I asked you."

"Jerk," Angelo said, and he pushed the reporter aside and opened the back door. "Let's go."

Aika faced the reporter as camera crews surrounded the taxi. "Angelo wrote Tony's biography anonymously. How would that make him famous?"

"Angelo's going to be famous now, isn't he?" the reporter said. "He knew this would eventually happen one day, right?"

"He didn't write it to become rich or famous," Aika

said. "He wrote it to celebrate his brother and to raise money for Asperger's research."

"And who are you?" the reporter asked.

"I'm Angelo's girlfriend and an editor at Random House," Aika said.

"So Angelo hooked up with you because of his book?" the reporter asked.

"We *met* at Random House," Aika said. "I didn't edit his book."

"Uh-huh," the reporter said. "It must be nice to be dating a writer who's already made a couple million bucks and won the National Book Award, huh?"

"What's your point?" Aika asked.

"No point," the reporter said. "Just seems to be two women here who like going for the gold. And there's going to be even more money in the future. I hear they're trying to get Johnny Depp to play the Sponge in a movie."

"I like Johnny Depp," Tony said, and the media flowed toward him and Trina.

"So do I," Trina said. "Have you seen all his movies?"

"Yes," Tony said. "I like him when he's a pirate. Captain Jack Sparrow."

Aika pulled on Trina's arm. "As far as I know, Tony's story is not for sale to any movie studios." She ducked under Angelo's arm and got into the taxi.

"Come on, Tony," Angelo said. "Let's go."

Shouting erupted:

"Tony, where are you going?"

"Are you going back to Brooklyn?"

"Why did your brother come to San Francisco?"

Tony let his eyes roam around the crowd. "I am going to ride the cable cars with Trina." He held the door for Trina, and she got in.

"So, did you have a good time with Trina last night?" a reporter asked Tony.

"Yes," Tony said.

"So she kept you up all night, huh?"

"No," Tony said. "I fell asleep on the couch."

"Right," the reporter said.

"My brother doesn't lie," Angelo said. "If he says he fell asleep, he fell asleep. Get in the taxi, Tony."

"So you're not sleeping with her, huh?" a reporter asked.

"No," Tony said. "But I want to."

Tony slid in, Angelo squeezed in, and the taxi moved forward and parted the crowd. Tony held out his hand, and Trina took it.

*Tony wants to sleep with me,* Trina said. *Knowing him, we will most likely sleep, but that's okay. That's more than okay. I need a man to hold me all night long.*

"We're going to have to hustle to make your flight," the taxi driver said, turning right on Hyde Street.

"We are riding the cable cars," Tony said. "We are not flying on an airplane."

"That's right, Sergei," Angelo said. "There's been a change in plans."

Sergei looked back. "The cable cars are right up the street. You could have walked."

"If you hadn't noticed," Angelo said, "we were surrounded by those assholes."

Sergei looked into the rearview mirror. "And those assholes are following us. I hate the paparazzi. Who's famous?"

"My brother Angelo is famous," Tony said. "He wrote a book about me."

"And who are you?" Sergei asked.

"I am Tony Santangelo," Tony said.

"Never heard of you," Sergei said.

"I wrote songs for Walter Little," Tony said. "I write songs for Naomi Stringer."

"I *have* heard of them," Sergei said. "That would make you Art E."

"Yes," Tony said. "But that is not my name."

"I heard you were in town," Sergei said. "You gonna give me a thousand-buck tip, too?"

"Just drive," Angelo said.

"We've got quite a parade behind us," Sergei said. "I might be persuaded to use evasive techniques to elude them."

"A hundred more bucks if you can," Angelo said. "Just get us away from them."

"Make it two, and you won't see any of them," Sergei said as they crossed California Street.

"Two hundred then," Angelo said.

Tony leaned over Angelo to look out the window. "There is a cable car."

Trina squeezed Tony's hand. "There are plenty of places to get on one."

"Yes," Tony said, facing forward again. "I see them all in my head. Sergei, go to Kent Street and Mason Street. We can park there and walk to a cable car."

"And then maybe we can go to Fisherman's Wharf," Trina said. "I know you're hungry."

"It is your dime," Sergei said.

"It will cost more than a dime," Tony said.

As they moved through traffic, Trina looked at their hands. *I wish Tony would take my hand. He offers me his hand and gives me the choice to take it, which is the mark of a true gentleman, but it would be nice if he grabbed my hand occasionally.* She smiled at Tony. *I'm still worried Angelo will take Tony away from me, so I have to make this day last. Fisherman's Wharf is a good place to waste a day, and tonight . . .* "If we're going to Cielo Azul for dinner tonight, Tony, maybe we should make reservations now. For four people this time, not two."

Aika smiled. "That sounds like a great idea."

"Okay," Tony said. He took out his cell phone.

Trina found the number in Tony's list of recent calls, dialed it, and pressed the speaker button.

"This is Cielo Azul. How may I help you?"

"This is Tony Santangelo," Tony said.

"Oh, yes, Mr. Santangelo," the man said. "Or should I say Art E.? We hoped you would call back."

"That's not what you said last night," Trina said. "You told him not to call back."

"Our apologies," the man said.

"*Your* apologies," Trina said. "I recognize your voice. Say *you* are sorry."

"I am sorry," the man said, "but you have to admit having Art E. call out of the blue like that was hard to believe."

"Art E. did not call you," Tony said. "I am not Art E. I am Tony Santangelo. I did not call out of the blue. You cannot make a phone call out of a color."

"Um, right, sir," the man said. "We can reserve our best table for you any time you like this evening."

"I am hungry now," Tony said.

"But we're not open for dinner until four o'clock, Mr. Santangelo," the man said.

"You answered the phone now," Tony said. "You are there now. I am hungry now. We will eat there now."

"Sir, only one of our cooks is here now," the man said. "The rest won't be here until—"

"You are there now," Tony interrupted.

"But I'm not a cook, Mr. Santangelo," the man said. "I only take reservations."

"We are coming now," Tony said.

Sergei looked back. "So now we're going to Cielo Azul? Please make up your minds."

"Take us to the nearest place to ride a cable car, all right?" Angelo said. "That restaurant won't be open yet, Tony."

Tony handed the phone to Trina. "Find the menu for Cielo Azul."

Trina located Cielo Azul's Web site and clicked the MENU button.

"We will all order now," Tony said.

"But sir—"

"We will order now," Tony repeated.

"Tony, you're being ridiculous," Angelo said.

"I am hungry," Tony said. "Trina, you order first."

Trina scanned the menu. "I'll have the couscous with a side order of lentil soup." She handed the phone to Aika.

"Did you get that?" Tony asked.

"Um, yes, sir," the man said. "Couscous with lentil soup. What else?"

"Oh, I'll have the beef tartare with *bottarga* on *koji* toast," Aika said. "Your turn, Angelo." She reached across Trina and Tony to hand Angelo the phone.

"This is nuts," Angelo said. "Um, you got a steak on this menu? I don't see anything but duck, lamb, chicken, and fish."

"The short rib is very good, sir," the man said.

"All right," Angelo said. "Give me that."

Tony took the phone. "I will have the sturgeon, the big-fin squid, and the lamb loin."

"You can't eat all that," Angelo said.

"I am very hungry," Tony said. "And for dessert I want black sesame cake and chocolate mousse."

"You're going to explode, Tony," Angelo said.

"I am not a bomb," Tony said.

"If you eat all that you might become one," Angelo said.

The man repeated the order. "We will have it ready for you as soon as we can."

"We will be there soon," Tony said.

"We'll do our best to have it ready," the man said. "Thank you for calling back, Mr. Santangelo."

"You are welcome." Tony turned off his phone. "I want to ride the cable cars now."

Sergei pulled the taxi to the curb.

"You are stopping," Tony said.

"I will wait until you decide what you are going to do," Sergei said.

Angelo sat forward. "You got somewhere else you have to be, pal? I told you I'd pay you two hundred bucks for losing the paparazzi." He looked out the back window. "I don't see any, so you'll get your money."

"You tell me we are going to the airport and then your brother tells me to go to Mason and Kent," Sergei said. "Then he tells me to go to Cielo Azul. Now you tell me to go to the nearest cable car. What's it gonna be?"

"I want to ride the cable cars now," Tony said.

"But we just ordered all that food," Angelo said.

"I know." Tony squeezed Trina's hand. "Ha ha. I am funny. Ha ha."

"Tony," Aika said, "what's so funny?"

"I am," Tony said. "Ha ha."

Sergei shook his head. "So we're going to the nearest cable car stop now instead of Cielo Azul?"

"Yes," Tony said. "To Mason and Kent. It is a good place to drop us off."

"You're confusing Sergei, Tony," Angelo said. "You're confusing me."

"I have a good sense of humor," Tony said. "Ha ha." Tony winked at Trina.

*Oh my goodness!* "We were never going to go to Cielo Azul, were we?" Trina asked.

"No," Tony said. "Ha ha."

"And we just ordered all . . . that . . . *food!*" Trina laughed loudly, and Aika joined in.

"I am funny," Tony said. "Ha ha."

Trina kissed his cheek. "You got him back, didn't you?"

"Yes," Tony said.

"We should really call them back and cancel the order, Tony," Trina said.

"No," Tony said. "They would not let me take you there. They must pay for being rude."

Trina shrugged. "But where will we eat tonight?"

"I like Johnny Foley's," Tony said. "I will have the fish and mushy peas again. I will play the piano for you."

"Tony," Angelo said, "we can eat anywhere you want to."

"We will eat at Johnny Foley's," Tony said. "You will hear me play, too."

Sergei smiled. "So . . . to Mason and Kent and the cable cars?"

"Yes," Tony said. "We are riding the cable cars now."

After Sergei parked the taxi on Kent and Angelo paid him *four* hundred dollars, they collected Tony's clothing bags and laptop case and climbed onto a moving cable car on Mason Street. While riding it through traffic to the end of Taylor Street, Tony scribbled a song.

"I will play it for you tonight," Tony said.

The media and paparazzi were waiting at the Bay Street turnaround and rode with them on another cable car to Fisherman's Wharf. They took hundreds of pictures of Tony and Trina holding hands, Tony ringing the bell, and Tony waving at people on the street. He answered none of the hundreds of questions they asked him because he was too busy sponging the city of San Francisco.

After eating fish tacos at the Codmother Fish and Chips, with fried Snickers and Twinkies for dessert, the quartet walked through the crowded and touristy Pier 39, giving Tony's fans photo ops as he wandered through Houdini's Magic Shop, rode a carousel on a white horse with Trina, and posed next to the guitars at the Hard Rock Cafe. A crowd of fans, camera crews, and reporters surrounded Tony as he watched the sea lions lounging on the docks, Alcatraz Island in the distance.

Tony read a sign to Trina: " 'Please do not feed our sea lion friends, thank you.' They are so big. We do not have sea lions in Brooklyn."

"They sometimes disappear," Trina said. "Some say they swim up the coast to Oregon. But they always come back."

"This is their home," Tony said.

Several sea lions barked.

Tony wrote another song.

On the cable car ride back to California Street, near Saint Francis, Trina's phone vibrated. *It better not be Robert,* she thought. "Hello?"

"I am so happy for you," Naini said. "Are you with him now?"

"Yes," Trina said.

"I am sorry I did not believe you, Trina," Naini said. "And I would have called sooner, but I have been so busy covering for you and working overtime."

"*You're* covering for me?"

"Yes," Naini said. "I volunteered. I have to warn you. ES is very cross. She cannot stand it when we cheer for you in the break room whenever we see you on television."

"You're cheering for little old me," Trina said.

"All the time," Naini said. "Look at Trina. One of the dark masses is doing great things. Ha! ES cannot stand to see you so happy."

"She can't stand to see any of us happy," Trina said.

"However, because you are not really sick," Naini said, "we think she will do something drastic soon."

"I'm not worried," Trina said.

"And you should not worry," Naini said. "You are an integral part of this hospital. Where will I see you on the television next? I have already seen you riding a carousel on Pier 39 today."

*That was quick!* "We'll be at Johnny Foley's again tonight."

"I will come down after my shift in the ER," Naini said. "I want to meet your knight in shining armor."

"We'll see you then," Trina said. "Bye."

After dropping off Tony's new clothes and laptop case at Trina's, they walked down to Johnny Foley's to eat more fish and chips and mushy peas while paparazzi lit up their meal with flashes from the sidewalk outside.

"That is so rude," Angelo said. "I have spots in my eyes."

"*You* chose a table near the window," Aika said. "We *could* be sitting near the bar."

"It is okay," Tony said. "They will have more pictures of themselves than they will of us. The light is wrong. They are taking pictures of themselves."

As they finished their meal, an older silver-haired man stopped by their table.

"Hi, I'm the manager, Patrick Kelly," he said. "How is everything?"

"Good," Angelo said. "You got a nice place here. You could put one of these in Brooklyn."

"Tony, are you planning to play again tonight?" Mr. Kelly asked.

"I want to," Tony said. "Aika and Angelo need to hear me play."

Mr. Kelly leaned over. "We'd like you to duel with tonight's pianist."

Tony blinked. "We will both play together."

"Right," Mr. Kelly said. "Tim Conroy's one of our very best, and he's looking forward to a showdown."

Tony picked up his root beer. "I will go play with Tim now."

The SRO crowds in the Cellar parted to let Tony and Trina through to the pianos amid cheers and applause. Tony walked up to Tim and shook his hand.

"May the best player win," Tim said.

Tony shook his head. "We will not duel. We will play together. You will see."

"All right," Tim said. "Let's do this."

Tony sat on the bench at the other piano. "You go first."

Tim played a jazzy tune with flourishes up and down the keyboard.

Tony nodded in time until adding to Tim's tune with flourishes of his own.

"This is incredible," Angelo said. "It's like Tony knows what Tim is going to play next."

At one point, the two pianists played the exact same notes until Tim had to stop because he was laughing too hard. While Tim stared at his fingers, Tony continued.

"Amazing," Tim said into a microphone. "That was my own composition, Tony. How could you know what I was going to play next?"

Trina slid a pencil-thin microphone in front of Tony. "I recognized your pattern," Tony said. "It is a good song." He stopped playing. "I will go first now."

"And I'll try to keep up," Tim said.

"Do not try to keep up," Tony said. "Add to the music. That is what music is for." He stood and pushed back the bench. "I will go slowly at first."

"Bring it on, man," Tim said.

Tony motioned Trina to his right and placed three of her fingers on a chord far to the right. "Play two times."

Trina played the chord. *Hey, it's the clang of the cable car.*

"Tim," Tony said, "we are going to ride the cable car now. This is called 'Cable Car Rock.'" He turned to Trina. "You decide when to ring the bell."

"Let's rock," Tim said.

And they did.

Tony tapped out a beat on the top of the piano with his left hand while doing a five-finger run in the middle.

Tim caught on and played the run.

Tony added a rumbling, thunderous bass.

Trina rang the bell.

"We are going downhill now," Tony said, and the song picked up tempo.

*Oh, and we're really moving now!* Trina thought. *We're on the Soul Train and a house party's breaking out!*

Tony stopped tapping the beat and added a light melody full of sunlight, while Tim improvised and played what music critics the next day would call "power chords reminiscent of early seventies rock and roll."

Tony slowed the melody.

Trina rang the bell twice.

Tony lifted his left hand from the bass while reducing the melody to a crawl.

Tim played one more bass chord.

Trina rang the bell.

Tim lifted his hands.

Tony lifted his hands.

Tony turned his head and smiled at Trina as the applause swelled around them.

*He's smiling,* she thought. *He's really smiling.*

"Angelo," Tony said into the microphone. "Angelo, root beer for everyone."

Johnny Foley's ran out of root beer in less than half an hour.

While the crowd toasted each other with frothy root beer, reporters surrounded Tony's piano.

"What do you think of our city?" a reporter asked.

"It is not Brooklyn," Tony said.

"So you don't like San Francisco," the reporter said.

"He only said it wasn't Brooklyn," Trina said. "He didn't say anything about not liking it."

"Let him answer," the reporter said. "I'm not talking to you."

Angelo towered over the reporter. "Hey, buddy. Lighten up, all right? Sometimes you have to rephrase your question and make it more direct. Tony, do you like San Francisco?"

"Yes," Tony said. "I like it very much."

"What do you like about San Francisco?" Angelo asked.

"It is different," Tony said. "It is the same. It is new. It is old. It is up. It is down. It is up again. It is a carousel with white horses. It is sea lions lying in the sun. It smells like the ocean. It smells like laughter. It smells like love."

The reporter shook his head. "What does love smell like, Tony?"

"Love smells like the old wood in the cable cars," Tony said. "Love smells like the water in the bay. Love smells like fish and chips at Codmother. Love smells like Trina's perfume. Love smells like Aika's hair. Love smells like Angelo's sweat."

"Hey!" Angelo shouted.

"All of that is love," Tony said.

"Are you saying that you love San Francisco?" the reporter asked.

"Yes," Tony said.

Trina looked into the crowd and saw Naini standing along the back wall. "Naini Mitra," Trina said in the microphone. "Naini Mitra, please come meet Tony."

Naini threaded her way to the piano and stood next to Tony.

Tony stared at Naini's shoes. "You have the same shoes I bought for Trina."

"These *are* a pair of the shoes you bought for Trina," Naini said. "Thank you."

"Tony, I'd like you to meet my good friend, Naini Mitra," Trina said.

Tony shot out a hand, and Naini shook it once.

"You have small hands," Tony said. "You are short. You have brown skin and brown eyes and brown and orange lips. I like your hair. It is long and squiggly and shiny."

"Thank you," Naini said.

Trina covered up the microphone. *If he starts talking about Naini's breasts and buttocks, I will be so embarrassed.*

"You are very pretty," Tony said. "You are from . . ." He sighed. "I am always wrong. Please tell me."

"I am from Bengali, a province in India," Naini said.

Tony nodded. "You have a pretty voice. It sounds like music. What does your name mean?"

"Literally, 'pupil of the eye,' " Naini said.

"You have pretty dark brown eyes." He pulled the piano bench forward. "I would like to play with you and Trina now."

*Good thing I'm covering this microphone.* "Excuse me?" Trina said.

Tony blinked.

"You mean you want to play the piano with us now, right?" Trina said.

"That is what I said," Tony said.

Naini sat to Tony's left. "What do I do?"

He put Naini's right thumb and pinkie on two different bass keys. "Play loud and fast." He put Trina's left thumb and pinkie on two different treble keys. "Play louder and faster. While you play, I will make your hands disappear."

A cameraman moved around the platform to capture the moment.

"Houdini's Magic Shop gave you this idea," Trina said.

"Yes," Tony said. He flexed his fingers. "Nothing up my sleeves . . ."

"You're not wearing sleeves, Tony," Trina said.

"They have already disappeared," Tony said. "Play . . . now."

Tony watched Naini playing her low notes. He watched Trina playing her high notes. He raised his hands in the air and clapped until the crowd caught on. He took a breath . . .

. . . and Tony's fingers became a blur.

"Speed piano," *Rolling Stone* would later call it, and at times, Naini's and Trina's hands *did* vanish as Tony played in between, above, and below their hands on the keyboard. Trina couldn't believe the ease with which he played between her fingers, and his fingers lightly brushed her hands like moths' wings.

Midway through the song, Trina distinctly heard the barking of sea lions.

When he finished the song, Tony grabbed both of their hands and raised them into the air.

The picture made the front page of *Bartaman,* the best-selling Bengali language newspaper in Calcutta, India.

Tony stood and put his arms around both women.

*This* picture appeared on TMZ.com with the caption: "Art E. has two brown gal pals now?"

"It was an honor to meet you, Tony," Naini said, hugging him tightly. She hugged Trina. "He is so wonderful," she whispered. "You are so lucky."

"I am," Trina whispered.

"May I hug him again?" Naini asked. "Please?"

"No," Trina said. "Tony's all mine."

Naini looked up at Tony. "If you are ever in Oakland, make sure to visit me."

"I will visit," Tony said.

Trina pulled Tony away from Naini. "No, you won't."

"I want to visit Naini in Oakland," Tony said.

"No," Trina said. "Bye, Naini."

Naini sighed. "Good-bye, Tony."

"Good-bye, Naini," Tony said.

After Naini left, Tony looked into Trina's eyes. "Naini is your good friend."

"Yes," Trina said. "So?"

"We should visit her in Oakland," Tony said.

"Naini only wanted *you* to visit," Trina said.

"Oh." Tony wrinkled up his eyebrows. "I do not understand."

"I'll explain later," Trina said.

Tony again looked into Trina's eyes. "You are tired."

"I am," Trina said. "Aren't you?"

"Yes," Tony said. "We have had a busy day."

"Let's go home," Trina said.

While Angelo and Aika did their best to forge a path ahead of them, Tony and Trina walked hand in hand out of Johnny Foley's and to her apartment, camera lights and flashes illuminating the night.

"You could stay with us at the Mark Hopkins, Tony," Angelo said. "We can see all of San Francisco Bay from our window."

"I am staying with Trina," Tony said.

*That's right,* Trina thought.

"That couch can't be good for your back," Angelo said.

"My back is okay," Tony said.

"Come on, Angelo," Aika said. "Tony's in great hands."

Angelo looked at Trina. "Does that couch fold out or anything?"

"No," Trina said. "If it did, it would swallow up the entire room."

"Are you sure you want to stay here, Tony?" Angelo asked.

"I am sure," Tony said.

"You'd have a big bed all to yourself at the hotel," Angelo said. "And the TV has the *real* weather channel."

*Jerk!* Trina thought.

"I am sure," Tony said.

"Let's go, Angelo," Aika said. "Good-night, Trina. Good-night, Tony." Aika hugged Tony, and then she hugged Trina.

"Good-night, Aika," Tony said.

Angelo stood in front of Tony. "Look at me, Tony."

Tony looked up.

"Get some sleep," Angelo said. "No messing around."

"I will try," Tony said.

"Did you hear me?" Angelo asked.

"Yes," Tony said. "Sleep. No messing around."

*Jerk! Jerk! Jerk!* Trina thought. *I know he "raised" Tony, but Angelo is seriously messing around with my love life.*

*If this is love.*

*If this can ever be love.*

# 29

In the apartment, instead of heading straight to the couch, Tony stood in the doorway to Trina's room.

*No weather watching tonight?* "Do you want to go to sleep now?" *With me. In my bed. Please?*

"I am wired," Tony said.

"I don't see any," Trina said.

Tony smiled. "Ha ha."

She hugged him from behind. "I'm wired, too." *Want to mess around? No, I can't say that!* "You've smiled at me twice tonight."

"I am practicing," Tony said.

"Why?"

"Your face glows when I smile at you," Tony said.

"Why don't you smile all the time then?" Trina asked.

"It hurts my face."

Trina smiled. "Smiling sometimes hurts mine, too." *Especially when ES is being particularly ugly and I have to smile and take it.* "Want to watch the weather together?"

"No," Tony said. "I want to watch you." He turned to face her.

Trina stepped in, resting her head on his chest. "Haven't you been watching me all day?"

"Yes," Tony said. "I want to watch you more."

"You sure were watching Aika at the pier today," Trina said.

"Yes, but I did not stare," Tony said. "I did not stare at her buttocks."

*Good to know.* "Did you stare at mine?"

"Yes."

*Better to know.* "And you couldn't take your eyes off Naini at Johnny Foley's."

"She is very pretty," Tony said.

Trina wrapped her arms around Tony's neck. "Prettier than me?"

"No," Tony said. "Naini is pretty. Aika is pretty. You are beauty."

*Best to know.* "I don't know if I like them hugging on you, though."

"They hugged you, too," Tony said.

"Not like they hug you," Trina said.

"I do not understand," Tony said.

She turned on the bedroom light and took his hand, leading him to the foot of her bed. "They hugged me mainly with their arms, Tony. They hugged *you* with their bodies."

"I still do not understand," Tony said.

"I will demonstrate," Trina said. She reached up and hugged Tony only with her arms, her body barely touching him. "That's how they hugged me." She then made contact with as much of her body as she could, her breasts pressed firmly into his breastbone, her hips tight on his thighs. "This is how they hugged you."

"I like this hug better," Tony said.

"So you know why I don't like other women hugging you this way," Trina said.

"I do not understand," Tony said. "This is a better hug. It is warmer. The other way is not a hug. It is a neck squeeze."

*How do I get him to understand?* "Do you like the way I hug you?"

"Yes," Tony said. "Very much. I feel your breasts on my stomach."

"Do you want me to continue to hug you this way?" Trina asked.

"Yes," Tony said.

"Then don't let any other woman hug you this way from now on," Trina said.

Tony nodded. "They can only neck squeeze me from now on."

"Good." She sat on the edge of the bed.

"I will watch you now," Tony said.

Trina took off her boots. *I have never had a man watch me undress completely. Is this what he wants to watch me do?* "You want to watch me take off my clothes?"

Tony's eyes widened. "I have already seen you naked."

"What do you want to watch me do?"

"I want to watch you sleep," Tony said. "You are tired." He touched the skin under her eyes with his index fingers. "So dark."

Trina tossed her boots toward the closet. "That's one of the reasons I am tired. I *am* dark."

"I like your color," Tony said. "It is a warm color."

"I know you do, but my supervisor at work does not like my darkness." She unbuttoned two buttons on her shirt. "Her name is Nurse Sprouse. She is a light-skinned black woman who makes all the dark-skinned nurses do most of the work and all of the really hard work."

"That is not right," Tony said. "Everyone should do equal work."

"In a perfect world maybe, but not in Nurse Sprouse's world," Trina said. "Nurse Sprouse is a heartless wench."

"What is a wench?" Tony asked.

"A woman who is not very nice," Trina said.

"You are nice," Tony said. "You are not a wench."

"I *can* be a wench," Trina said. *I want to be Tony's bed wench right now!* She unbuttoned another button.

"You are not heartless," Tony said. "You can never be a wench."

"Thank you," Trina said. She removed her shirt and tossed it into a corner.

"Go to sleep," Tony said. "I will watch you."

She undid her shorts and pushed them to the floor. "It will be dark. I will disappear."

"You are not magic," Tony said.

"My skin is so dark you won't be able to see me." *Unless we leave on the light. I've never done that before.*

"I will watch you with my hands," Tony said.

*This has taken a decidedly erotic turn. This man seems to see best with his hands.* "I'd like that." She pulled back her covers and wormed under them. "I'm ready for you to watch me with your hands now. Turn off the light, Tony."

"Okay." Tony turned off the light.

Trina closed her eyes. In a moment she felt strong fingers caressing and rubbing on her through the covers from the bottoms of her feet to the top of her head.

*As if he's playing me, as if I'm a piano.* "Are you playing a song on me, Tony?"

"Yes," Tony whispered.

"Which parts of me are the high notes?" Trina asked.

"Your face." He lightly touched her face.

"I assume my buttocks are the low notes," Trina said.

"Your toes are the low notes." He massaged her feet. *Oh, that's nice.* "But what if it starts to tickle?"

"I will stay in the middle then." He played what felt like a series of chords on her back.

"This is a nice massage," Trina whispered.

"I want to play you faster," Tony said.

"Go for it."

Tony played Trina's body from head to toe and back, digging "chords" into her back and shoulders and pressing hard against her buttocks.

*This man is making me squirm, pressing, pushing, running his fingers up and down my legs and my spine. This is intense foreplay. He has no idea what he's doing to me! Maybe that's why it's so intense!*

She turned to face him so his hands would press and caress her stomach, her thighs, and her breasts. *He has almost removed my bra! He's making a thong out of my underwear! I hope this song never ends. . . .*

Tony touched her nose with one finger. "That was the last note. You are an easy song to play."

"And you played me so well." *I want an encore! Now!* She adjusted her bra and underwear. "You can lie next to me if you want to." *On top of the covers where you're safe from hot, horny, and ready me.*

Tony lay beside her.

*That is a whole lotta man behind me. I hope he doesn't fall off this little bed.* "You can put your arm around me."

Tony rested his elbow on her hip, his forearm on her side, and his hand on her stomach.

*I'm not sure if it's right to force a man's affections, but I need to be held.* "If you get sleepy, you can stay here with me."

"Thank you," Tony said.

Trina pulled his hand up to her lips and kissed it. "Thank *you*." She held his hand against her stomach. "Are you comfortable?"

"Yes," Tony said. "I like how you feel."

"I like how you feel, too." *I am content. I am spooning with a good man. His hand is hot on my stomach. His thumb is inside my belly button, and his fingers are never still, stroking the tender skin just above my panty line.*

*I will not be able to sleep.*

She turned into him, his hand sliding over her side to her hip. "Tony?"

"Yes," Tony said.

"You're not asleep," Trina said.

"I am awake," Tony said.

"You have to be tired," Trina said.

"I am," Tony said. "But I cannot sleep because I am sleeping with an angel."

*So sweet.* "You're the angel, Tony."

"I am hot," Tony said. He took off his shirt and T-shirt. "This is better."

*I'll say.* She drifted her fingers over his chest. "*Much* better."

"You sleep," Tony said. "I'll watch."

Trina snuggled up against his chest and listened to his heartbeat. *His heart beats steadily, so steadily that it's almost hypnotizing. I know he can't see me.* She put his right hand on her hip, and Tony's fingers caressed her left buttock. *Now he can "see" me.* She kissed his chest.

Tony's fingers became still, and his breathing became regular.

*He's asleep already.*

She moved up and kissed his lips. *I've kissed you in your sleep. I hope you're dreaming of me.*

*I hope you're dreaming of us.*

*I hope I dream of us, too.*

# 30

Trina opened her right eye and saw a muscular, unshaven neck below her.

She opened her left eye and saw an unshaven Adam's apple.

*How did I . . .*

She looked down and saw a hairy chest.

She looked up and saw two dark blue eyes staring at her.

"Hi, Trina."

Trina blinked several times. "Hi, Tony." *How did I get on top of you, and why are your arms down at your sides? You should be holding me close to you.*

"You smile when you sleep," Tony said.

"I must have had a happy dream," Trina said.

"Tell me your dream," Tony said.

"I don't remember it." Trina sighed. "I don't remember most of my dreams. Do you?"

"Yes," Tony said.

"Did you have a happy dream?" Trina asked.

"Yes," Tony said. "I was dreaming about you."

Trina moved up Tony's body, lightly leaning her elbows on his shoulders. "What was I doing?"

"You were playing the piano with me at Johnny Foley's," Tony said.

"Like last night?" Trina asked.

"No," Tony said. "There was no crowd."

"Was Naini on the bench with us?" Trina asked.

"Yes," Tony said, "but she wasn't sitting or playing. She was dancing barefoot in a long dress."

*This is beginning to sound erotic.* "So while we played a song, Naini danced on the bench next to you."

"Yes," Tony said. "She has brown feet."

"What song were we playing?" Trina asked.

"I must write it first," Tony said. "I will play it for you tonight at Johnny Foley's."

"You actually *hear* music in your dreams," Trina said.

"Yes," Tony said. "And when I wake up, I try to remember the notes."

*Amazing.* "Do you hear lyrics, too?"

"Sometimes," Tony said. "Mostly it is the music."

"And I was in your dream making music with you," Trina said. "What was I wearing?"

Tony's eyes darted left and right. "I should not say."

"You can tell me," Trina said. "What was I wearing?"

"You were wearing blue underwear," Tony said. "They did not fit you very well. Your buttocks were sticking out of them."

*I was wearing a thong? Where has he seen a thong?* "Was that all I was wearing?"

"You were wearing the orange and black shirt," Tony said.

*I was a fashion nightmare in his dream!* "What were you wearing?"

"My clothes," Tony said.

*That's no fun.* "So we just . . . played the piano while Naini danced barefoot."

"I should not say more," Tony said.

Trina slid higher on his body, rubbing her nose on his chin. *I'm beginning to think we did more than play the piano in his dream.* "What else did we do, Tony?"

"We watched *SportsCenter*," Tony said.

Trina laughed. "We did what?"

"A television was on top of the piano," Tony said. "We played music and watched *SportsCenter*."

She crawled higher, rubbing her cheek against his beard. "And *then* what did we do?"

"We drank root beer and ate oatmeal and raisin cookies," Tony said.

*We had a catered dream.* "Did we get cookie crumbs on the keys?"

"Yes," Tony said. "But Angela cleaned them up."

"*Angela* was in our dream." *Our dream is getting crowded.*

"Yes," Tony said. "And Aika sat on top of the piano."

"What was Aika wearing?" Trina asked.

"I should not say," Tony said.

She held his face in her hands. "You *should* say."

"She wore a blue and black fuzzy bra and purple underwear," Tony said.

*Wow. This is quite an erotic fantasy.* "What did Angela wear?"

"A white apron," Tony said.

"Anything else?"

"No," Tony said.

*Three seminaked women.* "And Naini wore a long dress."

"Yes," Tony said. "Like women in India wear."

"A sari," Trina said. "Was she fully covered?"

Tony shook his head.

"What wasn't covered, Tony?" Trina asked.

"Her stomach," Tony said. "She has a brown stomach and a tiny belly button."

*So . . . Aika is wearing some kinky lingerie on top of the piano, Angela is walking around in an apron with her booty hanging out, and Naini is doing a belly dance while I sit on a cold piano bench in a blue thong and a ratty flannel shirt.* "What happened next?"

"I do not want to say," Tony said.

She kissed his nose. "You *will* say."

"I told you to take off Aika's underwear," Tony said. "I am sorry."

*Take off Aika's underwear?* "It's okay, Tony. You can't control what's in your dreams."

"I am still sorry," Tony said.

"Did I take them off?" Trina asked.

"No," Tony said. "You kept them on. Aika was angry with you. Angela said for you to give them back to Aika. Naini laughed and took off her sari."

*And this is where I went off on all of them in the dream, right?* "So now Naini is dancing naked next to you."

"Yes. She has very small breasts."

"And how did you respond?" Trina asked.

"I played the piano," Tony said.

*He had all that flesh around him, and he played the piano.* "And then . . ."

"And then I woke up," Tony said. "I have been watching you since then."

Trina rested her head on his shoulder. "Have you ever had a dream like this before?"

"No," Tony said.

"Did you ever have dreams with Aika or Angela in them before?"

"Yes," Tony said.

"Do they always wear the same thing?" Trina asked.

"No," Tony said. "Sometimes Aika wears her blue underwear, and sometimes Angela wears a black sweater."

"But you saw me in only blue underwear and a flannel shirt," Trina said.

"Yes," Tony said. "I am sorry."

"What are you sorry for?" Trina asked.

"Before I came to San Francisco, you were not in my dreams," Tony said.

*Oh, that's so sweet.* "I'm in your dreams now."

"But Angela and Aika are still there, too," Tony said. "I only want you in my dreams."

Trina hugged him tightly. "Tony, that was the nicest thing anyone has ever said to me."

Tony sighed. "Why was Naini in my dream? I do not know her. I know Aika, and I know Angela. Why won't Aika and Angela stay out of my dreams?"

*I'm no psychologist, but . . .* "Because you care about them. You may even love them."

"I do not know if I love them," Tony said.

"Sure you do," Trina said. "Do you ever dream of your parents?"

"Yes," Tony said. "We are back at our house with Tonto."

"You dream of the people you love, Tony," Trina said.

Tony blinked several times. "Why do I dream of you with only blue underwear and a shirt?"

*I am in no way qualified to explain this.* "I don't know. Maybe you like the way I look."

"I like the way you look in anything you wear," Tony said.

"Thank you. Did you, um, get excited when you saw me in your dreams?"

"No," Tony said. "I did not get an erection."

*He knows about erections. Of course he does. He's a forty-year-old man.* "Did any of the other women in your dream make you excited?"

"I should not say," Tony said.

*He was excited. I need to know who . . .* "Did Naini make you excited when she took off her clothes?"

Tony looked away. "Yes. She had a snake tattoo. It started on her small left breast and ended at her brown vagina."

"Didn't Jasmine have a snake tattoo?"

"Yes," Tony said.

*Some part of all of Tony's women was in his dream.* "Well, I wish I had your dreams."

"You wish to have Angela and Aika and Naini naked in your dreams," Tony said.

"No," Trina said. "I wish I had people I loved in my dreams. I wish I could see my grandmother again."

"Is your grandmother in heaven?" Tony asked.

"Yes," Trina said. "She raised me after my mama died. She made sure I went to college, but she died before she could see me graduate."

"I have never been to college," Tony said.

"You're still young enough," Trina said. "You could go."

"I am not smart," Tony said.

"I think you are one of the smartest men I have ever met," Trina said. "You are an expert musicologist."

"I am not a musicologist," Tony said.

"Yes, you are," Trina said. "You hear music in your dreams. You write music listening to cable cars, buses, and sea lions. Only an expert musicologist could do that."

Tony nodded.

Trina sighed and kissed his neck. "I wish I could remember all my dreams, but I don't need to dream about you if you're here with me. I think living a dream is better than dreaming one."

"I do, too." He lifted his arms and rubbed Trina's back.

*He has so much strength in his fingers. I feel like putty.* "What are you thinking about at this moment?"

"Your back," Tony said. "It is hot. It is sweaty. It has many muscles. My chest is hot and sweaty, too."

"Because you're pushing all my buttons," Trina whispered.

"You have no buttons," Tony said. "Your back is smooth."

"I meant that you are making me feel good," Trina said. She kicked her legs out, sat up, and straddled him.

Tony's eyes widened. "Are you having an orgasm, Trina?"

"No." *I wish!* "Why do you ask?"

"Aika has orgasms when she sits on Angelo like this," Tony said.

*No . . . way.* "You *saw* her?"

"Yes," Tony said. "The door was cracked. She shouted, 'Oh God, Angelo, I'm coming.'"

Trina pressed her hands into Tony's chest. "Do they know you saw them?"

"I told Angelo," Tony said, "but Angelo told me not to tell Aika."

"Don't *ever* tell Aika." She squinted. "I know this is none of my business, but why were you at their door?"

"I heard noises late at night," Tony said. "I liked the sounds. I wrote music to the sounds. Naomi Stringer will like the music."

*He has to be kidding.* "You made up a song while listening to your brother and Aika . . . getting busy."

"Yes," Tony said. "They were very busy. Aika was bouncing up and down. She has very firm buttocks. Aika likes to shout. I will now call the song 'Getting Busy.' "

"That's a good title." *And I think I just gave it to him. But I am going to have trouble looking at Aika from now on. She's so quiet! It's always the quiet ones who like to get their freak on. Of course, I'm quiet, too, but . . .* "You know what? I want to stay in bed with you all day."

"I am hungry," Tony said.

"We can eat in bed, too," Trina said.

"Okay."

Trina moved Tony's hands to her thighs. "You can rub my legs if you want to."

Tony rubbed Trina's legs, his thumbs pressing against her inner thighs. "So soft. So hot."

*So . . . erotic. Damn.*

"Tony, um . . ." *How do I ask this?* "Tony, have you ever . . ." *I can't say "have you ever been with a woman" because he'll say yes. This might work.* "Have you ever . . ." *Made love? I'm not sure he understands the phrase.* "Tony, have you ever done to a woman what Angelo does to Aika in bed?"

"No," Tony said. "I have not had sex."

Trina blinked. "But you know about sex."

Tony nodded. "Angelo told me about sex."

"What did Angelo say about sex?"

"He said not to do it," Tony said. "Ever. Never. Don't even think about it, Tony. I will be so angry with you."

*That figures.* "So how do you know about orgasms?"

"I asked Angelo what an orgasm was because a girl at school called me an 'orgasm gone bad,' " Tony said. "Angelo said to look it up. I looked it up in the dictionary."

"Do you still remember the definition?" Trina asked.

"An orgasm is 'the physical and emotional sensation experienced at the peak of sexual excitation, usually resulting from stimulation of the sexual organ and usually accompanied in the male by ejaculation.' "

*There's nothing about the female in that definition, and one hundred percent of the time there was no accompaniment with Robert. He came. He snoozed. I finished on my own.* "So you know how sex works."

"Yes," Tony said.

"How does it work?" Trina asked.

"I put my erect penis into your moist vagina," Tony said.

*So clinical!* "And then what happens?"

"We have orgasms," Tony said.

*Not every time, but . . .* "Would you . . ." *I can't ask him that! But I want to know if he really wants me physically.* "Would you like to put your, um, your erect penis into my moist vagina?"

"Yes."

*He wants me. A man wants me. Oh, I am so ready.*

Tony started to unbuckle his belt. "I want to do this now."

*I know I shouldn't have asked that, but it's been so*

*long!* "Um, Tony, you heard what Angelo said. No messing around."

Tony finished unbuckling his belt and unzipped his fly. "Sex is not messing around. Messing around is staying up too late reading my map books."

*Well, in that case . . . No!* "I think he meant no messing around as in no sex."

"Oh." Tony zipped up his fly.

"And we just met a few days ago," Trina said. "I'm not sure if that's what we should do."

"Okay." Tony buckled his belt.

*He gave up too quickly!* "I mean, *now.* Eventually . . . maybe."

"When is eventually?" Tony asked.

*Eventually was almost a few seconds ago.* "Tony, most people know each other for a long time before they have sex."

"How long?"

"It's different for every couple," Trina said.

"How long for us, Trina?"

*If he keeps squirming under me, about five seconds.* "I don't know. When the time is right."

"What time will that be?" Tony asked.

"I don't know, Tony," Trina said.

"But not now."

"No," Trina said. "Not now."

"I will wait until I know you better," Tony said. He dropped his arms to his sides.

*Hey, now!* "Um, it might not be *that* long."

"I can wait," Tony said.

"We're getting to know each other very quickly," Trina said, "so it might not be that long."

"I can wait."

*Now he's inert and lost in a zone again. Just when I start to get a rise out of him, I deflate him.* She flattened her body against his. "I don't know if I can wait that long, Tony."

"You are hot," Tony said.

*All this talk about sex has made me hot. Robert and I never discussed sex at all.* "Talking about sex makes me very hot."

"When I get hot I take off my clothes," Tony said.

"You want me to take off my clothes."

"You are hot," Tony said. "Yes. Take off your clothes."

*He doesn't have to tell me twice.* She took off her bra and panties and tossed them toward the door.

"That is better," Tony said.

"Yes, it is." She kissed his neck and massaged his chest. "You excite me so much, Tony."

"I do not know how I excite you," Tony said.

"Everything about you excites me." She kissed his neck, shoulders, and chest. She wriggled lower in the bed and kissed his stomach. When she started to feel him grow between her breasts, she gave his penis a gentle squeeze.

"Oh God, Trina, I'm coming!" Tony shouted.

Trina gripped the sides of the bed. *He almost flipped me off the bed with his legs!*

"I am sorry," Tony said. "I am sorry, Trina."

Trina crawled up his body and kissed him gently on the lips. "Why are you sorry?"

"You did not have an orgasm," Tony said. "I had an orgasm and you did not have an orgasm."

Trina kissed his cheek and held him tightly. *Who says Tony doesn't have any empathy? He apologizes—*

*and* means *it—because I didn't have an orgasm.* "We're going to be in bed all day, aren't we?"

"Yes," Tony said.

She looked out the window. "It looks like rain, too. It wouldn't be any fun to go outside in this rain."

"You are right," Tony said.

"And we're getting to know each other *much* better, aren't we?"

Tony nodded.

*So sweet, so innocent, so giving, so . . . pure.* "I think there might be time for you to give me . . ." She bit her lower lip. "An orgasm," she whispered.

"Trina, I am afraid," Tony said.

*So am I. This would be my first orgasm given to me by a man since George Bush was president. I might scare the hell out of Tony.* "Why are you scared, Tony?"

"I am afraid I cannot give you an orgasm."

*He almost did when I was fully clothed yesterday, when he was "playing" me last night, and a few moments ago when he was rubbing my inner thighs.* "Trust me, Tony. You won't have to do much."

"Teach me how to give you an orgasm, Trina."

*This has to be every woman's dream. Did I hear him correctly?* "You want me to teach you how to give me an orgasm."

"Yes."

*I heard correctly. Whoo. This is a lot of responsibility.* "Well . . ."

A phone rang from the other room. "Is that yours or mine?" Trina asked.

"Mine," Tony said.

*Shoot!* "I'll get it. You just . . . wait here."

Trina raced to the coffee table and picked up Tony's phone. "Hello?"

"Trina, is he up?" Angelo asked.

*He was definitely up a few minutes ago. And oh look. I'm completely naked.* "He's resting. Why?"

"What does he want to do today?" Angelo asked.

*He wants to learn how to give me an orgasm, and you just interrupted his first lesson.* "He hasn't decided yet."

"Let me talk to him," Angelo said.

*Oh no! I can't say he's sleeping because I just said he's resting. I have to trust Tony not to say the wrong thing.* She turned on the speaker and returned to the bed. "Tony, it's Angelo."

Tony picked up the phone. "Hello, Angelo."

"What are we going to do today?" Angelo asked. "It's raining to beat the band out there."

"I want to stay inside today," Tony said.

"And do what?" Angelo asked.

"Trina is going to teach me how to—"

"Get to the Museum of Modern Art," Trina interrupted.

"I know the way, Trina," Tony said.

"I'm going to teach you a new way to get there," Trina said.

Tony nodded. "Okay."

"That's not a good idea, Trina," Angelo said. "I took him to the Guggenheim Museum once, and he spazzed out. They made us leave."

"There were too many colors," Tony said. "They would not let me touch or smell the paintings."

"How old were you then?" Trina asked.

"I was eight," Tony said.

"Angelo, have you taken him to an art gallery since then?" Trina asked.

"No," Angelo said.

"I think he's changed a lot since he was eight," Trina said. "I can't guarantee there won't be too many colors, Tony."

"I like colors now," Tony said. "They are not as loud."

"You won't touch or try to smell the paintings, will you, Tony?" Angelo asked.

"No." Tony smiled.

"All right," Angelo said. "We're going to the museum. When should we pick you two up?"

"We can meet you there at . . ." She checked her alarm clock. "Eleven. It's not far from here. It's only a fifteen-minute walk."

"What did you eat for breakfast, Tony?" Angelo asked.

"I have not eaten yet," Tony said.

"I'll feed him, Angelo," Trina said. "Don't you worry."

"He likes Cap'n Crunch and bananas," Angelo said.

*That isn't happening.* "Okay. See you at eleven."

"Later," Angelo said.

Trina ended the call. *Whew! Now where were we? Yes. I'm still naked, and Tony is shirtless in my bed.*

"I am hungry," Tony said.

"We'll have to get brunch out," Trina said. "We can get something on the way. Taylor Street Coffee Shop is just around the corner." She straddled him. "So, you want me to teach—"

Tony swung his legs out from under her and left the bed. "I need to take a shower." He took off his pants and underwear and walked into the bathroom.

*He has to stop* doing *that!*

*Now we're both naked, and neither of us is getting busy.*

*This is so twisted.*

She went into the bathroom as Tony turned on the hot water. "Is it getting hot?" she asked. *I know I'm getting hot.*

"Yes," Tony said. "You need a shower, too." He held out his hand.

*I have never taken a shower with anyone but myself.* She grabbed Tony's hand. "I hope we both fit."

"There is room," Tony said. "You are slender."

Trina got into the tub and turned the lever for the shower, directing the spray away from her hair.

Tony handed her a washcloth. "I will watch you."

She rubbed soap into the washcloth and began soaping her body.

Tony reached out and touched the foam on her stomach. "So pretty."

"The soap?"

"Your stomach," Tony said. He looked down. "I am growing."

*Yep. He likes my stomach. A lot. All those one-piece-of-toast breakfasts are finally paying off.* "It's okay."

"Yes, it is," Tony said. He stepped closer and scooped some of the soap off Trina's breasts. "I am growing more."

Trina turned around and washed quickly, rinsed, and handed Tony the washcloth.

"You did not wash your hair," Tony said.

"I wash it every two weeks or so," Trina said.

"I can wash it," Tony said.

"We can wash it later tonight if you like," Trina said. "But we have to hustle now if we're going to get some breakfast and get to the museum by eleven."

Tony began soaping up his body. He reached out a finger and touched Trina's right nipple. "Does this hurt?"

*You're* killing *me, man!* "No."

"I am staring at you," Tony said. He washed under his arms and between his legs.

"What are you staring at?" Trina asked.

"Everything," Tony said. He stepped under the spray, rinsed, and turned off the water. "I will not wash my hair either." He reached out and held Trina's hips. "I want to give you an orgasm now."

"Are you sure?" *I will scream, and my neighbors will call 911.*

"I am sure."

Trina took his hand and put it between her legs. "Put your finger . . . here."

"It is a button," Tony said.

Trina closed her eyes. "Yes. It is a button. Your finger is on my clitoris."

"What do I do?" Tony asked.

*Nothing! I'm so close!* "Um, just . . . press my button." She felt Tony's hot finger press once, twice—

"Oh yes, thank you, oh God, thank you, Tony!" She opened her eyes and kissed him full on the mouth until her spasms subsided. "You are a fast learner." *And I am so embarrassed! He touched my clitoris twice! What is wrong with me?*

"I pressed your button twice," Tony said. "And you had an orgasm."

*He was counting, too!* She felt his penis poking her belly button. She put both hands on it and stroked it several times.

"Oh yes, thank you, oh God, thank you, Trina," Tony said. He looked down. "Much came out on you."

"It's okay," Trina said. *I could have had octuplets!* She turned on the shower and rinsed herself off. "Did it feel good?"

"Yes," Tony said. "Twice." He stepped close and put his finger on her clitoris again. "It is your turn again."

"I don't know if I can do it again so soon, Tony," Trina said.

"I will press your button three times this time," Tony said.

"Um, let's try . . ." *Oh, his hot finger covers it completely.* "Just . . . move it in small circles."

"Small circles," Tony said.

Trina closed her eyes.

"You are closing your eyes," Tony said.

"It helps me concentrate," Trina whispered.

"You are not having an orgasm," Tony said.

"Not yet," Trina said. "I'm close, though."

"What else can I do?" Tony asked.

She picked up his other hand and put it on her left breast. "Squeeze gently, and when I tell you to, squeeze my nipple hard."

"I do not want to hurt you," Tony said.

"You won't hurt me," Trina whispered. "I won't feel a . . . oh, shit, squeeze my nipple!"

Tony pinched her nipple and held it tightly.

Trina moaned and nearly fell back and out of the tub.

"Are you okay?" Tony asked.

"Oh yes," Trina said. "I am . . . feeling wonderful."

"You did not say 'Oh yes, thank you, oh God, thank you, Tony.'"

Trina smiled. "Sometimes I only moan like that."

"Your nipple does not hurt," Tony said.

"No," Trina said. "You squeezed it just right."

"Good." He stepped out of the tub and grabbed a towel, handing it to Trina. He took another towel and began drying himself off. "I must brush my teeth now."

Trina blinked. *So it's give Trina her second orgasm and go back to his routine. I'm standing in the bathtub panting while he brushes his teeth as if nothing has happened. The man is a machine! A sex machine who gave me two orgasms within ten minutes.* She smiled. *I just had two orgasms in ten minutes.*

She got out of the tub, wrapped the towel around her torso, and bumped him with her hip. "Um, I need to tell you something."

Tony took his toothbrush from her medicine cabinet and covered the bristles with toothpaste.

"Nod if you can hear me."

Tony nodded and started to brush.

"The next time you give me an orgasm, do you think you could hold me tightly afterward?"

Tony nodded.

"I like to be held tightly after I have an orgasm."

Tony only brushed for two minutes, spit into the sink, rinsed his mouth, and put his toothbrush back into the medicine cabinet. "I will hold you now while you brush your teeth."

Trina smiled. "It's okay. You can hold me next time." *And there will be a next time. There will be many next times.*

"I will hold you now," Tony said. He positioned Trina in front of the mirror and hugged her tightly from behind.

Trina looked into the mirror as she brushed. *I'm wearing only a towel and a naked man is holding me tightly while I brush my teeth. We have to make this part of our morning routine, too.*

"I will go get dressed in my new clothes," Tony said, and he left the bathroom.

"I'm sure they're wrinkled," Trina said. She tightened the towel under her arms. "We need to iron them."

Tony appeared naked in front of her. "I am not allowed to touch the iron." He looked down. "And I have no clean underwear."

*If this man goes out in public without underwear, the whole world will see his moose knuckle.* "We'll have to have Angelo bring you some."

"I will call him."

While Tony told Angelo to bring him new underwear, Trina took off her towel. *If he's naked, I'm naked.* She picked out a pair of black jeans and a red and black flannel shirt from her closet.

"I told him," Tony said. "He will bring the underwear here."

"You didn't tell him you were naked, did you?"

"No," Tony said.

Trina smiled. "You didn't tell him that I was naked, did you?"

"No," Tony said.

"Do you mind if I walk around the apartment naked?" Trina asked.

"I do not mind," Tony said. "Are you going to teach me how to iron now?"

*Ironing naked. Another routine I will definitely enjoy.*

Trina plugged in the iron, made the bed, and laid out Tony's pants. "Your shirt looks fine, so we'll only do the pants."

"It is a no-iron shirt," Tony said.

"There is no such thing as a no-iron shirt," Trina said. "You'll have to iron it eventually, but not today."

With a few sprays of starch, Trina speedily ironed one side of Tony's pants. "Were you watching?"

"Yes," Tony said.

Trina flipped the pants and smoothed out the cuff. "Your turn."

Though much slower than Trina was, Tony ironed the other side of his pants flawlessly.

"Please put them on now," Trina said. "And your shirt. You can't go to the door naked when Angelo gets here."

"No," Tony said. "But you are naked."

"So I'm flirting," Trina said.

"I like it when you flirt," Tony said.

*Her* phone rang. *What now?* She picked up her phone. "Hello?"

"Hello, Nurse Woods. This is Ellen Sprouse."

She covered the mouthpiece. "Tony, I'm going to need some privacy for this call, okay?"

"Okay."

Tony left the bedroom, and Trina closed the door behind him. "Hello, Nurse Sprouse. How are you?"

"Oh, I'm fine and dandy, Woods," Nurse Sprouse said. "How is your illness coming along?"

"I'm feeling much better," Trina said. "Thanks for asking." She opened a drawer and took out some black underwear, black socks, and a black bra.

"Oh, I *know* you're feeling better, Woods. I've seen you on the television with your boyfriend."

Trina pressed the speaker button and put on her underwear. "Okay. And?"

"You took two and a half sick days this week, Woods, and it is obvious you are not sick. I doubt you were sick the day you left early, too."

Trina put on her bra and sat on her bed. She grabbed her socks. "Okay. And?"

"The hospital administration has also seen you on

television, Woods. The whole world has seen you on television."

"Get to the point, please." She put on her socks.

"Because you lied about your absences, you will *not* get paid time off for them."

Trina sighed. "Fine. I gotta go. I'll see you Monday."

"Oh, you won't see just me, Monday, Woods. You have to go up before the disciplinary review board."

Trina sighed and shook her head. "Why?"

"For lying to a supervisor and dereliction of duty," Nurse Sprouse said. "These are serious charges."

"Miss Sprouse, I don't have time for this. Hold on." She turned off the speaker, covered the mouthpiece, and picked up her pants. "Tony, could you iron my pants, too?"

Tony opened the door. "Yes."

Trina handed him the pants. "Light on the starch. These are black jeans."

"One spray," Tony said. He laid the pants on the bed.

"Right."

Trina left the bedroom and sat on the arm of the couch. She uncovered the mouthpiece. "When do you need me to appear before the board?"

"Monday at seven AM sharp," Nurse Sprouse said. "Don't be late."

*Click.*

*Lovely. Most nurses in this situation get a warning for a first offense, so I'm not worried.* She looked at Tony intently putting expert creases in her pants. "That was Nurse Sprouse."

Tony didn't look up. "The heartless wench. You have to work today."

"No," Trina said. "No working today." She moved into the bedroom. "You do a really good job, Tony."

"Thank you," Tony said. "I like to iron your clothes."
*I think I am falling in love with this man.*

Trina jumped when Angelo pounded on the door.

"Hey, open up!" Angelo yelled. "I've got Tony's . . .
stuff."

Trina grabbed her jeans and put them on. "Go to the
door, Tony," Trina whispered. "And *please* don't tell
Angelo we've been walking around naked."

Tony smiled. "He would not believe me anyway."
He left the bedroom.

Trina closed the bedroom door and laughed as she
put on her shirt. *And neither would I.* She smiled at the
woman in the mirror. *Woman, you have lost your mind.
Walking around naked in your own apartment.*

She left three buttons open on her shirt.

*And if this is the life I'm going to have from now on,
I hope I never find my mind again.*

# 31

Trina listened through her bedroom door.

"What took you so long to come to the door,
Tony?" Angelo asked.

*One of us was nearly naked,* Trina thought. *And to
think that I used to be so shy.*

"Trina and I had to iron some clothes," Tony said.
"She taught me how to iron my pants."

"Your pants look great," Aika said.

"Thank you," Tony said. "Trina is a good teacher."

*Time to go out now,* Trina thought. *I don't want Tony telling them what else I've been teaching him.*

Trina kicked her underwear and bra away from the door and opened it. "Tony ironed my jeans, too."

Aika pouted. "You never iron *my* clothes, Angelo."

"Because you do not wear so many," Tony said.

"Hey, hey," Angelo said. "Let's go get some culture. The taxi's waiting."

Tony held up the bag containing his underwear. "I must put on my underwear first." He went into the bathroom and closed the door.

Trina stared at her hiking boots. *Please don't ask—*

"Has he eaten breakfast yet?" Angelo asked.

"Um, no," Trina said. "We were going to get brunch on the way at Taylor Street Coffee Shop. It's two blocks from here."

"I got a taxi waiting," Angelo said. "And Aika and I already ate breakfast like normal people, you know, at *breakfast* time."

"We'll get it to go then," Trina said, "and we can eat it on the walk to the museum. It's less than a mile from here."

"It's raining," Angelo said.

Trina went to the closet and took out two umbrellas.

"I want to go walking in the rain," Aika said.

Tony came out of the bathroom. "I am ready." He held out his hand.

Trina took it. "How hungry are you, Tony?"

"I am very hungry," Tony said.

*And I am very poor.* She took her purse from a hook in the closet. "Let's go eat."

While Angelo and Aika waited outside in the rain, Tony ordered two eggs and bacon to go inside the cramped Taylor Street Coffee Shop. "What are you eating, Trina?"

"I can eat some of your toast," Trina said. She opened her purse and found a crumpled ten.

It was just enough.

Trina held the umbrella while they walked and Tony munched on a piece of buttery wheat toast between forkfuls of eggs. She didn't know how she would pay the admission fee at the museum, but she didn't care. She was having a romantic brunch under an umbrella with a handsome man.

When they entered the San Francisco Museum of Modern Art, Tony held out his credit card. "I will pay," he said.

Trina smiled. "Thank you, Tony."

"I got this," Angelo said. He handed his credit card over Tony's hand.

Tony put his credit card back into his pocket. "Okay." Tony looked out into the first gallery. "I hear the colors."

"What sounds do they make?" Trina asked.

"All sounds," Tony said. "Some are not notes. I will write many songs about the colors today, and I will play them tonight."

"Can't you just *look* at the paintings today?" Angelo asked. "Do you have to listen to them, too?"

"There are so many songs here," Tony said. "I must write them."

"I'm only asking you not to write a song for a couple of hours," Angelo said.

"I will try," Tony said.

"You have a fantastic memory, Tony," Trina whispered. "You'll remember all those songs later, and then you can write them down."

"I will remember them," Tony said. "Yes."

Tony moved through the spacious museum until Pablo Picasso's *Les Femmes d'Alger* (*The Women of Algiers*) stopped him.

"She is blue," Tony said. "She has one white breast and one blue breast. She only has three toes. She has lost two toes. It should be easy to find two blue toes. The other woman has no face. I cannot see what she is looking at if she has no eyes. Why does she have one white breast and one blue breast, Trina?"

"I don't know, Tony," Trina said.

"She must have been very cold," Tony said.

Tony saw music in the lines and designs of Jackson Pollock's *Guardians of the Secret*. "This is not a painting," he said. "It is a symphony, but it has too much bass."

Henri Matisse's *La Conversation* made Tony squint. "The women are pink and orange. That woman's left arm is much skinnier and longer than her right arm. It is called *La Conversation*. Neither woman has her mouth open. They are not talking. They are listening to the colors shouting."

Tony and Aika talked about René Magritte's *Les valeurs personnelles* (*Personal Values*).

"How can a comb be larger than a bed?" Tony asked.

"It's a symbolic painting, Tony," Aika said. "It might mean we spend more time making ourselves look good than getting rest and sleep."

"A shaving brush," Tony said. "A match. A wineglass. Clouds on the wall. A mirror. A large pill. I do not have these personal values."

"Maybe the artist is trying to say that these are society's values," Aika said. "A comb and shaving brush are vanity. The match, wineglass, and pill represent vices. The artist is holding up a mirror on our lives."

"And we are living in the clouds," Tony said.

"Right," Aika said.

"The glass is empty," Tony said. "It should be full. If we change our personal values, the glass will be full."

Tony heard the violin playing in Georges Braque's *Violin and Candlestick.*

"The violin is playing very fast," Tony said. "The candlestick makes music, too."

"Light music," Angelo said.

"Yes," Tony said. "Light has music. The candlestick will play long after the violin strings break."

"Why?" Angelo asked.

"Light does not end," Tony said. "Light is eternal."

Robert Rauschenberg's *Collection* held Tony's interest the longest.

"Pink, blue, red, yellow, black," he said. "Drip, smudge, newspaper, cartoons."

"Hey," Angelo said. "Those are old newspapers from New York, Tony."

Tony squinted. "There is much violence. There is much death. There is much color. There is much humor. This is a colorful life." He smiled at Trina. "I will write all this as one song."

"I can't wait to hear it," Trina said.

Tony also couldn't wait to eat again. After a three-hour tour, they ate a late lunch at Caffe Museo, the high-end cafeteria inside the museum with decent orecchiette pasta and overstuffed pitas.

"This ain't Brooklyn," Angelo said, "but it's good, isn't it, Tony?"

Tony nodded. "My stomach is happy."

While they ate, an impromptu autograph session broke out for both brothers. While Angelo signed copies of Tony's biography and posed for pictures at one table, Tony signed napkins with a Sharpie at another.

Aika and Trina sat on either side of Tony and watched him laboriously writing his name. *He's trying so hard to make his autograph legible, and it still isn't. These people don't care about legibility, Tony. Scribble your name! Heck, give them your initials.*

A large-chested, wide-hipped woman in silvery designer slacks and a sequined black top prodded a young boy in front of Tony. "Hi, Mr. Santangelo," she said far too loudly. "I'm Alice Tilton, and this is my son, Kirk."

"Hello," Tony said.

"Well, say hello, Kirk," Ms. Tilton said.

Kirk didn't look up. "Hello," he said in a dull monotone.

*Kirk has Asperger's,* Trina thought.

"Eye contact, Kirk," Ms. Tilton spat. "Look Mr. Santangelo in the eye."

Kirk glanced up then back down at his shoes.

*Kirk sees everything in this room all at once,* Trina thought. *Too bad his overbearing wench of a mother can't see that.*

Ms. Tilton sighed heavily. "Kirk, this is the man you saw playing the piano on your computer."

Kirk nodded.

"Kirk plays the piano, too, Mr. Santangelo," Ms. Tilton said. "He is a prodigy, just like you were."

Kirk's eyes seemed to follow a dust mote floating in the air.

"Did you find all of them, Kirk?" Tony asked.

"Find all of what?" Ms. Tilton asked.

*Shut up, wench,* Trina thought. *Tony isn't talking to you.*

"I am speaking to Kirk now," Tony said. "Please listen."

Ms. Tilton folded her arms and shook her head.

*I've seen better "the nerve!" poses,* Trina thought. *Tony is much more aware of the world than anyone else believes. He shut up Ms. Tilton without telling her to shut up.*

"Kirk, did you find all the notes you were looking for today?" Tony asked.

Kirk shook his head slowly.

"Sometimes the notes hide," Tony said. "Sometimes the notes move very fast. You will find them. They like to hide. It makes finding them more special."

"There are too many," Kirk whispered.

*Oh, this is almost breaking my heart,* Trina thought. *Is this what Tony went through as a child?*

"There are many, yes," Tony said, "and you want to play them all."

Kirk nodded.

"You do not look at the notes on the page," Tony said.

"No," Kirk said.

"And it drives his piano teacher crazy, let me tell you," Ms. Tilton said.

Trina stared a hole in Ms. Tilton's head.

Tony ignored her. "Your teacher is mad at you because you do not look at the notes."

"Yes," Kirk whispered.

"Your teacher says you do not play the right notes," Tony said.

Kirk nodded.

"Your teacher makes you play the song until it is right," Tony said.

"Yes," Kirk whispered.

"You want to play something else," Tony said. "You want to play the notes you see, smell, taste, touch, and hear."

Kirk nodded.

"Your teacher is wrong," Tony said. "There are no wrong notes. It is always right to play something else."

Kirk smiled.

"Don't you tell him *that,* Mr. Santangelo," Ms. Tilton said. "I'm paying a large chunk of change so Kirk can have the best piano teacher in Northern California."

Tony looked only at Kirk. "Stop paying the teacher. Kirk is too good to have a teacher. Kirk will always be too good to have a teacher."

"How can you say that?" Ms. Tilton squawked. "You haven't heard Kirk play."

"I know he sees the notes," Tony said. "They are always in front of his eyes. He is looking for them now."

"But Kirk *has* to learn to read music," Ms. Tilton said.

"He already reads music everywhere," Tony said. "He sees the music now. He does not have to look at the paper anymore."

Kirk nodded.

"My teacher lasted one month, Kirk," Tony said. "Poppa sent him away."

"I am not going to . . ." Ms. Tilton sighed. "I was on a *waiting* list for this teacher for a *year!*"

"Kirk needs no teacher," Tony said. "Kirk knows that every sound is a right note. Every color is a right note. Every texture is a right note. There are no wrong notes."

Kirk looked Tony in the eye. "Yes."

"Keep looking everywhere for the notes, Kirk," Tony said. "The notes will always be there waiting for you. And do not practice anymore. Just . . . play."

Ms. Tilton pulled Kirk back to her voluminous hips. "Well, what do you know about raising a child with Asperger's? Kirk has to have discipline. He has to have a routine."

"Let him play," Tony said. "That will be his discipline. That will be his routine."

"Angelo!" Ms. Tilton shouted. "Your brother gives *lousy* advice! Put *that* in your next book about him! Come on, Kirk!"

Kirk didn't move. Instead, he extended his hand.

Tony shook it. "Keep playing, and ignore your mother," Tony whispered.

Kirk smiled again.

Ms. Tilton grabbed Kirk's hand. "Good-*bye,* Mr. Santangelo."

Tony smiled at Kirk. "Good-bye, Kirk. Remember the notes."

"I will," Kirk said.

Ms. Tilton dragged Kirk away.

Trina grabbed Tony's hand. "You just changed that boy's life forever."

"And the boy's mother hasn't got a clue," Aika said. She cut her eyes from Trina to another table. "Tony, will you be okay for a few minutes? I'd like to speak to Trina in private."

"I will be okay," Tony said.

Trina and Aika sat three tables away. "I just needed

some girl talk," Aika said. "And I can watch Angelo better from this table." She shook her head. "Look at all the women getting Angelo's autograph. He's in hottie heaven."

Trina watched Tony signing another napkin. "I don't have to worry about Tony."

"Sure you do," Aika said. "He's a man. And he still has a crush on me."

"I've noticed," Trina said. "It's hard not to notice when Tony tells you . . . Never mind. So, do you think Angelo—"

"When Tony tells you what?" Aika interrupted.

Trina sighed. "When he tells you that he dreams about you, Aika."

"Am I wearing blue underwear?" Aika asked.

Trina blinked. "You *know* about the blue underwear?"

"Oh my God, that was a guess." Aika frowned. "I'm so embarrassed."

"Did Tony tell you about the . . . the thong already?" Trina asked.

"No," Aika said. "Angelo told me. The first time Tony saw me at the Castle, I was going down to the kitchen for something to drink, and it was late, so I only wore a blue thong and a T-shirt. I didn't know Tony was watching me."

"Why would Angelo tell you about that?" Trina asked.

"So I'd remember to wear more clothes in the house," Aika said.

"Have you?" Trina asked.

"I always wear shorts now, yes," Aika said. "So I'm in Tony's dreams wearing a thong."

"Um, no," Trina said. "I'm wearing the thong."

"Really," Aika said. "You're wearing *my* thong."

"I'm wearing *a* thong," Trina said. "I don't know if it's *your* thong. Okay, yeah, it's yours, and in Tony's dream, he asks me to give it back to you."

"We have to cut back on Tony's consumption of root beer and sugar," Aika said. "He has too much going through his head as it is."

"Speaking of head cases," Trina said, "how am I doing with Angelo?"

"You're doing fine," Aika said. "Really."

"He seems to hate me," Trina said.

"He doesn't hate you," Aika said.

"I obviously don't feed Tony enough," Trina said.

"Don't worry about it," Aika said. "Angelo is Tony's overprotective parent. He's Tony's mother, father, and brother. It's the 'no one's good enough for my brother' kind of thing. I think you are *perfect* for Tony."

"Thank you," Trina said. "But I still think Angelo wishes I would vanish in a flaming ball of fire."

"He's only angry because you don't take any of his Brooklyn he-man shit," Aika said.

"Neither do you," Trina said.

"He doesn't stay angry with me for long. . . ." Aika smiled. "He's good at making up with me. *Very* good."

"Oh really?" Trina smiled.

"Yeah, he's gruff and huffs and puffs, but Angelo is really quite a teddy bear," Aika said. "Now if I can only get that teddy bear to pop the question. We've been seeing each other for a year. That's long enough, isn't it?"

"It certainly is," Trina said.

"This is going to sound wrong," Aika said, "but the more you pull Tony toward you, the easier it will be for me to pull Angelo toward me."

"It doesn't sound wrong," Trina said. "It makes perfect sense."

"But it's so selfish of me to think that, isn't it?" Aika blinked. "No, don't answer that. I have to be selfish at my age. I *need* to be married, okay? I'm forty-two and don't have many more years left to have children."

Trina grabbed Aika's hand. "No way. You're forty-two?"

Aika nodded.

*She has no wrinkles! How can a forty-two-year-old woman have no wrinkles and firm buttocks?* "I hate you," Trina said. "I thought you were younger than I am."

Aika squeezed Trina's hand. "You're good for my ego."

"And you're bad for mine," Trina said. "What's your secret?"

Aika leaned in. "Lots of good, hot, continuous sex."

Trina laughed. "There has to be more to it than that. Your skin is flawless. I'll bet you get carded every time."

Aika smiled. "I don't exercise, I don't use my treadmill, and I really don't watch what I eat. It's the sex. That's the only workout I get. Would you believe I used to be fatter?"

"No." Trina saw Angelo and Tony getting up. "I guess we're going." She stood, walked over to Tony, and hugged him. "Is your hand tired?"

"Yes," Tony said.

Aika hugged and kissed Angelo. "Get any phone numbers?"

"No," Angelo said.

Tony held out his hand, and Trina took it. "I did not get any phone numbers either."

She kissed his cheek. "Good."

"Why would they give me phone numbers, Trina?" Tony asked.

"So they could hook up with you later," Trina said.

"We would go fishing," Tony said.

Trina laughed. "Something like that." She rubbed Tony's hand. "Where to?"

"Johnny Foley's," Tony said.

"Again?" Angelo sighed. "Come on. There are hundreds of other places we could eat."

"I have two new songs to play," Tony said.

"It's only three-thirty, Tony," Angelo said. "They don't open the doors to that cellar place for five more hours. Why don't you come to our hotel so you can see the view from our room?"

"Okay," Tony said.

*The view, right,* Trina thought. *Jerk. Let's go see where you could stay instead of Trina's hole-in-the-wall.*

The rain turned to a fine, foggy mist as they walked from the museum to the Mark Hopkins, a San Francisco landmark a few blocks from Huntington Park and Saint Francis. Trina walked under sparkling chandeliers and around luxurious furnishings on the way to the elevators. When they got off on the fifteenth floor, she entered a spacious suite that was more an apartment than a hotel room. She washed her hands in a bathroom that was bigger than her bedroom and featured a bidet, a fancy toilet, and a tub big enough for two. She walked by a wide-screen TV on the wall, an executive-sized desk, and a fireplace to a glassed-in room with wicker chairs overlooking the city.

"Would you look at that view," Angelo said.

*I've seen it,* Trina said. *I live here. I can get as good a view from the top floor of Saint Francis.*

"I only see fog," Tony said.

"Wait until you see the view at night," Angelo said.

"I will only see more fog," Tony said.

Angelo put his hand on Tony's shoulder. "They have a full-size grand piano in one of the ballrooms."

*In* one *of the ballrooms,* Trina thought. *Whoop-de-do.*

"You could practice there," Angelo said.

"It is not my piano," Tony said.

"You play the pianos at Johnny Foley's," Angelo said.

"Because I play for Trina on them," Tony said.

*Give up, Angelo,* Trina thought.

"We could eat at Top of the Mark, my treat," Angelo said. "It's on the top floor. You can see the Golden Gate Bridge, Alcatraz, and the Bay Bridge from up there."

"I will only see fog tonight," Tony said.

"Okay, okay," Angelo said. "We'll eat at Johnny Foley's."

They ate more fish and chips and drank a pitcher of root beer at Johnny Foley's, and a huge crowd greeted Tony as he entered.

Tim vacated his piano and started the applause.

Tony sat, adjusted the microphone, and said, "This is called 'Dream Song.'" He smiled at Trina, who found enough room to stand sideways in the front row next to Aika and Angelo.

"Dream Song" oozed sex, and the crowd added ooh's and aah's. The first melody was slow and sure, the second melody faster, almost scampering. The third melody had a definite far eastern, Indian sound.

*Wow,* Trina thought. *He has just played Angela the*

*sure one, Aika the rabbit, and Naini the exotic Hindu goddess. I can't wait for my melody.*

The fourth melody had a little grind to it, and Trina thought she heard the sultry whine of saxophones. *Oh yes, Tony. Play me. Play me seductively.*

"Tony must have had *some* dream," Aika whispered in Trina's ear.

*You don't know the half of it,* Trina thought. *But my melody is the best. Look at all the people slow dancing around us. I'm sure a whole bunch of babies will be conceived to this song.*

Tim stuck his head between Aika and Trina. "He is fusing *four* different melodies into one continuous whole. Two is hard enough. Three is difficult. Four is next to impossible. How does he come up with these songs?"

"He dreams them," Trina said. "And then he plays them when he wakes up."

"I don't know anything about what he's got, but I wish I had it," Tim said. "That's the hand of God or something."

*Or the voices of the angels.* "I have a suggestion for you, Tim."

"I'm all ears," Tim said.

"Drink more root beer." She smiled. "You just need more sugar."

After some nice applause, Tony pushed back the bench.

The crowd cheered.

Tony smiled. "You like when I do not sit down."

The crowd cheered louder.

Tony leaned into the microphone. "This is called 'Colorful Life.' It will be loud." He took a deep breath and exhaled. "Get ready to rumble."

Playing the bass with both hands, Tony created quite a rumble. He kept the bass rolling with only his left before adding staccato bursts with his fists on top of the piano.

*That sounds like gunfire,* Trina thought. *This is* real *gangster music.*

Tony followed the gunfire with the distinctive wail of an ambulance. He took a breath and played a tune right out of the circus before playing a "conversation" between two loud women.

The ambulance returned.

The crowd laughed.

Tony stopped and looked at the audience. He blinked several times.

The ambulance returned.

The rest of the song took off at breakneck speed, ending with a terrible crash—

And the ambulance.

*I think we've all just heard a musical drive-by,* Trina thought.

A drunk took the opportunity during the applause to put a dollar in Tony's tip jar. "Play some Journey, dude!" he shouted.

Angelo reached out and grabbed the man by the shoulders. "He plays what he plays, pal."

"And I came here to hear some Journey!" the drunk yelled.

"Do you see Steve Perry up there?" Angelo asked.

"No," the drunk said, twisting away from Angelo's grasp. "But this is a piano bar. The pianist is supposed to take requests. Journey! Journey! Journey!"

In a moment, many in the crowd were chanting, "Journey! Journey!"

*This could get ugly,* Trina said. *This is a Journey town.*

"Just keep playing what you want to play, Tony," Angelo said. "Don't listen to them."

A few more drunk and boisterous men broke through the front row. "Journey! Journey! Journey!"

Trina crawled through them to Tony. "Do you know 'Don't Stop Believing'? That has a nice piano part in it."

Tony nodded. "I have heard that one." He picked up the microphone. "This is called . . ." He drummed on the top of the piano. " 'Don't Stop Believing.' "

The crowd roared.

Then Tony Santangelo from Cobble Hill, Brooklyn, New York, USA, played the living *hell* out of that classic Journey song as the crowd sang along. In yet another YouTube video gone viral, Tony ended the song by doing an incredible "drum solo" on the piano and the piano bench as the crowd sang the chorus a cappella for five consecutive minutes.

When he finished, the crowd gave him a three-minute ovation.

"Take a bow, Tony," Trina said.

Tony bowed.

Two minutes of furious noise later, Tony had drunk three glasses of root beer without a pause.

As Trina mopped Tony's face with some napkins at the main bar, Mr. Kelly approached. "Tony," Mr. Kelly said, "are you going to be here tomorrow night?"

"Why do you want to know?" Angelo asked.

"If we *know* Tony's coming," Mr. Kelly said, "we can promote him better."

"And increase your weekend cover charge from ten to twenty," Trina said.

"We always have a ten-dollar cover on Fridays and Saturdays," Mr. Kelly said. "I was thinking fifteen. We'll pay Tony for his time, of course."

"Tony has played here three nights in a row," Trina said. "And *now* you want to pay him?"

"I will play for free," Tony said, sipping his fourth root beer.

"No, you won't," Angelo said.

"What if we give him thirty percent of the gate?" Mr. Kelly asked.

Angelo scowled. "Tony is a living legend. Thirty percent? Are you crazy?"

"I will play for free," Tony said.

"You're not playing for free," Angelo said. "You shouldn't even be playing in this place anyway. You should be at the Hollywood Bowl or at Carnegie Hall."

Tony shook his head. "I will play for free."

Trina rubbed Tony's shoulders. "Are you sure?"

"I am sure," Tony said. "Music should be free."

"But Mr. Kelly plans to charge people to hear you play tomorrow night," Trina said.

Tony looked at Mr. Kelly. "Then I will not play."

Mr. Kelly sighed. "You won't?"

"Music is for everyone," Tony said. "Music should be free."

"You make a mint off drinks when he's here, don't you?" Angelo asked.

"Best three weeknights I've ever had," Mr. Kelly said. "And I have sold more root beer in three days than I usually sell in a year."

"If you do not charge," Tony said, "I will play."

"Okay," Mr. Kelly said. "No cover charge tomorrow night."

"I will be here," Tony said.

After Mr. Kelly left the bar, a man writing on a notepad moved over a seat. "Oh, that was good."

"What was?" Angelo asked.

The man read from the notepad. "'Music is for everyone. Music should be free.' I wonder what other musicians and singers will think about that." The man smiled. "Bobby Bodkins, Associated Press."

"You're taking what Tony said out of context," Trina said. "You're going to misquote him."

"It won't be a misquote, honey," Bodkins said. "'Music should be free.' Said by a living legend. *Twice*."

Trina dropped off her stool and stuck a finger in Bodkins's face. "That was a private conversation."

Bodkins shook his head. "Not when you're in a public place and especially not when you're a celebrity like Tony here. This is going to make headlines. Think I ought to get Naomi Stringer's take on this? Huh?"

Aika pulled Trina away. "No one will take this turd seriously, Trina. Let's go."

Tony slid off his stool and towered over Bodkins. "You are not a turd."

"Thank you, Tony," Bodkins said. "It's nice to know that *someone* here has manners."

Tony smiled. "A turd smells better."

Bodkins pushed by him.

"Do not misquote me on that," Tony said.

Trina laughed and hugged him. "You are so funny." She winked. "Let's get out of here."

"Yes," Tony said. "We must go."

Fewer paparazzi chronicled their walk to Trina's apartment building, and only one remained while Angelo and Aika waited for their taxi to arrive.

"We'll see you, what, around noon again?" Angelo asked.

"Let's play it by ear, Angelo," Aika said.

"Haven't we seen everything there is to see already?" Angelo asked.

"Not everything," Trina said.

"I want to go to Chinatown," Tony said. "It is supposed to be nice outside tomorrow."

"Good idea," Trina said.

"How about . . . seven-thirty?" Angelo asked.

"That's too early," Aika said.

"But that way I can make sure Tony gets a good breakfast for a change," Angelo said.

"Make it eleven or so," Aika said. "I want to sleep in."

Angelo sighed. "Okay, okay. Eleven." He turned to Tony as the taxi pulled up to the curb. "No messing around."

Tony said nothing.

"Did you hear what I said?" Angelo asked.

"I heard you," Tony said. "Good-night, Aika."

"Good-night, Tony," Aika said.

Angelo opened the back door, and Aika got inside. "*No* messing around," Angelo said, and he got in, closed the door, and the taxi rolled away.

On the way up to her apartment, Trina asked, "Why didn't you answer him?"

Tony smiled. "I did not want to lie to him."

*Oh, yes,* Trina thought. *We are messing around tonight.*

# 32

The second Trina closed the apartment door, Tony said, "I want to push your button."

"I need to wash my hair first," Trina said.

*I appreciate his enthusiasm—I really, really do—but how do I explain "I'm not in the mood yet because my hair is a wreck"? And what if I don't respond like I did before? I am wasted tired from the workout he gave me at the museum and the workout I witnessed at Johnny Foley's.*

"Okay," Tony said, looking at the floor.

"I'm going to need your help," Trina said.

"Okay," Tony said, smiling.

*He is so willing! Or am I manipulating him. Hmm. Maybe a little of both?* "I'm going to put on some different clothes first."

"I will wait in the bathroom for you," Tony said.

"I wash my hair over the kitchen sink," Trina said.

Tony blinked. "In the kitchen."

"Right," Trina said.

Tony wrinkled up his lips. "Not in the shower."

"No," Trina said.

"Okay."

Trina went into her bedroom and searched for something slinky to wear. She disrobed completely and put on some aqua-green panties and the orange and black flannel shirt. *These panties aren't exactly blue, but they'll have to do.* She unbuttoned the flannel shirt to her breastbone. *I am a mismatched woman about to have a man run his fingers through her hair.*

After getting the shampoo and conditioner and two towels from the bathroom, she went to the kitchen sink and ran some hot water mixed with a little cold water.

"I want you to stand behind me," Trina said. "I'm going to wet my hair first." She spread out the towel on the sliver of counter in front of the sink. "I want you to get close to me to make sure I get all my hair wet."

"Okay."

Tony moved closer.

*That's the way to do it,* Trina thought. *Get all up in my booty.*

She put her head under the faucet and soaked her hair. "Is it all wet?"

Tony moved even closer. "Yes."

*He's practically splitting my booty in two!* "Fill your hands with shampoo." She heard a long squirting sound. "Now work it into my scalp. If you need more shampoo, just add more."

"Okay."

Trina nearly fainted when Tony vigorously worked the shampoo into her scalp. She felt his bulge grow when she reached back to grab his buttocks. "You're good at this."

"Thank you," Tony said.

"It is all soapy?" *Am I all juicy? Oh, yes.*

"Yes," Tony said.

"Rinse your hands."

He did.

"I'm going to rinse off now," Trina said. "Stay very close to me so you can see any suds I miss."

Tony pressed hard against her. "I am close."

*I feel you, man. Whoo. And I'm getting closer.* "See any suds?"

"On your ears," Tony said.

She rinsed her ears. "See any more?"

"No."

Trina took the towel now pinned to her chest and wrapped it around her head. She dried her face and arms off with the other towel. "Now I put conditioner in my hair. Would you like to do it?"

"Yes," Tony said. "How much?"

"As much as your hands can hold." She removed the towel from her head and leaned over the sink. She heard Tony squirting conditioner for a long time. "Are your hands full of conditioner yet?"

"Not yet," Tony said. "I have big hands."

Trina undid another button to accommodate Tony's big hands. "Just . . . work it into my scalp and make sure you cover every bit of my hair."

Tony worked it in.

Trina nearly fainted again. "That feels good." Trina wiggled her buttocks against Tony. *And that feels big.* "Are you working it in?"

"Yes," Tony said. "It is slippery."

*You're telling me!* She undid one more button. "What do you see back there?"

"I see your hair, your neck, and your breasts," Tony said. "Your nipples are sticking out."

*Because this counter is cold!* "Are you peeking down my shirt?"

"Yes," Tony said.

"Do you like my breasts, Tony?" Trina whispered.

"Yes," Tony said.

"Have you worked all the conditioner into my hair?" Trina asked.

"Yes," Tony said.

"Rinse your hands."

Tony did.

"I have to wait a few minutes, and then I have to rinse out all the conditioner," Trina said. "And *then* I have to blow-dry it." She turned to face him and undid the last button.

"Your nipples are pointy," Tony said.

"Because the air is cold," Trina said.

"I will warm them," Tony said, and he covered her breasts with his hands.

*Where'd my breasts go?*

"Are they getting warmer?" Tony asked.

"Yes," Trina said. *And so is this room.* "I'm going to rinse now. Make sure all the conditioner disappears, okay?"

"May I still keep your breasts warm?" Tony asked.

"Yes," Trina said. "Don't let go of them." She turned and rinsed off her hair while Tony's hot hands squeezed and caressed her breasts. "Is all the conditioner gone?"

"Yes," Tony said.

Trina stood and dried her hair with the towel, Tony's hands firmly gripping her breasts. *I have a pair of man's hands where my breasts used to be.*

"Your breasts are soft and warm," Tony said.

"You can let go now," Trina said.

Tony removed his hands.

"Let's go to the bedroom so I can blow-dry my hair."

"Okay."

Trina dried her hair with a blow dryer, combing it out with her fingers, her shirt open, her forehead and nose sweaty.

"I am growing, Trina," Tony said. He looked down at his crotch.

Trina smiled. "How am I exciting you?" *So much! He's going to rip his pants!*

"Your shirt is open and I see your breasts and your nipples are sticking out and you have sweat on your forehead and your legs are naked and your panties are wet."

*Just hearing Tony saying all that excites me, too!* "And what do you want to do about it?"

"I want to push your button," Tony said.

"And what else do you want to do?" Trina whispered.

"I want to put my erect penis into your moist vagina," Tony said. "It is time, Trina."

Trina turned off the blow dryer. "Yes, it is." She threw back the covers, removed her shirt and panties, and parted her legs.

Tony took off his pants and underwear. "Tell me what to do."

"First we'll need a condom," Trina said.

Tony blinked. "I do not have a condom."

*Neither do I. Hmm.*

"Why do we need a condom?" Tony asked.

"Um, well . . ." *I shouldn't be worried about STDs with Tony since he has never been with another woman, but he* could *get me pregnant. Would that be so bad?*

"I will go get a condom," Tony said.

*I have a feeling we'd need a full box, and I don't want to wait any longer!* "No, it's okay." Trina stretched out her arms. "Come down here."

Tony crawled onto the bed. "I am excited, Trina."

"So am I." She hooked her legs around his thighs and felt the tip of his penis rubbing against her vulva. "You have never done this with another woman before, right?"

"I have never done this before," Tony said. "Tell me what to do."

"You're doing it, Tony," Trina said, and she guided him inside her. *That's . . . that's gooooood . . .*

Tony moaned and thrust several times. "Oh, Trina. I am coming."

*I want to cry! A man came the second he was inside me.*

Tony pushed himself up and looked down between Trina's legs. "I am a part of you, Trina. I see white and brown. It feels like a hand is holding me."

She pressed on his back. "You don't have to stop moving."

"I will not stop." Tony started a slow grind. "Am I doing it right?"

*Hell yes!* "You have a nice rhythm."

Tony smiled. "The bed is making noise."

"Are you going to write a song about this?" *Please say yes!*

"No," Tony said. "This music will stay in my head." He thrust deeper and looked down. "It is almost all the way in."

*That thing will never go all the way in.* "Don't stop."

He moved back slightly and picked up her legs. "I am going in and out of you."

"Yes," Trina whispered.

"You did not have an orgasm when I did," Tony said.

"It's . . . different this way," Trina said. "It takes me longer, unless . . . unless you press my button."

Tony used his right thumb to make small circles on her clitoris. "Like this?"

"Yes," Trina whispered.

"You are very wet," Tony said. "I hear squishing sounds."

"Because you're making me wet," Trina moaned. "You are exciting me."

"I do not know how," Tony said. "Tell me how."

Trina propped herself up on her elbows. "Your penis is thick and long and fills me completely. Your fingers are soft and smooth. Your muscles are big and well-defined. You're rubbing my clitoris. You're looking into my eyes. You're holding my legs tightly. Everything that's happening excites me." *Oh, shit, here I come!* She grabbed his buttocks and pulled him deep inside her. "Oh, Tony. Yes! Oh, yes!"

Tony slid his hands down her legs under her buttocks. "Oh Trina, I am coming, too."

*Oh, I'm going to be so sore tomorrow.* "Please kiss me, Tony," Trina whispered.

Tony pressed his lips against hers.

Trina shot her tongue into his mouth and tried to suck Tony's tongue out of his head.

Tony pulled back. "Your tongue danced with my tongue."

Trina smiled. "I was wrestling with your tongue, not dancing."

Tony looked down. "Where is my sperm?"

Trina turned him until she was on top. "It's inside me now."

"To make a baby," Tony said.

*My last period was . . . two weeks ago. I think.* "Maybe." She lay flat on his chest.

Tony rubbed Trina's back. "I am happy, Trina."

Trina closed her eyes. "I am happy, too, Tony." *I will never be lonely again. And he's still hard! How is this possible? He's still hard inside me.* "Tony?"

"Yes?"

"Do you really want to go to Chinatown in the morning?"

"Yes," Tony said. "I know all the streets."

"What if I want to stay here with you?" Trina asked. *And do this some more.*

Tony smiled. "Chinatown will still be there if we stay here."

She sat up and started to grind. "You're right." She braced herself on his chest. "Tony?"

"Yes?"

"Your penis is, um, still hard," Trina said.

"Yes," Tony said.

"This isn't normal," Trina said.

"I am doing something wrong," Tony said.

"Oh, no," Trina said. "You're not doing anything wrong. You're doing everything right. It's just that . . . after most men have an orgasm, they stop being hard."

"I am not most men," Tony said.

"No, you're not." She arched her back and moved her legs forward. "You are by far the best lover I have ever had." She pulled Tony's hands to her breasts.

"You are the only lover I have ever had," Tony said.

*Oh, this is so good! And we're talking while we're having sex.* "What goes through your mind when we're . . . making love?"

"There is so much," Tony said.

"What do you see?"

"I see your eyes and your teeth and the palms of your feet and your mouth and your breasts and your nipples and your firm brown buttocks and your vagina and your stomach and your legs and your button and your tongue."

She plunged down and stopped. "You see all that?"

"Yes," Tony said. "And I see gold and brown and tan and dark brown and black and white. I hear your breath. I hear your whispers. I hear your sighs. I hear your body moving against mine. I hear your moans. I smell your hair. I smell your sweat. I smell your vagina. I smell your breath. I taste your lips, your tongue, and your skin. I feel your hot skin. I feel your sweat. I feel your silky hair, your buttocks, your breasts, and your pointy nipples."

*He uses all of his senses to make love to me. I wish I could do that.* "Do you see, hear, smell, taste, and feel all that now?"

"Yes."

"It sounds intense," Trina said. *And I want more intensity.* She eased off of him and turned around, resting on her knees and her elbows. "What do you see now?"

"I see your firm brown buttocks and your vagina," Tony said.

*Oh geez. Talk dirty to me, man.* "Do you like my firm brown buttocks?"

"Yes."

She felt him squeezing her buttocks fiercely.

"They are soft and firm brown buttocks," Tony said.

"Put yourself inside me."

She felt the bed shift. She felt his hands on her hips. She felt his penis entering her. "What do you feel when you press against my firm brown buttocks?"

"I feel your hot legs against mine," Tony said. "I feel my hands on your hot hips. I feel my penis going into and out of your vagina. I smell your hair. I smell your vagina. I taste the sweat on your back. And I hear . . ." He began pumping her rapidly. "The things I hear, Trina."

"What do you hear?" *He is crushing my booty!*

"I hear music, Trina," Tony panted. "I hear very loud drums. I want to shout, Trina."

She reached down and furiously rubbed her clitoris. "Go ahead and shout, Tony. I'm about to come!"

"Trina!" Tony yelled.

*Holy shit! Tony can yell, and now I'm . . .* "Yes, Tony! Oh yes!" *Don't . . . stop . . . pumping . . . me . . . please! I see rainbows, rainbows, rainbows!*

Tony's body continued to slap against hers until he moaned and plunged himself deep inside her. "Oh, Trina, oh, God, I am coming. . . ."

Trina collapsed onto the bed.

Tony eased out of her.

Trina turned over.

Tony covered her, his head on her shoulder, his eyes staring into hers.

"Tony?"

"Yes."

"I know I've only known you for a short time, but is it okay if I love you?"

"It is okay," Tony said.

"You are by far the easiest man on earth to love," Trina said. "And not just because you are the world's greatest lover."

"I am not the world's greatest lover," Tony said.

"You are to me," Trina said. "I have never felt . . . anything I just felt. And my heart feels so happy right now. I love you, Tony."

"I am glad you love me, Trina," Tony said. "I want to love you, too."

She kissed his lips tenderly. "I know you do, Tony."

"I do not feel love," Tony said.

"Even if you don't feel you love me, you do," Trina said. "I feel your love for me. And one day, you will feel love for me, too."

"I need more practice," Tony said. "I want to practice loving you for the rest of my life."

Trina held him tightly, a few tears spilling from her eyes.

*I hope we live until we're one hundred and fifty.*

# 33

Angelo stood in the bathroom doorway, watching Aika bathing in the golden tub at the Mark Hopkins.

*I am completely in love with that woman,* he thought. *She's agile, voracious, soft, and gutsy. She could be Italian. I was ready to seal the deal and ask her to marry me, and then Tony went AWOL with Trina.*

*Trina is not a bad woman. She cares about Tony, talks to him, listens to him, touches him, holds his hand—all the things Aika does for me.*

*Well, almost all of them.*

Angelo tightened the towel around his waist, opened the suite's main door, and picked up a copy of the *Chronicle.* He flipped through the pages until he saw four headlines staring at him in the entertainment section:

ART E. WOWS 'EM AGAIN AT JOHNNY FOLEY'S
"MUSIC SHOULD BE FREE" SAYS ART E.
ART E. STIFFS CIELO AZUL
ART E.'S GAL PAL FACES SUSPENSION

He stormed into the bathroom, put the seat down on the toilet, and sat.

"What's wrong?" Aika asked.

"A little bit of everything," Angelo said, reading the first story. "Tony's all over the news."

"And not in a good way," Aika said.

"This first story is decent," Angelo said. "About his performance last night. But these other three . . ." He shook his head. "They ain't good."

Aika squeezed the washcloth and dripped soap onto her breasts and stomach. "Start with the *least* not good one."

"The owners of Cielo Azul are pissed at Tony and us for ordering all that food," Angelo said.

Aika smiled. "It was a delicious prank, though."

"Yeah," Angelo said. "And that reporter at Johnny Foley's was true to his word. He ran what Tony said. 'Music should be free.' It's even in the headline."

Aika lifted a silky, sexy leg out of the water. "It will blow over."

"I don't know if it will," Angelo said. "He even quoted Naomi Stringer. Listen to what Naomi said: 'I don't sing for free, but if Art E. wants to *give* me his music, I have absolutely no problems with that.'"

"She's an airhead," Aika said.

"Yeah, but a well-paid airhead who pays us a great deal of money for Tony's songs," Angelo said. "I need to give her a call."

"Later," Aika said. "You promised you'd join me. The water is so warm."

"Let me tell you about the last story first," Angelo said. "It seems Trina is about to be suspended from her job."

Aika sat up. "Why?"

"I'll read it to you," Angelo said. " 'Art E.'s gal pal Trina Woods, an RN at Saint Francis Memorial Hospital, faces a disciplinary hearing this Monday for "dereliction of duty," according to nursing supervisor and disciplinary review board chair Ellen Sprouse.' According to this, Trina told her bosses she was sick the past three days when she obviously wasn't."

Aika laughed. "So?"

"So?" Angelo said. "She lied."

Aika sighed. "She wanted to be with your brother. There's nothing wrong with that."

"But she lied, Aika," Angelo said. "If she lies about this, she might be lying about other things. Why didn't she take some vacation time or something?"

"I'm sure she had her reasons, Angelo. Now please get into this tub with me and soap me up and down before I turn into a prune."

Angelo rubbed his eyes. "I'm not in the mood anymore."

Aika stood and grabbed a towel. "And suddenly, neither am I. It's not a big deal, Angelo."

"It is to me." He left the bathroom and called Naomi Stringer. "Hey, Naomi? It's Angelo."

"Put her on speaker," Aika whispered as she walked out of the bathroom drying her hair.

"Hold on a second, Naomi," Angelo said, covering the mouthpiece. "Why?"

"I like hearing her ditzy ass talk," Aika said. "I need to learn more ditz speak."

Angelo turned on the speaker. "How you doing, Naomi?"

"What's this I hear about Art E. giving his music away for free?" Naomi asked.

"The reporter took it all out of context, Naomi," An-

gelo said. "Tony said, '*Music* should be free.' He didn't
say, '*My* music will be free.' He was talking about music
in general, you know, musicians being free to make
music any way they want to."

"Oh," Naomi said. "So what about what he said a
few days ago about that 'Trina' song? He said it was
only for Trina. I want it."

"I haven't even seen any lyrics for that song yet,"
Angelo said.

"The tune was bangin'," Naomi said. "I want it."

"I have to look at the lyrics first," Angelo said. "I
mean, if it's called 'Trina,' it's probably about Trina.
You want to sing a love song to a woman?"

"Maybe," Naomi said. "I know it will sell. What else
does he have for me?"

"He's been writing so many songs," Angelo said.
"I'll try to take a look at his scribbles and I'll get back
to you."

"It's such a shame about Trina, though," Naomi said.

"What about her?" Angelo asked.

"About her losing her job," Naomi said. "I read it in
the *Daily News* this morning."

"Trina hasn't even gone in front of that review board
yet," Aika said.

"Who's that?" Naomi asked.

"My girlfriend, Aika," Angelo said.

"Hey, girl," Naomi said.

Aika rolled her eyes. "Hey, Naomi." She threw her
towel at Angelo and jumped onto the bed.

"It was on TV this morning, too," Naomi said. "Send
me those songs, Angelo. Bye."

Aika looked out the windows at the rain. "Maybe
Chinatown isn't such a good idea today." She rolled onto
her stomach. "So what are we going to do instead?"

Angelo tossed his phone onto the nightstand. "We're going over to Trina's apartment and get some answers from Trina."

"She lied to her boss," Aika said. "Everyone does it. I've done it a dozen times since I met you."

Angelo sat on the bed and rubbed her back. "You have?"

"When I was trying to leave in the morning and you had to *do* me one more time or you begged me to do that *thing* to you one more time," Aika said.

"I didn't beg," Angelo said.

"You said please," Aika said. "I have learned that when you say 'please,' you're begging."

"Well, what Trina did was different," Angelo said.

"How is it different? You wanted more time with me, and I wanted more time with you. Trina wanted more time with Tony, so she lied."

"Yeah, but you didn't get caught being healthy on national television," Angelo said. "And you're not currently in danger of losing your job." He bounced off the bed. "I'm getting dressed."

"Why? We told them we'd play it by ear. It's only eight o'clock. They're probably still sleeping or watching the weather or . . ." She smiled.

Angelo turned. "You know something."

"I don't know anything for sure, but I have a feeling they're doing what we *should* be doing on a rainy day," Aika said.

"How do you know this?" Angelo asked.

Aika walked on her knees to the edge of the bed. "It's just a hunch. But say they are. Is that such a bad thing?"

"Yes," Angelo said.

Aika rubbed her breasts on his back. "They're both adults. It's allowed in this country. Get over it."

"I can't," Angelo said. "I'm scared she's going to . . . take him away from me."

She turned him around and held him close. "You'll never lose your brother's love, Angelo. There's no chance of that ever happening. None. You saw him the other day. He stuck up for you when I called you an asshole and you *were* being an asshole. You have his back, and he will always have yours. There's a lot of you in his personality."

"Yeah," Angelo said. "The best parts."

"So maybe this is a good time to let him go. Let him have his own life so you can live yours. He has proven he can function and thrive without you."

"I have been his legal guardian for so long," Angelo said. He laughed. "You know what Angela told me? She told me Tony retained her husband Matthew as his lawyer. That's . . . almost normal, you know?"

"It is."

"I just wish this wasn't happening so fast," Angelo said. "I hoped this day would come, but this is happening *way* too fast. Do you really think they're sleeping together?"

"I hope so."

"You hope so?"

"Yes," Aika said. "And I hope they're falling in love, because if they are, we'll have more time for each other if Tony has someone devoted to him like that, and he is obviously devoted to her." She removed his towel and pulled him onto the bed, stroking him firmly until he was hard. She wrapped her legs around him. "Show me how devoted you are to me."

Angelo entered her. "Is this good enough?"

"Oh, that's good," Aika whispered. "Don't move. Let me do the work." She used her feet to pull him deeper inside her. "And if they're a couple and they didn't live with us, I could shout louder."

Angelo held her hands. "Yeah?"

"And I'd even let you get me pregnant so we can start a family of our own," Aika said louder. "You can start moving now."

Angelo began thrusting.

"Because despite your arrogance, rudeness, and anger, I believe that we can make some beautiful children together," Aika panted. "And I haven't taken any birth control in over a month."

Angelo smiled. "Will the baby be Italianese or Japalian?"

Aika gripped his buttocks. "Neither sounds very nice. We'll just call them ours."

Angelo plunged deeper. "Them?"

Aika arched her back and howled. "Twins run in my family, Angelo. I want to have two. These walls are pretty thick, aren't they?"

"I guess," Angelo said.

"So get to work and make me scream. . . ."

# 34

The ringing of Trina's phone woke Tony, so he silently left Trina's bedroom and the peacefully sleeping Trina to pick it up off the coffee table. "Hello?"

"Put Trina on the phone," a man said.

"She is asleep," Tony said.

"Put Trina on the phone now," a man said. "This is Robert."

"Hello, Robert," Tony said. "How are you?"

"Put *Trina* on the phone," Robert said.

"She is sleeping," Tony said. "She is very tired. May I take a message?"

"You can *take* the phone to Trina," Robert said. "It is very important."

Tony blinked. "I will have her call you back."

"No!" Robert shouted. "This is a matter of life and death!"

"Oh," Tony said. "I will wake her then."

Tony went into the bedroom and shook Trina's leg. "It is Robert." He put the phone into her hand. "It is a matter of life and death."

Trina covered the mouthpiece. "Why did you answer it?"

"I did not want the ringing to wake you," Tony said. He smiled. "We are still naked."

Trina nodded. "Yep."

"I will take a shower while you talk to Robert." He went into the bathroom and shut the door.

Trina sat up, located her pillow at the foot of the

bed—*how did that get there?*—and leaned back on the headboard. "What now, Robert?"

"You're losing your job, Katrina," Robert said.

*Geez! Word flies so fast in the medical community, and I'm sure Nurse Sprouse broke quite a few HIPAA laws to make sure it flew faster.* "I haven't lost my job, Robert. I go before the disciplinary review board on Monday."

"The story is in the *newspaper,* Katrina," Robert said.

*I'm in the paper. How did an internal hospital affair become public knowledge? ES had to have made a phone call. I'm impressed. She actually did some work at work yesterday.* "What did the paper say?"

"That you lied to your supervisor about being sick," Robert said.

"And?"

"You *lied* to a supervisor," Robert said. "That alone should be grounds for dismissal, Katrina."

"What about all the times I lied for your sorry ass when you were too wiped out from studying," Trina said. " 'Hi, this is Robert Allen's fiancée. He has a touch of the flu.' 'Hi, this is Robert Allen's wife. He has a stomach virus.' You could have been dismissed from med school if it weren't for my lying."

"Don't you care about your livelihood?" Robert asked.

*Once again, he didn't hear a word I said.* "Oh, so it's okay if I lie for you, but it's not okay if I lie for me."

"What have I always told you?" Robert asked.

Trina pulled a sheet up to her neck. "You have *always* told me so many forgettable things, Robert."

"I've told you that you'll have to work twice as hard as the white people at that hospital for them to see you as half as good," Robert said. "One slip up and you're gone."

"You are so full of bullshit, Robert," Trina said. "I work for a light-skinned *black* woman. How does this figure into your racist theories?"

"From the way you talked about her, I always thought Nurse Sprouse was white."

"You *met* her once," Trina said.

"And she looked white," Robert said.

"Whatever." Trina sighed. "Look, this is my first time ever before the disciplinary review board. I'll get a slap on the wrist or a formal reprimand or another petty write-up in my file. That's all."

"They're going to fire you, Katrina."

"No, they aren't." Trina yanked the sheet off the bed, wrapped it around her, and stood in front of her mirror. *Look at you all wild-haired and wild-eyed. It's a good look on you.*

"They *are,* Katrina," Robert said. "You've been too public with your alleged sickness. They're going to hammer you. They are going to make an example out of you."

"At worst I'll get a week's suspension." *And that will give me even more time with Tony. I like how this is working out.* "That's the worst they can do to me for a first offense."

"Why would the story be in the *Chronicle* then?" Robert asked.

*Ellen Sprouse hates me and likes breaking HIPAA laws, that's why.*

"Saint Francis has to lower the boom on you to save face," Robert said.

"You're so melodramatic," Trina said.

"I'm looking out for your best interests, Katrina," Robert said.

"Are you? Should I feel gooey inside for this sudden burst of humanity from you, Robert?"

"You were once my wife, Katrina," Robert said. "I still care about you."

"No, you don't," Trina said. "You're worried about how this will reflect on you. You're worried the people at General will look at you negatively since you have a lying ex-wife."

"Who is *sleeping* with someone she just met," Robert said.

"Ooh, concern for my career and now jealousy."

"So you *admit* you're sleeping with him," Robert said.

"Yes, Robert," Trina said. "We are having sex, and lots of it, and it is *good.* I have had more orgasms in the last twenty-four hours than you gave me in ten years."

"You've lost your mind with that . . . that . . ."

"His name is Tony," Trina interrupted, "and he's very sweet." *The first few times we made love he was, but once I got him worked up, he was quite beastly in bed. And he lasted each time longer than Robert ever lasted*—cumulatively *over our entire relationship. I told Tony to wait, and he waited. I told him to come, and he came. Tony is the perfect lover.*

"He's sweet because he has the mind of a ten-year-old," Robert said.

"He has a higher IQ than either one of us does," Trina said. "And I love him."

"You expect me to believe that?" Robert asked.

"No," Trina said. "But it's true. I love him."

"So you'll throw your career away for an autistic musician who can't love you back."

Trina left the bedroom and stood in the bathroom doorway. *Tony cleans himself so well and so efficiently in that shower. I have to join him soon.* "Will there be anything else?" *I have an ache that needs soothing and a booty that needs massaging.*

"Katrina, please be careful," Robert said.

*Sincerity, too? My ears must be stuffed up.* "Why?"

"Because . . . because I still have feelings for you," Robert said.

"Bullshit, Robert," Trina said. "How can you have something for me now that you never had before?"

"Katrina, please," Robert said. "I'm not going to beg."

"Beg for what?"

"Another chance," Robert said.

Trina returned to her bedroom and shut the door. "Oh my God! Does this mean she dumped your ass?"

"We had a mutual breakup, yes," Robert said.

Trina jumped onto her bed and did a happy dance. "It really sucks, doesn't it?"

"It was a *mutual* breakup," Robert said. "She went her way, I went mine, and now I see you on television and I remember what we were like when we were just starting out. Do you remember those days?"

"I'm trying to forget everything about you, Robert." She opened the bedroom door and saw Tony toweling himself off in front of the sink. *Shoot, Tony's done. He'll be brushing his teeth soon.*

"Katrina, I have a little pull around here," Robert said. "If you should lose your job at Saint Francis, I can talk them into giving you a position here at General. I'm sure it will be probationary, but you can work through that. And then we can resume our dream together."

"Our dream ended in *my* nightmare, Robert," Trina

said. "I have started a new dream, and it will never, *ever* involve you. I am blocking you forever from my phone now. Good-bye." *I know I can't do that because of my cheap phone, cheap company, and cheap plan, but Robert doesn't know it.*

She stepped into the bathroom. "I wanted to shower with you, Tony."

"I must brush my teeth."

Trina stepped into the shower, turned the hot water on full blast, and watched Tony brush his teeth. *Ooh, shake it, Tony. Turn this way. That's it. Look at that wonderful ass that worked me all night long.* She removed the shower head from its holder with her left hand and directed the spray on her clitoris. She slid her right hand between her thighs.

"I am watching you," Tony said as he brushed. "I see you in the mirror. You are pressing your button."

*Busted.* "But I'm watching *you* while I do this. You're exciting me."

Tony spat into the sink and rinsed the toothbrush. He turned to face her. "I will watch."

*Hot pulsing water, my finger going round and round, a man in a tiny towel watching me with a smile on his face, remembering what he did to me again and again last night . . .*

Trina nearly fell out of the tub during her climax.

"You are finished," Tony said.

"Yes," Trina said. *I have never felt so free sexually. Tony's curiosity is going to make me go to sleep every night in bliss.*

Tony helped her out of the tub and put his hands on her shoulders. "I will be waiting in the bedroom."

*He wants more?* "Um, sure."

Trina wrapped a towel around her, left the bathroom, and peeked through the window overlooking O'Farrell Street. *Geez, there's more media out there now than ever before. I'm sure they want me to talk about the hearing on Monday, but I won't give them the satisfaction. I'm going into my bedroom and give my man some satisfaction.*

She saw a taxi moving through the crowd.

Angelo and Aika got out.

Angelo pushed through the crowd.

*It's only nine-thirty!*

*We're not dressed!*

*And Angelo looks pissed!*

# 35

"Tony!" Trina yelled.

Tony came out of the bedroom fully dressed. "Yes?"

"You're dressed," Trina said, scurrying past him to her dresser, pulling open the drawer and taking out some underwear and a bra.

"Yes," Tony said.

"When you said you were in the bedroom, I thought you'd be naked." She leaped into her underwear and put on her bra. She found a pair of black socks and yanked them on.

"I like when you take off my clothes," Tony said.

"I'll do that later," Trina said, crawling over the bed to her closet. "Go . . . watch the weather or something. Hurry. Angelo and Aika are on their way up."

"Okay."

She snatched some blue jeans from a hanger and stepped into them. *I haven't fed him, I'm half dressed, the wire in this bra is scarring me, the bed is unmade, and these jeans are wrinkled.*

The knock on the door made her jump.

Yanking a red sweater over her head, she raced to the door, opening it with a smile. "You two are up early." *That was actually pretty smooth. I know my hair is a wreck, but at least it's clean.*

Angelo walked past her with a newspaper tucked under his arm and stuck his head into her bedroom.

*That was rude.* "Good morning, Angelo. Why good morning, Trina. How are you? Did you have a good night's rest? Why yes, thank you, Angelo, for being so polite."

Aika smiled. "He's in a bad mood," she whispered.

"Isn't that normal?" Trina asked.

Aika nodded. "Yes."

Angelo opened the newspaper in front of Tony and placed it on the coffee table.

*I am a headline,* Trina thought. *I've gone from a nothing nobody to a headline with a picture of me at Johnny Foley's, and it's not very flattering. I look mean. I was tired, geez.*

"Read that," Angelo said, pointing at the "Art E.'s Gal Pal" article.

Tony picked up the paper, read the article, and put the paper down.

"So?" Angelo said.

Tony stared at the weather. "I read it."

Angelo sat beside Tony. "What did it say?"

"Trina lied," Tony said.

*Oh no!* Trina fell back against the closet door.

"What do you think of Trina now?" Angelo asked.

"I like her," Tony said.

"What I mean is," Angelo said, "can we trust her?"

"I can trust her," Tony said.

Trina pushed off the door. *Thank you, Tony.*

"How can you trust her, Tony?" Angelo asked.

"Trina lied so she could be with me," Tony said. "I am glad she lied. It shows she cares about me."

*I know Angelo isn't done yet,* Trina thought. *He can't be done. His eyes are still on fire.*

"But she broke a bunch of rules," Angelo said.

"I break rules every time I play the piano," Tony said.

Angelo pointed at Trina. "She might lose her job because she broke those rules. Tony, Trina is in a *lot* of trouble."

"She will not lose her job," Tony said.

"She's in the newspaper, for Christ's sake!" Angelo yelled.

"It is not a good picture," Tony said.

"You're right, Tony," Aika said, sitting beside him. "They always seem to put the worst possible picture next to a negative story."

*I didn't look* that *bad,* Trina thought. *Did I?*

"Don't you get it, Tony?" Angelo said. "Because of you, Trina is about to lose her job. Because of you, she lied. Because of you, all those people are outside waiting to ruin her life."

Tony stood. "I will go talk to them."

Angelo reached up and held Tony's wrist. "Oh no you won't."

Tony shook off Angelo's hand. "Yes. I will." He walked over to Trina, extending his hand. "Come with me, Trina."

Trina didn't take his hand. "I don't know, Tony. Your brother is right. It might not be a good idea to talk to them today."

"It is a good idea," Tony said. "I trust you, Trina. Do you trust me?"

"I trust you, Tony," Trina said. "I don't trust *them.*"

Tony grabbed Trina's hand and pulled her toward the door. "Let's go."

*He took my hand,* Trina thought. *He just snatched it up.* "Tony, I'm . . . I'm scared to go out there."

"I will keep you safe," Tony said.

"They're going to try to hurt me, Tony," Trina said.

"They will not hurt you," Tony said. "They cannot hurt you with their words."

"I know that, but . . ." Trina held his hand tightly. "They could hurt you."

Tony smiled. "They cannot hurt me. You said you loved me last night. Nothing can hurt me anymore."

"She did what?" Angelo shouted.

"Angelo, don't speak," Aika said. "Please don't say another word."

"She told him she loved him, Aika," Angelo said. "She's known him less than a week!"

"Because she *does* love him, Angelo," Aika said. "Can't you see that? Can't you feel that?"

"She said she loved him," Angelo said. "That's all. Anyone can say that."

"I cannot say 'I love you' and mean it," Tony said.

He held both of Trina's hands. "When you said I love you, I could not say it because I do not feel it in my heart. I can only feel love in my head. So now I want to use my head to show you my love."

Trina looked into Tony's eyes. "How?"

"By telling the shitheads outside the truth," Tony said. "Come on."

Trina laughed. "Their heads are not full of shit."

"Their heads are full of shit," Tony said. He turned to Angelo and Aika. "Then we can all go to Chinatown. I know all the streets."

Angelo stood. "You can't go out there alone."

"I am not going out there alone," Tony said. "I am going out there with Trina."

"I need to protect you, Tony," Angelo said.

"You must stay here with Aika," Tony said. "I cannot show her love, Angelo. Show her love. Show her love for me."

"They're out to get you, Tony," Angelo said.

"They cannot hurt me," Tony said.

"They're going to try," Angelo said.

"It is their job," Tony said. "My job is to protect Trina. I am going to show love for Trina now. Then we can go to Chinatown." He smiled at Trina. "Are you ready?"

Trina nodded. "Yes."

Tony winked. "Do not be scared. I will protect you."

# 36

"Tony, what do you think of your girlfriend losing her job?"

"Tony, are you giving your songs away for free?"

"Why did you stiff Cielo Azul, Tony?"

"Why'd you tell Kirk Tilton's mother to fire his piano teacher?"

*The wench went to the media about that?* Trina thought. *What an attention whore!*

Tony stood on the sidewalk and looked at the men and women in front of him. He stared at their tape recorders and cameras and microphones. He heard their shouts. He smelled the ocean. He tasted the toothpaste in his mouth. He felt Trina trembling beside him.

"Why won't you talk to us?" a reporter shouted.

"How do you feel about your girlfriend lying?" another asked.

Tony remembered stories the priest told at St. Paul's of how Jesus stood and said nothing. When a woman was caught in adultery, Jesus said nothing to her accusers. "He drew in the dirt," the priest said. "He could have had that dirt swallow up her accusers, but instead Jesus drew in the dirt." When Jesus stood before Pilate, He said nothing to His accusers. "Our Savior said nothing when with a *single* word He could have been delivered from His ultimate punishment," the priest said. "But Jesus said nothing."

Trina stood on tiptoe and whispered, "Are you going to say anything?"

"I am saying something," Tony said.

"By saying nothing," Trina whispered.

"Yes," Tony said.

*Smart man.* "I get it. But they don't."

"If they are quiet," Tony said, "they will hear me saying it."

"You might be waiting a long time," Trina whispered.

"I can wait," Tony said. "It is a beautiful day, and I am with you."

Trina gripped his hands tightly. "Thank you."

Tony made direct eye contact with reporters now, not widening his eyes. "Seas of faces, seas of spaces, no oasis, what's the basis for the human races," he mumbled.

The reporters quieted down.

"Hello," Tony said.

"Tony, what do you think of your girlfriend losing her job?"

"Why did Trina lie?"

"Do you believe piano teachers are worthless?"

Tony stared at the reporters in front of him. "Staring through him," Tony mumbled, "must unglue him, what land grew him, not a true him."

The entire crowd quieted down.

"I said hello," Tony said. "I do not know all your names or I would say hello with your name. I will try again. Hello."

A few reporters said hello.

"That is better." He smiled and looked into the sky. "Can you hear the birds now? They sing to us for free all day. We must listen to them. They have many words to say."

"Is he quoting song lyrics at us or what?" a reporter said.

"Shut up, man," another reporter said. "Let him talk."

"I came to San Francisco to meet Trina," Tony said. "I did not tell my brother Angelo I was going. I did not lie to him, but I did not tell him the truth. So, I lied, too."

*He's taking up for me,* Trina thought. *A man is taking up for me.*

"Angela and Matthew in Brooklyn helped me buy a plane ticket," Tony said. "Matthew rode with me in the taxi. It was the first time I was in a taxi. Katie helped me on the airplane. It was the first time I was in an airplane. It was the first time I was not in New York. Marie helped me find a taxi. Tino the taxi driver at the airport and Lily at Saint Francis Memorial Hospital here in San Francisco helped me. Jeanie and Terry the bellhop and Lu Chu who brought me food at the Huntington Hotel helped me. Natalya and Bea helped me at shoe stores. Carlos gave me a good haircut. Carmine made me laugh. William helped me with my new clothes. Hyun Ae made me a messy sandwich. Everywhere I go in Brooklyn and in San Francisco, people are kind. I am glad there is kindness in the world."

"What about your girlfriend?" a reporter shouted. "Do you think the disciplinary review board at Saint Francis will be kind to her?"

Tony smiled. "I saw Trina at Huntington Park. She looked up at the sun, and the sun turned her gold. I wrote a song for her. That is love. She rubbed her tired feet so I bought her shoes. Her feet do not hurt anymore. That is love."

*The first time Tony showed me love, I didn't know it was love,* Trina thought. *Now I know. I will never forget the lyrics to my song and I will never throw out the shoes he gave me.*

"Carlos gave me a good haircut and a shave," Tony said. "He talked to me. He gave me good advice. That is love. I tipped Carlos a thousand dollars. That is love. I tried to take Trina to Cielo Azul. The man did not believe me when I told him I was Art E. I do not blame him. I would not believe I was Art E. either. I am sorry I ordered all that food. I will pay them back for the trouble I caused. I will make it right. That is love."

Tony stared at the loudest reporter in the front row.

"I didn't have a question," the reporter said.

"You are listening instead of speaking," Tony said. "That is love, too. We went to Johnny Foley's to eat. Trina paid. She would not let me pay. Trina does not have much money, but she paid for me. That is love. I played the piano for Trina. I made her smile. That is love. People cheered for me when I played the piano at Johnny Foley's. That is love. Trina let me use her toothbrush. I left mine at the hotel. That is love."

Some reporters laughed.

"Trina gave me beef stew for breakfast," Tony said. "She told me to be careful, it's hot. That is love. She showed me the sights in San Francisco. We rode the cable cars. We looked at art. We watched the sea lions. We rode on a carousel. That is love. Trina taught me how to iron my clothes. That is love. She let me wash her hair. That is love. When I am nervous, she touches me and I calm down. That is love. I said that I would play for free tonight at Johnny Foley's. I said that music should be free. That is love. Trina said, 'I love you, Tony' last night. That is love. Today I read a newspaper story about Trina."

The reporters leaned in.

"Trina lied to her supervisor so she could be with me," Tony said. "That is love." He looked at the ground.

"Because I have Asperger's I cannot feel the same things other people feel. I cannot feel love. But I can show love. I have shown love for Trina today by talking to you. This is love."

*He may not feel it, but I sure do,* Trina thought. *Tony loves me.*

"We are going to Chinatown today," Tony said. "I know all the streets. If you come with us, you will not get lost." He looked up at Trina's front window and waved at Angelo and Aika. "We are going to Chinatown now."

*I will go anywhere with Tony,* Trina thought. *I will go everywhere with this man.*

# 37

Shown around the globe and translated into many languages, Tony's "That is love" speech struck some chords and plucked some heartstrings. Most of the media relaxed and simply reported instead of trying to make the news as they followed Angelo, Tony, Aika, and Trina around Chinatown.

The "Art E. Entourage" started at Grant Avenue and Bush Street at the Chinatown Gate, where stone lions guarded an entrance to Chinatown. Tony asked a Chinese woman what the Chinese characters on the gate meant.

"Peace, trust, respect, and love," she told him.

Tony smiled at her. "Trust in peace and respect love. Love peace and respect trust."

"Yes," the woman said. "You are right."

Then the entourage became tourists. They browsed the Chinatown Kite Shop, where Tony pronounced dragons "the fiercest flying warriors who play the notes with their wings." They posed for pictures in front of Chinese Hospital, where martial-arts legend Bruce Lee was born. They shopped at Dragon House, where Tony bought Trina a jade Chinese character symbolizing love. They ate sticky and garlicky sesame chicken with scallion pancakes and salt-and-pepper shrimp at the crowded House of Nanking on Kearny Street. They toured the incense-infused Kong Chow Temple, left a sizable donation, and learned that the color red warded off evil spirits, green symbolized longevity, and gold symbolized majesty.

"You are gold," Tony said to Trina. "You are a queen."

Trina kissed Tony often during the day.

Pictures of Trina and Tony appeared all over the Internet within minutes, and aside from several hard-core trolls, most of the comments were favorable: "They make a cute couple. . . . Those two are in love. . . . Her hair looks a lot better today."

At Portsmouth Square, Tony tried Tai Chi for the first time. At first he stumbled and looked awkward trying to mimic the tiny Chinese woman beside him, but once he felt the flow, he did fine. A photograph of Tony, Aika, and Trina doing Tai Chi appeared in newspapers as far away as Beijing.

Angelo begged off, citing an old high-school basketball injury.

Tony became instantly fascinated by men and women

playing Chinese chess, also known as *Xiangqi*. While two men played a speed version of the game and the press took hundreds of pictures, Tony studied the pieces and the moves.

"Like chess and not like chess," he whispered to Trina. "Like checkers and not like checkers."

Trina had difficulty following the lightning-quick action. "I don't get it," she whispered.

"Soldiers swim and then can move sideways," Tony said. "Soldiers can never retreat. Elephants cannot cross the river. Elephants can only move to seven positions. Horses cannot jump. Chariots are powerful. Cannons capture by jumping. Generals cannot face each other. Advisers cannot leave the palace."

"I still don't get it," Trina said.

"I will show you."

Once one man beat another, Tony sat in the loser's place. "I want to play. I am Tony Santangelo."

A wizened, wiry Chinese man nodded. "I am Tan Qin."

After the first move, Tony's and Tan Qin's hands moved so fast it was hard to follow the action. "Attack, attack, attack," Tony whispered continuously.

"Does he know what he's doing?" a reporter asked.

"Apparently he does," Trina said. "He's lasted a lot longer than the last guy did."

At one point Tony sat back and nodded his head. "Check," he said.

Tan Qin laughed. "You have surrounded my general." He extended his hand. "I am honored to lose to you."

Tony shook his hand. "You are very good at this game."

Tan Qin laughed louder. "Not today."

A man next to Angelo told him, "Your brother just beat a grand master. I have never seen Tan Qin lose."

"Are you sure Tony has never played this game?" a reporter asked.

"This is the first time," Angelo said. "I don't know how he does it. He learned chess in a day. That game looks harder."

Tony stood. "It is not hard. The pieces are like notes, and I played a melody with them."

Later that night at a cover-free, standing-room-only Johnny Foley's, Tony entered the Cellar and saw only one piano that was flanked by musicians with amplifiers, a man at a drum set, and several singers standing behind microphone stands. Mr. Kelly introduced Tony to his "accompaniment" for the night: Creedence Clearwater Revival guitarist John Fogerty; Grateful Dead drummer Mickey Hart and bassist Phil Lesh; jazz guitarist Calvin Keys; singer Tom Waits; jazz singer Faye Carol; and singer-actress JuJu Chan.

The press would call the ensemble "San Francisco's Finest plus One."

And they rocked Johnny Foley's as it had never been rocked before.

With Tony hammering away on the piano, the group recreated and redefined Led Zeppelin's "Ramble On" and "Nobody's Fault"; CCR's "Bad Moon Rising"; Jefferson Starship's "We Built This City"; the Pointer Sisters' "Slow Hand"; Sly and the Family Stone's "Dance to the Music"; and Journey's "Lights" and "Anyway You Want It."

Bootleg videos and audio CDs of this jam session

would number in the millions and "outsell" most genuine albums for the rest of the year.

Tony ended the night with Trina by his side on the piano bench in a soft golden spotlight. "I have finished your song," he said.

Trina smiled.

"For now," Tony said. "I am sure I will add many verses in the future." He kissed her cheek. "This song is called 'Trina.' . . ." And instead of singing, Tony chanted:

> If you *tell* me what is beauty,
> you might say this woman's booty,
> you might name a color or race,
> or you might show me a pretty face.

> But if you *asked* me what is beauty,
> it won't be a woman's booty,
> it won't be a color or race—
> it's sunlight's lace on Trina's face . . .

> Streams of gold shine all around her,
> I thank God that I have found her,
> I will remember this sunlight moment
> as long as I live, as long as I love . . .

> Streets of gold shine all around her,
> I thank the heaven that unbound her,
> I will remember her angel's face
> as long as I live, as long as I love . . .

As Trina rested her head on Tony's shoulder while the applause swelled around them, Tony said, "I love you, Trina."

Trina wept. "I love you, too, Tony."

Aika pulled Angelo away from the stage and into a dark corner, where she hugged him. "Tony just told her he loved her."

Angelo nodded. "I know."

"I think he's ready," Aika said. "Don't you?"

"He's ready." He kissed Aika tenderly. "I guess I had better call his lawyer. . . ."

# 38

Later at 2:00 AM, Tony sat with Trina on the purple couch, his arm around her shoulders, her head snuggling into his chest, while Angelo and Aika stood at the window, looking down on a few camera crews.

"Are you tired?" Trina whispered.

"Yes," Tony said. "But I am not sleepy."

Trina rubbed his chest. "Good."

Angelo left the window, moved the TV stand back, and sat on the coffee table. "Tony, look at me," he said.

Tony sat up straighter. "This is important."

"Yes," Angelo said. "This is important. I talked to Matthew a little while ago. I understand you hired Matthew to be your lawyer."

"Yes," Tony said. "I paid Matthew a retainer of fifty cents."

Angelo smiled. "Well, he couldn't legally be your lawyer before. We already had a family lawyer, but that's not what's important. I am going to pay Matthew five thousand dollars so he can officially be your lawyer."

"Okay," Tony said.

Trina sat up straighter and looked at Aika.

Aika nodded.

*Something big is happening,* Trina thought. *Something wonderful.*

"Matthew and I are going to work to release you from my care," Angelo said.

Tony stiffened. "You will not care."

"I'll never stop caring about you, Tony," Angelo said. "I can never stop caring about you. It's just the legal way for me to stop being your legal guardian. It's a way you can be your own man."

"I am my own man," Tony said.

"I know," Angelo said. "You've proved that, and now we're going to make it legal. You'll have immediate access to all the money you've earned and you can live wherever you want to." He smiled at Trina. "With whomever you want to. And if Trina is who you want and she wants you, then . . . that's good. That's fine by me. You have my . . . my blessing."

"You are not a priest," Tony said. "You cannot give me a blessing."

"I'm telling you," Angelo said, "that I'm okay with you . . . staying with Trina."

*Is this complete acceptance or is it more of a truce?* Trina thought. *I have to hug Aika. She had to convince Angelo to do this.*

"So, um, you can stay in San Francisco as long as you want to," Angelo said.

"I can live here with Trina," Tony said.

"If she lets you, yes," Angelo said.

"He has to stay," Trina said. "I will cry if you leave, Tony."

"I will not leave," Tony said.

Aika stood behind Angelo and put her hands on his shoulders. "The Castle," she whispered.

"And," Angelo said, "we'll be putting the Castle solely in your name so you and Trina could live there if you wanted to."

"Where will you live?" Tony asked.

"Aika and I will find our own place," Angelo said.

"No," Tony said. "I want you to have the Castle."

"Your money built it," Angelo said.

"But you built it for me, Angelo," Tony said. "I am giving it to you and Aika. I will need my piano first. And Silver. I do not need my rhythm machine. I am a rhythm machine now. And I will need all my notes and notebooks. And my map books."

"Of course," Angelo said hoarsely. "Right. All of that."

"If there is Hires Root Beer in the refrigerator," Tony said, "you can have it."

Angelo cleared his throat. "Yeah, we'll work all that out. And we'll also work out the next batch of songs you want to sell to Naomi. She really wants the 'Trina' song."

"It is only for Trina," Tony said. "Naomi can have other songs."

Angelo nodded. "I'll tell her."

"Tony, do you understand what Angelo is doing?" Aika asked.

"Yes," Tony said. "He is letting me be my own man."

"He is also giving you absolute freedom to go anywhere and do anything from now on," Aika said. "He won't be flying in an airplane to check up on you. He won't be telling you what to do and what not to do. You are going to make all your own decisions from now on. You won't even have to check in with him or call him to tell him where you are."

"I will still call him," Tony said. "He is my brother. I like talking to him."

Trina's eyes filled with tears. "I'll make sure you do."

Angelo stood and wiped his eyes. "We're going back to Brooklyn tomorrow, Tony. And I'm . . . I'm going to miss you, man."

"I will miss you, too," Tony said. "You can call me anytime you want to."

"You know I will," Angelo whispered. He swallowed hard. "You make sure you answer your phone when I call, okay?"

"I will not turn off the ringer," Tony said. He stood and extended his hand.

Angelo took his hand, pulled him fiercely to himself, and hugged him. "You're the best thing I ever did."

Tears streamed from Trina's and Aika's eyes.

Tony stood back from Angelo's embrace. "You are crying."

Angelo nodded.

"You are not happy," Tony said.

"Yes and no," Angelo said. "I'm sad to say goodbye, but I know you're in the best possible hands."

*That sounded like acceptance,* Trina thought. *Thank you, Angelo.*

"You can visit us any time you like," Tony said.

Aika stepped between Angelo and Tony, hugging him. "We will, Tony." She kissed his cheek. "Breakfast won't be the same without you."

Tony kissed Aika's cheek. "Wake up Angelo. He likes *SportsCenter,* too."

Aika pulled Trina to her feet and hugged her. "You are an amazing woman." She put her lips to Trina's ear. "And you can keep my underwear," she whispered.

Trina nodded. "Thank you." She looked at Angelo. "Thank you, Angelo."

Angelo nodded. "Take good care of him, okay?"

Trina stepped up to Angelo and hugged him. "I can't take care of him as well as you have, but I'm going to try. When he's not taking care of me." She kissed his cheek.

"That sounds fair," Angelo said. He took Aika's hand. "We, um, we better be going. We have an early flight."

"Good-bye, Angelo," Tony said. "Good-bye, Aika." He opened the door, and Angelo and Aika left. He closed the door. "I will miss them. I will miss them very much."

Trina took his hand and pulled him to the window. "So will I. We'll visit them often, okay?"

"Okay."

A taxi pulled up, Angelo opened the back door, and Aika got in.

Tony waved from the window.

Angelo waved.

"Good-bye, Angelo," Tony said. "I will miss you."

# 39

Tony sat unmoving on the couch, the television off, his eyes blinking rapidly.

Trina massaged his shoulders. "Are you okay?"

"I do not know," Tony said. "I am happy and I am not happy."

"How are you happy?" Trina asked.

"I am here with you," Tony said. "I will be here with you tomorrow, too. I will not worry that Angelo is taking me back to Brooklyn."

"You'll be here the day after that, too." She moved around the couch arm and sat in his lap. "And how are you unhappy?"

"Angelo and Aika will not be here tomorrow," Tony said. He sighed.

She held his face in her hands. "But that means we can sleep in without anyone knocking on that door and making us rush to get dressed."

"Yes," Tony said.

"And I can . . ." *Oh God, I hope I'm enough for this man.* "And I can . . . take care of you."

"I will take care of you," Tony said. He looked directly into her eyes. "I see you."

Trina stared back. "I see you seeing me."

"I am not scaring you with my eyes," Tony said. "I am not looking away."

"I know," Trina said.

"I am not looking away, Trina," Tony said. "I think it is love. I think love is looking someone in the eye and not scaring them."

Trina nodded. "That's a great definition of love." *Maybe the best one I've ever heard.* "Are you scared about being on your own?"

"I am not on my own," Tony said. "I am with you." He kissed her lips briefly. "I would like to make a snowflake child with you now."

"One for each knee," Trina said.

"Yes," Tony said. "But we will have to get a bigger house for hide-and-seek."

"It would be too easy to find our children here," Trina said.

"We would hear their laughter, and we would find them," Tony said.

"Isn't that the point?" Trina asked.

"Yes," Tony said. "That is the point. I will have to have my piano shipped to San Francisco. I would also like to go to the mountains. I have never been to the mountains. I would like to go to the beach here. I have been to Fire Island. It is nice. I want to learn how to surf at the beach here."

"We can go to the beach," Trina said, "when you take me to Los Angeles for the Grammy Awards. It's only a few weeks away."

"I have never been to the Grammy Awards," Tony said. "Angelo would not let me go."

"You can go now," Trina said. "You're your own man, right?"

"Yes," Tony said. "We are going to the Grammy Awards."

"So I can see you get your awards," Trina said.

"I have only one nomination this year," Tony said. "I will not win."

"How do you know?" Trina asked.

"You were not in the song," Tony said.

*He fills my heart with so many wonderful words!* "You say the nicest things."

"I like to say nice things to you," Tony said. "You smile when I say nice things."

"I have never smiled more," Trina said. She sighed. "But I might not be smiling too much on Monday, Tony. I might be losing my job."

"You will not lose your job," Tony said. "I will go with you to make sure."

Trina rubbed his arms. "You're not allowed in the meeting."

"I do not have to be at the meeting to make sure," Tony said.

"I appreciate your confidence, but I *did* lie, and I'm sure I'll be suspended for a while and not have enough money to pay some bills this month."

"I will pay them for you," Tony said. "I will also get you a new rain jacket."

*He is so practical!* "I want you to know I love you for you, okay?"

"I know you love me for me," Tony said. "You see how I am, and that is all I have to be."

"Right," Trina said. "I'm not a gold digger, am I?"

"You are gold," Tony said.

"I don't care how much money you have," Trina said, "as long as I have you to cuddle with and hold all night."

Tony blinked. "I do not know how much money I have. I must find out. Angelo will tell me." He dug his cell phone from his pocket and hit the number one. "Angelo, it is Tony. How are you? . . . I am okay. I need to know how much money I have . . . Okay. Thank you. Bye." Tony turned off his phone. "Angelo says I have around fifty million dollars."

Trina tried not to react, but she failed, her entire body shaking. "Fifty . . . million."

"Yes," Tony said. "Will that be enough for us to get a house?"

Trina nodded quickly. *Fifty . . . million. That's over . . . six hundred years of my salary.*

"Good," Tony said. "I want a big house with lots of hiding places for our children."

Trina tried to catch her breath. "I have to have a much bigger kitchen."

"I want lots of windows," Tony said. "We can watch the weather together without a television."

"Sure," Trina said. "You'll want a music room, too, right?"

"Every room in our house will have music in it," Tony said. "I want to look for a house now."

"It's two o'clock in the morning, Tony," Trina said.

"That is what the Internet is for, Trina," Tony said.

*Oh yeah!* Trina hopped off Tony's lap, got her net book, and returned to the couch. While it booted up, she asked, "How much do you want to spend on a house?"

"I do not know," Tony said. "I have never bought a house."

*Me neither.* She surfed to realtor.com and toyed with the first slider. "Um, could we spend . . ." Her finger grew moist. "A million?"

"I do not know," Tony said. "Let us find the house first."

*House first, cost second. This is how house-hunting should be done.* Then Trina did something she had never done on any Web site *ever*—she hit the HIGHEST TO LOWEST button.

*Wow. Thirty million.* She clicked on the 12,000-square-foot neomodern monstrosity. "What about this one?"

"No," Tony said. "I do not like the shape. It looks more like a turtle than a house."

She clicked back and saw a massive brick house on Franklin Street in Pacific Heights—*only a mile away from here!*—for ten million. "What about this one?"

"That is the one," Tony said.

"It's, um, it's ten million dollars, Tony," Trina said. "Do we really need something this big?"

"Yes," Tony said, clicking on the house. "It was built in 1900," he said. "That means it survived the 1906 earthquake. It is close to the cable cars."

*Ten thousand square feet, twenty-five times the size of this little apartment. Eight bedrooms, four and a half baths!*

"It has four stories," Tony said. "And a library for my map books."

*Six fireplaces, a state-of-the-art chef's kitchen opening to a spacious deck.* "It even has a guest kitchen and an apartment with a separate entrance, Tony."

"For when Aika and Angelo visit," Tony said. "It has an elevator, too. I like elevators."

"Walking distance to Whole Foods, restaurants, and Lafayette Park," Trina said. "It sounds perfect, Tony, but it costs ten million dollars."

"I want to look at the slide show," Tony said.

They watched forty-six pictures go by.

*Oh, this is a magnificent house! Look at the high ceilings! The crown molding! The pocket doors! A huge sit-down shower! Oh, and the views from the top floor are inspiring!*

"Do you like it, Trina?"

*Oh yes!* "I love it, but it's—"

"I will buy it for you," Tony interrupted.

"But we don't need ten thousand square feet, Tony," Trina said.

"You said you loved it," Tony said. "I like it. We will buy it."

"Are you sure?" Trina asked.

Tony nodded. "I watched your eyes while we looked at the pictures. They were happy. They were a child's eyes. I want to give you this house."

Trina hugged him. "I want you to give me this *home.*" She kissed him. "We can call the Realtor Monday to see if it's still on the market."

"Yes." Tony settled back into the couch. "And we will move in on Tuesday."

"Um, let's see how Monday goes first," Trina said. "It takes time to close on a house." *Or so I've heard.*

"If I pay ten million dollars," Tony said, "they will give me the house on Monday."

"I don't know about that," Trina said. "And I wouldn't offer them the asking price anyway."

Tony pointed at the screen. "This is the price of the house."

"That's the starting point for negotiations," Trina said. *As if I know anything about this.* "We'll put in a lower bid and see what happens."

"A lower bid," Tony said.

"Yes," Trina said. "Something less than ten million dollars. Say we offer nine million, and they drop it to nine million eight, then we offer them nine million two—"

"We will offer fifty cents," Tony interrupted.

Trina laughed. "For a ten-million-dollar house?"

"If they come down fifty cents, and we go up fifty cents," Tony said, "we will meet in the middle at five million."

*I can't fault his logic, but . . .* "We might offer, say, eight million in order to get nine."

"I like my way better," Tony said.

*So do I, but no one is going to part with a 10,000-square-foot house in pristine condition in Pacific Heights for five million dollars.* "Let's fill out this interest form and try to set up a tour for Monday. That way we won't have to call them at all, okay?"

"Okay."

Trina swung the netbook toward her. "What should I put for name?"

"Tony and Trina," Tony said.

"Um, you're the one buying the house," Trina said. Trina added "Art E." as Tony's middle name. "So they take us seriously," Trina said. "What time should I tell them?"

Tony blinked. "I do not know."

"How about eleven?" Trina asked.

"Okay," Tony said.

Trina listed both her and Tony's cell phone numbers and sent the e-mail. She held his hand. "Promise me you'll always dream with me like this."

"I promise to dream with you," Tony said.

"Do you want me to promise you anything?" Trina asked.

"Promise to teach me new things," Tony said.

"Like what?" Trina asked.

"Like how to cook beef stew or how to make sheets soft or how to make a bathtub shiny or how to wash dishes or how to give you more orgasms or how to wash clothes or how to drive a car or how to swim—"

"Hold up," Trina interrupted. "You want me to teach you how to give me *more* orgasms?"

"Yes," Tony said. "I want you to teach me other ways. I know if I press your button or you press your button or you put shower water on your button you will have an orgasm."

Trina stood and dragged Tony to the bedroom. "I'm going to teach you another way."

Tony took off all his clothes in less than ten seconds. "I am ready."

*Having a gorgeous naked man in front of me certainly helps our lesson.*

"Take off your clothes, Trina," Tony said.

*And having a man asking me to take off my clothes helps, too, but not as much as having him take them off for me.* "I want you to take off my clothes."

Tony unzipped her pants and pulled them down.

"Slowly, Tony," Trina said. "Build up some anticipation."

"How slowly?" Tony asked.

She bent down, pulled up her pants, and zipped her fly. "I'll talk you through it."

"Okay."

She closed her eyes. "Unzip my pants." She heard the zipper and felt his fingers. "Remove my pants a little at a time." She felt his fingers tugging at her pants, felt his fingers sliding down her thighs and calves. She felt Tony pick up one foot and then the other. "Stand up and unbutton my shirt from the top down. Count to . . . five between buttons." She felt his hands and fingers on her chest and then her stomach. "Take off my shirt." She felt his hands on her arms and shoulders. "Undo my bra and throw it somewhere." She felt his fingers on her back and heard the bra hitting the wall. "Now using only your teeth, take off my underwear."

Trina felt nothing for a solid minute.

She opened one eye and looked down. "Um, are you okay down there?"

"I am analyzing the problem," Tony said. He nodded. "Turn around."

*Gladly.* Trina closed her eyes, turned around, and felt hot hands on her legs, felt little nibbles at the tops of her buttocks, felt a nose go between her buttocks, felt herself getting moist as her underwear slid down her legs. One foot rose and then the other. "Lead me to the bed." She felt Tony's hand grab hers until her thighs contacted the edge of the bed. She reclined, resting her head on a pillow. "Now . . . spread my legs as wide as you can." She felt his hot hands gripping her ankles, and she started to pant. "Now put your tongue on my button."

"Small circles or big circles?" Tony whispered.

"Oh, it doesn't matter," Trina said. "Circles, lots of circles." She felt the tip of Tony's tongue on her clitoris.

"Your button is hard," he whispered. "It does not hurt."

"No," Trina whispered, reaching down and holding on to Tony's hair.

"I am sorry I keep asking questions," Tony said.

She felt his tongue making small circles. "Don't be." She felt him stop.

"How will I know you have had an orgasm this way?" Tony asked.

"I will pull your hair and try to strangle you with my thighs," Trina groaned. *Just don't keep stopping like that!*

"You will strangle me," Tony said.

"I'm going to try to," Trina whispered. "And when I do, that's when you spread my legs even wider and put yourself deep inside me, okay?"

"Okay."

Tony's tongue returned. Trina hummed Aaliyah's "Rock the Boat," and as she bucked her hips and cried out, she felt something hard and massive enter her. "Don't stop, don't stop . . ."

"You did not strangle me," Tony said.

"I'd be crazy if I did that, Tony," she said, reaching up and clawing at his chest.

"I am very deep," Tony said. "It does not hurt."

*It does a little, but I don't want to explain that to him now.* "Just . . . don't stop."

"I will not stop," Tony said, and he made the bed rock.

*Oh, I hope we're making a snowflake child to play hide-and-seek with in our new ten-million-dollar home.*

*And even if we aren't, we are going to rock this bed all night long.*

# 40

After spending most of Sunday in bed, interrupted only by a long shower and a quick trip to Brooklyn Pizza on Jones Street for Philly cheesesteak sandwiches and a large New York Specials pizza, and after another night of fierce and passionate bliss, Trina and Tony walked hand in hand through a gantlet of reporters in front of Saint Francis Memorial Hospital at 6:30 AM on Monday morning.

"Trina, how does it feel to be almost unemployed?"

"How does it feel to throw away your career?"

"Will you be going to the Grammys, Tony?"

"Trina, are you wearing the shoes Tony bought you?"

"Tony, how does it feel to be dating a liar?"

*I want to tell them I'm in love with Tony,* Trina thought. *I want to tell them I will miss this job so much. I want to tell them I will miss helping people with the wonderful people here. I want to tell them about the snowflake children we've been trying to make. I want to tell them I lied for love, but they'll only twist my words into more lies.*

"You are saying nothing," Tony said.

"I have learned a thing or two from you," Trina said.

"I am not a teacher," Tony said.

"You're the best teacher I've ever had," Trina said. "You've taught me that silence is loudest sometimes."

"Silence is very loud today," Tony said.

They entered the hospital and rode the elevator up to the fourth floor. When the elevator doors opened, a crowd of smiling and cheering nurses blocked their exit.

Trina hugged Naini and several of the other "dark" nurses. "What are you all doing here?"

"We are here to give you moral support," Naini said. "We are all rooting for you."

"Thank you," Trina said. "Thank you all." She pulled Tony out of the elevator. "This is Tony."

"Hi, Tony," the nurses said in unison.

"Hello," Tony said, his eyes looking around them.

*Is he blushing?* Trina thought. *My goodness! His cheeks are red. This has to be a first.*

One nurse took a quick picture of Tony with her cell phone. "Sorry," she said. "I couldn't resist."

Tony smiled. "It is okay. I hope Trina is in the picture, too. It is only a good picture if Trina is in it."

"Aww," the nurses cooed.

Tony blushed again.

"You should really get back to work," Trina said, taking Tony's hand and moving toward a door marked with a DISCIPLINARY REVIEW BOARD IN SESSION sign. "ES is on the other side of this door," she whispered. "I'll try to keep her occupied for as long as I can."

All the nurses but Naini scattered down the hallways. "I will be thinking of you." She hugged Trina tenderly, squeezed Tony's free hand, and left.

Tony blinked. "Naini hugged you with her whole body. Does Naini love you?"

"As a friend," Trina said. "She's nervous for me, Tony. Sometimes women hug each other like that to calm themselves down."

"Are you nervous?" Tony asked.

"Not if you're out here waiting for me when this is over," Trina said.

Tony's phone rang. "I do not recognize the number," he said.

"It could be the Realtor," Trina said. "Answer it."

"Yes, I am Tony Santangelo. . . . Yes, I play the piano. . . . Trina Woods will be with me. . . . Eleven o'clock today. I will see you then." He put his phone into his pocket. "We will go look at our house at eleven o'clock today."

*Yes! Our house!* "I don't know how long this will take, but I hope not long. Why don't you wait in the lounge at the end of the hall?" She gave him some change. "You can get something from the vending machine."

"Okay." He kissed her cheek.

Trina sighed. "Wish me luck."

"I wish you luck." Tony winked.

Trina smiled. "You winked at me, Tony."

"I must try to keep this relationship fresh."

She draped her arms around his neck. "After this weekend, we can only get fresher." She kissed him on the chin. "I'll see you soon."

"Okay."

Trina opened the door and walked toward a single white plastic chair in front of a long metal table, three ancient and balding white doctors sitting at attention on either side of Nurse Sprouse.

*Oh, this is fair. There's not a single person of color in here, ES included, and not a single real nurse.* Trina sat. *Let's get this over with. I have to go see my new house at eleven.*

"Before we begin, Miss Woods, do you have anything to say?" Nurse Sprouse asked.

*Oh now it's "Miss" Woods. The truth shall set me free? I doubt it, but here goes.* "I was not sick when I said I was, and I am sorry." *I've admitted my faults, now give me the punishment so I can get out of here and get down to Franklin Street.*

"Anything else, Miss Woods?" Nurse Sprouse asked.

"No."

"No explanation for *why* you lied to me," Nurse Sprouse said.

*I knew she couldn't let me get away that easily.* "I don't owe you that explanation. You wouldn't understand it anyway. Are we done here? Pass your verdict, give me your judgment, and send me on my way."

"What wouldn't I understand, Miss Woods?" Nurse Sprouse asked.

*Should I even care? I should. I have a lot of other nurses rooting for me.* "You wouldn't understand love, *Miss* Sprouse."

"Does this mean you were absent because you were lovesick?" Nurse Sprouse cackled to the doctors around her.

The doctors didn't crack any smiles.

*Are the doctors even alive? We may need a crash cart in here.* "I wasn't lovesick, Miss Sprouse. Not at the time. Love came a few days later."

"You're not making sense, Miss Woods," Nurse Sprouse said. "As usual."

"To *you,*" Trina said, looking at the doctors. "I don't know the rest of you, so I can't say you don't understand. I do know, however, that Miss Sprouse does not know what love is. She doesn't have a single clue." Trina leaned forward in her seat. "You see, gentlemen, it takes *love* to do this job."

"You obviously didn't *love* your job enough to follow all the rules and regulations," Nurse Sprouse said. "You obviously didn't *love* this job enough to tell your supervisor the truth. You obviously didn't *love* this job—"

"I already admitted I lied," Trina interrupted. "I will accept any punishment this board gives me. But I will not take any more punishment from you today, Miss Sprouse. I get enough of that on a daily basis." *And so do the women who sneaked off to wish me well this morning. I think I owe them a fight.*

"I do not punish you, Miss Woods," Nurse Sprouse said. "And I resent you saying that."

"And I resent *you*, Miss Sprouse." Trina smiled. "By the way, how many HIPAA laws did you break in 'leaking' the story to the press?"

Nurse Sprouse looked away. "I have no idea how the *Chronicle* got the story."

*Who's lying now? Should I continue this line of questioning? No. Let's get back to love so we can confuse ES some more.* "Gentlemen, I love this job. I love coming to work. I love helping patients. I loved a man enough to work double-shifts here to pay for his medical school. I still work two hours a night in the ER when I could be home resting my aching feet. I love working here at Saint Francis."

"All that is immaterial to these proceedings," Nurse Sprouse said. "Is the board ready to discuss—"

"I'm not through, Miss Sprouse," Trina interrupted.

"I asked earlier if you had anything more to say, and you said no."

*I thought I didn't. If I'm going to get in trouble, I have to get in trouble on my own terms.* "I had nothing more to say about what I *did*. I do have more to say about what I *do*." She scanned the doctors' expressionless faces. "Miss Sprouse has assigned me and many of my fellow dark-skinned nurses—Indian, Pakistani, Indonesian, Filipino, and of course, African and African American—the *worst* possible jobs at this hospital ever since she became nursing supervisor three years ago."

"I most certainly have not!" Nurse Sprouse squawked. "There is absolutely no truth to what she is saying!"

*Ooh, now she has some color in that light-skinned face of hers.* "While we 'colored' nurses empty bedpans, colostomy bags, do transport, and assist patients in going to the bathroom, Miss Sprouse's legion of 'white' nurses walk around with clipboards and pens and take extended coffee breaks and sit in the lounge for hours at a time gossiping and do everything they can to avoid actually doing any work."

"These are all lies, gentlemen, I assure you," Nurse Sprouse said. "These are lies from a liar."

"If I could, I'd bring all the nurses into this room and I'd say: 'Raise your hand if you've ever emptied *one* bedpan.'" Trina raised her eyebrows. "You would see a *forest* of dark hands go into the air. Walk around this hospital sometime. You will *see* the darker nurses much more often that you will *see* the lighter nurses. You will see the darker nurses actually working. They will not be *looking* busy—they *are* busy. They won't be rushing around the hallways to avoid work—they will be rushing around to go *to* work. If it weren't for us, this hospital would fall apart."

Nurse Sprouse shook her head. "Miss Woods is completely incorrect and has no proof of these unseemly accusations. She's just angry that she was passed over for the nursing supervisor position three years ago when I was hired."

"I'm not angry about that at all," Trina said. "If having your job would turn me into *you*, I'm glad I was passed over. I'd rather be of *use* to this hospital."

"Are you saying that I'm unqualified for my position?" Nurse Sprouse asked.

"No," Trina said. "I'm saying you're *useless*. I'm saying you're unqualified to be a nurse."

"I'll have you know—"

"Did you do a cursory exam on me when I told you I was sick?" Trina interrupted.

"What does that have to do with anything?" Nurse Sprouse asked.

*I need to show the board how incompetent you are.* "I know I lied about being sick," Trina said, "but as a nurse, Miss Sprouse, why didn't *you* do a quick exam on me?"

Two members of the board turned their heads toward Nurse Sprouse. The other four remained semicomatose.

"I took your word for it," Nurse Sprouse said, "which you have just admitted were lies. I will no longer take your word for anything."

Trina smiled. "What did you sign me up to do instead?"

"A refresher course on blood-borne pathogens," Nurse Sprouse said.

Trina cocked her head and squinted. "How did you make *that* determination if you didn't do a cursory exam?"

"Once again, I took your word for your illness," Nurse Sprouse said. "You were in the bathroom. That says diarrhea."

*What an idiot!* "And what *dangerous* blood-borne diseases are indicated by diarrhea, Nurse Sprouse?"

Nurse Sprouse closed her mouth.

Another doctor turned his head toward Nurse Sprouse.

"I'll refresh your memory," Trina said. "Only one blood-borne disease is indicated by diarrhea, and that is hemorrhagic fever, *Nurse* Sprouse. It's not hepatitis B, C, or HIV. If you *really* thought I had a blood-borne disease and if you knew that *only* hemorrhagic fever was indicated by diarrhea, why did you let me go home without an exam?"

"Because . . . because I took your word as another

nurse," Nurse Sprouse said. "But that's not *all* that this hearing is about. You have been derelict in your duty. You have been playing hooky from your job with your boyfriend the musician."

Trina sighed and smiled. "That's because I love him."

"And it's going to cost you today," Nurse Sprouse said. "Is the board—"

"I have worked here for ten years," Trina interrupted. "Until two weeks ago, I hadn't missed a single day. That's twenty-five hundred straight days without an absence of any kind. I have obviously kept myself healthy at a place where sick people come to get well, and unlike *Nurse* Sprouse, I am around these sick people all day. I even come into physical contact with them. I actually touch them. So, on the basis of one extended visit to the bathroom, *Nurse* Sprouse, you assumed *without* examining me that I had some blood-borne sickness which could *only* be hemorrhagic fever."

"You needed the refresher course on blood-borne pathogens anyway," Nurse Sprouse said. "All nurses are required to take that course once a year."

"I took it three months ago," Trina said. "Has the world of blood-borne pathogens changed so drastically in the last ninety days to warrant an *annual* refresher course only three months later?"

Nurse Sprouse narrowed her eyes. "The field of medicine is constantly changing, Woods."

*Where's the "Miss" now?* "*You* aren't changing, Nurse Sprouse. When's the last time you even *spoke* to a patient?"

"I am the nursing *supervisor*," Nurse Sprouse said. "I *supervise* nurses."

"You're still a nurse, aren't you? You walk by patients in need every day. I've heard them call out to you, and you keep on trucking. You routinely walk by patients that *you* could help and assign *us* to—"

"Because *that* is my job," Nurse Sprouse interrupted.

"It has made you heartless, Nurse Sprouse," Trina said. "There's no love in what you do. You're supposed to be here for the patients first. You have forgotten that."

"I think we've all had enough of your . . . assumptions and falsehoods," Nurse Sprouse said. "The board will now vote—"

"One more thing, Miss Sprouse, and then I will be silent." *This is a hearing, and they will hear me even if they don't listen to me.* "I have a great deal of pride in what I do, and I follow every procedure to the $n$th degree. Look at my file. Until Miss Sprouse arrived three years ago, my file contained no write-ups. None. I'm sure you gentlemen have looked at my file, and I'm sure you've seen the petty, picky, and ultimately immaterial things Nurse Sprouse writes us up for. Dresscode violations. Poor penmanship. Using a check mark instead of an $X$ on a form. These write-ups don't reflect the dedication we have to and for our patients. These write-ups don't reflect the love we have for this hospital. These write-ups don't reflect our worth, our abilities, and our expertise. They don't chronicle the times we stay long after our shift is through to sit with a patient who never gets anyone to visit during visiting hours. They don't chronicle the stress we face when a patient we've been caring for suddenly takes a turn for the worse or dies. They don't chronicle the number of times we bite our tongues when Miss Sprouse harangues us for a dress-code violation on days we'd rather not wear those depressing blue or gray scrubs because we feel the *patients* need to see something brighter to brighten *their* days. I know I shouldn't have lied to my supervisor, and I'm sorry. But trust me on this. I am the only *real* nurse in this room. Suspending me for any length of time will be detrimental to the patients of this hospital."

Nurse Sprouse rolled her eyes. "Are you through?"

"Yes." Trina folded her hands and placed them in her lap.

"Is the board ready to vote?" Nurse Sprouse asked.

The doctors nodded.

Nurse Sprouse smiled. "You may wait outside until we have rendered judgment, Woods. We'll call you back in when we're ready."

Trina stood, turned, and left the room, shutting the door quietly behind her. She walked down the long hallway to the vending area. *No Tony.* She backtracked to a nurse's station and waited until a chatty young LPN named Cathy noticed her. "Have you seen a tall, Italian-looking man recently?"

"Tony Sant-something from Cobble Hill something, right?" Cathy said.

*Oh, this new breed of airhead LPNs pisses me off.* "Yes. Tony Santangelo."

"He was a trip," Cathy said with a laugh. "He asked to see who was in charge of the hospital. Can you believe it? As if Dr. Canby would see *him.*"

"What did you tell him?" Trina asked.

"I told him that Dr. Canby would just *love* to see him," Cathy said.

*And that's where Tony is now.* "What did he say to that?"

"He said, 'Good,'" Cathy said. "He didn't get my sarcasm."

*And he never will.* "What did he say next?"

"He asked me to draw him a map to admin," Cathy said.

"Did you draw him a map?" Trina asked.

"*Yes,*" Cathy said. "Why are you looking for him anyway? He was strange. I'll bet he escaped from somewhere."

*Yes, he escaped from Brooklyn.* Trina wanted to jump over the counter and strangle Cathy with her long blond ponytail. "Have you been living under a rock lately? That was Tony Santangelo from Cobble Hill, Brooklyn, New York, USA, also known as Art E., the world-famous songwriter and piano player."

Cathy cracked her gum. "Okay. And?"

*She has no clue. This wench probably thinks Katy Perry is a gifted musician.* "How long ago did you give him the map?"

"About ten minutes ago," Cathy said.

*He's probably already there now. He'll find his way back. Tony never gets lost.*

A doctor poked his head out of the conference-room door and motioned to Trina with a wrinkled hand.

"I have to go back in," Trina said. "If Tony comes back, please tell him that Trina said to sit out here and wait, okay?"

"Okay," Cathy said.

"Repeat back what I said, please," Trina said.

"If Tony comes back, wait here because you said to," Cathy said.

*It will have to do.* "Thank you *so* much for your help," Trina said.

"Oh, you're welcome," Cathy said brightly.

*Idiot.*

Trina again sat in the chair. *Look how smug ES looks. She is arrogance personified.*

"Miss Katrina Woods," Nurse Sprouse said, "it is this board's determination that you be suspended for one week without pay."

*They're not firing me,* Trina thought. *I suppose that's a good thing. But wait. Nurse Sprouse is taking another breath. There's more. . . .*

"You will also be required to work any shift we deem necessary upon your return for a probationary period of three months, at which time—"

"This is complete and utter bullshit," Trina interrupted. "A week's lost pay for a first offense? Probation for three months after ten years of exemplary service?"

"Miss Woods!" Nurse Sprouse shouted. "If you continue in this manner, you will be terminated!"

Trina took a cleansing breath. "What was the vote?" she asked as she raked the doctors with her eyes.

"The board doesn't have to—"

"This board is messing with my profession and my livelihood," Trina interrupted. "I have a right to know. What was the vote?"

"The vote was unanimous," Nurse Sprouse said.

"Cowards," Trina said. "You all are cowards."

"Now where was I?" Nurse Sprouse said. "Oh yes. A probationary period of three months, at which time you will sit before this board again for the board to determine if you should return to full duty or be immediately terminated." Nurse Sprouse smiled. "I seriously doubt that calling these gentlemen cowards will help your cause."

"You gentlemen do not have the best interests of this

hospital in mind," Trina said. "You *are* cowards, and you're also fools. I'm sure Miss Sprouse bullied you into your vote. You don't know it yet, but you are going to regret this decision."

"Are you threatening me and the members of this board?" Nurse Sprouse asked.

"No," Trina said. "I'm predicting the future of this hospital. *I* care. My *heart* is in my work. Nurse Sprouse doesn't care. She has no heart. Soon patients will see this in the nurses at Saint Francis. She will rub off on them. Nurses are on the front lines. While doctors get a lot of the glory, nurses keep this place running. Nurses make patients happy. Nurses make this place profitable. You are cutting your own financial throat if you allow people like Miss Sprouse to dictate your consciences." She rubbed her eyes. "This is foolishness."

"Do you accept this reprimand rendered by the board, Miss Woods?" Nurse Sprouse asked.

*Hell no!* "What if I *don't* accept this reprimand?"

"Then you will be terminated immediately," Nurse Sprouse said.

"But you want me around, don't you, Miss Sprouse?" Trina asked. "It isn't punishment unless other nurses can see me *being* punished. I can't be an object lesson if I'm not here, can I?"

"I don't care if you work here or not, Miss Woods. Do you accept—"

"Do you know what many of the nurses call you, Miss Sprouse?" Trina interrupted. "We call you ES, and it's not because those are your initials. ES stands for 'evil stepmother.' And we call your two ugly stepdaughters ES Two. We've obviously given you an erroneous nickname because the evil stepmother in Cinderella was *much* nicer."

Nurse Sprouse smiled. "I take it that you are reject-ing this board's recommendation."

"I only reject *you,* Miss Sprouse, and everything you stand, oh, I mean, *sit on your fat ass for!*"

Nurse Sprouse stood, her body shaking and her face beet red. "That is *gross* insubordination, and you are hereby *terminated,* Woods!"

"What's gross is your fat ass, Nurse Sprouse," Trina said. "You know, if you actually did some physical labor here, you wouldn't have so much cellulite back there."

"Clean out your locker, turn in your ID, and vacate the premises at once!" Nurse Sprouse shouted. "You have one hour! This meeting of the disciplinary review board is now—"

The door to the conference room banged open, and Tony entered—followed by Dr. Morgan Canby, es-teemed president of Saint Francis Memorial Hospital.

"Hi, Trina," Tony said.

"Where have you been?" Trina asked. "I was wor-ried about you."

"I have been helping," Tony said.

Dr. Canby stood in front of Nurse Sprouse. "How did the board vote?"

"It was unanimous for suspension and probation, but that is a moot point," Nurse Sprouse said. "Miss Woods has been terminated for gross insubordination."

"Reinstate her now," Dr. Canby said.

"Excuse me?" Nurse Sprouse said.

"Miss Woods is to be reinstated immediately," Dr. Canby said.

"She said I had a quote, 'fat ass,' unquote," Nurse Sprouse said. "She said quote, 'what's gross is your fat ass,' unquote. This is *obviously* grounds for immediate—"

"I would have said much worse, Nurse Sprouse, after the way you have been treating her and the rest of the nursing staff," Dr. Canby interrupted. "Miss Woods, you are free to go."

Nurse Sprouse sat. "But I don't understand, Dr. Canby."

"This is Tony Santangelo, Trina's friend," Dr. Canby said, "and he—"

"You mean her boyfriend," Nurse Sprouse interrupted.

"I am her friend," Tony said. "Are you the heartless wench?"

"Tony!" Trina shouted, but she did nothing to conceal her smile.

"You are a heartless wench," Tony said. "I told Dr. Canby how you treat dark-skinned nurses. We have been walking around the hospital together, and all we saw were pretty, dark nurses working. We did not see many white nurses doing any work. They were standing around or sitting around and talking. You are the first white nurse I have seen today, and you are not working either. You are sitting on your fat ass."

"I am not going to stand for this," Nurse Sprouse said.

"You are sitting," Tony said. "You cannot stand for something if you are sitting."

Nurse Sprouse stood. "I am the *chair* of this disciplinary board—"

"You do have a fat ass," Tony interrupted. "It looks like lumpy oatmeal."

Trina pulled Tony away from the table. "Shh, Tony. Please. Don't make me laugh anymore."

"Nurse Sprouse, you are no longer chair of this board," Dr. Canby said. "And you and I are going to discuss what role—if any—you will play at this hospital in the future." He addressed the doctors. "You gentlemen are dismissed permanently from this board for your utter lack of discernment." He turned to Trina. "Miss Woods, no more calling in sick when you're not sick."

"No, sir," Trina said.

"And Tony, thank you for bringing this to my attention," Dr. Canby said.

"You are welcome," Tony said. "We will have lunch now, Trina, and then we will go buy a house."

Trina hugged him. "You're the boss."

Dr. Canby moved beside Tony. "We'll work out the details for that other thing soon, okay, Tony?"

"Okay."

Tony led Trina from the conference room directly to the elevator.

"What other thing?" Trina asked.

"I have given money to the hospital for Asperger's research," Tony said. The door opened, and they squeezed inside a crowded elevator.

"That's wonderful," Trina whispered. "How much?"

"Five million dollars," Tony said.

All talking ceased in the elevator.

"And in the future I will give more," Tony said.

They got off the elevator in the lobby.

Trina saw a mass of reporters waiting outside the main doors and guided Tony toward the emergency room. "I don't want to see them now, do you?"

"No," Tony said.

She led him through the ambulance bay and out to Bush Street. After seeing no reporters or cameras, she relaxed. "So tell me more about your donation."

"Dr. Canby will make a space for Asperger's patients to come and be helped," Tony said. "He thinks we should call it the 'Santangelo Asperger's Center.' I asked Dr. Canby if I could help, and he said yes. He wants to give me a job. It would be my first job."

"Doing what?"

"Talking to Asperger's patients and their families," Tony said. "I would be a counselor."

*What a perfect job!*

"I told Dr. Canby I would do the job for free, but he says I have to make at least one dollar," Tony said. "I also told him I wanted you to work with me."

"What would I do?" Trina asked.

"Dr. Canby said we needed the best nurse in the hospital to help us," Tony said. "You are the best nurse. You would talk to Asperger's patients and their families, too, and you would help them with medications they might need. Dr. Canby said we could have our own office together. I asked if I could have my piano there. He is thinking about it. We will need a refrigerator for root beer. We will need comfortable couches and chairs. I think the purple couch should be in our office. We will need many musical instruments. There is so much to do."

*Working side by side with my man, doing wonderful work—it's the perfect job for me, too!* "Have you already made the donation?"

"They were amazed that the money came through so fast," Tony said.

*I'd be amazed, too. Five million dollars!*

"I asked if Angelo and Aika could get a job there, too," Tony said. "Angelo knows more about Asperger's than I do. He could help many people. And Aika could help us write whatever we have to write. And then we could all be together again."

They crossed behind a cable car and went inside the BeanStalk Café. "Hello, Hyun Ae," Tony said.

"Tony from Brooklyn," Hyun Ae said. "You want the same sloppy sandwich?"

"I want two sloppy sandwiches today," Tony said. "And two root beers. This is Trina."

"Hello, Trina," Hyun Ae said.

"Hi," Trina said.

*Who is this man who can't stop talking, orders lunch for me, and introduces me to people?*

"We will sit at the first table," Tony said, and they sat facing Bush Street.

Trina held his hand. "I can't believe you did all you did in such a short time. Do you really think Angelo and Aika will relocate here?"

"No," Tony said. "They belong in Brooklyn. I will ask them, though."

"You really miss them," Trina said.

Tony sighed. "Yes."

Trina squinted. "You miss Aika a lot, huh?"

Tony nodded.

"Tony, I've never really pried, but I have to know something," Trina said. "What is your *specific* attraction to Aika?"

Tony stared into Trina's eyes.

"You like her eyes," Trina said.

"Yes," Tony said.

*So glad he didn't say her creamy, perfect complexion or her buttocks.* "Why do you like her eyes?"

"They are clear and happy like yours," Tony said. "They do not look around me. They do not look the other way. They see me."

*Aika's eyes accept Tony for who he is.* "Are my eyes clear and happy?"

"Yes," Tony said. "That is why I chose to come to San Francisco to meet you. I cannot wait to work with you. We can go to lunch together every day in the park."

"I'd like that, Tony," Trina said. "And by the way, you're already working with me."

"We do not go to work together," Tony said.

"We're working on a snowflake child, aren't we?"

"That is not work," Tony said. "That is love."

# 41

After eating the sloppiest, spiciest, and most delicious ham and cheese sandwich she had ever eaten, Trina let Tony drag her to a cable car for the ride toward Franklin Street. While they rode and Tony rang the bell several times, Trina's phone rang. *Naini.*

"The evil stepmother is gone!" Naini shouted. "And Inez and Danica will be emptying bedpans this afternoon! I cannot talk long. I have *rounds.*"

"Really? That's wonderful!"

"I am in charge of six patients," Naini said. "I just settled my first admission in a bed for the first time in six years. You are a miracle worker, Trina."

"Tony did most of it," Trina said. "He simply took

Dr. Canby for a tour of the hospital and pointed out the colors."

"Why did we not think of that?" Naini asked. "The simplest solution was right in front of us all the time."

"Naini," Trina said, "I have some sort of sad news."

"You are not quitting and running off with Tony, are you?" Naini asked. "No. This would not be sad news."

"Well, I won't be working with you anymore."

"But you were reinstated," Naini said.

"Yes, and I'll be working with Tony in a new Asperger's center Saint Francis is starting with Tony's donation," Trina said.

"How much did he donate?" Naini asked.

"Five million," Trina said.

Naini didn't respond.

"I *know,*" Trina said. "That's how I reacted, too."

"If he can donate . . . *that,*" Naini said. "I cannot comprehend this."

"Neither can I," Trina said. "And I have some even more sad news. We're on our way to look at a little house on Franklin Street across from Lafayette Park."

"It is not a little house," Naini said.

"No, it isn't."

Naini sighed. "Is his brother really in love with the Japanese girl?"

"Yes, and she isn't a girl," Trina said. "She's forty-two."

"No!" Naini shouted. "Life is so unfair! Oh, it is not unfair to you. But you are getting things out of order," Naini said. "Are you not supposed to be married before you get a house?"

"I guess," Trina said. *But for some reason, this sequence of events seems perfectly logical.*

"If you buy this little house which I know is not so little," Naini said, "I want your apartment."

Trina laughed. "You know how small it is."

"I do not care," Naini said. "I will not have to ride the bus, and Johnny Foley's is a few blocks away. Did I tell you how many phone numbers I got the other night?"

"No."

"I got three," Naini said. "One was a little drunk and a little cute, one was very drunk and very cute, and the last one was sober but only okay-looking. I do not understand why that is. Anyway, I have three more phone numbers than I have gotten in Oakland in eight years. Oh, I must go. I have a ninja patient."

Trina laughed. "How old is he?"

"*She* is ninety-seven," Trina said. "She has already kicked two LPNs, bitten a CNA, scratched an orderly, and karate-chopped her food tray. Bye."

Two women Realtors identically dressed in navy-blue blazers with white blouses and navy-blue pants met them in front of the Franklin Street mansion. "I *told* you," one of the women said. She extended her hand. "It is an *honor* to meet you, Art E."

"I am Tony Santangelo," Tony said. "This is Trina Woods."

The women introduced themselves as Jackie and Diane. "Like the song," Jackie said.

*Not like the song,* Trina said. *Unless Jackie was once a Jack . . .*

"We would like to buy this house today," Tony said.

"Splendid," Jackie said.

Diane, the older and thinner of the two, led them up a red-bricked pathway and opened a black wrought-iron gate. "The house lists for ten million," she said "What do you plan to offer?"

"I am offering eight million," Tony said. "This is where you say nine million five."

"Tony," Trina said. "Jackie and Diane have to take our offer to the owner first."

"Oh," Tony said. "Please call the owner now."

Jackie unlocked the massive entry door. "The Vances are on vacation in Switzerland."

Tony blinked. "It is eight o'clock at night there." He took out his phone. "They should be awake. What is their telephone number?"

"Um, Tony, can I call you Tony?" Jackie asked.

"That is my name, yes," Tony said.

"Tony, why don't we tour the house first?" Jackie asked. "Once you see all this house has to offer, you might think ten million is a bargain."

Tony walked inside and looked into every room of the first floor. "It looks just like the pictures on the Internet. I do not need to see any more. I want to buy this house for Trina today." He handed Jackie the phone "Please call the owner for me now."

Jackie took out her phone and found the number pressing the numbers into Tony's phone. "The Vances have had other offers," she said. "The last offer Mr Vance turned down was nine million seven."

Tony pressed the green phone icon.

Trina turned on the speaker.

"Hello?"

"Mr. Vance," Tony said, "I am Tony Santangelo, and I would like to buy your house today."

"Tony who?"

"Tony Santangelo," Tony said.

"He is also known as Art E., Mr. Vance," Trina said

"Oh, I've heard of you," Mr. Vance said. "The piano player who is all the rage on the Internet—and in Europe, too. You're *very* talented. Is that Trina with you?"

"Yes, Mr. Vance," Trina said. "How's your weather?"

"Cold and snowy," Mr. Vance said. "Just the way we like it. What are you offering me for my house, Mr. Santangelo?"

"I want to buy your house for Trina for eight million dollars," Tony said.

"Tony, my wife and I will not part with our house for a mere eight million dollars," Mr. Vance said.

"I can pay you the entire amount today," Tony said.

"No one can purchase a house like ours in one day, Mr. Santangelo," Mr. Vance said.

"I can," Tony said.

"Hmm," Mr. Vance said. "I suppose you can. But we would have to move out first, wouldn't we?"

"Oh," Tony said. "Yes. You have many nice things to move. It will take more than a day."

"We can make the *purchase* today, can't we?" Trina asked. "I know lawyers have to do their thing, and you do have a lot of beautiful furnishings to move. We are really motivated, Mr. Vance. We both love this house."

"I can appreciate that," Mr. Vance said. "But your offer is far too low, Trina."

"This is where you say nine million five, Mr. Vance," Tony said.

"I already lowered the asking price three hundred thousand dollars last month," Mr. Vance said. "Didn't Jackie and Diane tell you?"

"No," Tony said. "So you will not say nine million five."

"I am standing firm at ten million," Mr. Vance said.

Tony started to pull at his fingers.

*Oh, shoot!* "Tony and I will talk about it and ca`
you right back," Trina said.

"Okay," Mr. Vance said.

Trina pressed the OFF button.

"He would not say nine million five, Trina," Ton`
said, twisting his right ring finger.

Trina turned to Jackie and Diane. "What's the ap
praised value of this house?"

"Nine million seven and some change," Diane sai`
"But you couldn't rebuild this house today for ten mi`
lion. And because this is a historic property, you'll ge
a break on your property taxes."

"Do you think Mr. Vance will take anything les
than ten million?" Trina asked.

"I doubt it," Jackie said. "He's a tough customer. H
wouldn't budge off ten million three for almost a year.

"So this house has been on the market for over `
year," Trina said.

"Don't think that means anything to Mr. Vance`
Diane said. "He's as shrewd as they come, and this `
just one of his houses."

"What does Mr. Vance do?" Trina asked.

"He's an executive for the Gap," Diane said.

Tony blinked. "The Gap owns Banana Republic. `
wear Banana Republic clothes. I am wearing the`
right now."

*And Tony is a celebrity* . . . "Um, I need to use th`
bathroom."

Jackie directed her to a bathroom off the kitchen.

Once in the half bathroom, which was three time`
the size of her full bathroom, Trina redialed Mr. Vanc`
and kept the speaker off.

"Mr. Vance, this is Trina Woods."

"That was quick," Mr. Vance said. "Do you have another more serious offer?"

"I do," Trina said. "But first I have a question. How s Banana Republic doing, Mr. Vance?"

"What does this have to do with buying my house?" Mr. Vance asked.

*Maybe everything.* "Tony loves wearing Banana Republic clothing," Trina said. "In fact, in every video ou've seen him in he's wearing *your* clothes, so to peak. I don't know a thing about advertising, but I'm ure it wouldn't hurt if you had someone as handsome s Tony is to wear your brand. Imagine a commercial vith him playing the piano in your pants." *That didn't ound right at all!*

"What are you proposing?" Mr. Vance asked.

"If you sell your house to us for less than ten million," Trina said, "I'm sure I can convince Tony to wear Banana Republic exclusively in whatever he does. He nay even wear Gap clothes." *And you may only have to ay him a dollar.* "I know he will continue to perform t Johnny Foley's. And who knows? He might even lay at bigger places in the future."

"He's quite a showman," Mr. Vance said. "He would ell out any venue on the planet right now. Would you e interested as well?"

Trina blinked. "In doing what?"

"In wearing Banana Republic or Gap clothing," Mr. ance said.

"Me?" *He's not serious.*

"When Tony lifted you onto the piano at Johnny oley's," Mr. Vance said, "I said to myself, 'Now ere's an advertisement.' You had so much joy and onder in your eyes. You two make a visually arresting

couple. Have you ever worn Banana Republic tops o
dresses?"

"No," Trina said, "but I'm not exactly the type,
mean, you had Arlenis Sosa modeling for you a fe
years back, and she's tall, bronzed, and gorgeous."

"Our Banana Republic sales have declined over th
last few years," Mr. Vance said. "I've been telling ou
marketing department that we need some fresh faces
some real people to be in our ads to give that brand
boost. And here you both are. Would you be willing t
join Tony in a future ad campaign?"

"Mr. Vance, I'll be honest," Trina said. "I have neve
been able to afford Banana Republic clothing. I'v
been wearing nurse's scrubs for the last ten years. An
I don't know if I'd feel comfortable—"

"Nine million five and you both have to model fo
us," Mr. Vance interrupted. "Print, Internet, catalog
television. Is it a deal?"

Trina swallowed hard. "Wow. Are you sure?"

"I am," Mr. Vance said. "I have a great feeling abou
this."

"In that case, sure." Trina looked at her "fresh face
in the mirror. *You aren't half bad looking, old lad*
"Mr. Vance, I'm in one of your bathrooms making th
call, so Tony doesn't know I'm talking to you. Coul
you act as if Tony convinced you to go nine millio
five?"

"I would be delighted," Mr. Vance said.

"Thank you so much," Trina said. "I'll have him ca
you back."

"I'll be waiting for his call," Mr. Vance said.

"Bye." *I can't believe it! From almost fired nurse t
reinstated nurse to only nurse at a new Asperger's cer
ter to Banana Republic model in less than six hour*

*And in a few moments, Tony is going to buy me this house!*

Trina left the bathroom on shaky legs and handed the phone to Tony. "Do you think we should try again?"

"You said we would talk about it," Tony said.

"We don't need to talk about it," Trina said. "I was using an old bargaining technique. Sometimes you have to walk away from the table to get what you want."

Tony blinked. He looked at several side tables flanking a couch.

"The *bargaining* table," Trina said.

"We were on the phone," Tony said. "We were not at a table."

"Let me give you another example," Trina said. "When I bought my first car, I walked away from the salesman four times until he quoted me a price I could afford. I got the price to drop each time by walking away. Do you understand?"

"No," Tony said.

*How can I make this clearer to him?* "Mr. Vance wants to sell this house for ten million dollars. He already dropped the price three hundred thousand dollars. We have offered him eight million dollars, and now he's thinking about our offer because we stopped talking to him."

Tony nodded. "So the more we do not talk to him, the lower the price will go."

*Something like that.* "Right."

"If we do not talk to him for a week," Tony said, "the price will drop even more."

*I really screwed up that one.* "But someone else may give him an offer he likes by then. Why don't you call him now to see if he has reconsidered?"

"I will call him." He hit the redial button. "Mr. Vance, this is Tony Santangelo."

"Put it on speaker, please," Trina whispered.

Tony pressed the speaker button.

"I have been hoping you'd call, Tony," Mr. Vance said. "I have thought about your offer, and I am giving you a counteroffer of nine million nine."

Tony smiled. "And I will pay you . . . eight million five."

"Nine million eight," Mr. Vance said.

"Eight million nine," Tony said.

"Nine million seven," Mr. Vance said.

Tony started to dance. "Nine million . . . three."

"Nine million five and that's my final offer," Mr. Vance said. "I won't go any lower."

"He said nine million five, Trina," Tony said.

"Take the offer," Trina whispered.

Tony stopped dancing. "We will buy your house for nine million five, Mr. Vance."

"I'll have my lawyer contact your lawyer, Mr. Santangelo," Mr. Vance said. "Just give me your lawyer's name, and we'll get the paperwork started."

"His name is Matthew McConnell," Tony said. "He works at Angela's Sweet Treats and Coffee in Williamsburg, Brooklyn, New York, USA. When can we move in?"

"I'm certain you'll be in your new home by the end of the month or by the first week in February at the latest," Mr. Vance said. "Congratulations, Mr. Santangelo."

"Thank you," Tony said.

"Could you put Jackie or Diane on the phone for me please?" Mr. Vance asked.

Tony handed the phone to Jackie, and she and Diane walked out to the deck off the kitchen.

Trina hugged him. "Thank you, Tony!"

"We must go celebrate," Tony said.

"We just ate," Trina said. "I couldn't eat another thing."

"We will ride the cable cars wherever they take us," Tony said. "There are places in San Francisco I have not seen yet. I want to know my new city."

"Sure," Trina said. "That would be wonderful."

Jackie and Diane scurried up to them in the foyer. "There are *hundreds* of reporters outside the gate." Jackie handed Tony his phone. "*Hundreds.*"

"Is there another way out of here?" Trina asked.

Tony took Trina's hand. "Let us go talk to them."

"I thought you wanted to celebrate," Trina said.

"We will celebrate," Tony said. "But first we have to tell them the good news."

As soon as Tony and Trina hit the brick walk to the gate, the noise level increased and lights blinded them.

"Trina, how does it feel to be reinstated?"

"Did you just buy this house, Tony?"

"How much did you pay?"

"Are you getting married?"

"What role will each of you have in the new Asperger's center?"

"Is it true your supervisor has been fired?"

"Are the allegations of 'colorism' at Saint Francis true?"

"Why did you avoid us back at the hospital?"

Trina huddled behind Tony's back. "What are we going to do?"

Tony smiled. "We are going to give them something

to look at." Tony opened the gate. "Come inside and see our new home."

While most of the media swarmed the house, Tony and Trina sat in one of the two lower-level family rooms and answered questions.

"Does this mean you'll be living in San Francisco from now on?"

"Yes," Tony said.

"What about Brooklyn?"

"Brooklyn will still be there," Tony said. "We will visit Brooklyn often." He took out his phone. "Oh, I must tell Angelo and Aika the good news." He pressed the number one. "Angelo, I have just bought a house for Trina. . . . It is almost as big as the Castle. . . . The reporters are here asking me and Trina questions. . . . I let them in. . . . There was not enough room on the sidewalk. . . . They do not scare me." He smiled. "I will have Trina type Naomi's songs for you tonight. . . . I will call you later when we get back to Trina's apartment. Bye."

After the last reporter left their future home *three* hours later, Trina and Tony took a taxi back to her apartment, where Tony read off the lyrics to eight songs while Trina typed them.

"How does Naomi know the tune to each song?" Trina asked.

"I make a CD for her in my music studio," Tony said.

"And how are you going to do that here?" Trina asked.

Tony blinked. "I do not know."

"Maybe you can record the tunes at Johnny Foley's," Trina said.

"Yes," Tony said. "I can do them all live tonight." He called Angelo. "Trina and I are done with the lyrics."

Trina turned on the speaker. "And they're great, Angelo."

"How many?" Angelo asked.

"Eight," Tony said.

"That's all?" Angelo asked. "You were writing so many."

"That is all I want to give her," Tony said. "I am keeping some for myself."

"You don't sing," Angelo said.

"I will keep them instrumental then," Tony said.

"Or rap them like you did my song the other night," Trina said. "How many songs do you have in your head that could be only instrumental?"

Tony smiled. "Too many."

"Angelo, I think Tony needs to do a solo piano album," Trina said. "A live solo album."

"I could do that," Tony said. "I could do it at Johnny Foley's."

"Tony," Trina said, "you deserve a much bigger audience than that. And I've always wanted to see New York City."

"Yeah, Tony," Angelo said. "There are plenty of great venues here. How about the Brooklyn Academy of Music?"

"I was thinking more along the lines of Carnegie Hall," Trina said.

"I don't know," Angelo said. "They fill up their schedule at the Carnegie months and years in advance. Naomi had a tough time getting in there two years ago. Why not Madison Square Garden or the Barclay's Center?"

"It must be free," Tony said.

"You're kidding, right?" Angelo said. "They'd sell out tickets in an hour at any venue if you were doing a live show."

"It must be free," Tony said. "It must be free and in Central Park like Elton John did. It must happen this summer."

Trina gripped his hands. "That's a great idea, Tony. Wow!"

"Just think of it," Angelo said. "A half million people listening to you play live, and we'll have to see if any of the networks will want to run with it, too. I have always dreamed of you doing something like that."

"I will make your dream come true," Tony said.

"I'll make some calls and get the ball rolling," Angelo said. "This is fantastic!"

"Is Aika there?" Tony asked.

"She's at work," Angelo said. "I'll tell her the great news, though. Um, Tony, I need to speak to Trina privately."

"Okay."

Trina picked up the phone, turned off the speaker, and went into the kitchen. "What's up?"

"You two *have* to go to the Grammys," Angelo said.

"We'll be there," Trina said. "Tony asked me to go."

"He did?" Angelo asked.

"Yes," Trina said. "Do you think he has a shot at winning?"

"I don't know," Angelo said. "He's got some great competition this year. But anyway, they're giving Tony a lifetime achievement award."

"That's wonderful!"

"Don't tell him, and make sure he wears a nice suit," Angelo said. "He might not wear a tie, though. He hates ties."

"I'll keep that in mind," Trina said.

"I need to speak to Tony privately now," Angelo said. "If that's okay."

"Why wouldn't it be okay?" Trina asked.

"Well, now that you're his manager and all," Angelo said.

*Is that what I've become?* "I'm not his manager," Trina said. "Tony's managing himself. I am giving the phone to Tony right now." She put the phone in Tony's hand. "Angelo wants to talk to you in secret."

"Oh." Tony put the phone to his ear. "Hello, Angelo . . . I do not know. . . . Yes. . . . No, they do not. Great minds are great because they do *not* think alike. . . . I will. . . . I am not sad. . . . Okay. . . . I will try. . . . Good-bye." He turned off the phone. "Angelo asked Aika to marry him."

*So much for the secret, but why would Angelo want to keep that information from me?* "What'd Aika say?"

"I was not there," Tony said.

"Did she say yes?" Trina asked.

"I do not know," Tony said. "I was not there."

*I keep forgetting to ask direct, yes-or-no-type questions.* "Tony, are they getting married?"

"Yes."

"Well, that's great news," Trina said. "Why didn't he want me to hear about it?"

"You have heard about it," Tony said.

"You said you weren't sad," Trina said. "Sad about what?"

"Angelo thought I would be sad," Tony said. "I am not sad they are getting married. Angelo wants me to be the best man."

"You are the best man," Trina said.

"The man who is getting married should be the best

man," Tony said. "Angelo should be the best man, not me. I am not marrying Aika."

"Yeah, it doesn't make a whole lot of sense," Trina said. "Who are you marrying?"

"You," Tony said.

"When?" Trina asked.

"Soon." He kissed her hard on the lips.

*Soon! Yes! To Tony, "soon" means "right away."* She pulled back from the kiss. "Are you kissing me to keep me from asking you more questions about it?"

"Yes," Tony said. He kissed her again, and this time he didn't press as hard.

"I'll stop asking questions, if you don't stop kissing me."

"I will kiss you all night long," Tony said.

"All over my body," Trina said.

"All over your body."

*It's a good thing Tony's not a singer,* Trina thought. *He's about to lose the use of his lips and tongue for a few days. . . .*

# 42

"I hope you don't mind if I visit some of my friends at Saint Francis today," Trina said the next morning while they ate buttered toast and drank orange juice.

"I do not mind," Tony said.

"I know it's strange to go in to work on a day off," Trina said.

"It is not strange," Tony said. "You like your work."

"And until the Asperger's center opens, I want to try to take as much time off as I can so I can spend time with you."

"You cannot spend time," Tony said. "It is not money."

"But it's not good to waste time, is it?" Trina asked.

"No," Tony said. "Time is valuable."

"I should be done by eleven, and we can go out to lunch and eat it in the park if the press leaves us in peace."

"I would like that," Tony said. He finished his fourth piece of toast.

"Why don't you wait for me here?" Trina asked. "Get some extra sleep." She kissed his neck. "You earned it last night. You kissed every square inch of my body."

"I did," Tony said. "I made a map of your body with my lips."

*And I'm still tingling in places from those kisses.* "So you'll stay here and rest, right?"

"I have an errand to run," Tony said. "Please do not ask me what."

Trina looked up from her toast. "An errand, huh?"

"Yes," Tony said.

"Doing what?" Trina asked.

"You asked me what," Tony said.

"I'm just curious," Trina said.

"But I am trying to keep a secret from you."

"What if I finish visiting my friends earlier than eleven?" Trina asked. "Will you be close to the hospital?"

"I will have my phone," Tony said. "You can call me, and I will come to the hospital."

"You didn't answer my question," Trina said.

"I will be close to the hospital," Tony said.

"How close?"

Tony blinked several times. "I am going to Union Square."

Trina squinted. "You're going . . . to Union Square, huh?"

"Yes," Tony said. "On an errand."

Trina rubbed his hand. "There are a lot of nice stores at Union Square." *Including Tiffany & Co. Yes!*

"Please do not ask more," Tony said.

Trina smiled widely. "I won't ask you anything more about it. I like surprises."

"Surprises keep a relationship fresh," Tony said.

After walking Trina to Saint Francis, he backtracked down Hyde to Post Street and walked half a mile to Union Square—and Tiffany & Co. A doorman opened the door, and Tony walked directly to the back of the first floor to a showcase of engagement rings.

He stood at this showcase for thirty minutes while two sales associates talked to each other, waited on other customers who came in after him, and generally ignored his existence. Tony tried to make eye contact with them several times but failed.

A tall pencil-thin woman with a severe nose and far too much makeup breezed by him to wait on a new arrival, saying, "The silver jewelry is *upstairs*."

"I do not want silver jewelry," Tony said. "I want to buy an engagement ring."

The pencil-thin sales associate rolled her eyes and shook her head. "I will be with you in a moment," she said with a heavy sigh.

Tony waited twenty more minutes of moments while the pencil-thin woman waited on a woman who wore fur around her neck and then another woman who wore many diamonds around her neck, on her fingers, and on her wrists.

A younger long-haired associate approached Tony from behind. "Have you been helped?"

Tony turned. "No."

"Someone will be with you shortly," she said, and she, too, moved away to help another customer who had just walked in.

Tony pulled on his left ring finger. He located the pencil-thin woman and stood next to the woman she was helping.

"Oh, that will look divine on you, Faye," the pencil-thin woman said.

"I would like to buy an engagement ring now," Tony said.

"I told you I would be right with you," the pencil-thin woman said.

Tony twisted his left ring finger. "You have not been right with me. You have been wrong with me. You have helped four other people who came in after I did. I have waited my turn. It is now my turn."

The pencil-thin woman sighed. "Greta, could you help this *fine* gentleman?"

Greta, the long-haired associate, crept over to him at the speed of an arthritic sloth. "What may I help you with?" she asked blandly.

Tony stared into Greta's eyes. "You do not want to help me. Please get someone who can help me."

"Of *course* I want to help you, sir," Greta said.

"If you wanted to help me, you would not have walked so slowly," Tony said. "If you wanted to help me, you would not have walked past me twenty-seven minutes ago. Please get someone who can help me buy an engagement ring."

Greta exhaled, rolled her eyes, and slinked away—to *another* new arrival in designer sunglasses, shoes, and clothes.

Ten minutes later, Tony began twisting and pulling all of his fingers as he approached the pencil-thin woman once again. "My name is Tony Santangelo," he said. "I am from Cobble Hill, Brooklyn, New York, USA. I want to buy an engagement ring for Trina today."

The pencil-thin woman's mouth dropped open. "You're Art E."

"I am Tony Santangelo," Tony said. "I write songs as Art E. I have been standing here"—he checked his watch—"for one hour and seventeen minutes while you helped women with fur around their necks and women who wear lots of diamonds."

"Please *forgive* me, Mr. Santangelo," the pencil-thin woman said. "I didn't recognize you without your piano."

Tony blinked several times. "You are not forgiven. You should not have to recognize me to sell me a ring. You should have helped me right away. I do not want your help now." He remembered what Angelo sometimes said. "I want to see your manager."

"Oh, *that* won't be necessary, will it?" the pencil-thin woman asked. "I can most *certainly* help you find that *special* ring."

"No." Tony stared into her eyes. "I want to see your manager now."

"Our manager is busy at the moment," the pencil-thin woman said.

"You are lying," Tony said. "You do not know where

your manager is." He took out his cell phone and Googled "Union Square Jewelry." When the list appeared, he said, "If I do not see your manager in one minute, I will tell the media that you did not help me. The media likes talking to me, and I like talking to them. I will then buy Trina's engagement ring from Cartier, Brilliant Earth, or Edmund R. Weber Jewelers."

"Oh, you don't want an engagement ring from *those* places," she said. "You want only the *best* for Trina, don't you?"

"I will get the best for Trina," Tony said. "You go get the manager. You have forty-five seconds."

The pencil-thin woman picked up a phone and spoke in rapid, hushed tones.

"You have thirty seconds," Tony said.

With a few seconds to spare, a smiling woman bustled up to him. "Why hello, Mr. Santangelo," she said. "I'm Janine, Magritte's manager. How may I help you today?"

Tony looked at Magritte. "When you turn sideways, Magritte, you disappear."

Magritte took a deep breath.

Tony blinked. "Please turn sideways and disappear now, Magritte."

Magritte rushed away.

"She was not helpful to me," Tony said. "She did not see me. She should not work here if she does not see people."

"I see you, Tony," Janine said. "May I call you Tony?"

"That is my name," Tony said.

"I understand you wish to buy an engagement ring," Janine said.

"Yes," Tony said.

Janine peered into the showcase. "Do you see any rings you like?"

"No," Tony said. "These are not the right rings for Trina."

Janine brought a diamond solitaire up to the counter. "This is the classic Tiffany Setting in eighteen karat yellow gold, two and a half carats, and only fifty-two thousand dollars."

"It is not the right ring," Tony said. "I do not like it."

"Maybe you want a bigger diamond," Janine said.

"I do not know," Tony said.

Janine placed a pad of paper on the top of the showcase. "Well, what kind of metal do you think she'll like? Let's start there. Eighteen karat gold or platinum?"

"Trina is golden," Tony said. "Gold."

"Okay," Janine said, writing it down. "Now we'll choose the setting. Solitaire, three stone, pavé, diamond band, or side stones?"

"I do not know the difference," Tony said.

She pulled out a long display of rings. "These are all our settings. Which one do you like the best?"

Tony pointed at a ring. "That one sparkles the most."

"Solitaire." Janine wrote it down. "Now we'll decide on the cut of diamond you think she'll like. Round, princess, Lucida, square, emerald, oval, or cushion?"

"Round," Tony said. "Trina has round buttocks."

Janine smiled. "Okay." She wrote it down. "Great. We're making progress. What size diamond do you want?"

Tony pointed at a ring on the display. "Trina has small hands."

"Oh, but you want the diamond to stand out, don't you?" Janine asked.

"Yes," Tony said.

"So, four, five, six carats?" Janine asked. "Seven? Eight?"

"Six and a half," Tony said. "That is Trina's shoe size."

Janine chuckled as she wrote and said, "Six and one-half carats. Okay. What size ring does she wear?"

"She does not wear a ring," Tony said.

"You said her hands are small," Janine said.

"Yes," Tony said. "They are small but strong and brown and warm."

Janine held up her pinkie. "Is her ring finger about this big?"

Tony stared at Janine's pinkie. "No. Like your pointer finger."

"That will make it about a size six," Janine said. "She can have it sized if it doesn't fit." She tapped her pen on the paper. "That's all I need to know."

"What color will the diamond be?" Tony asked. "I do not want a regular diamond."

"What did you have in mind?" Janine asked.

"I want a chocolate diamond," Tony said.

"You want . . . a chocolate diamond."

"Yes," Tony said. "I want a chocolate diamond for Trina."

"Tony, it is customary to give diamonds like the ones in the display case for an engagement ring," Janine said. "Chocolate diamonds are traditionally given—"

"I do not follow customs or traditions," Tony interrupted. "I want a chocolate diamond for Trina."

Janine raised her eyebrows. "Okay, um . . . let me make a few calls to see if I can locate a six-and-a-half-carat chocolate diamond."

"You do not have it here," Tony said.

"No, Tony," Janine said. "Not in that size anyway."

"This is a jewelry store," Tony said. "You have diamonds. You should have chocolate diamonds."

"We have a small inventory of chocolate diamonds, Tony," Janine said, "and I know we don't have one that's six and a half carats."

"Oh," Tony said.

"We'll have to do Trina's ring as a special order," Janine said.

"Yes," Tony said. "Trina is special."

"It will take some time for the ring to be made," Janine said, "most likely in our flagship store in New York. Have you ever been there?"

"I lived in New York," Tony said.

"I mean, have you ever visited the Tiffany's in New York?"

"No," Tony said. "This is my first visit to a jewelry store."

Janine winced. "I'm so sorry it took so long for us to help you."

"Thank you for apologizing," Tony said. "But Magritte and Greta should be apologizing, not you."

"I'll call you when the ring arrives," Janine said, "but I really can't give you a specific time it will be ready."

Tony pulled on his left ring finger. "I cannot take it home today."

"No," Janine said.

"I can go to New York to get it," Tony said.

"That won't be necessary," Janine said. "We will have it shipped here when it's ready."

"I cannot buy Trina's ring today," Tony said. He twisted his left ring finger.

"I'm sorry," Janine said. "It may take a week, or it might take a month."

Tony pulled and twisted all the fingers on his left hand. "I do not want to wait a month. Why does it take a month?"

"We have to find the diamond first," Janine said.

"It is lost."

"It's not lost," Janine said. "We'll locate it most likely in Australia. That's where many brown diamonds come from."

Tony blinked rapidly. "You must find the diamond in Australia and send it to New York to make the ring and then send it back here. Trina's ring will travel seventeen thousand miles before she can wear it."

"Her ring will have wings," Janine said.

"Yes," Tony said. "Trina is an angel. Her ring should have wings."

"Because this is a *very* special order, Tony," Janine said, "we ask that you put down a deposit of thirty to fifty percent of the estimated total cost."

"I will pay the total cost now," Tony said. He took out his credit card and handed it to Janine.

"With a six-and-a-half-carat round brown diamond solitaire in eighteen karat gold, the ring will cost roughly . . . thirty thousand dollars," Janine said.

"Okay," Tony said.

Janine tapped the card on the showcase. "Are you absolutely *sure* you want to get Trina a chocolate diamond?"

"Yes," Tony said.

"Because we could get you a flawless six-and-a-half-carat diamond in no time at all," Janine said. "You could have Trina's ring in a matter of days."

"I will wait for the chocolate diamond," Tony said. "It will have a story to tell when it gets here."

"You're right," Janine said. "I'll only be a moment." Janine went into a back office for a few minutes.

Tony stared at Magritte. "I see you."

Magritte moved away.

He stared at Greta. "You are out of shape."

Greta slinked away.

Janine returned with the receipt.

Tony signed it as carefully as he could.

"Now this is just the estimated cost, Tony," Janine said. "If it costs more or less, we'll let you know."

"Okay."

"When are you planning to pop the question?" Janine asked.

"What question?" Tony asked.

"Will you marry me?"

"No," Tony said. "I am sure you are nice, Janine, but I am marrying Trina."

Janine laughed. "When will you ask *Trina* to marry you?"

"I wanted to ask her today," Tony said.

"You still can," Janine said. "If you describe the special ring you're getting her, I'm sure she'll understand why you don't have the ring yet."

"No," Tony said. "It will not be a surprise without the ring. Trina likes surprises."

Janine gave him a copy of the receipt. "I promise I will call you the second it arrives."

Tony blinked at the receipt. "I do not want Trina to see this."

"Don't show it to her," Janine said.

"I am not good at hiding things," Tony said. "If I hide it in my boots, it will get sweaty. If I hide it in a pocket, Trina will find it. She will find it when she puts her hands in my pockets. She likes to put her hands in my pockets." He nodded. "I will put it in one of my notepads." He stuck out his hand. "Thank you, Janine."

Janine shook his hand. "Thank you, Mr. Santangelo. Remember to come back to Tiffany's for Trina's birthday, and Valentine's Day, and your anniversary, oh, and Christmas, too."

Tony pulled and twisted his fingers. "I do not think I will come back here. It is hard to buy jewelry here. Good-bye."

Tony caught a cable car at the corner of Post Street and Powell, jumped off and caught another cable car at Powell and California, rode by the Mark Hopkins, thought briefly of Angelo and Aika, got off at Hyde Street, and walked two blocks to the main entrance of Saint Francis. He went directly to the information desk in the lobby.

"Hi, Tony," Lily said.

"Hi, Lily," Tony said. "I am looking for Trina."

"I saw her an hour or so ago," Lily said. "I am *so* glad you found her."

"I have not found her," Tony said. "That is why I am looking for her."

"I meant," Lily said, "I am so glad you came from Brooklyn to look for Trina. If it weren't for you, I wouldn't have met Tino. We've started dating. He's a really nice guy."

"Yes," Tony said. "Tino is nice. You will make big brown babies."

Lily laughed. "You're probably right. Would you like me to page Trina for you?"

"I do not know," Tony said. "She is visiting friends today. I will wait."

"Should I at least let her know you're here waiting?" Lily asked.

"Okay," Tony said.

"Trina Woods, please call the information desk," Lily said. "Trina Woods, please call the information desk."

"You said it twice," Tony said.

"Just in case she didn't hear it the first time," Lily said.

"Trina has excellent hearing," Tony said. "She hears me when I whisper. I whisper to her after we have sex. I whisper a lot."

Lily's phone rang. "Trina? Tony's here." She handed the phone to Tony. "She wants to talk to you."

"Are you okay?" Trina asked.

"Yes," Tony said.

"Did you have a successful errand?" Trina asked.

"Yes and no," Tony said. "But it is a secret, so do not ask anymore."

"Okay, I won't," Trina said. "I'll be down with Naini in a minute. She wants to treat us to Lahore Kahari for lunch to celebrate our new house."

"What is Lahore Kahari?" Tony asked.

"Google it," Trina said. "We'll be right down."

Tony handed the phone to Lily, Googled "Lahore Kahari" on his phone, and found it served Indian and Pakistani food. He did not know what "tandoori," "masala," or "vindaloo," meant, but he was sure Naini would know.

"Do you have a cast-iron stomach, Tony?" Lily asked.

"No," Tony said. "My stomach is not made of cast iron."

"You'll need one at Lahore Kahari," Lily said. "Tino has one. He took me there for one of our dates. Stay away from anything that's spicy and hot."

"Why?" Tony asked.

"You've never eaten Indian food?" Lily asked.

"No," Tony said.

"It can burn your tongue," Lily said.

"I do not want to burn my tongue," Tony said. "It is already tired."

"Thai Thai Noodle is excellent," Lily said.

"Thank you, Lily," Tony said. He left the information desk and stood in front of the elevators as people swarmed around him. When the elevators opened, Trina and Naini smiled and ran to him, each taking one of his hands.

"I would like to eat at Thai Thai Noodle," Tony said.

"Since when do you like Thai food?" Trina asked.

"Food made of ties," Tony said.

"No," Trina said. "Food from Thailand."

"A land of ties," Tony said.

Trina and Naini laughed. "Just come on," Trina said.

"I am funny," Tony said. "Ha ha."

"He knew what you were talking about, Trina," Naini said.

"Yes," Tony said. "I wanted to make you laugh."

Trina kissed his cheek. "I wish I could make you laugh."

They left the hospital and walked toward California Street. "I laugh all the time. Ha ha."

"I meant *really* laugh," Trina said.

"I laugh inside," Tony said. "I am always laughing in my head." He looked at Naini's hand holding his hand. "Trina, Naini is still holding my hand."

"She wishes you had another brother for her," Trina said.

"I do not," Naini said. "I want some photographer to take my picture today. When I hugged you at Johnny Foley's, they took a picture, and I have never received so many pokes on Facebook. If I hold your hand, they will take another picture. It will be good for my love life. Where are the photographers? My hair looks good today."

"Did they follow you around on your errand, Tony?" Trina asked.

"No," Tony said. He winced. "My stomach is laughing."

"You mean it's gurgling," Trina said. "Maybe we shouldn't eat Thai food today."

"No," Tony said. "It is laughing. It is saying rah rah rah rah."

Trina and Naini laughed.

"That is the sound my stomach is making," Tony said. "Rah rah rah rah."

Trina and Naini continued to laugh.

"It would make a funny commercial," Naini said. "I am hungry. Rah rah rah rah."

"Stop!" Trina shouted. "Wait. My stomach's rumbling now. Rah rah."

"You must say it four times," Naini said. "Rah rah rah rah."

Tony smiled at their laughter. He smiled at the people around them laughing at Naini and Trina laughing. He smiled for several people taking pictures of them with their phones. He squeezed Trina's hand.

Trina squeezed back.

He winked at Trina.

Trina winked back.

Tony decided that it was normal to laugh and hold
he hands of two beautiful women.

He wished he could give Trina her ring at Thai Thai
Noodle.

But he would wait.

*We will laugh again like this,* Tony thought. *I will
vait for more angels' laughter like this before I give
Trina her ring.*

*Yes.*

*I want the whole world to laugh when Trina gets her
·ing.*

# 43

Several calm, blissful, busy days and busier nights
later, Tony woke a little after 8:00 AM to watch the
weather outside Trina's front windows instead of
watching the weather on television. He saw a long black
:ar pull up in the street, and a tall black man in a black
:uit with shiny black shoes got out holding a bouquet
of red roses.

*That looks like romance,* he thought. *Roses and romance, poses and no pants.* Tony smiled. *My mind is
:unny today.*

A few moments later, Tony heard footsteps on the
stairs and then a knock.

Tony opened the door. "Hello."

"I have come to see Trina," the man said.

"Trina is asleep," Tony said. "I am Tony."

"I know who you are," the man said, stepping pas Tony toward the couch. "Trina!"

Tony moved around the man to stand in front o Trina's bedroom door. "Trina is asleep. Do not wake her. She is tired. I kept her up all night. We were mak ing a snowflake child."

The man's mouth opened wide. "Well, I am going t wake her up. In more ways than one."

"You brought Trina roses," Tony said.

"Obviously," the man said, shoving the bouquet int Tony's hands. "Make yourself useful and put these in vase, will you?"

Tony laid the bouquet on the coffee table. "You ar Robert."

"You're brilliant," Robert said.

"Thank you," Tony said. "You are an asshole and turd."

Robert frowned. "I'm sure she told you that."

"No," Tony said. "My brother thinks you are an ass hole. My friend Aika thinks you are a turd. I think you are an asshole and a turd."

"Trina!" Robert yelled.

"Do not yell," Tony said. "Only Trina yells in thi house." Tony smiled. "I make her yell, Robert. Thre times last night. She said, 'Oh, Tony, thank you, oh yes.' Tony smiled. "Sometimes she curses and growls. I like it when she does that. I have scratches on my back. D you want to see them?"

Trina's door opened, and Trina stuck out her head "Robert, what are you doing here?"

"I am talking to Robert," Tony said.

"I know that, Tony." She edged out the door. "I'n asking Robert why he's here."

Tony winked at Trina. "I am talking to Robert. You o back to bed." Tony's eyes traveled from Robert's iiny black shoes to his shiny, clean-shaven face. Why are you here?"

"It does not concern you," Robert said. "Trina, we eed to—"

"It concerns me," Tony interrupted. "Why are you ere?"

"Tony, I'm going to talk to the only other adult in ie room now," Robert said. "You go watch your eather like a good boy, okay?"

"The television is not on," Tony said. "I like watch-ig the weather outside the window now."

"Oh, that's special," Robert said.

"It is," Tony said. "It is a beautiful morning. Now ou will answer my question. Why are you here?"

*I've found a man with a backbone at last,* Trina iought. "Answer him, Robert. I have nothing to say to ou."

"He won't understand what I'm about to say," obert said.

"I am from Brooklyn," Tony said. "I speak asshole. I beak turd. You are an asshole and a turd. I will under-and what you have to say."

Trina smiled. *Is this the Italian in him, the Brooklyn him, or the real Tony in him? Go ahead, man! Kick obert's ass!*

"I came to try to win you back, Trina," Robert said.

"Trina is not a game to win," Tony said.

"It's just an expression," Robert said. "Oh, but you ave trouble thinking metaphorically, don't you?"

Tony smiled. "Metaphorically speaking, I do not ke the expression. Metaphorically speaking, love is

not a game with winners and losers. Metaphoricall
speaking, true love is only for winners."

Robert clapped his hands three times. "Bravo. Wi
that be another song, Art E.?"

"Yes," Tony said. "And it will sell a million copie
so I can buy Trina a house on the beach and a car s
she can teach me how to drive."

*Where is this cockiness coming from?* Trina wor
dered. *This man, this man. He continues to amaze me*

Robert took a step to his left.

Tony stepped to his right to block him.

"I want another chance, Trina," Robert said.

"I am her second chance," Tony said. "Trina will no
need a third chance."

Robert sighed. "Do you really want to spend you
life with this . . . this . . . chromosomal defect?"

"I am not a chromosomal defect," Tony said. "I am
unique member of the human race. I belong here. Yo
do not belong here."

"Trina, think about what you're doing," Robert sai
"Any children you may have with this . . . anomaly c
the gene pool . . . may get Asperger's. You are aware c
that?"

*Oh, that's low.* "Robert, I would rather—"

"Trina," Tony interrupted. "I am talking to Robert.'

"But he's ignoring you, Tony," Trina said.

"He cannot ignore me any longer." He took a ste
toward Robert. "I am here to stay. You are going t
leave. I do not want you to call Trina anymore. I do no
want you to visit Trina anymore. I do not want to se
your face anymore. Trina will not need your mone
anymore. She will not need those flowers. We wi
plant flowers at our new house."

Robert took a step backward. "I'm not going to lis-
en—"

"You are going to listen," Tony interrupted.

"Do you really expect me to take you seriously?"
.obert asked.

"Yes," Tony said. "I am seriously standing in front of
ou. I am seriously not letting you speak to Trina. I am
eriously thinking of punching you in the nose. I am
eriously thinking of hurting you. I am seriously think-
ıg of knocking you the hell out."

*Kick his ass!* Trina screamed in her mind. *Scuff his
ioes! Get blood on his shirt!*

"You're out of your mind," Robert said.

"I am never out of my mind," Tony said. "You would
ot like me if I were really out of my mind." He stared
ard into Robert's eyes.

Robert turned away.

"Trina is a good person," Tony said. "You took ad-
antage of her. She worked hard for you to become a
octor. You became a doctor. You left her for your mis-
·ess. You cheated. You had an affair. You slept with
ımeone who is not your wife. You hurt Trina's heart.
ou did not pay Trina enough alimony. You told Trina
·hat to think. You ordered Trina around. You did not
sten to Trina."

"I'm trying to listen now, Trina," Robert said. "I can
hange."

"You are a diaper that cannot be changed," Tony
ıid. "You are a bully like Nurse Sprouse the heartless
·ench. You bring Trina flowers. I bought her shoes.
ou bring her flowers. I gave her a new job. You bring
·r flowers. I bought her a house. You bring her flow-
·s. I will give her a snowflake child for each knee. You

bring her flowers. I give her love." Tony pointed to th
door. "It is not rude to point when the person in front o
you is rude. Robert, you will leave now. You will n
come back."

Robert turned toward the door and stopped. "Trin
you're not thinking this through."

"You did not think this through, Robert," Tony sai
"You thought you could get Trina back with flower
You cannot get love that way. Trina loves me, and I lo
her as best as I can."

"You're throwing the rest of your life away," Robe
said.

"No," Tony said. "She threw her life away when sh
met you. She has found her life again with me." Ton
grabbed the bouquet and shoved it into Robert's hand
Then he stepped around Robert and opened the doo
"Good-bye."

"Trina, you are going to regret this," Robert said.

"You will regret not leaving in exactly ten seconds
Tony said. "I am counting. I have an excellent sense o
time."

Robert turned and left.

Tony shut the door.

Trina ran to him, throwing her arms around h
neck. "You were wonderful."

Tony looked at Trina's arms. "This is a hug wome
give to other women when they are nervous."

Trina ground her hips into his legs and rubbed h
forehead on his chest. "Is this better?"

"I do not know," Tony said. "Are you nervous?"

"No," Trina said.

"Then yes," Tony said. "This is a better hug. It
much warmer."

Trina pulled Tony's arms up and placed his hands on
er lower back. "I didn't know you had it in you."

"I am a surprise," Tony said.

"Constantly," Trina said. "Thank you."

Tony looked at the couch. "You like surprises."

"I *love* surprises," Trina said.

"We will make love on the couch now," Tony said.
e lifted off her T-shirt and dropped her panties in a
ash.

"But there's not enough room," Trina said.

"I will sit," Tony said, unzipping his pants. "And
en you will sit. And if we hurry, Robert will get to
ar you yelling 'oh God, oh yes, oh Tony I am com-
g' . . ."

San Francisco,
California
and
Los Angeles,
California

# 44

The week before the Grammy Awards in Los Angeles was busy.

Mostly for Janine at Tiffany & Co. at Union Square. While movers took three days to carefully remove the Vance's furniture, window dressings, clothing, and artwork from "The Castle West," Angelo and Aika packed and shipped Tony's map books and piano to arrive in San Francisco within a week. While Trina gleefully picked out furniture for their house at DZINE, Tony found a quiet spot and called Tiffany's.

"Not yet," Janine said.

At Funky Furniture, Trina selected furniture for their shared office at the Santangelo Asperger's Center.

Tony walked out to the sidewalk and called Tiffany's.

"Soon," Janine told him. "I promise."

Tony signed a stack of legal documents Matthew sent, and Trina mailed them back to Brooklyn the same day. Tony was fitted for a charcoal Southwick suit at Cable Car Clothiers. He refused to wear any tie.

Trina didn't pout. "You look better without it," she said.

While Trina commissioned local fashion designe
Victor Tung to make her a one-of-a-kind crème dres
with hand-painted gold designs, Tony sneaked into
changing room and called Tiffany's.

"New York told me the last time I called that the d
amond had yet to arrive," Janine said.

"The diamond is playing hide-and-seek," Tony saic

"We know it's on its way," Janine said. "We're doin
the best we can, Tony."

"No," Tony said. "If you were doing your best, Trin
would be wearing her ring now."

While Trina got a manicure, pedicure, and her firs
ever facial at Nob Hill Spa, Tony sat in the waiting are
and called Tiffany's.

"I've located the shipment, Tony," Janine said. "
flew out of Darwin, Australia, to Honolulu, Hawai
yesterday. It should be in New York either late today (
tomorrow."

"Why can't it come to San Francisco?" Tony aske
"You can make it here."

"We don't make them here," Janine said. "It's ou
policy to—"

Tony hung up on Janine.

He called Janine back a minute later to apologize.

While Trina had her hair done at J. Roland, Ton
walked outside and called Tiffany's.

"It's there!" Janine cried. "It's in New York!"

"They are making the ring now," Tony said.

"All I know is that the diamond is at the New Yor
store," Janine said. "It will be ready soon."

"It will be ready in time for me to give it to her at th
Grammy Awards," Tony said.

"I don't know," Janine said. "We'll have to cross our fingers."

"I have been doing that a lot," Tony said. "My fingers need lotion."

Carlos gave Tony another great haircut, and Tony tipped him another thousand dollars. Naini crowded some of her things into Trina's apartment. Trina made first-class flight reservations to LA and secured a suite at L'Ermitage Beverly Hills for a week.

Everything was moving like clockwork.

Except the making of Trina's ring.

"I do not understand," Tony said to Janine. "They have the diamond. They should have the ring finished."

"It takes time to properly fit such a large diamond, Tony," Janine said. "You wouldn't want it to fall off, would you?"

"No," Tony said. "But if it did, I would glue it back on."

While Trina slept two nights before the Grammys, Tony crept through Naini's belongings out to the purple couch at 3:00 AM and called Angelo.

"I still do not have the ring, Angelo," Tony said. "I want to ask Trina to marry me, but I need the ring."

"Do you know what time it is?" Angelo asked.

"Yes," Tony said. "It is three AM here and six AM there. They are still making the ring at Tiffany's in New York."

"Be patient," Angelo said. "I've put you on speaker. He's perseverating about the ring again. Say hello to Aika."

"Hello, Aika," Tony said. "And I am not perseverating. I am worrying. There is a difference."

"Good morning, Tony," Aika said. "And please don't worry."

"I am sorry if I woke you," Tony said.

"It's okay," Aika said.

"I have been thinking of a solution," Tony said. "When you bring Silver to San Francisco, wait at Tiffany's at Union Square for the ring. I will send you the receipt overnight like I did with Matthew's papers. It will be there tomorrow. Then you can bring the ring to me in Los Angeles for the Grammy Awards."

"That's too much trouble," Angelo said. "Why don't I go to the Tiffany's here, pick it up when it's ready, and bring it to you when we fly out with Silver on Friday?"

"But I will already be in Los Angeles on Friday," Tony said. "Trina wanted to get there a day early to rest."

"It's okay, Tony," Angelo said. "We'll fly in to San Francisco on Friday, put Silver up in a kennel Saturday, and fly down to LA on Sunday."

"But I have the receipt in my wallet," Tony said.

"So you already paid for it," Angelo said.

"Yes," Tony said. "Thirty thousand dollars."

Tony heard what sounded like a *whump*.

"Ow, Aika!" Angelo shouted.

"You are hurt," Tony said.

"Aika just hit me," Angelo said.

"Why did Aika hit you?" Tony asked.

"You spent more for Trina's ring than I spent on hers," Angelo said. "She already hit me when I told her you got Trina a six-point-five-carat ring."

"But I have the receipt," Tony said.

"Don't worry about it," Angelo said. "Aika and I will go over to Tiffany's tomorrow and explain everything to them."

"Okay," Tony said. "You will call me when you have the ring."

"I'll text you, okay?" Angelo said. "That way Trina won't hit the speaker button and ruin your surprise."

"Okay," Tony said. "Thank you, Angelo."

"Hey," Angelo said, "what are brothers for?"

"They are for helping their brothers," Tony said. "And thank you for taking care of Silver for me, Aika."

"You're welcome, Tony," Aika said. "Now go back to bed."

"I am wired," Tony said.

"Then wake up Trina," Aika said.

"She is tired," Tony said. "I kept her up all night again."

"Were you snoring or something?" Angelo asked.

"No," Tony said. "We were making a snowflake child. Three times. How long does it take? We have had sex so often we should have had many snowflake children by now."

"Tony," Angelo said. "That's too much information, man."

"No, it isn't," Aika said. "Tony, I want you to go back into the bedroom now."

"I will wake up Trina," Tony said.

"That's the point," Aika said. "And thank you for waking us up, Tony. We need to be making a niece for you and Trina to spoil."

"That is too much information," Tony said. "Ha ha. Bye."

Tony crawled back into bed. He rubbed Trina's back. He squeezed Trina's leg. He caressed her buttocks. He slipped his hand between her legs. He pressed her button. He made small circles.

Trina stirred. "Again?"

"Yes," Tony said.

Trina turned to him. "Oh, all right. But make i
quick."

"I cannot make it quick," Tony said. "I can onl
make it good."

Trina smiled. "Then make . . . it . . . good."


As they walked hand in hand on the carpet in fror
of the Staples Center in LA on Grammy night, photog
raphers blinded Tony and Trina while reporters pelte
them with questions:

"Tony, do you think you'll win this year?"

"Trina, where did you get that dress?"

"Tony, where's your tie?"

"Trina, is it true you, Tony, and Naini Mitra are
triple?"

Tony put his lips near Trina's left ear. "A triple i
what you get in baseball when you hit it and get to thir
base. He said we are a triple."

"It's the press's way to stir up a mess," Trina sai
smiling for the next batch of photographers.

"I do not understand," Tony said.

"They think we are dating Naini," Trina whispered.

"We are not dating Naini," Tony said. "Why woul
we be dating Naini?"

"The media *wants* us to be dating Naini," Trina sai
kissing his cheek. "The press sees us hugging on yo
or holding your hands and they get weird about it."

"They get weird," Tony said.

Trina gently tugged his arm until she could put he

ips on his ear. "They think we're having sex with
Naini," Trina whispered.

Tony blinked. "But we have not had sex with her. I
only want to have sex with you."

"Good to know," Trina whispered.

"I will stop hugging her and holding her hand," Tony
said.

*That's my future husband,* Trina thought. "It's okay
f you hug her or hold her hand. I know you love me."
They posed in front of the Grammy Awards logo. "And
t's okay if you love Naini, too. She's my friend, and I
ove her to death."

"I hope you do not love her to death," Tony said. "I
would not want Naini to die." Tony felt his phone buzz.
*I have a text message,* he thought. *I do not get text messages. This means Angelo has the ring.* He looked
around at the crowds. *Now all I need is Angelo.*

Trina nodded at the main entrance. "Do you remember what we're supposed to say when the *Entertainment Tonight* reporter talks to us?"

"Yes," Tony said. "I remember."

Before they finally entered the Staples Center, *Entertainment Tonight* reporter Bryant Belton, at his un-
holy smarmiest, stood between Tony and Trina. "Tony,
darling, is it true you're going to go solo now?"

"I am not your darling," Tony said. "I am Trina's
darling."

Belton blinked.

"Yes," Tony said. "My brother Angelo is making
arrangements for me to play in Central Park this summer."

"Like Elton John did about a hundred years ago?"
Belton asked.

"No, like me," Tony said. "And it was not one hun
dred years ago. It was in 1980. I will not wear a duck
costume like Elton John did. I will wear Banana Re
public clothes."

"What about your collaboration with Naomi Stringer?"
Belton asked. "Will it continue?"

"Naomi will sing eight of my songs on her next
album," Tony said. "I am saving other songs for me."

Belton made a show of looking around them. "Where's
Naini, Tony? I expected to see her holding your other
hand, Tony."

Trina and Tony waved at the camera. "Hi, Naini,"
they said together. "Rah rah rah rah."

Belton's eyes popped. "So are you three a triple?"

Tony smiled. "Trina and I are a double."

Belton blinked. "Um, Trina, are you Tony's manager
now? Where's Angelo in all this?"

"Tony is his own man, Bryant," Trina said. "No one
manages him anymore."

"I love your dress," Belton said.

"You cannot have it," Tony said.

Once the show began, Tony took out his notepad and
tried to write in the near darkness.

Trina grabbed his hand. "Enjoy the moment, Tony.
Write about it later. Be a sponge. You'll remember
everything later."

Tony put away his pencil and notepad. "I will re
member." He let his eyes wander up and down the
aisles and to the rows on either side of them. "I wish
Angelo was here."

"He'll be here," Trina said. "You know he wouldn't
miss this."

When the spotlight hit him and Trina during the

reading of the nominees for best song three *hours* later, Tony smiled as the ovation continued for a solid minute.

"They are still clapping," Tony said.

"Because this is the first time they get to clap for you here," Trina said. "They didn't see you at Johnny Foley's."

"It has a nice rhythm," Tony said. He reached for his notepad but dropped his hand to Trina's knee. "I will enjoy the moment."

"And the winner for best song goes to . . . Alice Blazevich for 'Plastic Life'!"

Tony clapped as others around him stood and clapped. "Why are they standing?"

"They're glad Alice won," Trina said.

"I am glad Alice won," Tony said. "She writes many good songs." Tony stood and clapped.

Trina joined him. "Are you disappointed?" she whispered.

"No." Tony looked around him in all directions. *Where is Angelo?*

Trina squeezed his elbow.

*I am the only one still standing and clapping,* Tony thought. *I need more time to find Angelo. I will clap some more.*

In moments, others stood and clapped, and the applause became deafening. Tony still did not see Angelo anywhere, so he sat.

Trina rested her head on his shoulder. "That was so nice of you."

Tony's eyes darted around the Staples Center during several more musical numbers.

"Are you sure you're okay?" Trina asked.

"I am okay," Tony said.

"You wish Angelo and Aika were here," Trina said.

"Just Angelo," Tony said.

"Why not Aika?" Trina asked.

"I cannot tell you," Tony said.

After a commercial, Curtis Piccola, longtime music producer and Chair Emeritus for the Recording Academy board of trustees, stood in front of the podium. "The Grammy Lifetime Achievement Award is given to those who have made inspired contributions of exceptional artistic importance to the field of recorded music. At sixteen, our honoree wrote his first top-forty hit. Over the next twenty-four years, he added sixty—count 'em!—*sixty* more top-forty songs including three that won the Grammy for best song."

Tony's eyes continued to scan the crowd.

"Tony," Trina whispered, "he's talking about you."

Tony looked up at the stage. "Why is he talking about me? I did not win."

Trina kissed his hand. "You're about to get an award."

"I did not do anything," Tony said.

"Just listen," Trina said.

"Just one month ago," Piccola said, "this amazingly talented pianist wowed us all with his remarkable genius and skills, and I say, it's about time. Tonight, it is my privilege and honor to award Tony 'Art E.' Santangelo a lifetime achievement award. Tony Santangelo! Come on up!"

"But I have not lived a lifetime yet," Tony said.

Trina pulled him to his feet as the applause grew louder. "But you've done so much in your life, and they want to give you an award." She stepped out into the aisle as the spotlight found them.

"You will go with me," Tony said.

"It should only be you," Trina said.

"I would not be here if you did not love me." He kissed her cheek and took her hand. "Let us go for a walk."

As they walked, musicians and singers stuck their hands out into the aisles or gave Tony shoulder hugs. Tony shook as many hands as he could with his free hand.

"Do you know what you're going to say?" Trina asked.

Tony stopped at the foot of the stairs to the stage. "I have to talk."

"They expect you to say *something*," Trina said. "Even if it's simply a thank you."

Tony nodded. "I will say something."

Tony guided Trina up the stairs to the podium as the crowd stood and cheered.

Piccola handed him his award, and Tony placed it on the podium. "Trina would like me to say something." He smiled at Trina and then at the crowd. "Something." Tony stepped back from the podium.

Gradually, the audience began to laugh.

Tony held up a finger, and the laughter subsided. He reached into his suit jacket and took out his notepad. He began flipping through it, stopping occasionally, shaking his head, and flipping more pages.

He froze when he saw the receipt for Trina's ring.

He looked at Trina.

*I hope she did not see it.*

He put the receipt into his pants pocket.

The crowd laughed.

He put the notepad away and looked up into the orchestra backstage. "I see a piano," he whispered to Trina. "But it is not my piano."

"It has the same number of keys," Trina whispered.

"I can play it." He took Trina's hand and led her through the stage set and around light stands and wires to the piano, where a bearded man sat. "I want to play your piano."

The man stood and shook Tony's hand. "She's all yours."

While a man held a fuzzy boom mike over Tony, Tony turned to Trina, lifted her into the air, and settled her on top of the piano. "Hold on tight, Trina."

The audience laughed.

"Are you going to play your heart out?" Trina asked.

"No," Tony said. "I am going to play my soul out."

Tony Santangelo then shared his soul with the world.

Soulfully, smoothly, and masterfully, Tony blended old soul, gospel, and a healthy helping of the blues into a song that had the audience swaying. Two minutes in, he stood and kicked back the piano bench—

And he saw Angelo and Aika waving at him from the wings.

Tony kissed Trina and ran offstage, snatching the little blue box from Angelo. "Thank you," he said, and he sprinted back out to the piano, where he froze.

*Oh . . . my . . . goodness!* Trina thought. *It's a Tiffany's box!*

Tony kissed Trina again and ran off the stage. "Angelo, what do I say?"

"Say 'Trina, will you marry me?' "

"That is all," Tony said.

"It should be enough," Aika said. "It worked on me."

Tony blinked several times. "Angelo said 'Trina, will you marry me' to you."

"No, Tony." Aika hugged him. "Go ask Trina to marry you! Go!"

Tony ran back to the piano, set the Tiffany's box next to Trina—

And he resumed playing.

Laughter filled the Staples Center and swelled even more when Trina crossed her arms and shook her head. *He's teasing me!* she thought. *Give it to me! Give me my ring!* She moved the box into his line of sight.

But Tony tapped the top of the piano with his left while pounding the piano bench behind him with his right.

Then Tony stopped, stared at Trina, and asked, "Trina Woods, will you marry me?"

A hush filled the Staples Center.

"Yes!" Trina shouted.

"Okay," Tony said.

And he *still* continued to play, running his fingers up and down the keyboard at breakneck speed.

Laugher, amazement, and applause broke out. Trina couldn't stop shaking her head and smiling. *He asks me, I say yes, he keeps playing, the ring's right there— what is he doing?*

Angelo trotted out to the piano to some applause and put his hands on Tony's shoulders. "Give Trina the ring," Angelo whispered.

Tony's left hand rose off the keyboard while his right hand kept playing. He picked up the box and handed it to Trina.

"Open the box and take out the ring," Angelo whispered.

Tony stopped playing. He opened the box, took out the ring, and held it in front of Trina's eyes.

"Put it on her finger," Angelo whispered.

"Oh," Tony said. He slid the ring onto her finger.

Trina displayed the ring to the crowd. *This is the most beautiful ring in the world,* she thought. *And it's my color! I've never seen anything like it!* She reached out to hug him.

Tony *again* resumed his song.

Angelo hugged Trina, said, "Welcome to the family," and shook his head as he left the stage.

Trina watched Tony play and felt his love swelling around her. *Every note he plays is for me. Every sound he makes proves his love for me. I don't want him to stop! But I have to go to him. He came three thousand miles for me. I can move three feet for him.*

Trina slid off the top of the piano and stood next to Tony. She first picked up his right hand.

Tony's left hand played every bass note below middle C.

She slipped in front of him and picked up his left hand. "You can hug me now." She reached her arms up and grasped his neck. "If you want to."

Tony's hands stayed rigid at his sides. He looked into Trina's eyes. "I want to. I hold you in my mind all the time."

"I hold you in my heart," Trina whispered. "All the time."

Tony slid his hands from his sides to her hips then moved them to her lower back. "I will hold you forever, Trina." He pulled her to him, hugged her tightly, and dipped her almost to the piano keys, kissing her for a Grammy Award–show record two minutes and twenty-seven seconds as the crowd went wild.

Tony allowed Trina to come up for some air. "I am sorry I did that on television."

"I'm not," Trina said. "Do it again."

"I may not be able to stop," Tony said. "I have As-perger's. It will become a routine."

"Then don't *ever* stop. . . ."

Tony Santangelo and Trina Woods, his dark brown woman, received three *more* standing ovations that night at the Grammy Awards.

They were still dipping backstage an hour later. . . .

# Press Clippings

*February 20*

*San Francisco Chronicle*

### TONY MARRIES TRINA

AP (San Francisco) Tony "Art. E." Santangelo and Trina Ann Woods were married on February 18 in the opulent Court of Honor at the Legion of Honor in front of Rodin's *Thinker*, one of the most iconic sculptures ever created, while being serenaded by San Francisco musicians from Journey, Jefferson Starship, and the Grateful Dead . . .

Naini Mitra served as the maid of honor, and Angelo Santangelo, winner of the National Book Award for nonfiction, served as the best man. Matthew and Angela McConnell and Aika Saito ushered the bride down the aisle, and Angel McConnell was the sprinting, dancing flower girl . . .

The couple will honeymoon in Cobble Hill, Brooklyn, New York, USA.

### February 27

*Brooklyn Daily Eagle*

AUTHOR SANTANGELO WEDS SAITO

National Book Award winner Angelo Santangelo and Random House editor Aika Saito were united in holy matrimony on February 25 at St. Paul's in Cobble Hill with the groom's brother, Tony "Art. E." Santangelo providing all the music, including an original song for the couple entitled, "You Can Drink My Root Beer Now" . . .

The couple will honeymoon in Rome, Italy, near the Castel Sant'Angelo (The Castle of the Holy Angel) before continuing to Hiraizumi in northern Japan, the bride's ancestral home.

### March 15

*Apparel Magazine*

BANANA REPUBLIC PROFITS RISE

Thanks to a breakout ad campaign starring Tony "Art E." Santangelo and his bride Trina, Banana Republic profits have risen 5 percent in the last quarter, according to Gap executive Mark Vance.

"Not only do they look good in our clothes," Vance said, "but they have fun wearing them" . . .

## June 17

### Billboard magazine

### ARTY GOES PLATINUM; "SNOWFLAKE CHILD" GOES MULTI-PLATINUM

Naomi Stringer's album *Arty,* named in tribute to the man who supplied her with eight currently top-100 songs and a dozen others in the past, has gone Platinum, selling one million copies worldwide in its debut three months ago. "Snowflake Child" has become the number one selling single in the world with over two million sales worldwide.

As of June 15, "Sexy Hate" was No. 3, "Second Chances" was No. 5, "That's All You Have to Be" was No. 13, "I Only Want You in My Dreams" was No. 24, "Gettin' Busy" was No. 48, "That Is Love" was No. 79, and "Colorful Life" was No. 98 on *Billboard*'s Hot 100 . . .

## July 5

### New York Times

### ART E. ROCKS CENTRAL PARK

Tony Santangelo, aka Art E., rocked the Big Apple in front of a record crowd of an estimated 500,000 fans in Central Park and was seen by an estimated four hundred million television viewers worldwide yesterday, with Trina by his side . . .

He began his five-hour set with "Fog City," debuted "Love Is the Laughter of Angels," and ended the night by whispering "Trina" to his lovely bride . . .

During one of the many highlights of the event, Elton John, Billy Joel, and Alicia Keys joined Tony onstage in front of four pianos to play Elton John's "Bennie and the Jets" and "Honky Cat," Billy Joel's "Piano Man" and "It's Still Rock and Roll to Me," and Alicia Keys's "Fallin' " and "No One." The quartet ended with a soul-stirring, twenty-five-minute rendition of Chicago's "Hard to Say I'm Sorry" . . .

Proceeds from the sales of *Tony in the Park* CDs and DVDs will benefit Asperger's research worldwide . . .

## July 18

### Adweek

#### HIRES ROOT BEER SALES SKYROCKET

Thanks to Tony Santangelo's epic consumption of Hires Root Beer during his performance in Central Park two weeks ago, Hires Root Beer sales have risen 27 percent over this time last year.

"I hope he has many more live concerts in the future," Dr. Pepper Snapple Group CFO Miles Lawton said. "And I hope it's extremely *hot* wherever he has them."

## July 29

### *Billboard* magazine

#### *TONY IN THE PARK* GOES DIAMOND

Tony Santangelo's live performance in Central Park has gone "Diamond," selling ten million copies worldwide in only two weeks. If this sales trend continues,

*Tony in the Park* could eclipse Michael Jackson's record of twenty-nine million albums sold for *Thriller,* possibly by the end of August . . .


## August 1

### San Francisco Chronicle

WILLIAMS/RAMIREZ ENGAGEMENT
Mr. and Mrs. Robert and Lilian Williams are pleased to announce the engagement of their daughter Lily Genevieve Williams to Tino Julio Tomas Ramirez . . .


## August 15

### San Francisco Chronicle

SANTANGELO ASPERGER'S CENTER OPENS AT SAINT FRANCIS
The Santangelo Asperger's Center (SAC) is now fully operational and accepting patients and their families, according to Saint Francis Memorial Hospital president Dr. Morgan Canby.
"Tony and Trina Santangelo have been truly amazing at getting this center up and running so quickly," Canby said. "They've already met with a dozen patients and their families today, and they've received hundreds of referrals from around the world. And I've even heard music coming from their office."
According to SAC founder and counselor Tony Santangelo, therapy will revolve around music and art. "We will help people find all the notes and colors," Santangelo said. "We hope to do great things for good people."

*November 29*

## *Brooklyn Daily Eagle*

### Santangelo Daughter Birth

Angelo and Aika Santangelo welcomed the birth of Seiki Akari Santangelo on November 26 at Long Island College Hospital in Cobble Hill, Brooklyn. Seiki, whose name means "star and beginning," weighed seven pounds, four ounces . . .

*December 28*

## *San Francisco Chronicle*

### Tony and Trina Have a Baby

AP (San Francisco) Art E. has one knee covered.

Toni Angelaika Santangelo, nicknamed "Snowflake," was born to mega-recording star and composer Tony Santangelo and wife Trina on Christmas Day.

"It is the second best gift I have ever received," Santangelo said. "The first best gift was Trina's love."

For more information on Asperger's syndrome:

ASPEN—aspennj.org
The Autism Hub—autism-hug.com
Autism Research Institute—autism.com
Autism Speaks—autismspeaks.org
Families of Adults Affected by Asperger's Syndrome—faaas.org
National Autism Association—nationalautismassociation.org
OASIS: The Online Asperger Syndrome Information and Support—aspergerssyndrome.org
Organization for Autism Research—researchautism.org
US Autism & Asperger Association—usautism.org
WrongPlanet.net